What's a
Witch
to Do?

What's a Witch to Do?

A Midnight Magic Mystery

Jennifer Harlow

MIDNIGHT INK
WOODBURY, MINNESOTA

FIRST EDITION
First Printing, 2013

Book format by Bob Gaul
Cover design by Ellen Lawson
Cover illustration by Mary Ann Lasher-Dodge
Editing by Nicole Nugent
Family tree © Llewellyn art department

Midnight Ink, an imprint of Llewellyn Worldwide Ltd.

Library of Congress Cataloging-in-Publication Data
Harlow, Jennifer, 1983–
  What's a witch to do?: a midnight magic mystery/by Jennifer Harlow.
    p. cm.
  ISBN 978-0-7387-3514-6
1. Women priests—Fiction. 2. Witches—Fiction. 3. Werewolves—Fiction.
4. Paranormal fiction. I. Title.
  PS3608.A7443W47 2013
  813'.6—dc23
                          2012032918

Midnight Ink
Llewellyn Worldwide Ltd.
2143 Wooddale Drive
Woodbury, MN 55125-2989
www.midnightinkbooks.com

Printed in the United States of America

For Great-Grandma Honey and Auntie T—
both *real* witches.

The Goode and Knight Family Tree (1900–present)

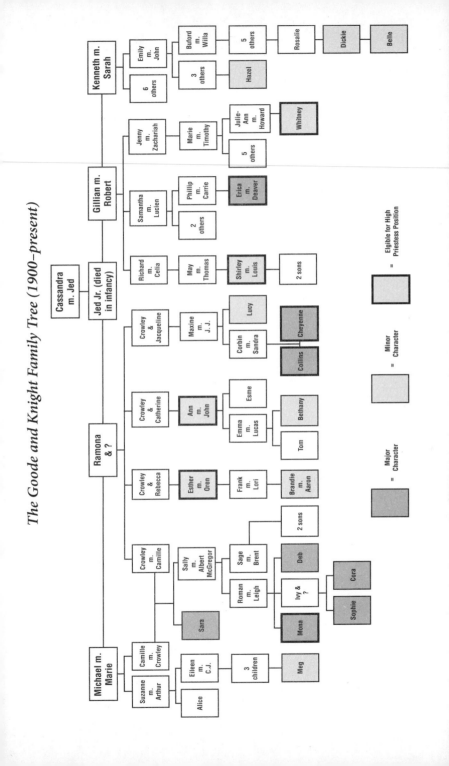

SATURDAY TO DO:

- *Hem Sophie's skirt*
- *~~Go to work~~*
- *~~Resupply herbs~~*
- *~~Confirm hall and playhouse for meetings~~*
- *Call Jocasta about wedding flowers*
- *Help Cora with her collage*
- *Go grocery shopping*
- *Make ~~20~~ 13 potions/spells/charms*
- *~~Make dinner~~*
- *~~Answer e-mails~~*
- *Girls' bedtime*
- *Kill self*

"Aunt Mona! Aunt Mona! Cora's bleeding!"

My heart skips a beat. Oh hell's bells. I drop the rosemary and wolfsbane onto the altar and sprint into the hallway, fear coursing through me. *Please don't let it be bad.* Cora's not in the pink bedroom she shares with her sister, but the blood trail begins at her white desk, continuing to the bathroom one door down. Both my nieces are at the end of the blood breadcrumb line. Sophie holds her younger sister's hand under the running faucet as the six-year-old weeps, blood splattered on her pink shirt like a Jackson Pollock painting.

"It hurts! It hurts!" Cora sobs as she bounces up and down.

I switch into emergency mode: calm and capable. "What happened?" I ask, grabbing a towel.

Sophie steps aside so I can take her place. "She was using the scissors! I told her not to!"

Ten minutes. I left them alone for ten flipping minutes, and they managed to break the rules and get maimed. They have so much of their mother in them it's frightening. "Let me look, sweetie."

I take her tiny hand from under the water. There's a deep gash about an inch long in her palm. Yeah, it's gonna need stitches. Bye bye, rest of the afternoon. I wrap the towel around Cora's hand and have her raise it above her heart to reduce the bleeding. She keeps whimpering and sniffling, blue eyes rimmed with tears. "It hurts."

I kiss her white-as-snow hair. "I know, sweetie. Guess what? We get to go see Nurse Luann again. I know how much you like her," I say mockingly. "Sophie, go grab yours and Cora's coats, okay?" I order, leading the wounded out.

"Do you think Dr. Sutcliffe will be there?" Sophie asks.

My cheeks flare up and butterflies sprout at the mention of that name. "I—I don't know. Probably not. It's Saturday."

Cora glances back at her sister. "But—but he could be, right?" Cora asks.

Oh goddess. Six and ten, and already suckers for a handsome face. They really are their mother's daughters. "I don't know! Sophie, the coats please! Come on!"

2

I hustle the bleeding girl down the wooden stairs. My purse, coat, and keys are on the table by the door. I grab them and push Cora out the door. It's cold for April in Virginia, but we just have to sprint to my blue Acura in the driveway. I help Cora into the backseat and scurry to the front. Sophie still hasn't come out of my three-story white Victorian house, so I honk the horn. My neighbor and great-aunt, Sara, always the busybody, steps out of her matching home. As usual she's dressed in a floral muumuu, and her gray hair resembles a permed helmet. "Mona Leigh, what is going on?"

I roll down the car window, all smiles. "Everything's fine, Auntie Sara. Thank you."

"Is that child bleeding?" she asks, hands on her hips.

"She's fine. Just a cut." I love the woman to bits, but she tends to embellish gossip. By midnight Cora will be at death's door undergoing a hand transplant.

Sophie careens out of the door with Cora's green coat in her arms and leaps off the lavender painted porch between the white columns instead of taking the steps, which I have scolded her for doing a dozen times. No time to yell now. I start the engine, give a wave and smile to Auntie Sara, and peel out of the driveway when my second passenger is in. "Seat belts."

Our destination is clear on the other side of town, so it takes ten minutes to get there. Traffic is never a real problem here, but if we had a rush hour, it would be now. All the families who journeyed to Richmond or Williamsburg today are making their way home for supper, so Courtland Street is backed up. Most of the small shops—mine included—are closed or closing, so the foot traffic has waned on the cobblestone sidewalks. Only Goodnight Diner and Ma's General Store have customers ambling in and out. As I drive under the "Goodnight Founders' Week" banner hanging above the street, through the windows I spot Tamara carrying plates of food to the Reverend Potter and his wife, Cece. That reminds me, I forgot to call Jocasta about the early delivery of the flowers for the wedding. Maybe Debbie did it. We really have to coordinate better.

Slower than I'd like, we leave the red brick commercial section of Goodnight for the massive park in the center of town. There are no kids on the playground, but Wayne Flynn walks his Great Dane while smoking his daily cigar. I don't know which his wife, Stacy, would mind more: the cigar or his checking out the teenager jogging by. Male teenager. No wonder Stacy has had a standing order for a male enhancement potion all these years. Poor woman.

As I'm driving over the railroad tracks through the south of town, which is just ranch-style homes lined with rusting cars, some on bricks, I glance back at the girls. Sophie whispers to her younger sister, who keeps nodding and looking at me, her small face looking almost guilty. Cora whispers back and Sophie shakes her head. "What are you two conspiring about back there?"

"Nothing," Sophie responds.

"My hand hurts," Cora whines.

"Almost there, sweetie pie."

Goodnight Medical Center is a four-story white building that from the outside resembles an office center except for the ambulance parked under the awning. I park in the lot, and we hustle in. Ancient Nurse Luann Smiley sits behind the reception desk, mouth pursed in displeasure when she lays eyes on us. The woman has carried a grudge against me for thirty damn years. As if I was the only child who's bitten her. That's what she got for poking me with a needle.

"Mona McGregor, twice in one month," Luann says. "What now?"

"Cora needs stitches," I say.

Luann rises, gazing down at the miserable girl. Sophie glares at her, and Luann glares back. Ever since Luann yelled at Cora for crying during an exam, Sophie has not hidden her feelings about Nurse Ratched there. Luann sits back down. "Were you keeping an eye on her?"

I scoff. "Yeah, Luann. I watched as she juggled three knives in front of me. We're thinking of selling tickets next time."

Her lips purse with disapproval. "I know this whole motherhood thing is new to you, but making sure the children live into adulthood is a big part of the job description."

I roll my eyes. "Just give me the damn forms to fill out. Please."

Still shooting us the evil eye, the old biddy hands me the clipboard. I snatch it away before retreating to the waiting area. It's odd that the biggest witch in Goodnight is one of the few who isn't one. Sophie and Cora sit next to me as I pull out my reading glasses and insurance card. The waiting room is almost empty with only first baseman Jace Brown and his teenage girlfriend, Amber Kermer, sitting off to the side, both visibly nervous but otherwise intact. Last month she came into the shop for a charm to ward off unwanted pregnancy. I gave it to her but only after a long lecture on modern birth control. Not thinking she listened.

As I'm copying my information down, the girls start whispering again and glancing at the reception area. Their excitement is palpable. I look up and my breath catches. Oh goddess. I was hoping he wouldn't be here, and also hoping he was. Dr. Guy Sutcliffe, the literal man of my dreams, is conversing with Luann at reception. Try as I might, I can't take my eyes off him. Each time I see him I want to relish it. He must feel me gazing at him like a lion does a zebra, all but licking my lips, because he turns my way. Oh, I really wish I had changed and put on makeup before coming here. Or at least brushed my hair. I quickly remove my glasses and smooth my hair, which is pointless when it's curly, but I do it anyway.

If I had ever made a list of all that I wanted in a man, he'd hit every item. Tall, thin, with chocolate brown hair with specks of gray, dark eyes hidden behind trendy glasses, and an ironic smile. And let's not discount the whole being a doctor thing, which of course makes all the other items moot. I like my men brainy and cultured, which are not qualities prevalent in the men of Goodnight—one of the many reasons that I haven't been on a date in years. That and I'm related to a large portion of the male population here.

I remember the first time I saw Guy in the diner three months ago. Tamara pointed him out, and my jaw dropped. Literally. I am a woman of discerning taste when it comes to men—much to a fault according to the entire town—so when I actually find someone who sparks my interest, it's a huge deal. Like, stop the presses huge. As Tamara is the go-to person for all the skinny on the citizens of Goodnight, she gave me the CliffsNotes version of his story. Forty, divorced with no kids, was living in D.C. but needed a change of pace and loved this area. It was as if someone had conjured my perfect man, and there he was eating pancakes.

Of course I wasn't the only woman in town who felt this way, and competition is fierce. He's dated at least two women I've heard of: my cousin Rosalie and Jana Garrett, a reporter at the local paper. Both women are the anti-me: skinny, sleek, charming, and who never leave the house in paint-spackled jeans and an old Goodnight Warlock's shirt sans makeup, even in an emergency situation. It's against the Southern Lady Code.

I've only spoken to him twice before, both on official business. The first was a week after the diner sighting when Cora needed a booster shot. I was so flustered I'm fairly sure I didn't say more than five words to him, then turned beet red when he flashed a smile. The second time went a little better, at least in terms of our interaction. Three weeks ago the school had to rush Sophie to the hospital when she went into anaphylactic shock after a bee sting. I came in, in near hysterics, and it was Dr. Sutcliffe who calmed me down with his soothing tone. She had to stay the night so I did as well, and before he left for the day he brought me a cup of coffee. I almost lost the ability to speak.

He spots us in the waiting area, gives a friendly smile and nod, and walks off. My cheeks are hot so I know I'm blushing again. I must be because Luann glares at me, shaking her head as if she can read my mind.

"Aunt Mona, I have to go to the bathroom," Sophie says, snapping me out of my hormone bubble.

"Um, can you hold it?"

Sophie leaps up. "No! I'll go alone! Be right back!" Before I can protest, she's sprinting away past reception and down the hall.

"Don't run in the hospital!" Luann shouts before turning to me. "Mona McGregor, you control your niece!"

I throw my hands up, shaking my head. "Yeah, I'll get right on that."

Luann plops herself back in her throne, grumbling about the youth of the nation or something. That woman gives spinsters like me a bad name. My wayward niece returns a few minutes later, and a few after that my cousin Collins, another nurse here, ushers us into an exam room where both girls jump up on the exam table. Collins is my second cousin, and we both have mousy brown hair, though she can afford highlights in hers. Wish I got her blue eyes though. Mine are as brown as mud.

"What happened here?" she asks, examining Cora's hand.

"I cut myself."

Collins checks Cora's vitals. "All normal." She turns to Sophie. "And how are you feeling after that bee sting, little miss?"

"A lot better, thanks," Sophie says.

"You girls excited about the wedding?"

"We're flower girls," Cora informs her.

"I know. We all get to wear matching dresses." Collins is my sister Debbie's maid of honor. "And aren't you in the Founders' Day pageant?" she asks Sophie.

"Yeah, I'm Mary Knight," Sophie replies.

"Well, I will try to make your stage debut," Collins says with a smile as she takes off her latex gloves. "Mona?" She gestures to the door. "I'm gonna steal your aunt for a sec."

I follow Collins into the hallway, leaving the door open to keep an eye on my little troublemakers. The moment I walk out, they start furiously whispering. They are so up to something. "She's okay, right?"

"Oh yeah. One or two stitches should do it," she says, writing in the chart. "Just what you needed, right? Want me to ask the doctor to prescribe you Valium to get through the week?"

"Tempting, but I need all twelve of my wits about me. Some speed might come in handy though."

Collins chuckles. "Are we still having class on Monday? I have a few questions about an illumination spell I found."

"That's the plan, but what with the preparations for the wedding, the coven meeting, the co-op, and the Founders' Day committee, not to mention work and my pretty hellions in there, I can't make any guarantees. If I have to cancel, I'll have Auntie Sara call." Hell, I'm tired just thinking about the next week. I'll be a zombie come next Sunday.

"If anyone can survive, it's you, my High Priestess. I'll light a fire under the doctor's butt and get you out of here."

"Thank you." She walks away and I return to the girls, who immediately stop talking as I enter. Cora looks down and Sophie smiles. "What?"

"Your lips look chapped," Sophie says. "You should put on some lipstick."

I sit on the stool across from them. "I will take that under advisement."

Sophie leaps off the table with my purse in hand. "I'm bored. I'll help you."

"No—"

She already has the lipstick out, and I'm too tired to struggle. Plus, she's right. I sit like a statue as my niece applies lipstick, powder, and pulls my hair back, fastening it with a barrette. Just as she clips it in place, Dr. Sutcliffe saunters in. Instantly, I become an awkward teenager again, wanting to hide behind my hair. No zits this time though. He looks up from the chart at me, and if I didn't know any better, I'd swear his face lights up as if he's seen a beautiful work of art. I've never had a man gaze at me like that. The butterflies in my stomach really like it. Happiness is replaced with confusion on his handsome face for a fraction of a second, but the gorgeous smile returns. "Um, hello," he says with a nervous chuckle.

"Hi," I say with the same reaction. What on earth?

Collins steps in too, and he blinks and shakes his head. I've flustered him. Usually it's the other way around. "Um, sorry." He looks at the beaming Sophie and smiles back. "What brings us in today?"

"Cora cut her hand," Sophie says.

"She did, huh?" he asks, slapping on gloves. After examining it he says, "Nasty cut there. How'd you do this?"

"Scissors," Cora says. "I'm not 'apposed to use them."

"No, you are not," I say.

Dr. Sutcliffe turns to me, flashing me a million-watt smile, which morphs into a nervous one before continuing his exam. Even Collins seems confused. "Accidents happen. You won't do it again, will you?"

"No, sir," Cora says.

"Collins, I'm gonna need a suture kit."

As she retrieves one from the cabinet, I get up and sit on the table, hugging my niece from behind. "Is it going to hurt?" Cora asks.

"Not too bad," Dr. Sutcliffe says before glancing at me with kind eyes. Goddess is he good-looking. Could be a male model. Collins returns and they begin to fix Cora up. She cries when he numbs her hand with a needle and I hug her tighter, whispering promises of ice cream when we get home. "There you go, the worst part's over," the doctor says. Five minutes of sewing and coy glances my way and he finishes. "All set."

"Thank you," I say.

"My pleasure."

"You did good," I say, kissing Cora's cheek.

Dr. Sutcliffe adds some notes to his chart. "Just keep it dry and bring her back in two weeks for suture removal."

"Okay," I say as I help her off the table.

As I'm getting their coats on, the doctor whispers to Collins. She tosses the kit in the trash and spins around. "Hey, girls. Let's go see if we can rustle up a lollipop or two for you being so good."

They all but run out of the room in search of candy. Collins raises an eyebrow at me before walking out. And now I'm alone with my fantasy man, who I think wanted to be alone with me. "Will she have a scar?"

"No," he says, back still to me. "I see Cora hasn't had her Hep B vaccination yet."

"Yeah, she and Sophie had to get every other kind a year and a half ago. That was a nightmare. I've been putting the rest off."

"They weren't vaccinated before?" he asks, turning around.

"Um, I have no idea. They don't remember ever getting shots, and I had no documentation. Hell, I don't even have their birth certificates. It was a fight getting them enrolled in school."

"What happened, if you don't mind me asking?"

I sigh. "My younger sister Ivy—who I had not seen in over ten years, mind you—showed up on my porch with Sophie and Cora for a visit. I wake up the next day and the kids are there, but Ivy and my emergency cash are gone. A week later a few boxes with toys and clothes arrived. That was the last we've heard from her."

"Jesus, I'm so sorry."

"It's been a learning experience to say the least."

"I can imagine. They're wonderful girls though. You should be proud."

"Well, thank you," I say, blushing for the nineteenth time today.

His sharp features soften again. "I'll, uh, give them the shots when Cora comes in next time."

"Okay," I say, following him out.

For a girl who just had a medical procedure, Cora is positively giddy, mouth curled into a smile as she sucks on her lollipop. Collins gives Sophie one too as we walk out. "Um, I'll see you girls in two weeks, okay?" the doctor says, patting Cora's head. Then those almost black eyes find mine. "Nice to see you again, Mona."

"You too, Dr. Sutcliffe."

"Please, call me Guy."

My new favorite name. "Guy."

11

"Goodbye girls, and thanks Sophie." What did she do? All four of us females watch as he struts away, off to help ease other's suffering. And yes, I do check out his heinie. He must feel it because he glances over his shoulder, looking at me with a private smile. Okay, I know it's been awhile, but either he's into me or the stress of my life is making me delusional. My past track record says the latter.

"Dang, Mona," Collins says, "get a room."

Or maybe my good luck's finally caught up with me.

· *Girls' bedtime/finish potions*

We return home to find Auntie Sara still on her porch, phone pressed to her ear. The three of us wave before running into the house, away from prying eyes. As I am a woman of my word, both girls enjoy ice cream before going up for their baths. This time used to be a massive struggle. If I had to guess, Ivy never made them do a damn thing, including bathing or brushing their teeth. They were almost afraid to get into the tub, as if they'd melt if a drop of water touched them. That damn *Wizard of Oz* set us witches back centuries in terms of progress. But if I learned anything from all the years I helped take care of my two younger sisters, it's that kids crave structure. Thanks to a bullwhip and rigid schedule, the girls felt safe for the first time in their lives, and within a month I didn't even have to ask them to bathe.

I flop down on the light pink couch in my cozy living room with a sigh as the water runs upstairs. The house is a treasure. Built almost a hundred years ago, it's held up beautifully. Hardwood floors, stone fireplace, all the original moldings. They don't make them like this anymore. The furniture is more modern, mostly from IKEA or Pier1. When the house officially became mine, I remodeled. It was far too old-lady chic. I painted the walls light blue but kept the dozens of pressed flowers and herbs in frames on the walls. It was Granny's hobby, I couldn't part with them.

With a sigh, I close my weary eyes. I am not going to make it through the next eight days if I'm this exhausted already. I'm pretty self-sufficient, once again almost to a fault according to everyone, but this week … I shake my head. There are very few times I wish I were married, or at least seeing someone, and this is one of them. Maybe a handsome doctor? No, don't get on that train of thought. If wishes were horses and all. But it was odd. I'm the first to admit I have no game or mojo. Never have. I'm told I have girl-next-door appeal, whatever that is. He was probably just bored. There is no way in hell he's interested in me. I'm thirty-five, plump (okay, fat), my hair has a mind of its own, I'm on the cusp of poverty, and I have two small children in my care. Oh yeah, line up, fellas.

But that last smile …

The ringing phone snaps me out of my head. I haul my exhausted bones off the couch and pick it up. Crap, I have four messages on the machine. "Hello?"

"Mona, it's Brandie," she says. Judging from the reluctance in her voice, I am not going to enjoy this call. "I've been calling for a dang hour!"

"I was out. What's the matter?"

"Okay, well I was trying out that new potion, the one that calms the mind? Well, I gave it to Aaron, and he just crashed to the floor like a ton of bricks. I can't wake him up! I've tried shouting, water, even a slap, but he won't wake up! He's in a coma or something. I don't know what to do!"

Cue the headache. "Brandie, I told you that you were using too much geranium."

"But it gives the potion more power!"

"Yeah, obviously. Okay, do you have the third lesson from December? The one about cleansing? Find it and follow it *word for word*. It should counter the other potion. He'll be fine by tomorrow morning, okay?"

"What if he isn't?"

"Then I'll pop by and see what I can do, but the cleansing potion should work."

"Okay. Thank you so much," she says, overeager as always.

"Have a goodnight." I hang up. Hell's bells. How hard is it to make a damn potion? There are step-by-step instructions. Yet most nights I get a crisis call from some witch who thinks he or she knows better than centuries of others, and as High Priestess it's up to me to fix their mistakes.

High Priestess. I really hate that title. Sounds like an eighties hair band. I inherited the title and the largest coven in North America when Granny died ten years ago. Did I want to? Hell, no. With Granny gone and Daddy dead five years before, I became the sole caretaker of my fourteen-year-old sister Debbie—Ivy had taken off the year before—this house, and the magic shop. I did not also need a hundred and fifty witches looking to me for spiritual guidance and witchcraft instruction. But I'd been training for years, ever since I got my first period and made a sinkhole in our backyard during a fight with Ivy. That's the mark of a High Priestess—control over earth/air/fire/water. I am the physical embodiment of the fifth element, aether or spirit, which unites the other four. I can't *conjure* the elements, but if they're around I can manipulate them to do my bidding. Think tornados, tsunami, bushfires, and earthquakes. I am literally a walking natural disaster.

In my own coven there are seven others with this ability, but the last High Priestess names her successor, and if anyone objects, the coven can vote for another replacement. That didn't happen in my case. I was groomed from age twelve to take over and had already assumed most of Granny's duties, including the management of Midnight Magic, so no one objected. Had they done so, I would have gladly stepped aside. I've found that no number of luck charms can ever change mine.

I press the button on the answering machine. *"Hey, it's Billie,"* my assistant manager says. *"I just e-mailed you three new orders. I'll have my twelve tomorrow. Bye."* One of the first things I did when I took over the shop was to set up a website where people can order potions and charms over the Internet. It's now over a quarter of our revenue.

"Hi, it's Debbie," my baby sister says. *"I was just wondering if you talked to Jocasta about the flowers. If not, I can do it tomorrow. Kiss the girls goodnight for me. See you tomorrow. Love you."*

Hell's bells, I cannot believe my baby sister is getting married in a week. I can't help it, I'll always think of her as the wide-eyed baby I used to feed and later walk to the school bus. I'm eleven years older than her. When Mommy died of an infection after having her, Daddy was shattered. He had two other kids to raise, not to mention a law practice, so he moved us down the street into this house with Papa and Granny. The three adults definitely did the brunt of the child rearing, but I aided as much as I was capable. I chased the monsters out from under Debbie's bed, took her to the park, and helped with schoolwork. But then Daddy was hit by a drunk driver when she was nine, Granny got cancer when she was twelve and died two years later, and Papa faded six months after that. So it was all on me. Teaching her to drive, counseling her on boyfriend problems, and helping her get into college fell on my shoulders. Thank the goddess Debbie has a good nature and a clear head on her shoulders. She not only got into the University of Virginia after two years of community college, but she found every available grant and scholarship to cover tuition. I scrimped and saved for the rest. Now she's marrying her college boyfriend, Greg, who just passed the Virginia Bar. A lawyer. My sister hit the jackpot.

The other two messages are from Brandie, as are the three messages on my cell. I delete them and consider taking the phone off the hook, but think better of it. Knowing Brandie, her poor husband will wake up covered in boils. It's happened before.

I'm starving and dinner didn't cut it, but I've used up all my Weight Watchers points on that cheeseburger today, so I grab some water and broccoli, lock the doors for the night, and check on the girls upstairs. I find Sophie at the desk cleaning up blood and the bits of paper Cora was cutting. Like her sister, she's as cute as a button with big blue eyes, straight light brown hair with bangs, and long limbs. As I watch her small body wiping up blood, a pang of regret hits me. She reminds me so much of myself at that age, taking care of everyone. It stinks being a forty-year-old trapped in a ten-year-old's body. I don't know if she was forced into it what with being the oldest—probably, based on what little they'll tell me about life with Ivy—or if she's just an old soul like me. Both, I'd guess.

"Hey, you don't have to do that," I say as I step in.

"I don't mind," she says, tossing the paper towels into her pink trashcan.

I pull her into a hug and kiss the top of her head. "I'm proud of you."

"Why? I should have been watching her."

"No, *I* should have been watching her. This one's on me." I kiss her again before picking up the scissors and clearing off the desk.

The collage Cora was making is a goner. "So what do you think for tonight? *Ferdinand* or start another *Encyclopedia Brown?*"

"Can we just watch *The Princess and the Frog* again?"

"Again? You can almost quote the whole thing."

"I know you have a lot of work to do," Sophie says as she sits on her bed underneath that Justin Bieber poster. He and Miley Cyrus fill every pink wall. I forbid anything *Twilight* in the house solely on principle. I personally know vampires, and they do *not* sparkle.

Normally I try to keep the TV consumption to a minimum, but I have too much work and not enough energy to protest. "Fine. Go take your shower then you can start the movie. The moment it's over, lights out okay? I will check."

"Okay, Aunt Mona." I give her one final kiss before beginning to walk out. "Aunt Mona?"

I spin around. "Yeah, honey?"

"I like Dr. Sutcliffe. He's super nice, don't you think?"

"I guess. I barely know him."

"But you think he's handsome, right?"

"I—I suppose." Oh hell, I'm so obvious a child can pick up my crush.

"I think he likes you too. You should ask him out."

"It's—it's not that simple, honey."

"I bet he'd say yes."

"Well, I will think about it." And I more or less run away from my niece after those words. Do not think about him. *Don't.* Keep busy. Never a problem for me. Cora is in the bathtub when I step in. "You okay? Keeping your hand dry?"

"Yes, Aunt Mona," she says, showing it off to me. "It itches."

"It will for a couple of days," I say. "Need help shampooing your hair?" She nods. I set my snack and the scissors on the counter before pouring water on her long, almost white hair and adding shampoo. In a couple of years it'll be brown like mine and Sophie's, but for now she can enjoy being a blonde. "And what have we learned today?"

"Don't use scissors unless you're there," she says in that chipmunk voice.

"No, don't use adult scissors period. You ask me, okay?"

"Okay."

After the bath, I detangle and brush her hair before leading her into my office so Sophie can shower. It's the smallest room, with sage-colored walls, bookcases along a whole wall, my oak table covered with herbs, an iron cauldron, and other altar items. Cora likes watching me mix potions. She and my fat old Russian Blue cat, Captain Wentworth (named after the hero from my favorite Jane Austen book, *Persuasion*), keep me company as I mix a fertility potion and anoint a gambler's charm before it's time for the frog and princess. I tuck the girls into their beds, switch on the electronic babysitter, and shut off the light. They'll be asleep before the happy ending.

The majority of our orders come from non-practitioners who stumbled onto the site looking for a love or luck charm. Love potions and charms are strictly forbidden per Wiccan law, so I just use a luck spell in its place. I can spot the real, genetic witches from their orders. A regular person would never want a "creating a familiar" spell or "opening new worlds" potion. I usually send those people a note inviting them to check out the coven website. Another one of my brain children. There are about fifty official covens in America, and we're linked to forty of them. We all share spells, concerns, or we just chat. It's hard to make friends when you have to pretend not to exist.

I finish eight of the thirteen orders before the smell of burning herbs and exhaustion get to me, and I can barely see. I'll finish the rest tomorrow. I clean up before picking up the Captain and checking on the girls a second time. Both have caught the train to the land of Nod. They really are good girls. We had some growing pains in the beginning but dealt with them soon enough. Once they realized I wasn't going to beat or abandon them, we got along great. From the little I could get out of them, I know they were dragged around Europe. Sophie speaks fluent French and Cora once mentioned the Piazza Navona in Rome. Goddess knows what my sister was involved with and with whom. I don't even know if the girls have the same father. I've tried to draw more out of them, but it's like they're scared to tell me. When Ivy showed up she seemed skittish, emaciated, and pale as a junkie. We didn't get a chance to talk before she vanished, leaving me with two shy, frightened children. Now I hope she stays gone.

I toss the Captain on my white fluffy bed, peel off my reeking clothes, and jump in the shower. I have a special scrub of my own making to remove the stench of potions. That bat guano for the banishment spell really gets into my pores. By the time I shower, exfoliate, put on my pajamas, and do my final check of the house, it's almost eleven. I climb into bed with a sigh. If I fall asleep this instant I can get seven hours before the Captain wakes me for breakfast. He curls up in his spot next to me on the other pillow. Always nice to have a male in bed. On a normal night I would plan for tomorrow, but tonight I close my eyes and pass out ...

But not for long.

I don't even have time to start a dream when the doorbell downstairs jolts me awake. It rings continuously, with a pound or two against the door thrown in for good measure. I sit up, my brain instantly booting up. This can't be good. The Captain meows as I hurl off the covers. I glance at the clock. 11:59. Who on earth would come at this hour?

That instinct single women living alone have takes over. Rushing over to my closet, I pull out my gun safe and punch in the code. My .38 special comes out. This is a safe town, but a gal can never be too careful. I sprint out of the bedroom into the hallway toward the girls' room. Sophie holds Cora in bed, petting her hair in an attempt to be brave for her sister. "You two stay here and lock the door."

"Okay," Sophie says as she leaps out of bed.

As I glide down the stairs, I hear their door shut and lock. The pounding starts again, weaker this time. My heart is racing as I approach the door, my grip on the gun tightening. I really need to install a peephole. "Who is it?" I ask.

"A—Adam Blue," the man says through the door.

Adam Blue? Who the ... the name's familiar. Come on, brain. Adam ... oh, Jason Dahl's Adam Blue. "Adam?" I ask, unlocking the door. When it opens, I gasp. I wouldn't recognize him. His face is a swollen mess of bruises and cuts. His clothes are torn, smudged with dirt and blood, and he has no shoes on. He holds his right arm against his chest. I think it's broken. "What ... "

"Help me." And with that, the werewolf collapses to my foyer floor.

Hell's bells.

SUNDAY TO DO:

- *Deal with bleeding werewolf on my doorstep*
- *Transmogrification potion*
- *Find our unexpected visitor clothes*
- *Drop-off/pick up Adam and send him on his way*
- *Send girls off with Debbie*
- *Go to work*
- *Lunch with Tamara and Clay*
- *Sunday supper*
- *Hem Sophie's damn skirt*
- *E-mail spell for class*
- *Dishes*
- *Feed the Captain*
- *Makes lunches*
- *Grocery shopping*

MIRACLE OF MIRACLES HE hasn't woken any of my neighbors. That'd be all I needed. After sticking the gun in my purse, I help Adam off the floor, throwing his one good arm over my shoulders. I kick the door shut with my foot. He's almost dead weight and is not a small man. Short yes, maybe an inch or two taller than my five six, but muscular like a boxer. I lose my balance on the stairs and fall against the banister. I hoist him up and continue on.

When we reach the hallway, both girls stand at their door, mouths agape and eyes bulging. "Who is that?" Sophie asks, shielding her sister who pokes her head around the side anyway.

"A friend," I say for lack of a better word. *Acquaintance* is more accurate.

"Is he dying?" Cora asks, almost elated with excitement.

"No. Sophie, go get me a big bowl of warm water, okay? Take your sister."

I lead the bleeding man into the spare bedroom across from mine. He falls onto the bed, and I flick on the lights before rushing to the bathroom for the first-aid kit underneath the sink. I get a damp towel and some extra gauze as well. The girls come in the bathroom as I stand. "What happened to him?" Sophie asks.

"I don't know, but he'll be fine. Thank you for the water, but now go back to bed. Now!" I holler. As I have more pressing concerns, I don't wait to see if they listen.

Adam lies face—well, what's left of it—up on the bed, breathing heavily with his eyes closed. I close the door before rushing over to him to survey the damage. He is a hot mess. His blood is already seeping into the bedspread. His right eye is swollen, a nasty gash at the hairline is still bleeding, and bruises discolor his entire face. His wrists are raw and blistering from, I'd guess, silver restraints. Nasty, but nothing compared to his swollen right arm, broken without a doubt. My biggest concern is the huge red wet spot on his left side. I pull up his shirt and remove his makeshift bandage made from soaked napkins. Sure enough there's a gaping wound. "Someone stabbed you?" I ask in shock as I press the towel against the gash.

"It's shallow," he says through the pain. "Didn't hit anything major."

"Will you be able to heal this?" Vampires and werewolves have super-healing, but I'm not entirely sure how much damage that encompasses.

"N—no," he stammers. "Used silver. Gave me something. Can't shift."

"A potion? Who? Who did this to you? They didn't follow you here, did they?"

"No. I made sure of it."

Well, at this point if they come, they come. We'll cross that bridge later. "Adam, you need a doctor. I'm calling Jason. He—"

Adam grabs my arm to stop me. "No! He can't know I'm here!"

Jason Dahl is the Alpha, or head werewolf, of the Eastern Pack up in Maryland with, at last count, twenty-four werewolves under his protection. He's also a member of the P.C.O., or Preternatural Co-Op, which is having its annual meeting a week from today. And guess who pulled the short straw for hosting duty?

The P.C.O. was the brainchild of the head of the preternatural police (the F.R.E.A.K.S., or Federal Something for Extra-Sensory and Kindred Spirits), Dr. George Black, after the Goodnight Massacre and Vampire/Werewolf War in the early eighties. He recruited Granny soon after. Since all of us preternaturals don't "exist," we tend to stick to our own kind, thus the co-op. We meet once a year to talk about potential threats, concerns, or needs. This way if a Lord vampire (the ruler of a vampire territory) needs a spell or advice, he knows a witch to call. It's probably why Adam chose my doorstep. But I thought Adam was Jason's Beta, or second-in-command. He must be in a whole heap of trouble to not want his Alpha to know he's here.

"Adam you might bleed to death. Whatever you did—"

"No! No," he says with enough force to knock over a mountain. "I just need to change."

"You—I have to wait eight hours to add the last ingredient in a transmogrification potion. I don't know if you have eight hours."

"It looks worse than it is, I swear it to you," he pleads with both his tone and blue eyes. "You cannot call him. No one can know I'm here. *No one.* Promise me. Please. *Please.*"

"Adam, I have two small children in this house. Whatever trouble you're in—"

"Mona, I swear on my pack, you won't be in more trouble by having me here. I would never put your life in danger. *Never.* I swear it."

And the weird thing is, I believe him. I trust him. Don't know why, but I do. What I do know is this is a bad idea. Very bad. I'll be in the center of a shit storm if I'm not already. If Adam's going against his leader and I assist, Jason might never forgive me, and he's not the warmest of men in the best of circumstances. In fact he's downright scary. His posture, the hard angles of his face, and especially the ice blue eyes that are always sizing you up as potential prey still freak me out. I've known him—we'll I've known them both—for eighteen years, and I wouldn't call either a friend. I only speak to Jason twice a year, once at the pack Christmas party and the other time at the summit, and that is more than enough. But Adam's his best friend; whatever he did, Jason will forgive him. And me.

Yeah. Right.

"I won't call Jason," I say. "I'll fix you up as best I can, you can stay here tonight, and tomorrow morning I'll help you shift, okay?"

"Thank you," he says, finally releasing my arm and falling onto the bed. "Thank you."

"Welcome. I'll be right back." When I swing the door open and step into the hall, the girls pop out of their room. "Didn't I tell you—ugh, never mind. Sophie, go upstairs to the attic. By the dressmaker's doll there should be boxes labeled 'Roman.' Get me some clothes out of them. Cora, go downstairs to the kitchen and get me the silver duct tape out of the drawer."

The girls obey, and I go next door into my office. In a wooden holder are the vials of potions I made tonight. Two are to relieve pain and I take them both, plus the sturdiest birch branch I have before returning to my patient. "Who's Roman?" Adam asks, I suppose to make conversation.

"My daddy," I say.

Cora runs in with the duct tape. "This it?"

"Yeah, thanks sweetie."

She hands it to me, then looks at Adam, studying him. "Hi."

Though I'm sure it kills him, he smiles at her. "Hi."

Mother's daughter, no question. "Cora, bed. *Now.*"

With a bright smile, she waves goodbye, and he does the same. "Thanks for helping," he calls as she leaves.

I pull the stopper out of the potion vial. "This is a sedative and pain reliever. It should work." I help raise his head, feeling soft hair under my fingers, and pour it down. Then the other. "I don't know how long it will take with your metabolism."

"Thank you." He watches as I amass my tools for repair, eyes narrowing in confusion as I pull out streams of duct tape. "What's that for?"

"I need to immobilize your arm so the bones don't shift. It'll heal wrong, right?"

"Yeah."

Sophie walks in, arms full of clothes, staring at Adam apprehensively. "Where should I put them?"

"Top of the dresser."

She doesn't want to come in, and when she does, her eyes never leave the interloper. He's smiling though. "Thanks for the clothes. Sorry if I scared you guys."

She sets her bundle on the dresser. "I don't get scared," she says, face affixed with a scowl. She crosses her arms across her chest. "What happened to you?"

"Sophie, go to bed and stay there this time or no TV for three days. I mean it." Still glaring at Adam, she stalks out, shutting the door behind her. "Is the pain waning?"

"A little." He blinks slowly. Yeah, it's working. "Don't … don't you want to know what happened too? You haven't asked."

"I have enough troubles of my own without taking yours on. Sorry. I want to be involved as little as possible, okay?"

"But you—" and he passes out. Score one for a super-fast metabolism.

First I set his arm with the branch and tape, then snip off his shirt. Though this isn't the right time or place, I can't help but notice that he has a nice chest in spite of the blood and bruises. Muscular and compact. After I wash the knife wound, I see he wasn't lying; it's not that deep but still oozes blood. I pack it with gauze, use all of my butterfly Band-Aids to close it, and cover it with a bandage. Hope it'll keep until morning. When that's over with, I rub burn cream onto his blistered wrists and wrap those too. He was held captive by a brutal bastard. If he finds us … *no*. Not going to happen. He said I wouldn't get into more trouble. Wait. *More* trouble? What the hell did he mean by that? Crap.

There's little link between us. I mean, I didn't even know he knew where I lived. I may have known him since I was seventeen, but we've barely spoken. He was always at the meetings or parties but off to the side in the background. In fact I noticed he's always sort of avoided me. The few times I'd strike up a conversation, I'd either get a single-syllable answer or nervous smile. Hell, I accidently bumped into him one time and he tensed up and pulled away like I had a flesh-eating disease. I figured he was shy or didn't like witches. But he did change my tire that one time.

It was two years ago the day after the pack Christmas party. I'd gotten up early to drive home, and of course I had a flat tire. It was cold, raining, I'd forgotten an umbrella, and I couldn't get the bolts off. Just my luck. Everyone was still asleep, and I sure as hell didn't want to wake them. I like the werewolves in the Eastern Pack, which is why I go to the party every year, but grumpy werewolves are never a good thing. Shivering and cursing at my car was a better option. After about ten minutes, Adam strolled out with an umbrella and blanket for me and changed my tire. I made small talk about the party but was once again treated to almost silence. He handed me the tire iron, gave a quick nod, and ran back inside without another word.

We are so even now.

When I'm confident he won't bleed out, I toss a blanket over him and return to my office to start on the potion. Transmogrification, or shape-shifting, is one of the most complicated and dangerous potions. The ingredients have to be perfect in both proportion and freshness or it won't work—or worse, will half work. Think Jeff Goldblum in *The Fly*. I'd do a simple counter-spell, but I don't know which spell to counter.

It takes an hour to assemble the base, but I have to wait another eight hours for the concoction to simmer before adding the catalyst. By the time I canvass the house again, retrieve the gun, check on my three slumbering charges, change out of my bloodstained pajamas, and get back into bed, it's two a.m. I pass out five seconds after my head hits the pillow.

· *Get the werewolf out of my damn house*

The sound of voices and laughter draws me out of a dreamless sleep. Normally it's the Captain meowing for his breakfast that gets me up, but he's not in his usual spot. I check the clock. 8:47 a.m. Crap, it's almost time to finish the potion. Oh, I really hope Adam didn't die in the night. Way things are going, it wouldn't surprise me.

Cora's high-pitched giggle echoes through the house. Then another. I pull my tired body out of bed and shuffle into the hall. "My favorite is Sandy. She knows kung-fu," Cora says.

I step into the guest bedroom, a little taken aback by the sight. A much-improved Adam sits up in bed, Cora right beside him, and Sophie in the rocking chair in the corner, all eating cereal and watching cartoons. "Morning," I say.

"Aunt Mona, Adam watches SpongeBob too," Cora says.

"Does he now?"

"It's the one show all the kids in the pack agree on," he says sheepishly.

"And he likes Lucky Charms," Cora says. "I brought him breakfast in bed!"

"That's very sweet of you," I say.

"He's feeling better," Sophie says, lacking her sister's enthusiasm.

"I can see that."

"Pretty sure it was the Lucky Charms that did it," he says to Cora, who giggles again.

Our guest is quite the lady charmer. "Okay girls, I gotta check his bandages. Why don't you finish breakfast downstairs?"

Cora pouts but climbs off the bed, milk sloshing onto the bedspread. It's a goner after the blood, so I don't say anything. After they leave, I shut the door.

"They're great girls," Adam says.

I take the bowl off of his lap before lifting his shirt. "Thank you." His bandage is soaked through with blood. "It hasn't stopped bleeding."

"When I change it should heal."

I give him the once over, examining his face and chest as he watches me. His eye isn't swollen anymore, the gash in his head is pink, and all the bruises are yellow. "You're looking good. You're damn lucky." I stand from the bed. "The potion will be ready soon. I just need to get the final ingredient from you." I take the scissors from the first-aid kit and clip off a few strands of his light brown hair from the tips. "You grew this before your last change, right? It should be untainted by the potion you were given."

"Okay," he says. "I need a safe place to shift though."

"Already thought of that," I say as I walk to the door. "I'm gonna get ready. Can you dress yourself?"

"I can manage."

"Good. We'll leave in half an hour."

I'm about to walk out when he says, "Mona?"

I turn around. "Yeah?"

"Thank you. You didn't have to—"

"Of course I did. Just get dressed, okay? I have a busy day today."

I take a quick shower and put on clothes but don't bother with hair or makeup. No time. As I lace up my sneakers, I phone my assistant Billie at the shop, telling her I'll be late before running into my office to check the potion timer. Ten minutes left.

"Hello?" my sister Debbie calls from downstairs.

"Aunt Debbie," Cora shrieks, running down the hall from I'd guess Adam's room.

Sure enough when I step into the hall, Sophie walks from there out toward the stairs. Popular guy. As I pass the room a hand grabs my arm. Adam pulls me toward him. "No one can know I'm here."

"She's my sister," I say, yanking my arm away.

"Mona you can't trust *anyone.*"

"I can trust my sister."

"You don't understand," he says desperately. "I need to tell you—"

"He's up here," Cora shouts downstairs. "His name's Adam, and he's a real werewolf!"

I cock an eyebrow. "Moot now. Excuse me."

Debbie and her fiancé, Greg, stand by the front door, gazing up at me with confusion. They're quite a pair. Her auburn hair is long and curly, but it suits her long face and huge almond eyes. She takes after our mother with lean limbs and freckles across her nose. Greg is every bit the lawyer in preppy clothes complete with popped collar, sandy blonde hair, and regal features. He's a good man and even asked me for Debbie's hand in marriage. I'm a sucker for good breeding.

"Werewolves are real too?" Greg asks me. They've been together for four years, and he's still not used to the whole preternatural thing.

"Vampires too," I say with a smile. "Welcome to our world."

Debbie rubs her fiancé's back. "Why is there a werewolf here?"

"Million-dollar question," I say after a peck to her cheek. "It's co-op business. Just don't tell anyone, okay? It's a little sensitive." I glance down at the girls. "The same goes for you too. You can't tell anyone else. Not your friends, not anyone in the family, alright? Pinkie promise?" I hold out my pinkies for them.

"Pinkie promise," they say.

"Good. Now go get dressed! There's a lot of wedding stuff Aunt Debbie needs help with today. Go on." Reluctantly, they go back upstairs. "Coffee?"

Debbie and Greg trail me into the kitchen, which is a mess with milk and Lucky Charms littering the counter. I roll my eyes and get three cups. "So he just showed up last night?" Debbie asks.

"Yeah. Someone did a real number on him."

"And you let him in? Mona, you could get in trouble or something."

"Or more trouble," I mutter into my cup.

"What?" Debbie asks.

I sigh. "He's leaving today. No one will ever know he was even here, okay?"

"Then why are the police outside?" Greg asks.

I choke on my coffee. "What?" I cough. I run out of the kitchen toward the front door. Sure enough when I get outside Deputy Roy Timberlake is three houses down inspecting a red Explorer with a missing window as Auntie Sara, who holds my wayward cat, talks his ear off. Oh crap. She looks over at me. "Oh, Mona!" For being in her mid-eighties, she sure can walk fast. Debbie and Greg join me on the lawn just as she reaches us. "Deborah. Gregory."

"Hi, Auntie Sara," Debbie says.

The Captain meows in Auntie Sara's arms, so she hands him to me. "I saw him on my lawn about to go to the bathroom. You really must keep a closer eye on him."

"I will," I say, nuzzling his grayish fur. "What's Roy doing here?"

"I called him, and it's a good thing I did! That car is stolen, and there's *blood* inside."

"Oh my word," I say, pretending to be scandalized. "Where was it stolen from?"

"Roy said a bar parking lot in Richmond. I noticed it first thing this morning and called right away."

"I'm sure it's nothing," Debbie says.

"Deborah Jean there was a criminal on this street last night while we slept, completely defenseless. I didn't hear a thing, did you?"

"No. Quiet night," I say with a smile.

"Well, whoever it was might still be around. You better keep those girls inside today."

"They're going with Debbie today, but I'll be careful," I say as I start back to the house. "Have a nice day."

Our smiles drop the moment the front door shuts. The Captain yowls and jumps out of my arms, skittering under the couch in the living room. "What's up with him?" Greg asks.

"I'm here," Adam says behind us. We all spin around. He slowly takes one step at a time down the stairs. Daddy's clothes are too long on him but otherwise he looks good; contrite but good. I definitely wouldn't call him handsome, he's not a head turner like Guy, but he is interesting looking with thin lips, close to flat nose, and buggy blue eyes. I shake these thoughts away to focus on the problem at hand.

"You stole a car?" I ask.

"I had no choice," he says.

"How dare you just show up and drag my sister into your mess," Debbie snaps.

"I had no choice."

"You listen to me," Debbie says, taking a step toward him, "if any harm comes to my sister or nieces because of you, it won't matter that you're a werewolf. I will hunt you down and skin you alive, do you understand me?"

"The last thing I want is for any harm to come to your sister. You have my word on that."

I don't know if it's the sincerity in his voice or set mouth, but like me she believes him. Her shoulders slump a tad, but she still turns to me. "Is he a man of his word?"

"We'll see," I say.

Like all Southern ladies, the girls have perfect timing. They stroll onto the landing fully dressed, Sophie in jeans and a butterfly shirt, her light brown hair pulled into a ponytail. Cora's put on her brown corduroy jumper and pink long-sleeved shirt. "What are you talking about?" Sophie asks.

"Grown-up stuff," I say. "You ready?"

33

"We're helping with the wedding," Cora informs Adam. "I'm a flower girl."

"Really?"

"Yeah. My dress is pink. That's my favorite color."

Obviously put off by the crushing six-year-old as her jaw sets, Debbie says, "Come on girls. Lots to do today. Those birdseed packages aren't going to ribbon themselves."

Greg and Debbie help the girls on with their coats before Greg ushers them out the door. "Bye, Adam," Cora chirps. "Feel better!"

Sophie half smiles at our guest as she walks out. Debbie gives Adam one more glare before shutting the door behind herself. With two less things to worry about now, I start up the stairs past my guest.

"I'm sorry for all the trouble I've caused," Adam says.

"It's fine. I gotta finish the potion and get a few things. We'll leave in about five minutes."

In my office, right as the buzzer dings, I add his hair into the cauldron. The requisite green vapor poofs up—the movies got that part right—and I funnel the liquid into a glass vial. I still have to invoke the magic when we arrive at the farm. Otherwise I'd just give it to him and boot him the hell out. Nothing is ever easy. I pack up the potions from last night, a few other trinkets I need, my four biggest crystals, and my glasses before returning downstairs. Pretty sure I'm forgetting something, as usual, but there's no time to think about it.

Adam sits on the couch, grimacing in pain as he tries to put on Daddy's loafers. "They don't fit."

I can see blood seeping into his plaid shirt. "Stop bending. Hold on." I run to the closet and get my pink flip-flops. They're still small, but he can walk in them. "These will have to do."

"Thank you," he says, standing up with a grunt.

"I'll pick you up a new change of clothes later." I reach into my pocket and pull out a Celtic amulet, handing it to him. "Put that on."

He does. "What does it do?" he asks, examining it.

"Nothing yet." Closing my eyes, I place my hand on the amulet and the other on his forehead. As I pull the magic into me, much like drawing breath into my lungs, my hands tingle with heat. It's amazing whenever I do this. Right. Every cell of my body feels as if it's full of light and energy. Like I'm connected to all the power of the universe. Which I kind of am. Thirty seconds later, I open my eyes and he's vanished. He's gone.

Damn, I'm good. "There."

"What did you do?" his disembodied voice asks.

"Turned you into the invisible man. Only works for a couple minutes though. Come on." I pick up my bag and purse before opening the front door. I can tell by the noise of the flip-flops that he follows me outside. Auntie Sara maintains her usual post on the porch, eyes glued to the deputy talking on his radio. She and I wave as I walk to my car. I open the passenger side on the pretense of putting my stuff onto the floor. "Hey, Auntie Sara?" I call to buy time.

"Yes?"

The car shakes a tad when Adam climbs in. "You have fun at the bake sale! Save me some pig cookies."

"Of course, dear. You have a good day at work."

"I will." I shut Adam's door and get in on my side. It's a little odd hearing someone breathing beside me without seeing them. I'll drive like the wind to the farm. I want this over with. I start the car. We ride past the deputy who waves to me and I him. "Are you sure that car can't be traced to you?"

"My fingerprints aren't on file, and I stole it from a bar a few blocks from where I was held, but I can't be sure. Can I take this thing off? It's making me hot."

"Not until we get out of town." The streets are fairly empty, even the sidewalks, as the majority of the town is still at church. Even the diner has only a few customers. Tamara spots my car from inside and waves. I do the same.

"Friendly town," Adam's disembodied voice says.

"Well, don't start house hunting yet. You get healthy, and you get gone. I don't care where you go, or how you get there. I am running very low on charity right now."

My companion doesn't say a word for a few seconds, doesn't even breathe, but I can feel him. It's as if there's a ghost in the car. "Mona," he finally says, "there's something I need to tell you."

The last person who said that to me was a doctor who then told me my grandfather had lapsed into an irreversible coma. My stomach clenches. "What?"

He sighs. "I think someone inside your coven is trying to kill you."

The knot loosens. Oh hell's bells, he almost gave me a coronary for nothing. He might as well have said Debbie was a pod person. "That's insane," I chuckle. "Kill me?"

"Yes," he says as serious as cyanide.

"What? No."

"Yes."

"No."

"Mona. *Yes.*"

This man has lost his mind, but I'll play along. "Okay, for the sake of argument, let's say this is true. You know this how?" I ask, still chuckling.

"Because until last night ... I was one of the people who was supposed to kill you."

· Have a nervous breakdown

I know smoking is bad. I do. I'd whip the girls if they ever tried a cigarette. And I'm such a hypocrite, because here I am in their empty school parking lot, puffing away. I'm supposed to be a role model, and I'm smoking and pacing like a caged animal. I only smoke in times of extreme stress or depression, and boy do both of those apply now.

My hit man sits half in and out of my car, silently watching me go nuts, concern all over his now-visible face. A concerned hit man, doesn't that go against the code? "Okay, you need to start at the beginning," I say, taking another drag.

"About three days ago, a rogue werewolf contacted Jason. He does mercenary work, primarily against other preters. He was approached by Alejandro, Lord Thomas's second-in-command, about taking out Thomas. And you."

"Me? Why me? I barely have any contact with the Lord of Richmond or any vampire."

"The rogue didn't ask. The only reason he told Jason was he recognized your name and knew you were a ... *friend* of the pack," he says with a scoff.

"How'd he know that?"

"He used to be in the pack, but left about twelve years ago. He's been to the Christmas party a few times since." Meaning I've probably met this man. "Anyway, it was ... decided I would approach Alejandro pretending I wanted in on the plot. That I wanted to kill Jason and become Alpha. Basically, it was a 'I'll take care of yours if you take care of mine' deal."

"So who wants me dead?"

"I don't know. I only dealt with Alejandro. He wouldn't even say her name."

"Her?"

"As in, 'This was all her idea.' I got the impression she and Alejandro were lovers."

I take another drag of my cigarette. "As far as I know there's no one in my coven sleeping with a vampire." I shake my head. "When was this supposed to happen?"

"Sooner rather than later. We were just getting into the details last night when some vampires busted into Alejandro's house and dragged us out. Lord Thomas must have discovered the plot, so that was the end of Alejandro. I barely escaped, and you know the rest."

My mind is going a million miles a minute. "B—But wait. Alejandro's dead. There isn't a hit man. So whoever wants me dead has no one to do her dirty work."

"So she'll probably just do it herself."

I stub out my cigarette. "Fuck. We need to call George. Get the F.R.E.A.K.S. here. The girls will just have to stay with Tamara or Debbie, I don't know."

"For how long? Whoever it is, is going to need to plan. A new time table. It could be tomorrow or six months from now before she tries again."

Crap, he's right. I can't go into hiding. I have two small children in school and nine million other responsibilities. "What do you suggest? Because this is new territory for me. I guess we could call Jason. He might have some ideas."

"No," Adam says vehemently. "I would not recommend that."

"Why the hell not?" I snap.

"The pack is going through its own problems right now. He'll feel that with Alejandro dead, the threat was neutralized."

"Then I'll convince him it's not."

It takes effort, but Adam pushes himself into the standing position. "Listen, I know Jason a lot better than you do, okay? You can call him for advice, sure. But you cannot tell him I'm here."

"Why not?"

He hobbles over to me, his slightly bug-eyed blue eyes meeting mine point-blank when he stops. "Because. He'll order me back to Maryland, and I'll have to go. Then you'll be in this alone."

I tense from toenails to top at this thought. For once the idea of being alone terrifies me. Normally I welcome it. I fear I'm about to burst into tears, and there is no way I'm letting him see me like that. I turn away. "And why—why would you help me?"

"I have my reasons."

"Them being?"

"My own."

I groan in frustration. What the hell am I going to do? Deep breath. The one I take doesn't help a lick. Okay, stick to the plan for now. Get him healthy, go from there. Be strong. After a second to compose myself, I spin back around. "Well, you're no good to me injured. Let's get to the farm."

With shaking hands, I open my car door and climb in. My hands don't stop vibrating as we drive to the Hackett Farm five miles outside of town. Adam keeps glancing at me, but I keep my eyes on the road. "I'm sorry," he says.

"Every problem has a solution. I just have to think and find it."

"I have some suggestions," he says.

"All ears."

"You need to act as if nothing happened. Whoever she is, she's probably feeling desperate right now. If she knows you're onto her, that might make her more dangerous. Just try not to be alone and isolated. Big crowds."

"Not a problem this week. What about the girls?"

"This entire plan was a power grab. Whoever this woman is wants your position. The only way to become High Priestess is for the old one to die, right? Hurting the girls won't accomplish that. Besides, you're one of the most powerful witches in the world. You can protect them better than anyone."

My ego swells a little. "How do you know so much about witches?"

"I ... did my research."

We ride in silence the rest of the way as the wheels in my head turn. Of course with every rotation I see my mangled, bloody body left in an alley being feasted on by dogs. Okay, I really have to lay off the horror movies.

The Hackett Farm was one of the most prosperous tobacco farms in the county a hundred years ago. Now the only remnant of the once great plantation is the decaying gray barn missing about fifty percent of its roof and walls. It's isolated, with the nearest family seven miles away and one dirt road in and out, so kids come out here to party and engage in lascivious acts. This was one of my sister Ivy's favorite spots to raise hell. I only came out here when I had to pick her drunken butt up.

After helping Adam out of the car, I locate the potion in my purse and hand it to him. "Go wait inside. I have to set up the perimeter." As he pads to the barn, feet slapping in pink flip-flops, I retrieve my four quartz crystals. I walk around the perimeter of the barn, placing one outside at each corner. When I put down the last one, I call the magic into me to energize them. It flows from my finger to the crystal like electricity. Feels good every time. I stand up and peer through a gap in the wall. Adam has been watching me this whole time. "So nothing physical can come in or out," I explain. "Try putting your hand through."

He tries to reach for me, but my invisible fence stops him. "Impressive."

"How long do you think you'll need?"

"Earliest I can change back is two hours. After that I'll need a minimum, bare minimum, of three hours sleep."

"Okay. I guess I'll just, um, come get you in two hours?"

"Okay," he says, nodding. He holds up the potion. "Should I drink this now?"

I nod. Adam steps away from the wall into the center of the barn. He all but chokes on the disgusting potion, hacking his lungs out when it's all down. Magic time. I close my eyes, reaching out to the three ley lines that run through this town. They're invisible paths of energy that I draw from to boost my power. My entire body tingles and all that power is siphoned into my body, filling me like a vessel. I reach out to the ingredients in the potion coursing through Adam's body. All originate from the earth, and I am a part of that earth. Most witches need to say a few words or an invocation, but I just need to concentrate. Another trait of a High Priestess.

Adam is of this earth, and I sense him too. His heart, his mind, especially his soul. And the wolf inside him. It's angry. He wants to come out and roar. I call to it, all but stroking his metaphysical fur, and he comes running. The force of the wolf busting out nearly knocks me down. My eyes fly open just as Adam expels a blood-curdling scream. He falls onto his knees, howling like a man on fire. The change is just as painful. Bones breaking, skin stretching, organs rearranging. Perhaps fire would be preferable. I've never seen a werewolf change, and I don't want to break that streak now. This is private and should stay that way. As he shrieks, cries, and groans in pain, I run back to my car. He'll be fine.

It's my own neck I'm worried about.

· *Go to work*

Okay. Next crisis. On the drive back to town, I'm still reeling from information overload. I need to organize my thoughts. Someone I know wants to kill me. As in dead. As in no more tucking the girls in at night. No more lunches with Tamara and Clay. No more *breathing*. How the hell did this happen? I am not the kind of person other people want to kill. I'm not a werewolf who chases after rogues that attack people. I'm not a vampire who leaves bodies in his wake. I'm a witch, the pacifists of the preternatural world. I don't even squish spiders. Hell, Goodnight hasn't had a non-domestic homicide since the early eighties when three vampires slaughtered my cousins Emma, Lucas, and Tom for harboring a runaway witch. People still talk about it.

I keep glancing in my rearview mirror for strange cars. Goddess, I haven't been this paranoid since the one time I smoked pot. How long have I been in danger and not even known it? And who the hell would want me dead? Someone who wants to be High Priestess.

42

That narrows it down. There are only seven others who are candidates, and all are my relatives. I am more likely to be killed by someone I—

A honking car drives right in front of me. I slam on the breaks as Jeff Pinker flips me off. I just ran a red light. I never run red lights. I'm gonna get myself killed before someone else can do it. I think I'm going to throw up.

I park in the lot around the corner from my shop. It's half full now and by lunchtime it will be packed. Wish it was that way now. As I pass each empty car, I tense up, convinced my murderer is hiding behind one to pop out and shoot me dead. My paranoia only gets worse as I move down the cobblestone sidewalk past all the tiny curio shops that comprise downtown. Since I know about ninety-nine percent of the population in town, they smile and nod as I pass. I keep glancing at their hands for weapons. How the hell am I supposed to act normally with the Sword of Damocles hanging over my head?

Midnight Magic is nestled between an antique shop and Lady Catherine's Tea Room, which is owned by a man named Duke. We get a decent tourist trade here, mostly from upper-scale and sophisticated older women searching for some Southern gentility. Except my customers. Since we're the largest occult shop within a hundred miles, I find myself waiting on New Agers along with those Southern ladies looking for homeopathic remedies to stave off aging and hipsters who've read the Harry Potter and Twilight series. Money's money.

The store was opened in the early twentieth century by my great-great-grandmother Ramona, my namesake. She was High Priestess at the turn of the past century and was rumored to have had an affair with Aleister Crowley, a self-proclaimed witch who I later learned was just batshit crazy. Supposedly he's my great-grandfather Crowley's father. It was quite the scandal, one of many surrounding Ramona. Her reputation is hard to live up to.

We only have one customer inside when I walk in, my cousin Bethany. Strange. I was just thinking about her family. She was the sole survivor of that massacre in town when she was a child. On a normal day I'd strike up a conversation, but now I'm afraid she'll pull out a knife and stab me. She is over by the athames, or ritual knives. Maybe being in the house while her family was slaughtered cracked her. Not that she's a High Priestess, but still. Not taking any chances.

Billie stands at the counter reading a magazine. The majority of genetic witches try to blend in, but not Billie. Her spiky hair is dyed blue this week and today she sports a bat nose ring, but the black ankh tattooed on her neck draws the attention first. At least her dozen other tattoos are hidden by her jeans and Misfits hoodie. I had to institute a dress code when I hired her. She looked too much like a walking ad for Hot Topic, and my other employee, Alice, who's worked here part-time since Granny's days, kept lodging complaints about unprofessionalism. So I compromised, which means they both grumble to me on occasion.

I walk past Billie into the back room without a word. The front of the store is all retail: books, jars of herbs, oils, jewelry, incense, posters, candles, even joke magic tricks all cramped together in stands that make it hard to move around. One entire wall is covered with ancient bookcases filled to capacity with occult books. There are a few shelves on the walls with statues and candle holders. I have to keep the crystals, herbs, and oils behind the counter or customers couldn't get to anything.

The back room is where the real magic happens. My office/altar/ storage space. I flip on the lights and toss my purse on the ancient table. My cell phone is in there somewhere. Billie strides in, towering over me as usual. She's over six feet tall and skinny. She could be a model if not for the attitude. "How many did you get done last night?" she asks.

"Eight—no, six."

"That's it?"

"I know. If you can cover the front, I'll get the rest done today."

"We had three new orders this morning."

"Then I'll do them too!" I snap. We're both taken aback. I'm known around town for my calm demeanor, so yelling is not a common thing. "Sorry."

"Stressful night?"

"Understatement." I pull out my cell. "I need to make a few calls."

"Okay," she says with a cocked eyebrow. "I'll be out front if you need me." With another concerned glance she walks out, shutting the curtain behind herself.

Could it be her? She's worked with me for five years ever since leaving her coven in Orlando when her girlfriend got a job in Richmond. No way. She doesn't have an ambitious bone in her body. I spent two weeks begging her to officially become assistant manager. And she's not an aether. No, right now there is a short list of people I trust implicitly, and Billie is one of them, along with Tamara and Clay, Debbie, Auntie Sara, and Adam.

Adam? Okay, maybe not him. He'll earn his place when he stops being so damn withholding of information.

I sit down in front of the computer and pull up my password-protected address book with all the co-op telephone numbers. I'll try George Black first, seeing as he's the head of the preternatural police, and this is right up their alley. He picks up on the fifth ring.

"George Black," he says.

"George, it's Mona McGregor. I have a problem." I lay out everything Adam told me.

"Oh, Mona, I'm sorry. I have no idea what to tell you."

"Tell me you'll send someone to help me, George." My voice is terse even to my own ears.

"I can't. I'm sorry. The team's already on an investigation in Idaho. They just arrived last night. There's a wraith slaughtering people."

"Then just send us one agent. Just not the vampire," I say with scorn. "You know why."

"Mona, I don't have a person to spare. We recently lost two members. The best I can do right now is contact the FBI and have them look into it. Or your local police."

Not gonna happen. The county sheriff is married to one of the candidates, my cousin Shirley. He wouldn't appreciate me accusing his wife of sleeping with a corpse and plotting murder. "So after years of friendship and me helping you out on multiple cases, when I need you, the F.R.E.A.K.S. won't lift a finger to stop me from being iced? Thanks, George."

"Mona—"

I hang up. Of all the nerve! After all … the phone rings, the display lighting up. It's George, but I just hit "end." *Okay, calm down, Mona.* I take a few deep breaths that don't help. That Valium Collins mentioned might work, but since I'm fresh out and a calming potion takes too damn long, on to option two. I dial Jason's cell. He answers on the second ring. "Jason Dahl," he says in that harsh tone he always has.

"Jason, it's Mona McGregor."

"Mona. What do you want?" This guy does not know the meaning of the word *manners*.

"I want to know why you didn't tell me someone put a hit out on me."

His end is quiet for a few seconds. Even his silence is intimidating. Thick even. "I wanted to get all the facts before I contacted you. How did you find out?"

Okay, in normal circumstances, I'd tell the truth. It goes against the co-op's spirit to lie to other members, but if half of what Adam said is true—and I'm literally betting my life that it is—then I have no choice. "Lord Thomas of Richmond called me last night. Apparently he discovered Alejandro's plot, and unlike you thought I should know."

He's quiet for a second, his breathing ragged. "He killed Alejandro? Did he say anything else?" he asks, voice like an ice pick.

"Like what? He doesn't know who wants me dead, if that's your concern."

"Mona, has Adam contacted you at all in the last few days?" he asks, voice tinged with fear, not an emotion I thought him capable of.

"Why would he?" Not technically a lie.

"If he does, would you have him call me?"

"Jason, what about me? I could still be—"

"You'll be fine. I have to go." And he hangs up on me.

The bastard! Both of them! I am literally vibrating with rage. What the hell is the purpose of the co-op if I'm the only one who cooperates with the others? Hell's bells, I cannot believe this. Well, next time either of them needs a favor, they can forget it. Screw them both.

There's only one more person (and I use the term loosely) that I can call, but he won't get my message until tonight. I'm not as friendly with Lord Thomas as the other members since he only attends summits once every three years if that, but he's my last hope. I leave a message. "Thomas, this is Mona McGregor from the P.C.O. I, uh, there's no easy way to say this." I sigh. "Your second, Alejandro, along with one of my witches, was plotting to kill us. I understand, uh, that your end has been taken care of, but any help you can give me to find my wicked witch would be much appreciated as ... she might still want to kill me. Ha ha. So please call me. Soon. Thank you." I'm about to hang up when I remember, "Oh, and if Jason Dahl calls, could you please tell him that you were the one who filled me in on this whole mess? I'd appreciate it. Bye." I hang up and thump my head on the altar.

Okay, now what?

I've read enough mystery novels to formulate a plan. I can do this. What would Stephanie Plum do? Sleep with two gorgeous guys then have her car blow up. Okay, not applicable. Miss Marple. What would Miss Marple do? Identify potential suspects.

Assuming this is a power play for my job, there are seven women in line for Priestess, all cousins of one stripe or another: Shirley, Whitney, Erica, Ann, Esther, Collins, and her sister Cheyenne. I can't see eighty-three-year-old Ann or sixty-seven-year-old Esther sleeping with a vampire, and Whitney is fourteen, so for the time being I'll discount them. That leaves four.

Shirley Andrews is a distant cousin I've had few dealings with. She's in her fifties with two grown children, a sheriff husband, and a driven attitude. She won't be happy until her husband is mayor or a senator. She barely associates with the rest of the coven unless it's an election year. The only reason I know she's an aether is Granny wrote her name down in a ledger that keeps track of all of us. If I was running against her husband for mayor then I wouldn't put it past her to put a hit on me, but not for the run of the coven.

Next there's Erica Fitch, who was my only real competition when I became High Priestess. She's in her early forties but looks much younger thanks to constant glamour spells and trips to the plastic surgeon. Being a former trophy wife then rich widow is hard work. At age twenty-two she caught the eye of the richest man in the county, Deaver Fitch III, much to the chagrin of his first wife. Erica and Deaver were only married for three years before he mysteriously died of a stroke at age fifty-two in the middle of sex with his young bride. The entire town suspected she offed him, but there was no proof. She's been the merry widow since, though her exploits with not only the young blue-collar boys in town but the upper echelon gentlemen in Richmond do tarnish that image.

She easily could have met Alejandro in Richmond at some point, though why she'd want to become High Priestess is beyond me. Growing up she regularly attended coven meetings, but those tapered off when she got married. Now she comes about once a year, mainly to catch up with old friends. The past month I have seen more of her as she's on the Founders' Week committee with me, and what a joy that has been. I do not enjoy high and mighty people putting me and everyone else down once a week. I almost want it to be her just so they can haul her liposuctioned butt away. Maybe she's just bored and decided, "Hey, maybe that High Priestess job might be fun for a little while. I killed once, what's one more time?" Possible.

Finally, there are the twins: Collins and Cheyenne Bell. I personally trained them as aethers when puberty hit. It's rare to have two High Priestesses in one family, but since they're identical twins it wasn't too surprising. We have the same great-grandfather Crowley who, like his alleged father, left multiple bastards in his wake. Three that we know of. Granny and Auntie Sara were the only legitimate children. The Great Ramona forced her wayward son to marry his powerful cousin Camille, the supposed next High Priestess. Great-Grandma Camille died of the Spanish Flu before this came to pass, but Ramona lived until her late nineties, and by then Granny was old enough to take the reins.

Like most of my second cousins, Collins and Cheyenne come from the illegitimate branch of the family. Not that anyone save their grandmother Maxine cares anymore. Family is family, at least to me. I'd cross Collins off the list even before Shirley. She practically lived at my house growing up, what with those abusive asshole parents of hers. She even stayed with us for a few months just to get away from them. Then Granny died, and I had to send her back to said assholes. She went to live with her grandmother a few days after that. She and Debbie have been best friends since kindergarten. Hell, she's Debbie's maid of honor. I've known her all her life, and she doesn't have a malicious bone in her body.

Now Cheyenne...

For identical twins, those two could not be more different. Their parents are drunken, abusive, disgusting assholes whose fights are legendary. Collins told me she spent years tending to her parents' wounds so becoming a nurse was always a foregone conclusion. They never hit the girls though. Granny and I asked. We tried to informally adopt Cheyenne too, but she was a vicious child. Beating up Debbie, stealing, shouting obscenities at us. She hasn't gotten much better with age. Poaching boyfriends, an arrest for drunk driving, and the inability to hold a job are her claims to fame in this town. She does attend coven meetings regularly but is constantly questioning me and making snide remarks. I have heard on more than one occasion that she's been dabbling in the gray and even black magic. Anything that takes away a person's free will, like love potions, is gray. Black is classified as anything that harms another living creature. Both are illegal. If a witch is guilty of either, I'm duty bound to contact the F.R.E.A.K.S. and excommunicate them from the coven. Right now all I have are rumors and a hunch. I was going to start digging more into the rumors after the wedding, but I guess I'll have to start now. So how?

The curtain is pulled aside, and Billie pokes her head in. "Hey, some guy's asking for you."

My body tenses. Another hit man? "Who is he?"

She smiles mischievously. "I told you. Some guy."

Great. I stand and walk into the store, my heart leaping into my throat when I lock eyes on the man at the counter. She was right, he is some Guy. "Dr. Sutcliffe," I say with a nervous laugh. He looks gorgeous in his dark blue jeans and plaid sweater with white shirt underneath. "Um, hi!"

"Hi," he says, blushing just like me.

Neither of us says another word for seconds, we just coyly smile at one another. Billie eyes us both, then clears her throat. "May we help you with something, doctor? We're having a sale on Harry Potter items."

"Oh, uh, no. Thank you." He clears his throat. "I was just stopping by to check on Cora. How is her hand?"

"Fine. She said it still hurts and itches a little though."

"That's normal. It means it's healing. The discomfort should stop in a day or two."

"She'll be happy to hear that," I say.

More awkward silence where we gaze at our shoes. Billie clears her throat again. "Sorry. Frog in throat. I'm going in the back to get some water. Excuse me." She winks at me as she passes. I really hope he didn't see that.

When the curtain shuts, Guy and I smile nervously at each other. "So … you own this place?" he asks.

"Yeah, it's been in the family for generations."

He glances around, taking it all in. "I've never been in a magic shop before. It's … interesting. Are there a lot of Wiccans in town?"

Really only about fifteen who practice the religion. "Enough."

"And you're the, what do they call it, 'High Priestess' is it?"

"Who told you that?"

"Collins. I never would have pegged her or you for a Wiccan. I always imagined someone like Stevie Nicks or Goths singing to the moon. Not that there's anything wrong with that," he backpedals. "Or the religion. To each his own and all." Oh my goodness, I've flustered him again. A handsome man is clumsy around me. I like it. "I didn't insult you, did I?"

"Not at all."

He shakes his head. "Sorry. I don't know what's the matter with me today."

"It's just one of those days," I say with a chuckle.

"I guess," he says, averting his eyes. "So … have you always been Wiccan?"

"Pretty much. It's the family religion, not unlike being a Baptist around here."

"And you perform spells? Do they work?"

"Most of the time. They're really just a way to focus and meditate on what you want. We don't sacrifice animals or anything like that."

"Oh, no, I know you don't. The websites said so." He was researching witches? There go the tingles again. He blushes again at his slip. "So uh, Founders' Week is this week, right? What's that usually like?"

I shrug. "Don't know. We haven't had one in fifty years, since the three hundred mark."

"But you're on the committee, right?" Has he been checking up on me? "What, um, events do you suggest I hit?"

"Well, you missed the crafts fair yesterday, but you can make the bake sale at the Methodist church today. My auntie's making pig cookies. They're delicious. I'm really just coordinating the festival on Friday. It's gonna be great. We have games, rides, even fireworks. Sophie's actually in the pageant that day."

"I'll definitely have to go then," he says.

"Um, here," I say, handing him a yellow flyer on the counter. "This has the schedule."

He reads it. "'Bachelorette Auction?'"

"Yeah, it was my cousin Erica's idea," I say, rolling my eyes.

"Are you in it?"

"No, no," I say with a chuckle. "Hell no."

"Why not?"

"Because..." Nobody would spend a nickel on me, "I'm too busy."

"To go on a date for charity? That doesn't sound like you."

"But you don't know me very well," I point out.

He raises an eyebrow. "Maybe you can sign up for that auction, and we can remedy that." Oh hell's bells. Did he...does he mean...I'm speechless, but singing like Maria on the Swiss Alps inside. I'm also so red now I'm closer to purple. I manage a bright smile, which he returns. Thank the goddess customers come in. Tourists, since I've never seen them before. Guy glances back at them, then at me. "I'll let you get back to work. Think about what I said."

"I most definitely will," I say, trying to stay composed.

He walks toward the door, but just as he steps out he pokes his head back in. "See you around, Mona."

"Bye, Guy." The moment the door shuts, I squeal and jump up and down. The tourists are taken aback, but I could give a hoot.

Billie, who probably had her ear to the curtain the whole time, rushes out. "You have to do that auction."

"He is interested in me, right? I'm not just going nuts?"

"No way. He totally wants in your pants. You're doing the auction Wednesday, right?"

"Yeah, I guess. I don't know what to do. This is unprecedented. I haven't been on a date in ten years. I don't know how to act. I don't know if I'm supposed to call him. I suck at flirting. You heard me, I was...horrible."

"You did fine, *obviously.* All you have to do is show up at the country club Wednesday. I have a feeling he'll handle the rest."

Now I just have to live that long.

• *Pick up the werewolf*

Time flies when you have fifteen potions to concoct, customers to assist, a survival plan to make, and a fantasy wedding to envision. Adam's had three hours to play wolf when I return to the barn. I did make a quick stop at Walmart to get him some clothes and toiletries. Hope they fit.

As I approach the barn, I hear growling and furious digging. When I'm a few feet away, the sounds stop. "Adam?"

Just as I get within a few feet, out of nowhere a big brown ball of fur crashes into the side of the wall, the whole barn shimmying. Slats of wood fall and slide to the ground, one from the roof landing a foot away from me. I gasp and step back as the growling inside intensifies. Through an opening I see rows of sharp teeth snapping as a claw reaches through a hole in the ground. He found a way around my gate.

I've never seen a werewolf after a transformation for this very reason: they're scary as hell. Whatever the man weighed as a human, he weighs as a wild beast. Like Adam's normal hair, his pelt is light brown with blonde highlights. Those razor sharp talons continue digging in the dirt in an attempt to get out and eat my liver. But I don't have time for a hissy fit. I push my fear aside, square my shoulders, and march back to the barn. "Adam Blue, you stop that this instant!" Using my power, I reach into the ground and tell it to close up the hole. There's a small tremor. The dirt redistributes as the wolf whines and backs away. "Bad boy!"

The wolf stares at me, at first baring his fangs and growling, but then his still bright blue eyes lock on mine. As if a switch was flicked, he calms. The growling is replaced with panting while the vibrating hair along his spine flattens. Guess he remembers me. "Can you understand me?" He keeps panting, pink tongue lolling out of the side of his mouth. I'll take that as a yes. "I'm going to change you back now, okay?" He whines a little. "I know, but I need you human. Sorry. Hey, the full moon is next week. You can come back then." The wolf walks up to me, still whining. He's a good-looking wolf, majestic as hell. I have the strongest urge to run my hand through his soft fur. I don't though. I like my hands attached to my body, thank you.

"Sorry." I close my eyes again, calling to the ley lines. The wolf literally howls in agony as I infuse him with power. It finds the man inside the beast and jerks him out of they abyss. Like before I don't wait and watch the change. I cover my ears as I sprint back to the car. The Dixie Chicks can't drown out his screams. That poor man. Werewolves definitely have the short end of the preternatural stick.

About five minutes later, the noise ceases. Taking a pair of sweats with me, I walk back, picking up the nearest crystal to break the seal. Adam lays on the ground in the fetal position, slick from sweat and the sticky ectoplasm that aides the change. Naked. He's naked. Hell's bells.

I haven't seen a naked man in fifteen years, though Dennis didn't look near as good. He was stringy where Adam is muscular. Sculpted even. I can't help it, my eyes dart to his butt. Even has dimples. *Damn.* I turn purple again. "Adam?" I ask as I quickly turn my back to him. I hold out the clothes behind me. "Brought you clothes!" I can hear him stand and shuffle toward me. He takes the clothes, and I start power walking away. "Meet you at the car!"

After a minute or so enduring visions of dimples dancing through my head, he meanders out of the barn like a sleepwalker and gets in the car. The moment he rests his head against the window, he falls asleep. He'll be out most of the day, I know that much about werewolves. Birth twice in one day takes it out of even the strongest person. Not so ferocious now. I've heard stories of wild wolves unable to control their temper and ripping men apart. They aren't nearly as bad as I'd imagined. Besides that initial scare, he was rather pleasant. He probably would have let me pet him.

Back to the house we go. Auntie Sara is at the bake sale today, and everyone else could care less, so I help him walk to the front door. When we get inside, I stay by the door. "Bathroom is the first door on the right upstairs." I hand him the Walmart bags. "Here. I got you some extra clothes. I hope they fit. You'll be staying in the guest bedroom where you were last night. Help yourself to anything in the fridge. If there are any problems, all my numbers are by the phone in the kitchen."

"I'm staying?" he asks.

"We'll get into all of that later, okay? I'm already real late. You get some sleep."

I'm about to shut the door, when he says, "Mona?" I step back in and turn around. "I'm sorry if I scared you back there."

"You didn't. Actually, you looked kind of cute with your tongue hanging out."

"Oh," he says with a tiny chuckle.

"Just sleep, okay? I'll be back to check on you later." I shut the door.

Time to rally the troops.

• Lunch with Tamara and Clay

Goodnight Diner is, without debate, the heart of the town. There isn't a citizen who doesn't patronize it at least once a week to sample their down-home breakfast or best barbeque in the county. The lunch rush has dwindled by the time I arrive, so there are actually tables available. As I walk in, Tamara spins around from the kitchen with two trays full of food. Her hay-colored hair is pulled back into a ponytail, and smudged eyeliner rims her large brown eyes. She's stick thin and muscular from all the whizzing around with heavy trays. We met the first day of high school in English class. Her family had just moved from Charlotte and she didn't know a soul. I wasn't exactly popular, but I had a good circle of friends. The rest have moved out of town, but we keep in touch. Only Tamara and Clay remain.

Clayton McGregor is another second cousin, though from my nonmagical grandfather's side. He waits in the back booth fiddling with his cell phone. That man loves his online poker. He's my brother from another mother. His mother and mine became fast friends when they were each pregnant with their respective firstborns. Clay and I played in the same bassinet, on the same playground, and then went through school with most of the same classes. I'm sure if we weren't related we would have married by now. He's moderately attractive with brown hair, small hazel eyes, receding chin, and always a bowtie. He even asked me to marry him once, but I've never had a single lustful thought about him. About two months after he proposed to me he got engaged to Jolene, who he has been divorced from for two years. She cheated, the bitch. Never deserved him.

"Hey," I say as I sit. "Sorry I'm late."

He puts his cell away. "You're always late. How's Cora? I heard about her hand."

"Two stitches, no big deal."

Tamara slides into the booth next to Clay with a sigh. "I hate Sundays. How's Cora?"

"Jeez, does the whole town know?"

"Cora and the stolen car are the hot topics of the day," Tamara says. "Care to comment? Clay here needs a quote." Clay is one of three full-time reporters at the *Goodnight Star*, our local paper.

Before I can say a word, Tamara starts talking again. "Oh, before I forget, that gorgeous doctor was in here asking questions about you."

"What doctor?" Clay asks.

"The new one. You've seen him. Tall, thin, Yankee, mediocre tipper?"

"Him? Why would he ask about her?" he asks with distaste.

"Thanks, Clay," I mutter.

"Guess, *mo-ron*. I saw him walk to her shop right after." She looks at me. "Did he ask you out? Because I got the distinct impression he wanted to."

"Not exactly," I say.

"Wait, I think I played golf with him once," Clay chimes in. "Blackish hair? Snooty attitude?"

"He does not have a snooty attitude," I protest. "He's wonderfully nice."

"He kept complaining about how small the course was. The man could play though."

"Shut up, Clay. No one cares about golf," Tamara says. "Did he ask you out or not?"

"He asked if I was going to the bachelorette auction, then *strongly* suggested I sign up."

Tamara squeals. "I knew it! He likes you! Oh Mona, how exciting! It's finally going to happen for you. I just know you two are gonna get married! You're so damn picky, and finally someone picked you right on back. I always said it only takes one," says the woman on her third marriage.

"Tam, calm down. He hasn't even officially asked me out yet."

"He will at the auction, I know it. You'll have to buy a new dress, but I'll do your hair and makeup."

"Tam, stop it," I say.

"How can you not be excited about this? A hot *doctor* wants you. I'd be dancing in the streets if I was you."

"I have other things on my mind."

"What could be more important than the first date with your future husband?"

So I tell them. They both know all about us preternaturals. Hell, only a few in town don't. They also know to keep their traps shut.

"Holy shit," Clay says.

"Yeah," I say, sipping my water.

"I don't believe it," Tamara says. "No way. Out of everyone in this town, you're the least likely to be murdered."

"Adam has no reason to lie, and Jason confirmed it."

"But … kill you?" Tamara asks. "To become queen of the witches? All you do is complain about how crappy it is. Why would anyone want to do it?"

"Hell if I know. I'll ask her before she shoots me."

"And you can't abdicate or step down?" Clay asks.

"There are only two ways out: die or be censured for black magic."

"Then go start sacrificing some goats to Satan," Tamara suggests.

Clay and I shoot her a look. "What can we do?" Clay asks.

"I need help investigating the four women, Erica and Cheyenne especially. Between the two or you, not a piece of gossip slips past. Any ammunition or rumors about them might be useful. Just be discreet. Whoever this is doesn't think I know. She could get desperate if she does."

"I spend thirty hours a week with Cheyenne in this diner, and let me say she does not have the brainpower to put together a hit. But I have heard the rumors about black magic."

"I'm gonna talk to Meg and Belle tomorrow to see if I can get more out of them," I say. "Their names keep popping up in the rumors too."

"And I'll pull everything the paper has on Shirley and Erica," Clay says. "Maybe call a friend at the Richmond paper."

"Thanks. Oh, Tam, start telling people I just picked up my cousin A.J. from Boston. That'll explain why I have a strange man living in my house this week."

Tamara falls back in the booth. "This is insane, Mona."

"Believe you me, I know it. I'm really just worried about the girls. I'd send them to Debbie's or Sara's, but for how long? And what if whoever it is kidnaps them or something? I guess I'll just keep Adam around them until this is over, I don't know."

"And you trust this guy?" Clay asks.

"Enough. I mean he—"

Cheyenne Bell, in all her glory, steps into the diner with her grungy boyfriend of the week, Bruce Nettles. She's a pretty girl, full and lithe like her twin, but lacking Collins's grace. Her hair is platinum blonde, her black shirt and skirt are both tight, and she always reeks of cigarettes. I can smell them from here. She kisses Bruce before stepping into the back of the house. "Guess I should start my spying now," Tamara says as she turns back around. "If she's upset her vampire boyfriend croaked, she ain't showing it."

"She might not know, she might not care," I counter. A second later, Cheyenne strolls back out, fastening her black and white checkered apron, which matches the floor. I catch her eyes, and she half smiles before returning into the back room. That was odd. "There is definitely something up with her."

"I'll see what I can get out of her," Tamara says as she stands. "Is there anything else I can do? Do you want Lonnie's shotgun?"

Clay and I scoot out as well. "I don't need it," I say, "but thanks."

We three musketeers move to the door and exchange hugs. Cheyenne eyes us as she pours Ned Larder's coffee at the counter. I have the strongest urge to leap across it and shake her until she admits everything, but I don't. I need more information before I confront her. It's the Miss Marple way. Clay escorts me out and down the street toward the shop. I do love Southern manners.

"There has to be more we can do," he says.

"Clay, I can't think of anything."

"I really think you need to take an extended vacation until this blows over."

"I have two small children in school, a shop to run, a festival and wedding to put on, and a gaggle of preternaturals coming to town for a summit. Not to mention I can't afford a vacation, and the problem will just be waiting for me when I return. I'm screwed."

"Well, I'll start digging on Erica. Those vampires too. I'll just say I'm doing a profile piece on her."

"I appreciate it," I say, hugging him when we reach my shop.

"If you need *anything,* call me day or night."

"Thanks." I notice Billie watching through the window and pull away. "Gotta get back to work." Clay nods, pecks my cheek, and walks down the sidewalk.

When I step in Billie has her pierced eyebrow raised. "Does the doctor have competition?"

"Funny," I say, taking off my coat. "Can you come into the back for a sec?"

"Am I in trouble?" she asks, following me.

"Actually, I am. And I need your help."

· *Close up shop*

On Sundays we close the shop at four, and in spite of the drama, Billie's incessant questions, and schemes to sniff out the witch, I manage to get a decent amount of work done. I only have a backlog of two potions to finish tonight. The bigger task will be going through all my ledgers and computers to be on the lookout for combinations of ingredients that can be used in black magic. I'm pretty good if someone orders them all in one clump, but if there are separate orders over a period of time, I can miss it. Fun times ahead.

I pull up to the house next to Greg's Land Cruiser. Just as I do, Sheriff Louis Andrews crosses the street, waving at me. Wonderful. He's in his mid-fifties, balding, and far too overweight to be a peace officer. Shirley must be a hell of a cook. All smiles, I climb out of the car as he approaches. "Afternoon, Mona."

"Sheriff. How's Shirley doing?" She plotting my death these days?

"Great. Looking forward to the wedding."

"Really? I heard she got into an accident the other night in Richmond."

His eyes narrow with confusion. "Accident? Wasn't her. We haven't been to Richmond in months."

"Oh, my mistake."

"Funny you mentioned Richmond though. We found a stolen car from there this morning. There was blood inside. Don't suppose you know anything about that?"

"No," I say, shaking my head. "Sorry."

"The odd thing is nobody's reported a missing car from town, and no stranger came to the hospital with odd wounds."

My stomach seizes up, but I don't show it. "You think whoever it was might still be around hiding out?"

"That's what my gut tells me," Andrews says. "Just be on the lookout, and be vigilant."

"Well, I have my cousin A.J. staying this week for the wedding, so me and the girls should be safe as houses."

"Good. If I have any follow-up questions, I'll pop by."

"Okay," I say as I head toward the door. "Give Shirley my best." I don't drop my smile until the door shuts. Crap, the one week I'm hiding a werewolf, all my neighbors decide to reinstitute a Neighborhood Watch. Just my damn luck. A jubilant Cora and scowling Debbie walk in from the living room. "Howdy," I say.

"Aunt Mona, Adam's still here!" Cora says with a huge smile.

"I know," I say, taking off my coat and putting down my purse.

"I tried to wake him, but he fell back asleep."

"And he was naked," a still scowling Debbie adds.

Oh hell. "Well, he was very tired." I clear my throat. "Hey, why don't you go and draw him a picture while I talk to Aunt Debbie, okay? I bet he'll love that when he gets up. Nice surprise for him."

"Okay," she says, scampering into the other room.

"Why is he still here?" Debbie asks, folding her arms. She looks just like Mommy when she does that. My heart aches. "The sheriff came to the door asking all sorts of questions and told the girls to look out for strangers."

"Well, if anyone asks, he's our cousin A.J. from Boston, okay? He's Great Uncle Cal's grandson here for the wedding."

"Why would…" She groans. "Mona, what the hell is going on?"

In any other circumstance, I wouldn't tell her. This is the week of her wedding, and she's my baby sister. I've spent my life protecting

64

her. But like the girls and my friends, she can be used to get to me, so I spill.

"What?" she shouts.

"Shush! I don't want the girls to know!"

"The naked man upstairs was in on a plot to kill you? And he's still in this house asleep when he should be protecting you?" She spins around and runs up the stairs two at a time. Crap. I follow close behind. Without knocking, she storms into the spare bedroom where Adam slumbers. I'm almost sad to see he's put on pajamas. "You! Werewolf! Wake up!"

He stirs, blinking those baby blues to focus. "Oh. What time is it?"

"Time for you to do some talking. How are you going to protect my sister and nieces from a freaking murderer, huh? Is sleeping part of you plan?"

"What—"

I grab Debbie's shoulders and steer her out of the room. "Sorry. Excuse us." I push her across to my bedroom, shutting the door. "Will you calm down?"

"No! Someone wants to kill you! The week I'm getting married! I need you! If you die who's gonna walk me down the aisle? Or teach me the summoning spell?"

"Gee Debbie, sorry my possible death is affecting you so," I say sarcastically.

"Sorry, sorry," she says plopping down on my bed. "This is just a lot to take in. I mean if you die, that's it. You're my family, Mona. You're all I have left."

I sit next to her, taking her hand. "Nothing is gonna happen to me, okay? Put it out of your mind. We'll find the person and have them arrested." I kiss her cheek. "But I'm gonna need your help."

"How? Anything."

"I need you to discreetly ask around the coven about the others. Especially Cheyenne, Collins, and Erica."

"Collins? She wouldn't do this," she says. "You're like a sister to her. She loves you."

"She might have information about Cheyenne."

"Well, if it's anyone, it's that cow," Debbie says.

"We need proof." And I need to stay alive long enough to find it. There's a knock on the bedroom door. "Come in." Adam steps in, now dressed in black jeans and camouflage T-shirt. Without the bruises and ectoplasm, his impish face is just a few degrees shy of handsome. "You're looking better. How you feeling?"

He shuts the door. "Good. Tired."

"Lot of that going around," I say. "Debbie, give us a minute?"

Debbie stands and walks past Adam, giving him the evil eye. "I'll order the pizza."

"She's tough," Adam says after the door shuts.

"She's scared. Getting married, now this. Finding you naked didn't help matters."

"Yeah, sorry about that," he says, blushing a little.

I rise from the bed. "Just wear pajamas from now on. Impressionable young girls around and all."

He raises an eyebrow. "Does that mean I'm staying?"

"So it seems. No one else is rushing to my rescue anytime soon."

He nods sadly. "I'm sorry."

"Yeah, well, I'm used to it," I say with a shrug. He just looks at me with pity. I don't do pity. "What do we do now? I have my spies out in full force collecting intel. I've identified potential suspects. I've established your alibi. I've whipped up a few protection charms at work, and dinner's on the way. What next?"

He seems suitably impressed, even raising an eyebrow. "I guess we eat pizza."

"Best damn idea I've heard all day."

· Sunday Supper

The girls, Debbie, Greg, Adam, and I all sit around the dining room table scarfing down pizza and apple juice. The dinner of champions. I figure if I'm dying soon, screw Weight Watchers, I'm going to enjoy fat, sweets, and empty calories as much as I can. Though my eating habits are positively dainty compared to Adam's. He shovels an entire pepperoni and sausage pizza into his mouth in record time, having warned Debbie to order extra. Cora giggles and tries to do the same, barely chewing, but I yank the piece away with a scowl.

"Hungry there, uh, Adam?" Greg asks as he exchanges a glance with Debbie.

"Sorry," Adam says with his mouth full. "I haven't eaten all day."

"You shouldn't talk with your mouth full," Sophie sneers. "It's rude."

Adam takes a few seconds to chew and swallow. "You're right. I apologize."

Sophie's sneer doesn't waver as she sips her juice. We eat in silence for a few seconds. Cora smiles brightly at Adam, who smiles back. Greg and Debbie exchange another look, neither too happy with our latest addition. My house, I have to play host before the atmosphere goes from frosty to arctic. "So girls, it looks as if we're having a guest stay with us for a few days."

"Him?" Sophie asks.

"Yes, and if anyone asks, he's our cousin A.J. from Boston here for the wedding."

"Why do we have to lie?" Sophie asks.

"You'll understand when you're older," Debbie says. "Your aunt has a reputation to maintain. We don't want the entire town thinking she's Paris Hilton, do we?"

"But why does he have to stay *here?*" Sophie asks.

"Because he's our friend," I say, "and since he is a guest in this house, we will treat him accordingly, okay? So drop the attitude."

"But—"

"Not another word. You are being rude, and you know better."

Sophie tosses her half eaten slice down and stands. "This sucks!" she says before running off. Um…okay. Debbie, Greg, and I are all speechless. This is not normal behavior for her. She does silent seething, not temper tantrums. Something is really wrong. I excuse myself from the table and follow her as the unfazed Cora chatters on about all that she wants to do with Adam. Tea parties and movies are on tonight's agenda. He'll be worn out by tomorrow.

The girls' bedroom door is shut, so I knock. When there's no answer, I let myself in. Sophie lies face down on her bed and doesn't look up when I step in. "Soph?"

"What?"

"You need to go downstairs and apologize."

She flips over, indignant rage written all over her face. "No! I hate him!"

"What is your problem?" I ask, shutting the door.

"He's bad! You told us never to lie, and now he's making us all lie! Someone hurt him, and now they're going to hurt us!"

Wow. I knew she was precocious, but now I think she might be a freaking genius. That or she can see there's trouble. It wouldn't surprise me if my sister was into some pretty bad stuff and the girls got dragged into it. And here I am doing it all over again. I join her on the bed. "Nobody is going to hurt us, okay?"

"I heard Aunt Debbie yelling. Someone wants to … " She can't finish. Her lower lip quivers, but she bites it to stop it. She refuses to cry. Even in the hospital after the bee sting when she almost died, she didn't cry once. Damn my sister.

"Hey, hey," I say, taking her hands. "No one is going to hurt me or you or your sister, okay? I'm gonna make sure of it. I promise."

"You can't know that," Sophie whispers.

"Would you feel better if you spent the week with Aunt Debbie or Miss Tamara?"

Sophie sits up, eyes like telescopes. "No!" she shouts, suddenly terrified. "Oh please don't send us away! Please! Don't send us away!" She grabs a hold of me for dear life. "I can protect you! I can, I swear it! Just don't make us go away! *Please!*"

I'm momentarily shocked by her vehemence. What the hell did Ivy do to this poor girl? I wrap my arms around her tiny body, enveloping her to keep out the bad. "Okay, it's okay, baby. You don't have to go anywhere. You're not going anywhere. You're staying right here with me, I promise."

"I can protect you, I can," she says quietly, squeezing me even tighter.

"Hey," I say, extracting her. I meet her blue eyes. "You listen to me. It is not your job to protect me, it's my job to protect you. Got that? Now, I made a promise, okay? Nothing is going to happen to me or any of us, so don't you spend a minute worrying about it. You just keep doing what you always do: go to school, keep a close eye on your sister, and be ten years old. Can you do that for me?"

She shakes her head. "Okay."

I smooth her hair then kiss it. "Thank you. And be nice to Adam, please. He's here to help us."

"Why?"

Good question. "Because he's a good guy," I say for lack of a better answer.

"Cora's in love with him."

"Cora's also in love with the mailman. She'll get over it." I kiss my niece's head again and stand. "Come on. You have an apology to make."

I hold out my hand and she takes it, lacing her fingers with mine. And we re-join the family for Sunday Supper.

I just pray it's not our last.

• *Hem Sophie's damn skirt*

The rest of the night runs smoothly. After dinner Debbie and Greg reluctantly leave, Adam returns upstairs to his room to rest, and the girls get ready for bed. In between all of this, I plant the charm bags I whipped up at work and some crystals around the perimeter of the house. Magical security system, better than ADT. If someone breeches it, I'll get a psychic heads up. I also line black salt at every entrance to ward against people who want to do me immediate harm. Keeps bad energy away. A person who wants to kill me certainly fits.

I read to the girls and sing them two songs before kissing them goodnight. I'd join them in slumberland but still have a few things left on my To Do list. I'm happy to find "feed Captain," "make lunches," and "dishes" all done for me. Adam even remembered the juice boxes. All that remains (that can be done tonight) is to hem Sophie's skirt. I grab a beer, my rarely used sewing kit, and plop down on the sofa in front of the television. For the first time in days, I have a few minutes to myself to relax. I don't even mind the Captain meowing from inside the fireplace. He's crawled up the flue, the silly thing. I'll go through my grimoire tomorrow and see if I can locate a spell to make him more comfortable around Adam.

About halfway through *Game of Thrones* and with two bleeding fingers, I hear footsteps on the stairs. A second later Adam strolls in. We smile at each other as he slips his hands in his pockets, rocking back and forth on his feet in the doorway. I guess I'm not alone in not knowing how to act around a virtual stranger in my space. "Mind if I get a beer?" he asks.

"*Mi casa es su casa,*" I say.

He disappears then reappears with a beer, sitting on the sea green armchair next to me. "Oh, I like this show."

"Yeah, me—fucking hell!" I say as I prick my finger with the damn needle again. I wince and stick the bleeding digit into my mouth. "Crap."

"Here, let me ... " Adam says, reaching for the skirt.

"What?"

He puts his beer on the coffee table. "I can do it. Give it here."

Reluctantly, I hand him the skirt and needle. "You can sew?"

He raises an eyebrow. "You can't?"

I give him the stink eye. Smiling, he sits back and starts hemming. "Wow. I am impressed," I say.

"Well, we werewolves rip a lot of clothes. If I didn't know how to do this, I'd be bankrupt. Also useful if you need a quick field suture."

"Need a lot of those? Field sutures?"

"Enough," he says with a half smile.

He has a nice smile. It melts years off his already youthful face. I wonder how old he is. Werewolves age slower than humans, so he could be anywhere from twenty-five to sixty-five. He hasn't changed much through the years, either. Never even changed his haircut from the short-on-the-sides-and-floppy-on-the-top style. I fold my arms across my chest. "You know, we've known each other for eighteen years, and I just realized the only thing I *really* know about you is that you can change a tire."

"You remember that?" he asks with genuine surprise.

"Of course. It was the nicest thing anyone's done for me in years."

"Really? That's sad."

"It is what it is. So how old are you?"

"I'll be forty-three next week," he says, still sewing.

"Happy early birthday," I say.

"Thanks."

"Do you have a job? A career besides being Jason's Beta?"

"Me and some of the other wolves have a general contracting business we run. I didn't do so hot in school, didn't even graduate high school with the dyslexia, but I found something to suit me." He holds up the skirt. "I'm very useful with my hands."

"Obviously," I say with a smirk. "The girls must love you."

His smile wavers a little. "I do alright."

"Ever been married?"

"Haven't even come close."

"Hard to believe. Good-looking guy like you, handy around the house." Great butt doesn't hurt either.

"Next subject, please," he says.

"What, some girl break your heart?" I ask with a fake pout.

He looks me square in the eyes. "Next. Subject."

Touchy. "Okay, favorite food?"

"Veal Parmesan. You?"

"Blackberry pie. Favorite color?"

"Green."

"Purple. Favorite TV show?"

"Anything football. Especially when the Ravens play. A bomb could go off, and I wouldn't move from the TV. Yours?"

"We're watching it. Were you born a werewolf?"

"Yep. My grandfather was Alpha before Frank Dahl. I took over Beta duty under Jason when Frank was murdered."

"I remember that. I'm so sorry." A few years ago some nasty werewolves tried to take over the Eastern Pack and killed a lot of wolves, including the Alpha Frank Dahl. Jason stopped them and became Alpha. "What about siblings?"

"I had a brother, but . . . he was killed then too," he says with a hint of regret. "Mother as well, if that's your next question. Dad died of cancer years before that. He was human."

Great, I feel like crap now. He's here to help me and I'm dredging up the most painful time of his life. "Sorry. My parents are dead too, and one sister might as well be. Or if she shows her face around here again, she soon will be." He smiles at my last statement. "And I'm sorry about earlier with Sophie. She's—"

"Scared," he finishes. "I didn't take it personally. Besides, I'm used to surly people. Us werewolves are notorious for it. Jason especially, but you know that already."

"Yeah, he is not my favorite person at the moment. He was really worried about you though."

"I know," he says with uneasiness.

"Do you like working for him?"

"He's been my friend for over thirty years. I'd die for him in an instant. The pack is my life."

I know how that is. "Then why—" My psychic security system goes off inside my head like a buzzing bee. Three times. Three people cross it. "Someone's outside."

The knock on the front door jolts us both. Adam and I exchange a worried glance before standing up. As he quietly pads to the door, I peek out the front window. There's a familiar SUV with "Top Dog Construction" written on the side. It takes me a second to place it. "Of course," I mutter.

"Who is it?" Adam mouths.

"Coming, Jason," I call as I walk toward the door.

All the color drains out of Adam's face. I gesture for him to go into the kitchen, and he does. I move to the front door. *You can do this.* Taking a deep breath, I open it. Jason Dahl and two other imposing werewolves stand on my porch with matching scowls. The Alpha glares down at me with stone cold ice blue eyes like a husky. He'd be a decent-looking guy if he ever smiled. Six foot four, overly muscular, with sandy blonde hair, hawk-like nose, and sharp cheekbones. It isn't just his physicality that puts a person on edge. The air around him grows a little stiller when he's there. The only people I've seen him smile at are his wife and kids, otherwise he's expressionless or sporting this scowl. Quite honestly he scares the shit out of me. And now he's pissed off. At me. Gulp.

"Jason. This is unexpected," I say with a smile.

"I need to speak with Adam. Right now."

"Adam? He's not—"

"Stop it," Jason says, voice booming. "The vampire didn't cover your lie. I know he's here. I can smell him."

I cross my arms. "I don't appreciate your—"

"It's okay, Mona," Adam says behind me. I spin around as he walks toward us.

"Aunt Mona?" Sophie asks she walks onto the landing above.

"It's okay, Soph. Go back to bed." Her eyes narrow at the wolves before obeying.

The men exchange a guilty look. "Let's not do this here, okay?" Adam says.

"Agreed," Jason says.

Adam steps onto the porch. "Give me a minute?" Adam asks Jason.

The surly werewolf eyes me, then says, "Fine. We'll wait in the car." He nods at me. "Mona."

I nod back. "Your Alphaness." Jason's glare grows stronger, but he walks toward the SUV with his flunkies. "So much for the co-operation part of the co-op," I say to Adam.

"He's just angry right now. I'll talk to him."

"What about you? Will you be okay? He won't hurt you, will he?"

"I'll be fine," Adam says. "Sorry about this whole mess."

"Stop apologizing for everything. You tried to help when everyone else wouldn't. It means more to me than I can say. Thank you."

Now, I'm not the touchy feely type, but I follow my instinct and move toward him, putting my arms around him. He did endure physical torture, not to mention the mental torture of Sunday Supper, for me; I think he deserves a hug for that. He stiffens at first, but after a second he embraces me back. I kiss his cheek and pull away, but he doesn't let me go for a few moments. "Um, Adam?"

My voice breaks whatever spell he's under. "Sorry," he mutters, stepping away. "I better go. They're waiting. Um, bye." The man practically sprints off the porch toward his friends. Jason, who has been watching the whole exchange through the car window, gazes at me, hard face almost sad. Didn't know he was capable of that emotion.

Weird. Adam jumps into the car, and it speeds off before the door's even closed.

And that's it. I'm completely on my own now. I should be used to it, years of practice and all, but … Tears spring into my eyes, and I push them away. Crying never does a lick of good. *You are solid steel, High Priestess. Indestructible.* "It's okay," I whisper to myself. "It'll all be okay."

Yeah, not even I believe it anymore. I shut my front door.

· *Clean the Captain*

I lull the girls back to sleep after evading their million questions with platitudes that sound hollow even to me. There's no real way to make, "We're screwed," sound good. When they're down, I want nothing more than to join them. Just one last thing to do, and now that Adam is gone, I can do it. It takes some coaxing, and a tin of tuna, but the Captain crawls out of the fireplace. He puts up little protest, mostly due to the tuna, as I carry him into the kitchen and use a wet towel to wipe the soot off him. I kiss the top of his head. "You won't abandon me, will you, Captain Wentworth?" He purrs, which I take to mean no. I almost start weeping but once again stop myself.

A few deep breaths, a few seconds of digging my nails into my palms do the trick. I don't cry. I am tough, I am capable, I am … scared shitless. At least with a werewolf on the team, I had a fighting chance. Someone to guard the girls when I couldn't be around. Someone who faced killers before and came out alive. Damn Jason. Damn them all. I'd be there for them if they needed it. Hell, I have. Recently even. And Adam … damn him for giving me false hope. Okay, that one's not on him. He had to go back, I know that and I don't fault him for it. A relative stranger or his family, no choice there. No, I raised my own hopes, and I know better. After thirty-five years, I should know at the end of the day I can't really rely on anyone but myself. I'm just an idiot who—

The magic security system alerts me that a person has crossed the perimeter. The Captain lifts his head and hisses before jumping off the counter and barreling toward the living room again. Oh hell. A second later, the doorbell rings. It's been a little over an hour since the wolves left, but I'm still on edge. For the first time ever, I don't feel safe in my own home. At least the girls don't wake up this time. "Who is it?" I ask when I reach the door.

"Adam."

For some reason it feels as if a thousand pounds lifts when I hear his deep voice. A smile stretches across my face as I swing the door open. He does not share my joy. He plods in, head hung as if he's been through the Spanish Inquisition. "You're back," I say, my smile wavering.

"Uh, yeah," he says, still not looking at me.

The SUV, with Jason sitting in the passenger seat glaring at me, drives off. Not thinking I'll be invited to the pack Christmas party this year. I shut the door and turn back to Adam, who is halfway up the stairs already. "What happened?"

He stops the climb but doesn't face me. "I can be, uh, very persuasive."

"But he—"

"I don't want to talk about it right now, okay?" he snaps.

"Sure. No problem." He nods and continues up the stairs like a sad puppy. I suddenly feel like a total piece of crap. Goddess knows what that bastard said or did to him because of me. "Adam?" He turns around at the landing and glances down at me. "Whatever happened … thank you. For coming back."

He nods. "Welcome." He starts walking again, but then turns around. His brow furrows as he says, "We have, uh, until Saturday night."

"To find out who wants to kill me? What happens Saturday night?"

He doesn't answer. "Goodnight, Mona." And he walks away.

MONDAY TO DO:

- *Find out who wants to kill me*
- *Hem that damn skirt*
- *Go to work*
- *E-mail spell for class*
- *Founders' Day meeting*
- *Teach class*
- *Grocery shopping*
- *Stay alive*

THE ALARM BUZZES AT seven, and I smash the clock with my fist. I groan and pull the covers back over my head. I don't want to get out of this bed. Ever. In here nobody wants to kill me, I have no endless To Do list, and I can ignore ominous statements uttered by werewolves. I succeeded in pushing all bad thoughts away last night as I fell asleep, but they've returned to torture me in the light of day.

I won't let them. There's no time. Gotta get the girls off to school. I toss the covers off, grab my robe (seeing as we have a gentleman in the house), run a comb though my hair, and brush my teeth. I debate slapping on makeup but realize there isn't time. Those girls are slugs on school days. When I leave my bedroom, I notice the other two bedroom doors are open. Adam's room is a mess with the bed unmade and clothes on the floor. The girls aren't in their room either.

I find the threesome in the kitchen, the model of domesticity. Adam stands at the stove making eggs as the girls sit at the table sipping orange juice and watching *Dora the Explorer* on the tiny television on the counter. Okay, I'm momentarily stunned. This is just so ... nice. "Morning all."

They glance at me, Adam saluting me with the spatula and the girls smiling. "Aunt Mona! Adam came back!" Cora says, grinning from cheek to cheek. "He's making breakfast!"

"I can see that," I say as I step in.

"Just scrambled eggs," Adam says as if it's nothing. Nobody's made me breakfast since Granny died.

"I'll take it," I say, pouring myself some coffee.

"Hope you don't mind. I used the last of the eggs. And you're out of—"

"Everything," I say, pouring the last of the milk in my coffee. "I'll see if I can fit it in today."

"I want to go grocery shopping," Cora whines.

I sit at the table. "We'll see." Adam serves us each a spatula full of eggs before joining us at the table. "What do we say?"

"Thank you, Adam," the girls say in unison.

"You're welcome." He and I share a grin and start eating. "Are you girls looking forward to school today?"

"I have pageant rehearsal," Sophie says.

"You're in a pageant?" Adam asks.

"Yeah, but I just have two lines."

"Have to start somewhere," Adam says.

"Crap, that reminds me. I have to finish your skirt. Is it—"

"I took care of it," Adam says.

"When?"

"I've been up since five."

"Oh. Thank you."

"Not a problem," he says with a wink.

Okay, now I'm blushing for some unknown reason. I *really* wish I had put on makeup. I start playing with a strand of my hair. "Uh, hurry up and eat girls. We don't want to be late."

They finish in record time and excuse themselves, running out of the kitchen to get dressed, leaving Adam and me alone. I sip my coffee and watch Dora on her adventures so I don't have to look at him in case my cheeks flare up again. "We should probably start talking strategy," Adam says.

Good. Yes. Work. "Well, I have to go to the shop today, then I have a committee meeting at three, followed by class here at five. Good news is I'll have contact with three of my four suspects then. I'll see what I can get out of them."

"Then I'll just shadow you," Adam says.

"Actually, the girls get out of school at three. I don't usually work Mondays and only have a half-day on Tuesday, but since I'm not working this weekend I have to go in. I had planned on having Auntie Sara watch them, but I think you should do it."

"Is that wise?"

I set my fork down. "Look, let's get on the same page right quick. My top priority is keeping those girls safe, my life is a distant second.

I can protect myself. They can't. So I'd feel much better knowing you're around them when I can't be. Is that okay with you?"

He smiles. "As you wish."

"Good. Now I just don't know how I'm going to explain you being around me all day without arousing suspicion."

"I thought of that this morning. If you're in the store all day, I can work on it. Fixing it up. Do you have any tools I can use?"

"Up in the attic there's a whole setup. Saws, power drills, stuff I don't even know the name of. They were my grandfather's."

"I'll take a gander," he says, grabbing his plate and Sophie's.

"Oh, you don't have to do that. I'll clean up. You made breakfast. Least I can do."

"Okay," he says with a sheepish smile. "I guess I'll be in the attic." He leaves, and the moment he does, my damn cheeks return to their normal temperature. Gonna have to get a handle on that.

I finish eating, stick the plates in the sink (they can wait), and rush upstairs to throw on some clothes. I choose my favorite outfit: black jeans and purple beaded V-neck top. It shaves ten pounds off. Wish I had time to straighten my hair, but I don't, so I clip the sides back with barrettes. After copious amounts of makeup and hair gel, I look halfway decent, close to pretty even.

The girls wait by the front door, and Sophie helps Cora on with her backpack. "Did you get your skirt and top?" I ask Sophie, who nods. "What about your protection charms?" They both show me the black cloth bags I made yesterday. "Good. Adam, I'm taking the girls to the bus stop," I call out.

"Coming," he shouts back.

"He's coming with us?" Sophie asks.

"Yeah, and he's gonna pick you up after school too, so be nice and listen to him."

Adam hustles down the stairs, throwing on the jean jacket over his black top and blue jeans I got for him yesterday. I lead the parade out with Sophie behind me as Cora takes Adam's hand, leading him out. The other parents are marching toward the corner as well. I wave to Millie Peterson and her son Gabe. "You girls remember the story about Adam, right? He's our cousin from Boston here for the wedding."

"We *know,*" Sophie says.

"Mona Leigh!" Auntie Sara calls from next door as we pass her house. Damn. The spry old thing walks off her porch to intercept us.

Seeing as it's rude to run away from her, we stop. "Morning, Auntie Sara."

She examines us, especially Adam who keeps a pleasant smile on his face. "Who is this man, Mona Leigh, and why was he coming in and out of your house at all hours last night?"

"He—he's our cousin A.J. from Boston, here for the wedding," Cora says excitedly. She looks at me for approval, and I smile.

The bus rolls down the street toward the stop. "I'll take them to the corner," Adam says. "Be right back."

"Have a good day at school," I say, quickly kissing them both. "Remember what I said." Adam and the girls trot toward the waiting bus, and I'm left with my skeptical great-aunt. "Yeah, I picked him up from the airport yesterday. He wanted to come for the wedding, and he's gonna help me fix up the shop a little."

"I do not know of a cousin A.J. from Boston," she says with certainty.

"He's from Papa's side. A.J. is his brother Cal's grandson, Joan's son. We've been e-mailing for years, but he's never been here before." Wow, I never knew I was such a good liar.

"I think I feel my ears burning," Adam says as he strolls back.

"I was just telling Auntie Sara about your grandfather Cal and mother Joan, and how we've been e-mailing for years."

He nods. "True. Mona's mentioned you many a time, Miss Sara. All good though."

"And who were those men you went out with last night if you've never been here before? They looked familiar."

Crap. "Uh ... "

"Well, Mona's not the only member of my extended family I've gotten in touch with," Adam says, smooth as silk. "We went out for drinks."

"Uh huh," she says with skepticism.

Time to end this while we're still ahead. "Auntie Sara, we really need to get going. I'm opening the shop alone today." I kiss her cheek. "See you later. Oh, and A.J. will be watching the girls this week so you don't have to."

Poor Adam gets the stink eye again as she pulls me aside. "Him? But you barely know him."

"He's family and I trust him." I kiss her cheek again. "Love you."

"It was nice to meet you," Adam says with a wave. After we start walking, he asks, "Think she bought any of that?"

I glance back at Auntie Sara, who is still glaring at us and shaking her head. "Hell no."

· *Open the shop*

Monday's are the slowest day at the shop. All the tourists have gone back to work along with everyone else. This is usually my only day off with Billie manning the shop, but not this week. She switched Saturday for today so I can prepare for the coven meeting and co-op that day. I've decided to just close the shop on Sunday, seeing as the entire town will be at the wedding.

This schedule used to work, but since the girls came into my life, it isn't cutting it. I get to be home for them on Monday and Tuesday, but Wednesday, Thursday, and Friday they're either in the back room watching TV or with Auntie Sara. Saturday I splurge on a babysitter, which eats up the day's profits. Sunday they're with Debbie or Tamara and her kids. It's bad now, but I'm dreading summer vacation. They hated the camp I sent them to last year. Okay, I'm getting ahead of myself. Deal with the problems I have now, not future ones. Who knows, I may be dead by then. Lucky me.

The store's been open two hours now, and we've had but one customer. The downtime allows me to remain in the back working through the online orders while Adam measures the ancient bookcases in the front. I had an e-mail from George Black profusely apologizing for yesterday. He offered assistance short of sending the team here. I still don't know what to ask him. I just sent him a list and brief description of each of the women. He's been investigating for decades, he'll know better what to do than I.

Adam walks in, Papa's old leather tool belt wrapped around his waist. "How old are those bookcases?" he asks. "The shelves are about a hair's breadth from splintering."

"I have no idea," I say, adding the nightshade to the charm bag.

"Well, you need new ones. Not to mention the display shelves are in the same condition, you have three rotten floorboards, and the sign in the window needs painting. I don't even want to talk about back here. You need a new pipe on that sink, it's completely eroded."

"Adam, you don't have to actually fix anything."

"If I'm going to pretend, I might as well do it for real."

I shake my head. "No, you're already doing more than enough. I mean, I'd pay you but I can't really afford—"

"Hey, I'm stuck here, right? You don't want me to die of boredom, do you?" he asks with that boyish smile.

"I just, I..."

"Okay, I'll make you a deal. I do this for you, you let me have all of your grandfather's old tools up in the attic."

"You really want them?"

"Oh yeah. You have no idea how much that stuff up there is worth. I should be feeling guilty, not you, okay?"

The store bell rings. Oh goody, a customer. "Okay, fine, but I'll cover the materials."

"You got it. I'll start a list. Pick them up later."

I swear I feel like I have a fairy godfather. With an amazing smile.

Collins waits at the counter, still in her peach scrubs with her light brown hair in a bouncy ponytail. The girl spends her days saving people, there is no way she's a murderer. "Hey, are you here by yourself?" she asks as I step out.

"Not exactly. Did you just get off work?"

"Yeah, I pulled a double. I just came to get the ingredients for tonight. I'm out of almost everything. We're still having class, right?"

"Yep. My house, five o'clock." I start putting all the herbs into baggies. "I think we're going to do a defensive spell and charm. I don't teach nearly enough. I e-mailed it out this morning."

"Can't wait."

"Just so I have a preliminary headcount, do you think Cheyenne will be there?"

"I think so."

I continue to weigh the herbs. "How has she been lately? I saw her at the diner yesterday. She seemed out of sorts."

"Who knows," Collins says behind me. "I barely see her outside of coven class. We're not exactly close anymore."

I turn back around, all smiles. "It's just … people have voiced concerns about her. That she's dabbled in illegal spells."

"Well, I don't know anything about that. It wouldn't surprise me."

The curtain to the back room opens and Adam strolls out, scribbling on his pad. He glances up and smiles at Collins, who smiles back. "Um, Collins this is my cousin A.J. He's here for the wedding. A.J., Collins."

They shake hands. "Nice to meet you," Adam says. "Excuse me." He lifts up the partition at the counter and moves back toward the bookshelves.

I can't help noticing Collins checking out his butt. A tiny, barely noticeable stab of anger forms inside. I quickly push it away. "But what about you? How are you doing? We didn't talk much at the hospital. Been awhile since we have. Are you seeing anyone?"

"Not really, not anymore. Hey," she says, leaning on the counter, "what's up with you and Dr. Sutcliffe? I'm surprised I haven't found you two making out in the supply closet yet."

"Um," I say, quickly glancing at Adam who glances back, "I don't know."

I start ringing her up, but she isn't letting up. "He practically grilled me about you. Twice." She scoffs. "He even asked me what your favorite flower is. Told him I had no idea."

"He's a very nice man," I say. "Your total is 37.87."

She starts digging in her purse. "Hey, can you add tannis root and a bloodstone? I lost mine."

I grab those and she pays. "Here you go," I say as I hand her the bag.

"I am going home to sleep until class. See you tonight. Nice to meet you, A.J." And with smiles for us both she departs.

I clear my throat. For some reason I feel uncomfortable at present, as if the air is thicker than normal. "So uh, what do you think? You have more experience with dangerous people than I do."

"She seems perfectly nice," he says, removing the last of the books from one of the shelves. "But that doesn't mean jack at this point."

"I helped raise her. She was at the house almost every day. She's a good girl."

"Just don't put up blinders. Some of the wolves who attacked the pack were family. I used to hunt with the guy who shot me. Hell, he arranged for me to lose my virginity."

"You got shot?" I ask.

"Silver shot to the back and shoulder with a shotgun," he says as he measures the shelf.

My mouth drops open. "Holy shit, Adam. I'm so sorry."

"Nothing to be sorry about. I survived. A lot of others didn't." I have no idea what to say, so I say nothing. He half smiles to reassure me and stands. "I need to, um, remove the statues to measure this," he says, pointing to one of the shelves on the wall with various statues of deities. "Are all the shelves the same size?"

"No clue."

"I was thinking, this place is pretty claustrophobic, especially the floor space." He is not wrong. "What if I line the wall with one continuous shelf, or even two. That way you can get rid of some of these displays, and the place will look cleaner. I did the same to this bookstore in Baltimore. It really helped."

I envision his suggestions and smile. "You know, I never thought of that. I think it will work. You're a genius!"

The bell rings as two of my witches, Hazel and Lucy, enter. Adam retreats to the back of the store to measure the walls. I get them their herbs and oil for tonight's lesson, and we chat about the wedding. As I hand them their bag, the bell rings again and in walks a man holding a huge vase of red roses. "Mona McGregor?" the delivery man asks. Hazel's and Lucy's eyes pop out of their heads. I nod. "Sign here."

"Um, okay … " I say, signing.

"Oh my word, who are they from?" Hazel asks as he departs.

"No idea." I take out the card. Hell's bells.

Dear Mona, a little incentive for Wednesday. Guy.

A smile spreads like wildfire across my face. Someone sent me flowers. A *man* sent me flowers. This has never happened before. Sure I'm not a big fan of roses, bluebells and violets are more my speed, but … holy shit!

I notice Adam staring at me and immediately drop my smile. "They're from no one. Excuse me." I take the vase with me into the back room away from prying eyes. A lady does not speak about her beau in mixed company.

"When did she get a boyfriend?" Lucy asks in the other room.

"I wonder who he is," Hazel responds. The bell rings a few seconds later as they leave. It's just flowers. Men send flowers every day. Okay, why am I so darn uncomfortable about this? It's like the already heavy air just gained ten pounds. Maybe it's because this is all so new to me. I'm out of practice how to react when a man is publicly wooing me. Not that one ever has. The sad truth is that I've only ever been in one relationship, if it could be called that, and that was fifteen years ago. Dennis was an anthropology student at UVA, doing his dissertation on the roots of Wicca. He was here for all of two weeks and never called after he left. I found out later he had a fiancé. That was my one foray into love, or at least sex. Since then I've only been on a handful of dates and each time came to the conclusion that men are usually nothing but trouble, and I have enough of that in my life already. Then I saw Guy … I sigh. He really does like me. A gorgeous doctor likes me. Crap, now I have to go to that damn auction, and I have nothing to wear. See? A man's complicating my life, and we haven't even been on one date. He better be worth it.

• *Supply shopping/lunch*

My employee Alice, a forty-year veteran of the store, arrives an hour later so I can take my lunch break. A quiet Adam and I take this opportunity to run to the hardware store down the street for supplies. He's barely said a non-work-related word to me since the flowers. I do like a man who doesn't pry.

There's still time left after we drop off the hardware at the shop to grab some take-out at the diner. It's bustling so we're lucky to snag two seats at the counter to place and wait for our orders. Our luck doesn't end there. Cheyenne runs to and fro behind the counter with plates, her emotionless eyes sliding over me as she passes. "That's Cheyenne," I tell Adam.

She passes again but this time her gaze locks on Adam. She stops in front of us, licking her red lips and smiling seductively. "Well, hello," she purrs.

"Hello," Adam says with a matching smile. I have the strongest urge to smack his arm.

"Are you the mysterious cousin everyone's been buzzing about?" she asks.

"I have a feeling I am."

I clear my throat. "Sorry, Cheyenne, we're in a hurry."

She doesn't take her eyes off Adam. "What can I get you two?"

"I'll have the Cobb salad to go, dressing on the side," I say. If I eat healthy starting now maybe I can lose ten pounds by Wednesday. Yeah, right.

"Can I have two hamburgers, both rare, and fries on the side?" Adam asks.

"A man with a hearty appetite. I like that." With a coy grin, she leaves to place our order.

"Can you please not fraternize with the enemy?" I ask in a low voice.

Cheyenne glances over her shoulder at Adam, who smiles. "If she likes me, I might be able to get her to open up."

"In more ways than one," I mutter.

"Mona!" Clay calls behind me. Adam and I turn to find him approaching. He's sporting the green-and-black bowtie I gave him for Christmas. He kisses my cheek. "Hi. I was just having lunch with Griff. Who is—"

"A.J. You know, *our* cousin A.J. From Boston?"

It takes Clay a second, but he gets it. "Right! Our second cousin who's staying with you. Right. Nice to meet you. Cousin."

The men shake hands. "You too."

"Clay is my oldest friend, and he works at the paper. He's helping on that project I told you about."

"I actually have made some progress on that front," Clay says, glancing at Cheyenne, whose eyes keep finding Adam. Hussy. "Let me just say bye to Griff, and we can go back to your shop," he says before returning to his editor.

Adam moves to get up. "Be right back." He walks toward the bathrooms.

The second he's out of sight, Cheyenne hustles over to me, brimming with excitement. "Please tell me he's not my cousin too."

"Nope." Sadly.

"And he's staying at your house? Will he be there tonight?"

"Yep, but I think he has a girlfriend in Boston."

"So? I have a boyfriend."

Already guilty of infidelity, can cold-blooded murder be far behind? "Doesn't he live in Richmond? I thought I heard you were spending a lot of time there."

"Cheyenne!" Shane, the manager of the diner, shouts through the partition. "Come on! Hustle!"

"Fuck. See you tonight," she says as she walks away.

Crap. I'll try interrogating her tonight if I can pry her tentacles off Adam.

Clay plops down in the vacant seat next to me a second later. "What did she say?"

"That girl is pure evil. No question."

Adam returns a minute later and our food arrives a minute after that. Can't beat that service. Cheyenne winks at Adam as she hands him the bag. He winks back. I suppress an eye roll. "Friendly town," Adam says as we walk out.

The shop is quiet with only one customer browsing books, so I leave Alice out there and shut the back room curtain. Adam immediately digs into his first burger, red juice dripping down his chin. I hand him a napkin. With their superfast metabolism, werewolves need lots of protein and carbs. I've seen one devour an entire turkey and still have room for pie.

Clay grimaces as Adam licks the blood off his fingers. "So you're a werewolf, huh?"

Adam narrows his eyes at me. "He knows about preters?"

"My entire life has revolved around witchcraft and the co-op since I was born; he figured it out after a couple of years. Everyone in town kinda knows the deal."

"I won't tell about you though," Clay say indignantly. "Hell, who'd believe me?"

"What did you find out, Clay?" I ask.

"I called my friend at the *Richmond Standard.* She covers the social scene there. I gave her the names, and she cross-referenced them. It seems that Erica and that vampire Thomas Wellington and Alejandro Agguire regularly attend parties together. They have for years."

"So she knows them. Not surprising."

"Well, according to Samantha, the rumors have swirled for years that Thomas and Erica were sleeping together. It's just rumors though."

"Wouldn't shock me," I say, "but if she's sleeping with Thomas, why not conspire with him, not Alejandro?"

"Maybe she was sleeping with both of them," Adam suggests.

"I'll call him tonight and try to find out what that shithead bastard found out before he offed Alejandro," I say. "What else?"

"Nothing on Shirley or Collins. I did find an archived article about Cheyenne from three years ago. She was arrested for drunk driving."

Bad girl, but I already knew this. "Keep focusing on Erica. See if you can dig up any more on her relationship with the vampires."

"Roger, roger. I better get back to work. That article on the library renovation isn't going to write itself." He kisses my cheek. "I'll call when I have news." He spins around to walk out but stops halfway when he spots the roses. "Oh my God. Did that doctor send you those?"

I glance at Adam, who picks at his fries, and say, "Um…yep."

"Wow. That's great. Are you going on Wednesday?"

"There's kind of a lot going on, Clay."

"There's always time for love, Mona. I mean, you've had your sights set on him for three months, and he obviously likes you enough to spend a hundred bucks on flowers."

"Goodbye, Clay," I say in sing-song with a tiny wave.

"Fine. Nice to meet you, Adam." Adam nods and Clay walks out, leaving me mortified. I stab some lettuce and stuff it into my mouth. I'm not used to having a private life, but I certainly know I don't want it discussed.

"So you met this doctor three months ago?" Adam asks.

My eyes narrow. "Yeah. Why?"

"Because if I'm going to keep you safe, I need to know the people in your life, boyfriends included."

"He is not my boyfriend, and he has *nothing* to do with the woman trying to kill me. He's a doctor. From D.C. He doesn't know a thing about witches or vampires."

"How can you know?" Adam asks. "I don't like the timing. Has he seemed interested in you this whole time or is this a recent occurrence?"

I open my mouth to protest, but the words don't come out. It is kind of odd that after three months he chooses *now* to start courting me. The few interactions we've had prior to Saturday were friendly but certainly not flirty. Well, there was that look he gave me after

Sophie's bee sting episode. I was sitting on her hospital bed with Cora in my lap playing war with a crumply deck of cards, and he was at the door, looking most impressed. He even winked at me. Maybe that's when the seed was planted. That's gotta be it. It has to be. Right? Because if it's not … no. Not going there. Of course a great, handsome, smart man like Guy Sutcliffe could like me. Good things like this happen, they do, and now they're happening to me.

I scoff. "So the only way a man can be interested in me is if he's evil? Is that what you're implying?"

"Of course not. I—"

I pick up my salad and stand. "Guy is not trying to kill me, he's trying to sleep with me, thank you very much. That doesn't make him crazy or evil, it makes him the smartest man in town, present company included. Because I am a caring, vibrant, passionate, strong woman who would happen to make the best damn partner in the state, and Guy just happens to be intelligent enough to recognize that."

I start walking toward the door, but Adam grabs my arm. "Mona, I—"

I jerk my arm away and look him square in the eyes, indignant rage emerging from my every pore. "My entire life has been about others since I was a kid. Their wants, their needs. I am a good friend, a good sister, a good aunt, and a good spiritual leader." I bite my lower lip. "I kept my family together through sickness and death. I am raising children that are not my own by myself. I help women reach their full potential. And I'm happy to do it, I really am. I'm good at it. *Damn* good. It's what I was put on this earth to do. But what about me? It's never been about me. I don't get what I want, hell I barely get what I need, and right now, I need this. I need to believe that something good can happen to me. Because if it can't... then why the hell am I fighting so hard to stay alive?" I shake my head. We're both breathing heavier than normal. "I am *entitled* to some damn happiness. I've earned it, threefold. And now it's come to call. Don't you dare tarnish it."

I avert my eyes and stalk out. Adam doesn't follow.

Alice stares at me through her glasses, looking very concerned. I plop my salad down on the counter and lean against its solid bulk, once again trying to fight back tears. Alice rubs my back. "Having a bad day?"

"Having a bad life."

• *Founders' Day Committee Meeting*

Things pick up in the afternoon with most of my class swinging by for ingredients. As I'm ringing them up, each and every one of their eyes dart to Adam, who scrapes paint off my window like a maniac. Step one of the renovation: re-paint the name of the store. It hasn't had so much as a touchup in twenty years, so the words have chipped off. I decided on midnight blue with yellow to represent moonlight. If it turns out half as good as the sketch Adam made, I'll be happy.

Right now, though, I'm alternating between mortified and angry, mostly at myself. I can't even look at him, working away over there. For me. I spend as much time as possible in the back with the online orders, and when he comes back for a tool, we don't even acknowledge each other's presence. This is especially hard when Alice goes on break, and we're both stuck in the front. I try to read a book as he stencils.

I should apologize, I *know* I should apologize. He was just pointing out the obvious, but I can't. If I do, I'm admitting to myself that he might be right, and I'll lose all hope. And right now I need some fucking hope in my life. The potential that life won't always be like *this*. When I think about the years ahead of me, I feel desolate. I work my ass off to scrape by, deal with everyone's crises, and raise the girls until Ivy inevitably returns to snatch them away from me. I'll just keep getting older, watching my body decay, having everyone go off to live their own lives. I'll end up like Auntie Sara, alone and angry, living vicariously through others whether they like it or not. Looked down on and pitied. Hell, maybe I should just off myself and save my unknown enemy the trouble.

Alice returns before my thoughts grow even darker. "Adam, time to go," I say.

"Fine." He collects his tools as I go into the back to get my purse, coat, and sanity. He walks in just as I zip up my case. "Where's your meeting?" he asks.

"Just up the street." I toss him my car keys. "You take the car. I'll get a ride home."

"Do you want me to escort you there?"

"No, the streets are filled with people, I'll be fine. You better go or you'll miss their bus."

He nods. I put on my coat and take a step to leave. "Mona?" he asks. I turn around. "I'm sorry if I offended you. I didn't—"

"I know. I'm sorry too. I shouldn't have lost it like that. I'm just on edge." I give him a quick smile. "Don't let them have too much sugar, or you'll really feel my wrath."

"I definitely don't want that," he says with a smile back.

"I'll be home about four thirty." I wave and step out.

No one attacks me as I walk down Courtland Street toward Goodnight City Hall, the oldest building in town. Two of the people I'm helping honor this week, Courtland Goode and John Knight, constructed it three hundred fifty years ago when they first settled here. They and their families landed with the rest of the colonists but quickly broke away from the others, migrating west until Anne Knight—daughter of John and my great-to-the-twentieth-power-grandmother—told them to stop when she sensed the ley lines.

The town really owes itself to Courtland and Anne. The legend goes that John Knight, a witch in England, had two daughters: Anne and Mary. When one of their neighbors saw Anne literally playing with fire, the entire extended family fled before she was accused of witchcraft and hung. On the passage over Anne Knight met Courtland Goode, the handsome reverend's son, and they fell madly in love despite the popular belief that witches were the spawn of the devil. That rumor was most likely started by an actual demon, not that it mattered. Millions of witches were killed in the most heinous ways, and to this day we're feared and reviled. But none of this mattered to Courtland. He saw past the prejudice to the woman underneath. Courtland left behind his family—hell, everything he ever believed in—for Anne. From them came the town. And me.

City Hall is a two-story brick building with a bronze bust of Anne out front. Originally they wanted a statue of John and Courtland, but my great-great-grandmother Ramona led a protest down the street to have it changed to Anne. Except for sleeping with a drug-addicted crazy man, she was a woman after my own heart.

The six other committee members stand or sit around a table in the conference room. We've been working for months to pull this festival together. Like most things in this town, the government is run by the women. Magdalena Rogers, our mayor of ten years, is at the head of the committee with Eileen Merriman and Yvonne Cliff, both retired schoolteachers, doing the brunt of the work. My old classmate Jocelyn and I basically assist them when needed. Erica, who now sits at the table, manicured fingers tapping away on her iPhone, left the planning and execution to us. She just connected us with the concession company and donated ten grand for cleanup.

I smile at Jocelyn as I enter but make a beeline for my glamorous cousin. Like Shirley, she's descended from Ramona's sister Gillian, so we're *distant* cousins. It shows. Ms. Erica Fitch is tall and thin with flaming red hair and brown eyes. It's easy to see why she attracts the attention of powerful men, including vampires. There isn't an inch of her that isn't coiffed, tight, or manmade to look beautiful. As I sit, her eyes acknowledge me, but nothing more. "Afternoon," I say.

"Afternoon," Erica says coolly as she puts away her phone.

"I don't know about you, but I'll be glad when this festival's over."

"Me too. Of course then I have this *massive* silent auction I'm helping out with at the end of the month. I know I'm spreading myself too thin, but I'm such a giver, you know? How can you not help those who can't help themselves?"

Oh gag me. "Are you coming to the coven meeting Saturday? Or the wedding?"

"The wedding, yes. I've been friends with the Walkers for ages. I hope you won't be offended if I sit on their side at the wedding."

Where all the posh people will sit instead of us country bumpkins. "Of course not, but I'm barely even thinking of the wedding. I have serious co-op problems."

"Oh? Did those evil doggies give you fleas?"

"No, actually it's our pale friend in Richmond."

"Tommy?" she asks with surprise.

"Yeah. He's been making noises about withdrawing his support and telling others to do the same. I've been trying to call him, but he won't return my calls. You know him, right?"

"We have met on a few occasions," she says with a private smile, no doubt reliving their sexual Olympics.

"Well, Alejandro called me Friday night, and I've been leaving messages for him as well." I gaze at her to gage her reaction, but she remains impassive. Could just be the Botox. "I really, *really* need Thomas to call me back. This affects the entire coven. I hate to ask, but can you have him contact me?"

"What makes you think he'll listen to me?"

"You can be very persuasive, Erica. It doesn't even have to be him, you can try Alejandro. Just one phone call. Please? For the coven?"

Okay, my logic behind this gambit is that if she wants me dead, there's no way in hell she'll waste a precious second of her time doing me this favor. And since her murder plot went awry, she'd stay as far away from Thomas as possible. On the other hand, if they are lovers, she'll jump at a chance to call him, even for me. So if she calls him, she's probably innocent. If she doesn't, then she's either a bitch or wants to kill me. Miss Marple, eat your heart out.

"Of course I will," Erica says with a gracious smile. "Anything for the coven."

Mayor Magda hustles in, her arms filled with file folders. We, being good minions, snap to. Those standing quickly find seats as our taskmaster hands us each a file. We go over the order of events, all our specific jobs from here on in, the progress of the mural for the pageant. After twenty minutes of discussion of who is providing what for the silent auction at the country club, I feel like stabbing myself in the eye with a pencil. Quite a few times, I glare at the oblivious Magda for roping me into this. She cornered me at the grocery store and pretty much told me she was recruiting me for this committee. She is not a woman a person says no to, which makes her a good mayor.

"In other news," Magda says, "I was at the Goodnight Museum where DJ Ray from WQRG was broadcasting and promoting the festival this week. The museum had record numbers of attendees this week and tomorrow's performance of *The Crucible* is sold out. And both the bake sale and arts and crafts fair were rousing successes. We also forecast making ten thousand dollars at the bachelorette auction on Wednesday. We've had fourteen participants sign up, including our very own Erica Fitch and former homecoming queen Naomi Ferguson."

We clap at this stunning achievement. "And please know I have been promoting the heck out of this event too," Erica says, "both in town and Richmond. I am more than sure we will surpass our goal." On her alone, she no doubt adds in her head.

"And thank you, Erica, for organizing the event," Magda adds. "I'll meet with you on Wednesday to coordinate at the club. I think that's it. We seem to have everything well in hand. If I have any follow-up, I will call you. See you all on Thursday for prep."

We all stand and Jocelyn mutters to me, "That's over an hour of my life I'd like back."

I chuckle as I push in my chair. "Hey, can you give me a ride home?"

"Sure," Jocelyn says.

Erica begins tottering away on her five-hundred-dollar heels. "Just give me a sec, okay?" I rush after Erica, tapping her on the shoulder. She spins around. "I ... " Okay, do I really want to do this? It has a huge potential to blow up in my face, making me the laughingstock of the town. Or worse, it could break my heart. But Daddy didn't raise no coward. "I want to sign up for the bachelorette auction."

Her eyes just about bug out of her head. "What? Really? *You?*"

"Yeah. It's not too late, is it?"

"What—You—What," she stammers. "Are you sure? I mean, you…I don't think it's your scene, Mona. Most of the men attending are, well, not your type. You wouldn't enjoy yourself." She pats my shoulder. "I'm just looking out for you."

I so want to punch her surgically altered nose, but being a lady I instead plaster a smile on my face. "That's really sweet of you. Really. But I promised a certain gentleman I would participate, and I cannot bring myself to let him down. I'm sure you understand."

"And who is this gentleman?"

My smile grows wider. "Let me sign up and see."

Erica's eyes narrow as she tries to figure out my angle. As if I'd sabotage her event. "Well, it's your life, Mona. Don't say I didn't warn you."

Though it sickens me, I hug her tiny form. "Thank you, Erica." I let her tense body go. "I really appreciate it. Don't forget to call Thomas for me! See you Wednesday!"

I rush over to the confused Jocelyn waiting for me by the door. "What on earth was that about?"

"A leap of faith."

· *Witchcraft for dummies*

Ah, just what every woman wants to be greeted by after a long day: the noise of a band saw. The whirring grows louder as I enter the house. Auntie Sara pounces on me the moment I shut the door.

"Is he going to continue with that racket during the class?" she shouts. "I cannot stand it a moment longer!"

I set my bag down and start toward the source of the noise, the backyard. Auntie Sara has begun setup for the class in the living room, dining room, and kitchen by laying down plastic sheets on all tables and setting out extra copies of the lesson. In half an hour there will be twenty witches here, and there isn't a single one who isn't messy. We used to meet at the high school chemistry lab, but then the old principal retired and the new one is a Baptist and didn't want evil spread through his high school—his words, not mine. So I sacrificed my upholstery and carpet for the furtherment of education. I should put a curse on that damn principal.

When I get outside, with Auntie Sara right on my heels, I find Adam behind Papa's old wooden stand using an electric saw to cut planks of wood. There's a whole stack of them off to the side. He's not the only one hard at work. Sitting in the grass, Sophie and Cora have their own project, painting lumber with dark varnish and deep concentration, as if they were working on a masterpiece.

Adam shuts off the saw when he notices me and takes off his safety glasses. "Oh hey."

"Aunt Mona, we're painting!" Cora says with a huge grin.

"I see that."

"Before we went to the grocery store, we stopped by the Home Depot and got the wood for the shelves," Adam says. "Had a little luck too. They had some already cut to fit the bookcase. The girls are working on those now."

"You went grocery shopping too?" I ask.

"They were right next door to each other," Adam says.

"Oh, well, thank you," I say, most impressed for some reason.

"You're welcome," he says with a nod.

"Young man, are you going to—" Auntie Sara starts.

The man completed my most hated chore; I'm not going to have him lectured. "Auntie Sara, can you please finish setting up?" I ask with a sweet smile. "Everyone should be arriving soon. I'll be in there in a minute."

"Fine," she says, still eyeing Adam, who holds his pleasant façade. She retreats inside.

"That woman does not like me," Adam says when she's out of earshot. "She barely let me in the house when we came home. Then she tried to grill me about myself. That's when I started sawing."

"She's just protective."

"I can appreciate that. How'd your meeting go?"

"Dull, but Erica was there in all her bitchy glory. I asked her to call Thomas for me."

"Think she will?"

"If she's innocent, she will. And as much as I can't stand her, I don't think she's the one. Being High Priestess is all about respect and guiding others, and Erica wants precious little to do with us lowly small-town folk."

"Just don't let your guard down around her," Adam warns.

"Speaking of, both Collins and Cheyenne will be here shortly. Can you keep an eye on the girls in case the spells hit the fan?"

"Sure thing."

"Thanks," I say as I reach across and rub his hard biceps in appreciation. His body jerks in surprise as if I've just electrocuted him. I quickly pull away. "Sorry. Sorry, I just thought because werewolves like to be touched—"

"No, no, it's fine. It's fine," he mutters, embarrassed to hell. "I'm just going to get some water. Excuse me." He all but flees inside.

Okay, no idea what that was about. Note to self: don't touch him. I turn my attention to the girls, walking over and sitting on the grass next to them. "How was school?"

"Boring," Sophie says.

"I got a check plus on my spelling test," Cora says.

"That's great. And did you have fun with Adam?"

"He let me get Twinkies," Cora says, "*and* Oreos."

"He did, huh?" I ask, petting her hair before I stand. "Well, you have fun painting. I have class. You two stay here and keep working."

Adam walks back out with three juice boxes. We pass each other, but he just nods. "For my assistants," he says as I step inside.

I barely have time to change clothes and grab a snack from my now fully stocked fridge before my students start arriving. The majority of them are younger and female, from sixteen to twenty-five, with a few exceptions on both accounts. It's open to everyone, but since I mainly do beginner potions, the more advanced witches approach me one-on-one for help. As they set up their mixing bowls, I move from room to room to check on them. The space at the kitchen counter with a perfect view of the backyard is the first to fill up. The ladies are doing less prep and more staring out the window and whispering about the man measuring and marking lumber. One eligible bachelor comes to town, and all the women go into heat.

"Oh please tell me he isn't a cousin," Belle says to Meg.

I needed a reason to pull them aside to grill them about Cheyenne. This'll do. "Belle, Meg, I need you two to come with me right now, please," I order.

The girls, both in their early twenties and petite, exchange a worried look but follow me out of the kitchen and up to my office. "Are we in trouble?" Meg asks when she walks in.

"No," I say as I shut the door. "I just need to speak with you."

"What about?" Belle asks.

"Cheyenne. In the past month, a few people have come to me with rumors about you two, her, and black magic. I want to hear your side before I decide what to do."

All the color drains out of their faux tan faces as they exchange another petrified look. "We—we don't know what you're talking about," Meg says.

"If you come clean now, I will take that into consideration, and what you tell me goes no further than this room."

They glance at each other again. "You'll, like, give us immunity or whatever?" Belle asks.

"Immunity?"

"Like if we confess you won't kick us out of the coven?" Belle asks.

"It was Cheyenne's idea, anyway," Meg adds. "We didn't want to. Honest!"

"We were just kind of bored," Belle says. "And we didn't hurt anyone. It didn't work."

"What exactly did you girls do?"

"We were hanging over at Cheyenne's, like, two months ago," Meg begins. "She said she found this grimoire with these awesome spells inside. Stuff you wouldn't teach us, so we thought we'd try one out."

"It was just a little hex," Belle adds. "We tried it on Brittney to give her some boils because she was flirting with Cheyenne's boyfriend earlier, but it didn't work. We're so sorry. Please don't kick us out! We'll never try black magic again, we promise."

"What else was in the grimoire?"

"Bad stuff," Belle says. "Stuff to trap spirits and jinxes and ones that required animal sacrifices."

"Was it hand-written or a printed book?"

"It was a small black notebook with spells written or glued in," Meg says.

"Do you know if she still has it, or if she's tried other black magic spells?"

"We're not really all that close," Belle says. "We only went to her house because we were leaving Dixie's Bar at the same time."

"Well, have you heard anything? Rumors? People talking about how she, or anyone, doesn't like the job I'm doing, or that they have anything against me?"

Both girls shake their heads no. Crap. "Are we in trouble?" Meg asks.

"Well. You did try to harm another person, that can't go unpunished. You're both banned from class for the next two weeks, starting tonight. Use this time to reflect on how stupid what you did was. That spell could have backfired, or worse. Now, go pack up your kits and I'll see you in two weeks. And don't tell *anyone* what you've told me, not even Cheyenne, alright?"

"Yes, ma'am," the girls mutter.

"Go on," I say. The girls scurry out of the room like a shot. I follow a few seconds later.

Okay, so Cheyenne has a book of black spells. Interesting but not definitive. Even I have a book or two on black magic. It's only natural for witches to dabble in the forbidden, and I speak from experience. When I found out Dennis had a fiancé, I hexed him. I don't know if he became impotent, but Granny found out and ripped me a new one. But if Cheyenne has skirted the dark side once and is actually adding black spells to the book, then that's a horse of a different color. She wouldn't go to the trouble of accumulating them unless she planned to use them.

Through the kitchen window, I view the wicked witch of the hour in my backyard dressed in super-tight jeans and an obscenely low-cut top, chatting with a smiling Adam. I'm no expert in flirting, but even I am not oblivious to what's going on back there. Her I'm not surprised by; but him ...

He leans in and speaks, causing her to burst into laughter and "accidently" place her hands on his pecs. With her, he doesn't flinch or act as if her hands are coated in acid. A stab of I-don't-know-what pierces my chest, and I bristle. He must like 'em whorish and evil. No accounting for taste.

"Oh lord," Collins says behind me. "That man doesn't stand a chance."

I turn around and find her and Debbie staring out the window too. "Eww," Debbie says.

"Hey, how you two doing?" I ask.

"Tired," Debbie says. "This wedding is sucking out my soul."

"Well, just remember, this time next week you'll be in the Bahamas sipping mai tais with your charming husband."

Collins puts her arm around Debbie. "And we will be here not so quietly hating your guts."

Auntie Sara rushes in, lips pursed in disapproval as always. "Everyone's arrived."

"Thank you," I say. "Attention everyone! Please go into the dining room so we can begin." All the women in the kitchen obey, and I poke my head out the back door. "Cheyenne, class is about to start."

"I gotta go," she says to Adam with a pout. "Think about what I've said."

"Oh, believe me, I will."

I suppress an eye roll as she walks past me. His eyes follow her, but when they meet my hard ones, he smiles sheepishly. This time I don't stop my eyes from revolving.

All nineteen women and three men wait around my table, where I take my place next to Auntie Sara at the head. Most students have their pads out except lazy Cheyenne and Debbie, who already knows the spell. Debs just likes to come to see all her friends and lend a hand. Cheyenne keeps glancing in the direction of the backyard and even gives a little wave. This will not be a fun class for her.

"It's recently come to my attention that I have not been giving you a well rounded education," I start. "Now, I know no one in this room is guilty of performing black magic, but not all witches are as honest as the Goodnight Coven. I realized you need to know how to properly defend yourselves against those … monsters," I say as my eyes dart to Cheyenne, who is still gazing into the backyard. "So we will spend the first half practicing a protection spell, and the other making a charm bag. Auntie Sara?"

Auntie Sara flicks her fingers at me while saying, *"Efflo aeris,"* and I sneeze. Ivy used to drive me nuts with this hex, among others. Auntie Sara does it again, but this time I hold up my hand to focus my power and say, *"Reverto,"* and Auntie Sara sneezes this time. "Now, please note that this is an all-purpose deflection, but it won't work with some higher-level hexes or if the witch attempting a hex is drawing more power from the ley lines. Still, it's a good start. Okay, break into partners and take turns. Sara and I will move around and observe."

I spend the next half hour strolling around the house watching a lot of people sneeze. Most get it quickly, both the hex and deflection, except for the few near the backyard who can't unglue their eyes from a sweaty Adam. Those ladies require some glares before returning to the task at hand. Sophie and Cora keep giggling as Rosalie Dupres gives Cheyenne a sneezing fit, snot running down her nose. That's what she gets for not paying attention. After the fourth try, Cheyenne rushes for a tissue.

Since she's culled from the herd, I follow her to the bathroom. "Are you okay?"

"Fine," she says after blowing her nose.

"You know I thought you, of all of them, would find this easy as pie."

"I'm just a little distracted," she says as she tries to step around me out of the room.

I block her way. "Yes, my cousin is very distracting. At least you seem to know the hex."

"Yeah, well, everyone's known that one since kindergarten," she says defensively.

"And what other hexes do you know? I hear you've been working on some others."

Her eyes narrow but before she can comment Auntie Sara rushes in. "That fool Brandie has a nosebleed from sneezing too much. Blood's pouring everywhere."

"Hell's bells." Great, instead of grilling a suspect, I have to go ice a nose.

When that crisis is over, I call them back into the dining room to demonstrate how to make a charm bag to ward off hexes. This proves to be less dramatic, just mixing herbs and stones and infusing them with magic. We even finish ten minutes early. I work the rooms, saying goodbye to those who don't stay for wedding talk. Debbie holds court in the living room with about seven cousins gushing about her dress and lingerie for the honeymoon. Just talking about it makes her glow. My crowning achievement, that girl.

"She's so happy," Collins says as she sidles up beside me by the front door. "We should all be so lucky."

"Yeah," I say with a sigh. "Hey, I have a few minutes if you want to work on that illumination spell."

"That's okay. Debs and I are going back to my place to tackle the never-ending wedding crap. The seating charts still have to be done."

"Hey, Mona," Brandie, whose nose is still red, says, "I can't find my black water vial."

"Brandie, what the heck are you doing with black water anyways?" Collins asks.

"I don't have it for black magic, just luck," she whines.

"If I find it, I'll keep it for next time," I say.

"Thanks," she says as she leaves. "See you Saturday at the coven meeting!"

"One of these days she's gonna blow up the whole town," Collins says.

Time to do some detecting. "Hey, I almost forgot, what is the name of that restaurant in Richmond you recommended to Debbie? The one downtown near Croatoan?" Which just happens to be Lord Thomas's base of operations. "I'm thinking of taking her there after the co-op."

"I have no idea what you're talking about," she says.

"You go to Richmond a lot, don't you? Can you think of another place?"

"I really don't get there that often. Just take her somewhere in town."

"Yeah, maybe." Okay, time to switch tactics. "There is something else I wanted to speak to you about. In private."

"Sure." A few girls wave goodbye as we move onto the porch. I lead her toward the swing where we sit. "What's up?"

"Okay, this is something I have been considering for some time, and I want to run it by you before I do it." Collins nods. "How would you feel about being named my successor?"

She does a double take, eyes narrowing. "I'm sorry?"

"As of right now, if I die, Erica Fitch is next in line for High Priestess. Now, I chose her ten years ago because she was the only viable option. That's changed."

"Why me?" she asks, nose crinkling.

"You've got a good head on your shoulders, you're talented, and the others respect you."

"People don't respect me," she says with a scoff. "Not like you."

"Yes, they do. You've come a long way, Collins. You're disciplined like no one else here. You have power inside you. And most importantly, you care about people. Everyone knows it." I pat her hand. "Now, I don't anticipate dying anytime soon, but I'd still feel better if I name you."

She mulls this over, indecision all over her face. "I mean, you can if you want, but ... "

"What?"

She shifts uncomfortably in the swing, pulling her hand away. "Well, and I don't really mean to offend you, but the coven is your whole life and ... I—I don't want that for myself. I got my own problems without taking on other people's. I mean, it's great you do, but it's not for me. I don't want to be at everyone's beck and call twenty-four seven. Sorry."

I stop myself from taking a literal breath of relief. "That's okay. Like I said, it was just something I was thinking about."

She nods. "And I am beyond flattered that you think I could fill your shoes, I really am. You have no idea what that means to me." She smiles humbly before standing. "I'm gonna go rescue Debbie." She starts walking toward the door but stops halfway and turns around. "Okay, I know I'm wasting my breath, and I can't really believe I'm uttering these words, but ... have you considered Cheyenne?"

"Cheyenne? Why?"

"I know what everyone thinks about her, but that's just one side of her. She's just always wanted the job, and maybe if she had a chance of getting it, she'd turn onto the straight and narrow. When she applies herself, she can be really powerful. She taught me quite a few things."

"I'll think about it," I say.

"Just putting it out there," she says as she walks inside the house.

I can now breathe that sigh of relief. I knock Collins down the suspect list to the bottom. If she wanted the post, she'd jump at the chance for me to name her. That's a load off. One down, three to go.

I settle into my seat with a smile to enjoy a few moments of peace. I love this swing. I'd never leave it if I could. I've spent hours out here reading and watching people go by as a gentle breeze blew. I catch the faint whiff of honeysuckle. Wish I could stay here and pass out, but it is not to be. Cleaning up is next on the agenda. I'm about to push my tired carcass upright when Adam and Cheyenne walk out, he with his hands in his pockets and she brushing against him more than necessary. "So ... just think about it, huh? We usually get there around ten and get fun around eleven," Cheyenne says.

"I will definitely think about it," Adam says with a huge grin.

"Don't make me wait," she says in sing-song. She steps off the porch. "See you tonight!"

"Maybe," he says.

While still walking she turns around, backing toward her car. "Definitely."

I roll my eyes and rise, walking past him with a hard glare. The bridal party and Auntie Sara are just leaving, and I kiss my sister goodbye. And then there were four. I guess I'll work on the kitchen so I can make dinner, oh joy and bliss. The table and counters are covered with herbs and used tissues from all the sneezing. Yuck. I just finish with the counter when Adam walks in. The kitchen is small so it's hard to ignore him, but I do my damndest. He glances at me before opening the fridge, pulling out a huge package of hamburger. "I'm going to make spaghetti and meat sauce," he says. "Do you have any oregano?"

"You don't have to make dinner, you've done enough," I say shortly.

He drops the meat on the counter right next to me. "Fine." The werewolf stalks outside to the backyard, and a few seconds later that saw starts again. Okay, is *he* pissed at *me*? I'm not the one planning on necking with a psychopath. Whatever. He should just be glad he's a werewolf so he can't catch anything from her. I'll bet Typhoid Mary had nothing on that hoochie.

I find the rest of the dinner ingredients and get to work. Since I spend most of my day cooking up potions and charms, by the end of the day the last thing I want to do is more of that. I only cook a few times a week, and before the girls came I was just a master microwaver. I turn on the news and pour myself a glass of wine as I cook. Murder and rape are rampant per the TV. Wonder if I'll end up as a top story. If they use my driver's license photo, I'll die a second time. I switch the station to *The Big Bang Theory*. When I'm done with dinner, that's it. I'm sending the girls off to bath and bed, climbing into mine, and passing out.

Just as the water begins to boil, Sophie and Cora stroll in, their faces and hands covered in varnish. Without protest they go upstairs to shower. I tidy up the living and dining rooms, sighing the whole time. Collins is right about me. I have no life. I work, I clean up after people, and I sleep. Even if by some miracle I get a life, I'll be too exhausted to live it. Whoever wants my job must be out of their mind. Or a *mo-ron*.

I set the table and dish out dinner. There was too much meat, so I also fry up two burgers for Adam. Just because I'm a little disappointed in him doesn't mean I should be rude. He's deep in thought, glaring at the wood he's cutting as if it owes him money, when I poke my head out. "Dinner," I shout.

He looks up at me, still scowling. "Thank you."

The girls are still showering, so soon it's just him and me at the small table. I sip my wine and keep my eyes on the TV, picking at my food. He eats with gusto, no doubt gathering fuel for tonight's physical exertion. "This is very good."

"Uh huh," I say. "What did Cheyenne say?"

"Nothing pertinent."

"What's your impression of her?"

"Um ... uninhibited," he says with a chuckle.

"Did you get around to talking about me?"

"A little."

Freaking blood from a stone. "Well, try and remember the mission when you're dirty dancing with her tonight. Just my life on the line, is all."

He sits back in the chair and folds his arms across his chest. "Why are you mad at me? I told you I'm gaining her trust. Nothing more."

"Just don't whore yourself out on my account, okay?"

He cocks his head to the side. "Would it bother you if I did?"

I open my mouth to protest, but shut it. I smile instead, and say, "I don't give a damn who you sleep with, that's your business. Just don't use me as an excuse. That's all I'm asking."

Thank the good goddess the girls chose now to walk in. They sit and we adults smile as if everything is hunky dory. The rest of dinner is spent chatting about their day. They especially loved the hardware store. I doubt they've ever been inside one, judging by how awed they sound talking about it. I miss the days when plumbing supplies brought excitement. To be young again.

The doorbell rings just as we finish eating. Adam and I exchange a concerned glance before we both stand to answer it. "Stay here," I tell the girls. Adam beats me there. He hangs by the stairs, but as I walk closer, I hear the sound of two children arguing on the other side of the door, and don't even need to ask who it is. Tamara and her fifteen-year-old son Shawn and ten-year-old daughter Piper, in her white karate outfit, stand on the other side when I open it. My godchildren resemble their father, DeShawn, tall and good looking with light brown skin and black hair. Even in this day and age, it was a minor scandal when Tamara married an African American. He was a wonderful man, just a lousy husband. He cheated on her with at least three women, though she gave as good as she got. She married husband number two a week after the divorce. That one lasted a year. Lonnie is number three.

"Hey, guys," I say.

The trio walk inside, and Tamara kisses my cheek. "Hey, girl." She locks eyes on Adam, and her eyes expand to alien proportions. "Um, *hello.*"

"Tamara, this is Adam."

Adam extends his hand. "Nice to meet you."

"The feeling is definitely mutual."

Jeez Louise, I'm gonna have to start handing out drool buckets at this rate. "Hey, there's spaghetti on the stove. Help yourselves," I say to the kids. "Tamara? Wine?"

"Read my mind," Tamara says. After we get the kids situated, Tamara and I pour our wine and retreat onto the porch swing, where we've spent many a night talking. The evening is crisp but not cold; in other words, lovely. "You didn't tell me he was so cute."

"If you like that type."

"What? Handsome and chivalrous? You gone lesbian on me?"

I sip my wine. "I have other things on my mind, Tam."

"Fine. You're uncomfortable talking about it, big surprise. So fill me in on the rest."

We spend about fifteen minutes talking about my investigation. About halfway through, that frigging band saw starts again. "You hear anything yet?" I ask over the noise.

"I tried talking to Cheyenne, but she was less than receptive."

"Well, maybe Adam will have more luck tonight. They have a date."

Tamara wrinkles her nose. "What? Is he insane?"

"I guess," I say with another swig. "He is a man after all. Well, most of the time."

Tamara's eyes narrow. "It bothers you, doesn't it?"

"What? No! Stop looking for romance everywhere. This isn't a Jane Austen novel."

"Uh huh," she says.

"Besides, a girl shouldn't date two men at once. It's unladylike."

"Shut up!" She smiles from cheek to cheek. "The doctor asked you out?"

"Sort of. He sent me roses and told me to attend the auction on Wednesday."

"Oh my God! That is so romantic! Are you going? You *have* to go."

"Signed up today, goddess help me. I mean, I'm not insane in thinking he's into me, am I? Because Adam suggested he might be part of the plot to kill me."

"Well, then Adam's an idiot. He must be if he's going out with Cheyenne."

"He's only doing it to get information out of her," I concede.

Tamara shakes her head. "Who cares? You've landed yourself a gorgeous—"

"Mona Leigh!" Auntie Sara shouts, mad as a March hare, from her side window. "Will you please tell your guest to stop that horrible racket? I am trying to watch the news!"

"Yes, Auntie Sara," I say. "Come on. Let's go check on the kids." Sophie, Cora, and Piper are all watching *iCarly* in the living room, stuffing their faces with contraband Twinkies. The kitchen is empty except for a clean table and running dishwasher. Huh. I could get used to having such a houseguest. My excellent lodger and Shawn are in the backyard, the teenager having a blast with the saw, judging by his smile. "We had a noise complaint," I shout. Shawn shuts off the saw.

"Sara?" Adam asks.

"Who else?"

"What are you guys working on here?" Tamara asks.

"We're making shelves for Miss Mona's store," Shawn says.

"You're fixing up the store?" Tamara asks Adam.

"Just putting up new shelves," Adam says.

"That's nice of you," Tamara says. "Aren't you just a fine, upstanding gentleman."

Like every other female today, she devours him, giving him a full-body scan with a glint in her eyes. He gives her a humble smile as I suppress an eye roll. This is getting more than a little annoying. The guy's not a model or anything, for goddess's sake, but there is that tool belt . . .

"Hey, I gotta get the girls ready for bed," I say, maintaining my calm. "It's getting late."

"Oh, right," Tamara says. "We better boogie. School night and all. Nice to meet you."

"You too," Adam says.

Tamara takes my arm and drags me inside. "I want one," she whispers as we walk. "Can I borrow yours for the night?"

"Um, he can hear you," I say. "Werewolf, remember?"

"What?" We turn around and see Adam give a little wave. Tamara chuckles nervously. "Kidding."

"I charge by the hour," Adam calls. "Plus tips."

"And I am more than sure you are worth every penny," Tamara says.

"Gross, Mom," Shawn says. I second that.

I escort them out of the house to Tamara's Malibu. Her kids, who haven't stopped bickering since they could talk, squabble as they get into the car. "Oh, I almost forgot," Tamara says, moving to the trunk.

She pops it open and pulls out a pump action shotgun and cartridges. "Lonnie said you can keep this as long as you need it."

"I don't want that thing," I say.

She thrusts it into my arms. "Tough. Put it under your bed for when Mr. Fix-It isn't in there."

"What? He's not coming anywhere near my bed," I whisper.

"Oh, Mona, what am I going to do with you?" She kisses my cheek. "Have a nice, cozy night with the hunk sworn to protect your body."

"Bye, Tam," I say with a little wave.

The car pulls away as I slowly stroll back to the house. Why is it that everyone assumes when a man and a woman inhabit the same space for a period of time they'll fall into bed with one another? I've known Adam for eighteen damn years; if he had any designs on me, he would have acted on them by now. Or at least given me a damn sign. Instead he went out of his way to avoid me until now. I recall at least three instances off the top of my head where he saw me approaching his group and walked away. If I'm honest, it kind of hurt my feelings. I wasn't even worth a stupid conversation to him. Which makes this whole thing so strange. There is something that I am not seeing. Why—

My train of thought is derailed when a silver Lexus parks right in front of my house. My breath catches when the driver gets out.

Guy Sutcliffe. Here. At my house. Looking edible in a white dress shirt with the sleeves pushed up and black slacks. "Hi," he says as his eyes narrow. "Um…"

I follow his gaze to the shotgun slung over my shoulder. Oh goddess. "Oh," I say with a chuckle, "I was just taking my shotgun for a walk. It gets fussy if I don't."

"Oh," he says, shutting the car door. "Wait, what?"

"I'm joking. It was a joke? Apparently a bad one."

"No, right," he says. "Sorry. I'm a little slow today. Twelve-hour shift."

And he came here! I suppress my giddy jumping. "Well, would you like to come in for some tea? Might perk you up."

"I'd love some tea," he says, walking up to the house. He follows me inside, both of us glancing at the other and awkwardly smiling. "I hope you don't mind me stopping by like this. It was on my way home."

"No, I'm just surprised you knew where I lived."

"I, uh, got the address off Cora's chart."

The girls are still in front of the TV when we step in. I don't want them to see the shotgun. "Make yourself at home. I'll be right back."

I take the steps two at a time and sprint into my bedroom. He's in my house. The man of my dreams is in my house! I jump up and down squealing for a few seconds before regaining my composure. I stash the gun into my closet with the cartridges going in my dresser. With that done, I rush into the bathroom to brush my hair, add lipstick, and gargle with mouthwash just in case. Of kissing!

When I swan back downstairs, Guy is wedged between the girls on the couch examining Cora's hand. "Are you keeping it dry?" he asks.

"I hold it up in the bath like this," she says, demonstrating.

"Excellent," he says.

"Girls, don't bother the doctor," I say. "He's had a long day." I grin at him. "Come on. Let's get you that tea." Guy follows me into the kitchen. Thank the goddess Adam isn't in the backyard anymore. "Hot or cold, sweet or unsweetened?"

"Sweetened iced, if you have it."

I pull out a pitcher of just that. "Dr. Sutcliffe, you are south of the Mason-Dixon. I dare you to find a home without cold sweet tea in the fridge."

"Well, I beg your pardon, ma'am," he says, trying to copy my accent.

I pour. "You are forgiven. This once," I say, handing him a glass. I guess flirting is like riding a bike, though I never thought I'd learned in the first place. "Save any lives today?"

"Not really. Things are pretty quiet around here."

"Is that a good or bad thing?"

He shrugs. "A little of both. I wanted a slower pace, and I got it," he says, not sounding all together thrilled. "It's just different."

"What made you decide on Goodnight?" I ask.

"There was an opening, and it has a certain Southern charm. I always wanted to live in the deep South. Painted porches, sweet tea, sitting out on a swing enjoying both."

"Well, I think I can help fulfill that fantasy. Come on."

Guy shadows me back into the living room where the girls are whispering to each other, stopping when they see us. That is beginning to bother me. I'm not a big fan of secrets, and I'm about to say something when the footsteps on the stairs cause us all to look that way. Adam wanders in, and my back involuntarily straightens. It feels strange having Adam and Guy inhabit the same space, as if the combination sends uncomfortable ripples through the atmosphere. I think they feel it too. After the initial surprise, they grow a little suspicious of one another, almost examining one another like animals ready to pounce. Most odd.

"Hello," Adam says.

"Um, A.J., this is Dr. Guy Sutcliffe. Guy, this is A.J."

"He's our cousin from Boston in for the wedding," Cora says.

Guy's posture softens a little. "Oh, nice to meet you." He extends his hand. After an uncomfortable second Adam takes it, squeezing so tight Guy winces and pulls away. "Nice grip."

Adam doesn't utter a word.

"Um, we'll be out on the porch if anyone needs us," I say lightly tugging on Guy's shirt.

"Nice to see you girls again," Guy says as we walk to the door. He half smiles at the scowling werewolf. "Have a ... nice night."

I shut the front door when Guy steps out. "You'll have to forgive my cousin. He's a tad grumpy today."

"No, it's fine," Guy says as he sits on the swing. "Exactly how many cousins do you have in town?"

I sit as close to him as I dare, leaving about two feet between us. "I've actually lost count. We're an old family."

"And you've always lived here?"

"Born, lived, and will probably die right here."

"That must be nice, having roots. It's hard to get them up in D.C."

"Blessing and curse, like most things in life," I say, sipping my own tea. "I've known these people all my life, but on the flipside they've known *me* all their lives, and people in small towns have long memories. I'm still getting heat from Nurse Luann about biting her thirty years ago."

"Yeah, she mentioned that," he says with a chuckle.

"See? So watch out. Just saying."

He sips his tea, glancing over at me with a sly smile. "And what will me sitting on this swing with you do for my reputation?"

I beam back. "You'll be considered a very smart man with excellent taste in women."

"Huh. Accurate so far." He scoots closer to me so our legs touch. He's touching me. My entire body tingles with anticipation. "And if I, I don't know…" he says, lifting up his arm and draping it around my shoulders. I almost *die* on the spot. "Do something like this, what do you think they'll say?"

"Um…" I seem to have forgotten the English language. "Good. Good things."

He proudly smiles and takes a sip of the tea, the blue and purple bracelet on his wrist falling a little. I've seen that before. Where— "So did you get my flowers?"

"What? Oh, those were from you? I thought they were from one of my other gentlemen callers."

"You have others?"

"Oh tons. I'm beating them back with a stick. Though you're in the lead."

"My good old-fashioned Southern courting skills are that good, huh?"

I shrug. "You lose points for not wearing seersucker and asking me to dance a reel."

"I will have to remember that for next time," he says with another smile.

We swing for a minute, and I enjoy every moment of it. The feel of his body beside mine. The weight of his arm on my shoulders. The way his thin lips pucker just after he sips the tea. He must feel me staring because he turns, his eyes meeting mine. His smile starts small, as does mine, but they grow in time with each other. The smile of anticipation. My cheeks grow hot again, but I don't break the gaze. He is so handsome, like something out of a movie. He moves first, lips slightly parted for what's to come, and I follow his lead. This is really happening. Please let me remember how to kiss. I close my eyes.

"Oh my God! They're going to kiss!"

My eyes fly open, as do Guy's. Both our gazes whip toward the window behind us. Cora, with her mouth now covered by a hand, is being dragged away by her sister toward the couch. And the mortification hits ... *now*. Guy chuckles and shakes his head, but I want to go hide in a closet. The mood is dead. "Uh, I guess I better go," he says as he stands.

"Yeah," I say, standing too.

He hands me his empty glass. "Well, thank you for the tea and Southern etiquette lesson."

"Always glad to help."

"Um, so I'll see you Wednesday night?"

"I'll be there. Will you?"

"Wouldn't miss it for the world." He takes my hand and brushes his lips across the top. Cue melting. "Goodnight." With another smile my way, he steps off the porch toward his car, giving a quick wave before climbing in. I wait until I spin around before letting a huge smile form on my face. I feel like I'm floating on a cloud. Is it too soon to be looking for a wedding dress? Probably. I'll start *after* our first date.

The girls are sitting side by side on the couch with expressions of dread on their cute faces when I come inside. I fall from my cloud and drop the smile to glare at them. "What have I told you about spying on people? It's rude."

"Sorry," Sophie says.

"Are you going to marry Dr. Sutcliffe? Can I stay here in my pink room?" Cora asks.

"No one is getting married." Yet. "Now, both of you get upstairs. You've lost TV privileges for the night."

"Aww, but—" Sophie says.

"Zip it. Upstairs. Scoot."

Moping, the girls turn off the TV and tread upstairs. It's almost time for them to head off to bed anyway. With a sigh, I walk into the kitchen and stick our glasses in the dishwasher. So close, I was *so close*. Next time I won't wait. Before he says a word, I'll press my lips to his and give him what for. Next time.

The back door is open and I can hear quiet sawing. Through the window, I see Adam still at his post using a manual saw to cut another plank in relative quiet. He sneers at the wood, sweat dripping from his nose onto the wood. I fill another glass with water. He doesn't stop sawing when I step outside. "Here. Thought you might be thirsty."

He glances at the glass. "I'm not."

"O-kay," I say, pulling my hand back.

"Is your boyfriend gone?"

"He's not ... yeah, he's gone. He just stopped by to make sure I got the flowers."

"Oh," he says over the gentle noise.

I stand here for a few seconds, water in hand, as he picks up the pace. The excess wood lands on the concrete, and Adam brushes his forehead, bits of wood sticking to it. I have the strongest urge to wipe the sweat and wood from his brow but hold back. That's the sexual frustration urging me on. He does look pretty adorable disheveled like this. "Well, I'm gonna get a little work done, and get the girls to bed. Excuse me."

Just as I step into the house, his voice stops me. "Mona?"

I turn around. "Yeah?"

"I'm going to say this, and I don't want you to take it the wrong way. This has nothing to do with you as a person, okay?"

"What?"

"I don't like that guy."

"Yeah, we all kind of picked up on that," I say.

"It's not…" He shakes his head. "There's something off. I don't know what it is, but I can feel it. Something is wrong about him. I just don't want you to get hurt."

My back straightens. "Noted. Thank you for your concern. I'll let you get back to work." I step inside before he can say another wretched word.

He's wrong. He wasn't on that porch. Guy's a doctor, not an actor. He couldn't fake the lust and kindness I saw in his eyes. No, it was genuine. And lovely. Adam's just paranoid.

I'm staking my heart on it.

· Get the girls ready for bed

The girls go off to bed with little fuss, and I get the majority of my work done, though I seem to be missing a few oils and herbs I need. I was sure I had enough, but it wouldn't surprise me if I just forgot to write down that I needed more. My brain can only handle so much.

After a shower, I check on the slumbering children and the big baby downstairs still hard at work in the backyard. He's gonna wear himself out if… oh my. My breath catches when I see him shirtless and sweating, muscles rippling as he saws back and forth. Without a word, I spin on my heel and scurry out of the kitchen before I'm caught ogling my houseguest. My libido is worn out from the past few days, and I'm afraid one more shock will make it break down and do something…unladylike.

Work. Investigation. Focus on that. So I get my cell phone, go out on the front lawn to activate the perimeter, and dial Lord Thomas as I sit on the swing. He answers on the fifth ring. "Thomas Wellington."

"Lord Thomas, this is Mona McGregor."

"High Priestess McGregor. I was wondering when you would phone."

"Well, I almost called last night but decided I should calm down before we had this conversation."

"Always wise. I do apologize for literally throwing you to the wolves. I had no choice. Mr. Dahl was…more than a tad upset and concerned as to the fate of his friend. He would not believe me unless I produced the Beta. From the message you left, I assumed he was with you. He is well? My men tend to take their tasks very seriously."

"He's fine."

"Do tell him I hope there are no hard feelings. I did not know he was a double agent."

"I'll tell him."

"And you? How are you? Has our mystery witch made herself known yet?"

"No, but I'm looking into it, as I'm sure you are as well. I thought we could pool information, as she now has a reason to be pissed at you too. You know, *cooperation*? You are familiar with the meaning of that word, right?" He doesn't dignify this jab with an answer. I sigh. "I've narrowed it down to four possible, two probable suspects: Cheyenne Bell and Erica Fitch. Has Erica called you yet?"

"Erica? No," Thomas says.

"Well, have you found any clues that might lead us to his accomplice?"

"There were women's undergarments and spell paraphernalia in Alejandro's house. However, he was quite popular with the fairer sex, so a multitude of women were seen leaving his home. Try as we did, he would not give up the name."

"So you have nothing, either."

"They were careful. Was the wolf's information any better?"

"No. Alejandro never gave any indication as to who she was."

"Then we will have to soldier on as we are. If I uncover anything pertinent, I shall phone."

"Same here. And if Erica calls, let me know. I set up a little test for her."

"I will. Have a good night." He hangs up.

"Any news?" Adam asks behind me through the window.

People have no sense of privacy anymore. "No." Damn it! Our dead ends have dead ends. I return to the house and am relieved to see Adam's shirt is firmly on his torso. Very firmly. Kind of clinging. I lock the front door and hand him the keys. "Here. You can take my car for your date tonight. Just lock the door behind yourself. I'm going to bed."

"I don't think I'll go," he says.

"Why not?"

"I don't want to leave you unprotected."

I sigh. "Look, you were right, and I was wrong. The date was a good idea. Anything you can get out of her will be helpful at this point, so go. Please."

"You don't … mind?"

"I'm not your keeper," I say wearily. "And I have a shotgun, a pistol, and the elements to defend myself. Don't worry about me. This has to be done. Go. Maybe even try to have fun. You deserve it."

"Fine then. I will. Excuse me." He brushes past me without another word.

Goddess, why are all werewolves so moody? We women got nothing on them.

I do one final sweep of the house before jumping into bed face first. It's odd not having the Captain waiting for me on his pillow, but he refuses to come out of the chimney. Add that to my To Do list: cat love potion so he'll tolerate Adam. It's not illegal to use on animals, at least I don't think so. That's a theoretical debate for tomorrow.

I shut off my lamp and snuggle into bed. I fall asleep to the rhythm of the shower in the next room and visions of me walking down the aisle in Granny's wedding dress.

I'm jolted awake a short while later by the knowledge that someone is breaking the perimeter: Adam on his way out. Hope his date is as frustrating as mine was.

TUESDAY TO DO:

- *Cat love potion*
- *Continue investigation*
- *Find a dress for auction*
- *Work*
- *Paint front window*
- *Organize store for renovation*
- *Lose thirty pounds by tomorrow night*

12:52 A.M. OKAY, THE psychic alarm system is getting on my nerves. I wake again as someone walks through it. I listen as the door opens, closes, and keys are set on the end table downstairs. Adam. He walks up the creaky steps and finally the bedroom door shuts across from mine. I fall back asleep ... until the phone rings. "For fuck's sake." I pick up the portable, turn it on and off, then on again to leave it off the hook. No way. Not tonight. Within seconds, I'm asleep again.

What the fuck?

I sit straight up in bed, every one of my nerve endings buzzing with warning. There are goose pimples all over and the hair on my arms stand on end. Danger. I've never felt this before, but instinctively I know the cause.

I am in such deep shit.

"Aunt Mona?" Sophie calls, voice filled with terror.

I leap out of bed and run to the door. Both girls stand in the hallway, Cora clutching onto her shaking sister. They're as petrified as I am. "Are you okay?" I ask, trying and failing to hide my own fear.

The door across from me swings open, and we all almost pee our pants. Adam steps out, hair wild from sleep. "What's the matter?"

"You don't feel that?" I ask.

"What?"

"Demon," Sophie says, voice quaking. "There's a demon outside."

"A demon?" Adam asks.

"You two, my office, *now!*" The girls spring next door with me close behind. Oh fuck, this is not good. This is as far from good as we can get. The girls huddle in the corner while I get to work. Off the top of my head I know they don't like white musk and myrrh, so I light those incense sticks. I go through my shelves, knocking things down left and right.

Adam steps in. "Mona, what—"

"Shotgun in the closet, shells in my underwear drawer," I say as I fumble with the top to the carnation oil. He runs out.

"What's it going to do to us?" Cora cries, tears streaming down her face.

I bend down right at her level, meeting her eyes. "Nothing," I say with utter certainty. "It is not going to do *anything* to you. Adam and I will make sure of it."

"Promise?" she sobs.

"On my life."

"They—they hate sage and sea salt," Sophie says. "It hurts them. Hyssop too. It burns them like acid."

How she knows that is a question for later. "Then burn some," I say, anointing them with carnation oil. "Now, you two stay here. Run some black salt across the floor, okay? It shouldn't be able to cross it."

"Don't leave!" Cora shrieks.

Her voice cuts me so deep it brings tears to my eyes. "I have to, sweetie. I have to get him away from the house. But if anything happens to me, you call 911 and wait for them in here, then go to Auntie Sara's, okay?" I quickly kiss each of their cheeks and rise. I grab some sage, hyssop, a silver athame, and two protection amulets. I light the two herbs. "Lock this door and black salt it, okay?" Sophie nods her head. "Love you. It'll all be fine."

I shut the door and run into my bedroom just as Adam sticks a cartridge into the shotgun. "Will this work on a demon?"

I retrieve the gun safe from the closet. "Aim for the head. That'll stop anything." I press in the code and pull out the .38. "Come on." He follows me down the hall and stairs. I hand him one of the amulets and the hyssop on the stairs. "Put that on," I whisper. The house is dark, and I don't want to give away our location, so we carefully pad into the living room.

"Could it be in the house?" Adam whispers.

"No, the perimeter hasn't been breached. It must sense it," I whisper back. "Still. Backyard first."

He takes the lead through the living room to the kitchen, checking every corner with the muzzle of the shotgun pointed there. My heart is beating like a jackhammer and every muscle is wound up, but Adam just seems focused. He's faced life-and-death situations before, he'll know how to handle this one too. At this moment, I'm so relieved he's here I could kiss him. He looks out the kitchen window into the backyard. "I don't see or hear anyone."

The telephone rings, and I shriek and damn near pee my pants. He must have hung up the one in my bedroom. There goes the element of surprise. Adam isn't fazed. He unlocks the back door and storms outside, gun first. I follow close behind, my gun not as steady as his. He checks everywhere, scanning for the enemy. Nothing. I can still feel the son of a bitch nearby, prickling my skin with his unnaturalness. Front yard then.

The telephone continues ringing as we retreat inside and through the house. Without hesitation, Adam throws open the front door and rushes onto the porch. He stops right at the steps, gun and eyes roving the horizon. I don't see anything but an empty street. Adam's head cocks to the side as if he's listening to the night. His nose starts twitching. "I feel something," he whispers. The amulet to protect against psychic attack heats up against my collarbone. I wince. "Stay here and cover me," Adam says.

Before I can protest, he leaps off the porch and races in the direction diagonal to Auntie Sara's house. Just as his bare feet hit the sidewalk, a pickup down the street roars to life. When Adam sprints toward it, the truck pulls away, tires screeching as it does a U-turn. It hops the curb and speeds away with the werewolf in hot pursuit. He's no match for the truck though. When it peels around the corner, Adam stops in the middle of the street and groans in frustration. At least my skin doesn't hurt anymore.

"Mona!" Auntie Sara stage whispers to my right. She steps out onto her porch, clutching her robe in one hand and pistol in the other. "Is it gone?"

"For now."

· *Figure out how to kill a damn demon*

Judging from the twenty voicemails and house phone ringing off the hook, I'd say the demon woke up the whole town. Every witch he came within fifty feet of sensed him. I know this because it's in the book right in front of me, which Auntie Sara brought over. I sit at the kitchen table with Cora curled up in my lap as I scan the pages. She hasn't let me go since I retrieved them from the office. Sophie was throwing ingredients into the cauldron as Cora watched. I think it was a protection spell. I grabbed them and dragged them downstairs with me into the kitchen, where we've set up camp.

Adam hands Auntie Sara a cup of coffee, which she takes with shaky hands. Sophie sits across from me staring at her sister, face set in stone. Adam plops down in the empty chair beside me, sliding a coffee cup over. "Thank you," I say.

He nods. "So … a demon. I thought they were just myths."

"Says the werewolf," I say with a crooked smile. It's all I can muster right now.

"I cannot believe you lied to me," Auntie Sara says to me.

I had no choice but to tell her everything after she saw Adam chasing the demon, shotgun in hand. "I'm sorry."

"What do you know about demons?" Adam asks me.

"Not a whole lot. It's not something I ever thought would come up. They're rare, at least the kind I think this one is."

"There's more than one type?" Adam asks.

"There's the kind you summon and the kind that just sneaks through the dimensional cracks," Auntie Sara instructs. "With the latter, you get your basic demonic possession. They're weak, so they need a host body. The summoned kind is a specific demon. They have specific traits and powers, depending on who was called."

"What do they look like?" Adam asks.

"Human," Sophie says. All eyes dart to her in surprise. "He'll look like whoever gave the blood for the ritual." Auntie Sara, Adam, and I all share a concerned look, and Cora grasps me harder. "The murder of something innocent, usually an animal, helps open the doorway. It comes out of the portal, looking like a demon. It's … " She shakes her head and winces. I get a chill. "It's unnatural. It doesn't belong here and can't survive, so the witch gives her blood and then it takes human form." She looks down at the table away from our stares. "Um, it'll look, sound, act, even bleed like us. I guess it sort of *is* us. Just … a little more. And powerful."

"So it can be killed," Adam says.

"It's not as simple as that," I say. "It's like a psychic on steroids. If you summoned the demon in charge of fire, it can make you spontaneously combust from twenty yards away. If it can read minds in its dimension, it can invade your mind and trap your consciousness inside yourself here."

"And it's strong," Sophie adds. "Probably as strong as you. And it heals fast too."

My stomach clenches again. "What—what else do you know about them, honey?"

"People can't tell what they are, but we can because we're from here and they're from there. They don't like us because of it. And they don't like it that they have to listen to the person who brought them here. But they only have to do one thing, and then they're free. We can trap them, though, with sigils and spells. They can't hurt us then. Not even with their brains. And they don't like certain smells, and silver hurts them real bad."

"An—anything else?" I ask, trying to keep my voice steady.

She just shrugs.

I clear my throat. "Okay um, girls why don't you go in the living room and pop in a movie?"

Cora burrows deeper into my chest. "No, I don't want to leave you," she cries.

"I'll be in here. I'll be able to see you the whole time, okay?"

"Come on," Sophie says as she stands up. "We'll watch *Toy Story 3.*"

I manage to extract the child from my body and get her to her feet. A stoic Sophie takes her hand and leads her into the living room. My stomach clenches in fear. Oh hell, what on earth am I going to do?

"Mona, how did she know all of that?" Auntie Sara asks. "You don't think—"

"Auntie Sara, that is a 'not now' question, okay?" The telephone starts ringing again, sending splinters into my already throbbing temples. "Can you just field calls for me?"

"And what am I supposed to tell them?"

"The truth?" My brain is swimming. I rub my temples to focus. "Tell them we're having an emergency meeting in the morning, time and location in an e-mail to follow."

"Okay," Auntie Sara says as she stands. She grabs the portable phone and walks out.

I glance at the girls sitting on the couch, then at Adam. He plays with his cup, but his weary eyes stay on me. "Are you okay?" he asks.

I don't know what it is about those words, or maybe it's his gentle expression, but I almost burst into tears. Tentatively, he places his hand over mine, squeezing it. No, not now. That simple gesture shoves me over the edge. I gasp and cover my mouth but a few tears make it to my eyes. I shut them. Using all my willpower, I push them away. If I break now I won't be able to pull myself together again, so I do what I do best. I swallow my emotions so deep an archeologist couldn't find them. I pull my hand away and wipe the stray tears off my face.

Problem. Fix the problem first. "Um, what did you find out from Cheyenne? What time did she get to the bar?"

"She was there when I got there at ten thirty. We talked until about twelve thirty, when I walked her to her car and came back. We woke up here at four thirty, so she had plenty of time to summon it."

"What did she say?"

"About you? Not a lot. She thinks you're prissy, unimaginative, and holier-than-thou. Her words, not mine."

"I don't give a shit what she thinks about my character flaws! In between the make-out sessions did she give you any indication she hates me enough to do all this?"

"I don't know. I couldn't get much out of her, I'm sorry."

I stand, practically making the chair fall back. "Well, I can't do much with *sorry*, can I?"

I can't breathe in here. I need to breathe so I can think. I stalk into the backyard, taking in huge gulps of air. Instantly, I feel like a jerk. Because I am one. I can't keep doing that. Adam is in no way, shape, or form deserving of my ire.

Even still, a second later he steps outside to check on me. "Mona?"

"I'm sorry," I say, "I'm so sorry. I don't mean to snap at you like that, I really don't. I'm not normally like this, I swear."

"I know you aren't."

"I have no idea what I'm doing, Adam. A killer? Now a demon too? What the hell am I going to do?"

"We'll figure it out."

"How? I can't think. I can't . . . " Shit, the tears are trying the damndest to get out. I take a ragged breath. "I am *so scared.*"

"I know." He steps toward me, and the next thing I know his arms are around me, pulling me into his warm body. Dear goddess, does this feel wonderful. He's so solid and even smells good, like hyssop and soap. "I know," he whispers. He simply holds me, my head on his shoulder and hand against his racing heart. I just want to melt into him. He'll keep me safe. For a fleeting instant all the world fades except for me and him, and I can actually believe everything will be okay as long as he never lets me go.

But only for an instant. I'm too realistic for false hope. Lust, be gone. I pull away, my back straightening to gain some respectability back. "Thank you. That helped."

"Happy to oblige," he says, for some reason unable to look at me.

I step away and turn my back to him. Okay, I can think now. This is good. "So um, I have a request to make of you."

"Anything."

I knew he'd say that. "I need you to take the girls away from here. Take them to Jason's or your house or wherever, and keep them safe for me."

"That's not a good idea."

I spin around. "The hell it isn't! There is a fucking demon here to kill me!"

"Then you come with us."

"I can't! I can't leave everyone here with a demon on the loose. Just take them and go!"

"I am not leaving you alone here!" he says with enough force to punch through a wall.

"This isn't your fight."

"Yeah, it is."

"The game has changed. It's too damn dangerous around me now. Just take them and go. Please!"

"*No*. I made a promise and I take promises very seriously."

I throw my arms up. "I absolve you! Take them and go!"

"No!" Sophie shouts from the door. I spin around as she leads her sister toward us. "If you send us away, we'll just come right back! We will!" she says, voice shaking. "I can protect you! I can! I know what to do! Please!" She looks at Adam, eyes wild. "Don't take us away. Please, don't take us away."

"Sophie—" I say, my voice breaking along with my heart.

"We are not going anywhere," Adam says to Sophie. "I promise."

"You can't—" I say.

He grabs my arm and yanks me away from the girls, all but dragging me to the other side of the yard. "Now, you listen to me," he says in a low voice. "You are letting your fear cloud your judgment, and you are scaring the hell out of those girls there. More than even the demon is. Is that what you want?"

"No, but—"

"We are not leaving, do you hear me? Do not mention it again." He takes a deep breath to regain his composure. "Look, I know you're used to doing everything on your own, but you *cannot* do this alone. You can't. So I am here to protect you and those girls so you don't have to. But to do that, we all need to be *here*. United. A cohesive unit working together. A pack, okay? And since you aren't thinking clearly right now, I'll do it for you. If you die, who will take care of them? They need to be near you, a *strong* you. If they go away and you die, they will never, ever recover. They have lost too damn much already."

"It could kill them to get to me," I whisper.

"Mona, if that thing wants them and is as powerful as you say it is, it won't matter where they are. It will find them and use them anyway. At least here they have you and me and an entire army of witches in this town to go through first. And I will *die* before I let anything happen to any of you. Do you believe me?"

I absolutely do. I shake my head.

"Good. Then trust me on this. We're sticking together. We will be cautious, but we will not let fear dictate our lives. We stick to the plan. We fortify this place and ourselves as best we can, we find who summoned this thing, and we stop her. You … and me. I am not going anywhere. I *swear* it to you."

I have the strongest urge to hug him again, among other things I won't admit to. He's so sincere I can't help but feel … relief. At least that's what I think it is. It's a new sensation. Takes me awhile to get used to it. "Okay," I whisper. "Okay."

"Then let's get started." He turns away from me and walks over to the waiting girls, picking up Cora as if it was the most natural thing and holding his hand out for Sophie. She looks at it, but after a second of indecision, puts her hand in his. He leads them inside, off to find a way to save my life.

This time I let the tears flow. Because I can.

· *Run emergency meeting*

The only space big enough to fit the entire coven, all one hundred fifty of us, is the Goodnight Playhouse next to the museum. I find it rather fitting to be standing on the stage where *The Crucible* will be performed tonight, what with it being about witches in peril. I just hope things end better for me than it did for them.

As the edgy women and men filter in, Billie, Auntie Sara, and Debbie stand at their respective doors handing out packets I've put together on Demonology 101. Research, sigils, spells, anything I could find in the three whole books Granny and Auntie Sara had on the subject. Everyone is abuzz and chatting with each other about their experiences, so it sounds like a football game in here. The phone tree is a wonderful invention and an effective one, given the size of the crowd. Even Shirley showed up, though she hangs in the back looking put out as always. Her husband, the sheriff, stands on-stage with me sporting the same expression as his wife. As he's married to a witch he knows all about us, and since the demon passed right by his house and scared the hell out of said wife, he's agreed to help. It must be catching.

My backup is dropping off the girls at school, among other things. We decided since I'm the target, we'd send them to school where at least four teachers are witches. We loaded them up with charms, amulets, and even black salt just to be safe. As an added precaution the teachers are going around the campus carving or spray painting sigils outside just like we did at the house. Casa McGregor now a magical fortress with the strongest barrier spell I could find. Nothing can come in or out without my or Adam's say-so.

As the last witches arrive, I scan the crowd for my prime suspects. Erica isn't here yet but Cheyenne sits in the back, a huge pair of sunglasses covering her face though we're inside. Summoning a demon

142

does take a lot out of a witch. That or she's hung over. Probably both. Collins is one of the last stragglers, still dressed in her scrubs. She kisses Debbie's cheek and finds a seat. Let's get this show started.

"May I have everyone's attention?" I shout. Those standing and chatting take their seats. After a few more seconds the auditorium grows quiet. "I want to thank y'all for being here on short notice, including Sheriff Andrews. I know this isn't your jurisdiction as such, but I'm sure we all feel better knowing you're involved." The sheriff nods. "As y'all are aware of by now, a demon was sensed by multiple people in this room, myself included." The murmuring begins anew, but I hold up my hand to quiet them down. "Okay, everyone settle down. There is no need to panic. There have been no sightings since six this morning, so for all we know it was just passing through town." Yeah, right.

"How did it get here?" my cousin Dickie shouts.

"It was summoned, by whom I don't know."

"Was it someone in this room?" a woman asks.

"I have no idea, but if it was I implore that person to come to me so I can help you send this thing back before it hurts someone. Whoever you are, you are dealing with the darkest magic there is. What you brought here is more powerful than you can imagine. Whatever the reason you summoned it, it is not worth yours or anyone else's life." The audience shifts uncomfortably, and everyone scans the auditorium for signs of guilt. My eyes stay affixed to Cheyenne, who still hasn't taken off her sunglasses. "If anyone has any information on people in this coven even dabbling in black magic, it is your duty to tell me. I promise this will all be kept confidential."

"Well, what do we do?" Brandie asks. "Is it going to try and kill us?"

Only me. "As I said, what it's doing here—if it's still even here—I don't know. But considering what this thing is, we need to take precautions. I already have people at the school warding it, so don't be afraid to send your children there. I have also provided you with an overview on demons and spells to protect against it. They're a little more advanced, so those of you who struggle please don't hesitate to ask for help. Anyone who has time today and is willing to help, please raise your hand." About a third of the group does, mostly the older women. "After this meeting I will be opening the shop so you can get the supplies you need, and Billie, Alice, and I will be there all day to offer assistance as well.

"As I said, these are only precautions. There is no need to panic. I do ask that those of you who sensed this thing send me an e-mail with your address and the time you felt it so we can track it. Also, if you sense it today, call me immediately."

"Promise to answer this time?" someone shouts.

"Yes. Sheriff, anything else to add?"

Sheriff Andrews steps beside me. "I know this is out of my purview, but if you feel you are in danger, call 911. The dispatcher will notify me, and I will notify Mona."

"Thank you," I say as he backs away. "Okay, that's all for now. Get back to your normal lives and live them. Just be vigilant. Trust your instincts. Thank you." The moment I step backstage with Andrews the cacophony of voices starts again. "When we can get the trajectory of the demon I'll call you, and you can search the area where it originated from. Maybe the witch left a clue there."

"Shirley mentioned that sometimes a human sacrifice is needed," Andrews says.

"That's rare. Most of the time it's just an animal. It really depends on how powerful and schooled the witch summoning it is." I pause. "Any luck on the license plate?"

"It belongs to Brooks McBride. He didn't even know his car was missing until I told him. Stolen right outside his farm. I'm heading over there now."

"His farm borders Hackett Farm, right? I'd check there for the altar. There'll be strange drawings, blood, salt, and it will probably smell like sulfur."

"Okay. If I find it, I'll call." He walks away, off to find the demon. The man has my vote come election time.

"Mona?" Debbie asks behind me. She, Billie, Collins, and Auntie Sara all walk toward me. "What now?"

They stare at me expectantly, apprehension all over their faces. I'm their leader, the person with all the plans and answers. But I don't. Beyond getting everyone protected, I haven't a clue what to do next. I don't know how to find this demon, let alone the person responsible for bringing it here. I'm out of ideas. But as I look at them, fear in all their eyes, I straighten my back and hold up my head. They need me, and a general never lets down her troops.

"What now? *Now* we fight back. No one brings a demon into my town and gets away with it. Y'all with me?"

"Hell yes," Billie says with a smile.

"Good. Then let's find the bastard."

· *Find the demon*

There isn't time to think or be tired. There's a crowd outside the shop when Billie, Alice, and I arrive, all clamoring to demon-proof their lives. Within an hour, I'm out of every type of amulet, altar, oil, and rune that can be converted into a protection charm. The herbs go even faster. I have to start sending people to the grocery store to get their sage and cloves, though I doubt Kroger's has burdock. I've already ordered more but it won't arrive until tomorrow, which means I have a lot of pissed off, scared witches yelling at me. I let them.

Things slow after hour two, and by hour three the place is damn near empty. I send Alice to help the ten witches who called the shop for assistance and leave Billie up front to handle the stragglers and telephone calls so I can get a few minutes of peace in the back. Adam glances up from the computer and map as I enter. Since he couldn't work on the shelves with a stream of witches filtering in, he took it upon himself to track the demon and coordinate with the sheriff. The map of the town next to him has a few dozen dots with times written on them, starting right on the northern outskirts of town and ending on the south side where farms begin again.

"Sheriff called again," Adam says. "The blood at Hackett Farm wasn't human."

"Thank the goddess for small favors," I say as I fall into the chair next to him.

"And George Black e-mailed you. All the women except for Cheyenne don't have criminal records. What's more interesting, she was given a speeding ticket last month two miles from Lord Thomas's club, Croatoan. He's still waiting for the financial statements."

"Did he write anything about the demon?"

"Just what we already knew. He did say the second it harms someone, he'll send the team to help us catch it. Until then, neither it nor the person who summoned it can be arrested."

"Well, it's nice to know that when this thing explodes my brain with its mind, the F.R.E.A.K.S. will stop by to mop it up." I rest my aching head on the table and close my eyes. "I want to sleep for a year."

"You just need to eat something."

"I don't want to get up. People will just keep asking me questions or hollering at me. I hate being the leader. Cheyenne must be batshit if she wants this job. Hell, at this point, all she'd have to do is ask."

"You don't mean that. You're too damn good at it."

"One of the witches under my supervision raised a demon right under my nose. Priestess of the Year for me."

"This isn't on you, and considering the circumstances, I think you're doing a hell of a job. They all know what to do, how to protect themselves, and they know no matter what, you'll get them through this."

"You sound so sure."

"Tell me I'm wrong."

I sit up, once again looking at him in awe. Who is this guy? "Shut up."

He grins again, and I get a little flutter in my tummy. His whole damn face lights up when he smiles. Not many people's do that. They should. The fluttering grows worse when he pats my hand. "Come on," he says, pulling me up. "I think we both need a shitload of caffeine and sugar. I'm buying."

"No. The yelling will start again," I whine.

"I won't let anyone yell at you," Adam says.

I pout. "Promise?"

"I'm your bodyguard, and that includes stopping irate witches from getting in your face." He holds out his hand. "Come on." I take it.

Billie is cleaning up the herbs when we walk out. Her eyes immediately dart to our clasped hands, and she raises an eyebrow. I hadn't even realized we were still hand in hand. I pull mine away, using it to smooth my hair. "We'll, uh, be back." Eyes to the ground and hands in my pockets, I lead the way to the diner. That was a close one. I've given the gossip mongers too much to work with this week already.

When we're about two stores down, my cell rings again. Can't I get even ten freaking minutes of peace? Nope. Never. I answer. "Hello?"

"Mona?" Brandie asks, voice quaking. "Oh thank God."

I touch Adam's arm, and we stop walking. "Brandie, what is it? Are you okay?"

"I—I felt it, I mean I *feel* it. I think it's nearby. Can you come?"

Adam and I exchange a knowing glance then take off running toward the parking lot. "Brandie, I am on my way, okay? Have you put up the sigils I gave you?"

"Um, yeah," she says, "I—I don't see anyone outside."

We reach my car and leap in. "Stay away from the windows, okay? It can sense you too."

"It can?" she asks on the verge of hysterics.

"Just start burning sage. We'll be there in a few minutes. You'll be fine. It doesn't want you."

"How—how do you know? Aaron's been catting around with someone. She might have brought it here to kill me!"

Adam raises an eyebrow, and I shrug. The phone beeps to tell me I have another call. "I doubt it, okay? Be there in three minutes. Just stay indoors." I switch to the other call. "Yes?"

"Mona, it's Meg," she whispers. "It's here."

"I know. I'm already on my way. Just burn sage and stay behind the sigils. It can't get you. I'll be there soon." I hang up. "They live a few houses apart," I tell Adam.

"What do you think it's doing there?"

"Cheyenne lives down the street from them." I drive over the railroad tracks into the south side with its tract houses almost on top of each other and separated by chain link.

"Do we have a plan?" Adam asks as I make a quick right onto Cheyenne's street.

"You're supposed to be the tactical expert. I—"

I feel it. That same prickling of skin sprouting gooseflesh and rock in my stomach. I slow the car down, scanning the houses and cars for people.

"Mona?" Adam asks.

"Tell me when you feel it too."

We pass Brandie's house with the GTO on bricks in her driveway. The twisted lines like ivy made up of incantations is painted on the door. At least she can get sigils right. There's no movement between the houses or in the parked cars. Meg's house, which she shares with Belle, is two down. There's nothing out of the ordinary there either. Cheyenne's is the last house on the right with the dying lawn. Her car isn't in the driveway. There aren't any sigils either.

"I think I feel it," Adam says. "Keep driving." I just see more of the same, a whole lot of nothing but houses in need of paint and a million cars until we reach the next intersection. "Turn here and park."

I do as he says, stopping in the only space available, in front of Maxine Bell's ranch house, Cheyenne's grandmother. "Okay, it's around here. Now what?" I ask.

"We find it and kill it," he says before getting out of the car. "Pop the trunk."

My Girl Scout leader would be proud to know I follow the "Be prepared" motto even after all these years. Shotgun, salt, spray paint, potions, charm bags, silver daggers, even holy water. "Here's what we're going to do," Adam begins, taking out the potions and shotgun. He hands me the bag with the rest. "You're going to drive back toward Cheyenne's, stopping a house or two down. I'll be shadowing you through the backyards. You get out of the car and walk to her house. If it's outside, it'll try to take you there." He pulls out the pentagram amulet that matches mine. "This thing makes it so it can't affect you psychically, right?"

"Right. It can't get into our mind or spirit, but if it can throw a car with its mind or bend space/time, they won't do a lick of good."

"If it could do either of those, it would have last night when you were on the porch. We'll just have to take that chance. So it comes into the open for the attack, I come out firing, hopefully blowing its brains out."

"If you can't?"

"Then while I keep its attention, you draw that trapping sigil. I'll do my best to get it in there, and you send it back to hell. Sound good?"

"Sounds awful, but I don't have any better ideas."

He rubs my arm. "You'll do great. Just keep your eyes open." He steps away, but then a second later turns back around. "Look, if something happens to me … I want you to run. Don't try to save me, just run. Pick up the girls and drive to Jason's. Vivian will convince him to help you. She likes you. Force him to take you in. Don't—"

"Nothing is going to happen," I say forcefully. "Not to you, not to me. You promised, right?" I squeeze his hard biceps before shutting the trunk. "You die, I swear I'll bring your ghost back and make your afterlife a living hell." I squeeze one last time. "Be safe."

"You too."

As I move toward the car door, my partner rushes to the nearest house. I start up the car, turn around in Maxine's driveway, and slowly drive back toward Cheyenne's. The only citizens outside are old Cray Bradshaw talking to a pretty brunette I can't place at the moment. They ignore me as I pull into the one spare spot on the street. There are so many cars parked I can't keep my eye on them all. I shut off the engine but can't move. I don't want to get out of this car. I know the demon can get me in here, but I don't want to be exposed. And Adam's out there. He's not afraid. He's tough. Brave. Of course *he* has a shotgun, and I have spray paint and sage. Still. I'm not leaving him out there alone.

I throw the door open, grab the bag, and force myself out of the car. Every muscle in my body is strained as I stand. The birds chirping on the power lines above work my nerves. What if the demon can control animals? I could become the star of *The Birds II*. They don't swarm, but I still don't loosen up as I walk toward Cheyenne's. My skin is actually starting to ache now from the demon's power, like it's stretched too thin, but the street remains quiet. What the hell is it waiting for?

The amulet around my neck heats up like last night, and I press it against my chest. He's trying something psychic. Maybe when that fails he'll come at me physically. Having no idea what else to do, I walk up Cheyenne's driveway to the door. Still nothing. I'm close to quivering in terror now. Maybe it's inside. I glance back but the only signs of life are Cray and his chatty companion. Okay, I can't just stand at this door. I touch the door handle and deadbolt, closing my eyes and calling the magic. I whisper, *"Patefacio."* The locks click and I step inside, locking them again behind myself. Nothing attacks me in here either. The amulet cools.

Cheyenne's house is not in the best shape with cigarette burns on the carpet and cheap posters of rock bands on the walls complete with ratty second-hand furniture. I especially love the beer can pyramid on the coffee table surrounded by ashtrays full of joints. I open the sliding glass patio door and step into the backyard with plastic green table and chairs covered with more beer cans. "Adam?"

He steps from the side of the house. "Nothing."

"It tried to put a psychic whammy on me again," I say.

"Then it has to be in a car or house watching you."

"Then why not attack—" And the prickling stops. "Feel that? It's gone."

"It must have realized you were protected and left to regroup," Adam suggests.

"You think?" Somehow I don't buy that. "Should we chase after it?"

"We don't know which way it went. We'll track it through calls like before."

I check the bag for my cell. Not there. "My cell's in the car. Crap." I sigh. "Okay, you start searching the house. We're here, might as well make the best of my felony B&E. We'll stay until we get a tip."

"You're the boss," he says with a smile.

I rush through the house and back outside onto the empty street. My cell is on the dash where I forgot it. No new calls. With most people at work it'll be harder to find him, especially if he leaves town again. Just have to get lucky, I guess.

I walk back toward the house, but as I'm about to step inside, a woman shouts, "What the hell are you doing?"

I spin around and find Maxine, Cheyenne's grandmother, striding down the sidewalk. She's a tiny woman with wild gray hair and is dressed in stained blue sweats as always. She looks a lot like Granny, as they were half-sisters, though Granny's scowl didn't turn you into stone like Maxine's. "Hello, Miss Maxine," I say with a smile as I step back out.

That petrifying scowl doesn't waver. "I'll ask again, Mona McGregor, what the hell are you doing going to my granddaughter's house when she's not there?"

Oh hell. "I, uh … demon. You didn't feel the demon?"

"Of course I did," the old woman huffs. "What does that have to do with you breaking into Cheyenne's house?"

"Uh, Meg said she saw a man go in. We thought it might be the demon. Door was unlocked and all."

Almost on cue, the door opens. "There's no trace of it," Adam says as he steps outside beside me, shotgun swung over his shoulder. "If it was here, it isn't now."

If possible Maxine's scowl grows scarier. "Who is that?"

"My cousin A.J. Cal's grandson. He's my backup. A.J., this is Cheyenne's grandmother Maxine."

He nods at her. "Nice to meet you." He turns to me. "It's not here. We should go."

"Yes, you should, before I call the sheriff," Maxine says.

Adam shuts the front door. "Ma'am," he says with a grin. We start down the driveway. Out of the corner of my eye, I watch as Maxine folds her arms over her chest and follows us toward the car just in case we make a break for it. Adam climbs in the car, but I turn back to Maxine. "I didn't see you at the meeting this morning. If you like I can bring you the protection packet I gave out. You really should put up a sigil at least."

"Don't you talk down to me, Mona Leigh McGregor. I know how to protect myself a lot better than you."

"I didn't mean—"

"Just because you're the High Priestess and live in that fancy house don't make you better than me, little miss."

There's no point fighting with this woman. Many have tried, all have failed. You can't reason with crazy; you literally get spit on. "I am sorry if I offended you. Have a nice day." After another smile, I jump into the car and drive away as fast as I can, the old witch glaring even as we turn the corner. "Bitch."

"What was that all about?"

"Oh, uh, old resentments. Daddy loved your granny best, so I must take it out on everyone, including people who never met the bastard. Not really her fault. Couldn't have been easy growing up illegitimate back then. Cheyenne probably bought into her poison." I shake my head. "You find anything in there?"

"I barely had time to check the closet."

"We need to get back into that house. The demon was around there for a reason."

"We'll think of something." He pauses. "We make a good team."

I couldn't agree more.

• *Happy Family Fun Time*

With no new calls, I drive around town aimlessly for half an hour on the off chance I'll sense it. No such luck. We do use the time wisely though. Having no fresh leads and a growling stomachs, we return downtown ready to implement "Operation: Hoochie House," the closest thing to a plan we have, revolting though it may be. I relieve Billie so she and Adam can go to the diner for lunch. Adam returns ten minutes later with our cheeseburgers, a piece of blackberry pie for me, and a date for tonight with our prime suspect. He'll get her out of her house so I can break in and search it. Easy and hopefully effective. Though when he tells me it's on, for an instant— mind, just a fleeting, barely-even-there instant so I don't even know why I'm mentioning it—jealousy rips through my body like a vengeful spirit eating my soul. But just for an instant. Okay, *several* instants. Only about twenty or so.

The rest of the relatively customerless day is spent installing bookcase shelves and prepping for the rest for the renovation, which means cleaning and moving merchandise. The store is even more cluttered and claustrophobic than usual, but I can see how it will all come together in the end. The day's events and manual labor soon begin to take their toll. I'm yawning every thirty seconds. After I break into Cheyenne's house, I'm going straight home and flopping into bed. Adam leaves at two thirty to pick up the girls, and seeing as I'm the boss and it isn't nearly as fun remodeling without the odd appreciative glance at my handyman, I decide to close early. We had a banner day fiscally speaking; probably the best ever. I'll thank the demon before I send him back to hell.

Billie drops me off at the house just before five. All is quiet, except for that saw. Doesn't bother me as much tonight. Actually, it's comforting. I take a step off the sidewalk onto the lawn but can't make another. Crap, forgot about the invisible fence. I tap the crystal embedded in the ground, step in, and tap it again to re-energize it.

Good to know the thing works. When I walk inside, a wonderful smell wafts from the kitchen, roasting chicken I think. That takes me back. Granny was a great cook, and the house always smelled like cookies or glazed ham. Mommy was the same. She loved her Julia Child cookbook. Being a child at the time, all I wanted were hot dogs and chicken nuggets, which Granny provided before I had to go home and eat leek soup. I didn't inherit the cooking gene from either side of the family.

"Honeys, I'm home!" I shout from the door.

As I hang my coat, the saw is replaced by thumping of shoes on hardwood growing closer until Cora bounds in from the living room. "Aunt Mona, Adam stuck a can of beer up a chicken's butt! It was so cool!"

"Probably the oddest sentence ever uttered," I say as I kiss the top of her head.

"I'm painting some more. It's fun!"

Adam, covered in sawdust and trailing it behind himself onto my floor, saunters in, his hair plastered to his forehead from the sweat. "Hey."

Damn does he look cute all messy like that. "Hey."

"I told her about the chicken," Cora says. "It was funny."

I raise an eyebrow, and he grins. "It's for dinner. You marinade the chicken with beer, season it, then stick the can in it, and roast it in the oven. It's my specialty."

"Can't wait," I say with a smile. The man made dinner. If this were a hundred years ago, I'd swoon. Instead, I gaze down at my niece. "Is your sister in the backyard?"

"She's upstairs. With the door locked," Cora whispers. "She won't let me in."

I look at Adam, who nods. "She's been up there since we got home."

"Is she okay? Did something happen?"

"She wouldn't say," Adam says.

Great. I wanted to postpone this conversation until I had at least three working brain cells, but as always I'm not that lucky. I smile down at Cora. "Hey, can you do me a favor? Will you paint me two shelves before dinner? Gotta hurry though."

"Okay," she chirps before running off.

"Good luck," Adam says to me before following her out.

The door is still closed and locked when I get there. "Sophie?" I ask as I lightly knock. There's no answer. "It's Aunt Mona. May I come in?" Still nothing. "Hon, you need to let me in. We gotta talk." Silence. "Fine. I'm unlocking this door and coming in now." I try the unlocking spell, but she must have a counter-spell on. Luckily I had plenty of practice the old-fashioned way when Debbie was a teenager. With the aid of a bobby pin from my room, I get open the sucker in thirty seconds.

My ten-year-old troublemaker lays on her bed with a book in her hands and ankles crossed. I'm so not buying the little angel show before me. "Why didn't you open the door?"

"I want to be alone. I'm reading."

I step in and shut the door. "Well, I just wanted to check on you. See how school was."

"It was fine," she snips. "Can I read now?"

I thought I'd have three more years before I had to deal with a moody teenager. Got an early bloomer on my hands. I'd rather tangle with the demon. I sit on the bed next to her, and she tenses a little. "Are you still scared about the demon? Because the whole town—"

"I don't want to talk about it, okay? I just want to read."

I lie down beside her like Daddy used to do with me so I can hold her, but there's something off about the pillow. It's too lumpy. "What is this?" I ask. Sophie's eyes grow with fear as I reach under, pulling out two books, three charms, and a small mortar and pestle bowl used to grind herbs. There are herbs in there, but I can't tell what kinds. "What are you doing with all this?"

"I . . . nothing."

Both books are on black magic from Granny's collection. "What were you making? Something from one of these books? Sophie—"

"It was just a potion so you could freeze the demon, I swear."

"Sophie, you shouldn't be making something so dangerous or even reading these books. It's unsafe."

"But I have to protect you and Cora! You don't know how to do these!"

"And you do?" Her mouth snaps shut. Her eyes grow even wider from fright. "Honey, I know you don't like talking about what happened with your Mom, but—"

"I don't want to talk about it."

"Hon, it might help—"

"I don't want to talk about it!" she screeches before shoving me. "Get out! Get out!"

I'm so shocked by her vehemence, I obey. "Okay. I—I'm going."

She flops onto her side so she's facing the wall with her back to me. I collect the contraband and slink out of the room, shutting the door behind myself. That did not go well. With a sigh I retreat into my bedroom, shut the door, and fall into bed. That zapped the last of my energy and then some. I rub my gummy eyes to clear them.

Goddess, it's worse than I thought. That girl is traumatized to hell, they both are. Cora still wets the bed, Sophie once or twice too, usually after night terrors. Until about three months ago, one or both spent most nights in my bed. I tried the therapy route after half a month of straight night terrors, but Sophie barely uttered a word to the woman, and Cora just drew pictures of butterflies and flowers. They were both relieved when I told them they didn't have to go back. I'm so out of my depth here, and helpless is not something I do well.

After a scorching shower to wash the day away, I blow dry my hair then braid it for tonight's escapade. Then comes the wardrobe. All black from tips to toes doesn't suit me, but a night in jail would suit me even less. Adam and Cora are still hard at work in the back-yard while rice boils on the stove. There's sawdust all over the floor and counters, so I sweep before setting the table. The timer rings just as I fill the last glass with apple juice. The saw stops outside—gotta be impressed by werewolf hearing—and a second later Adam appears at the back door.

I hold up my hand to stop him. "Wait. I just cleaned."

He glances at himself and chuckles. "Oh." He takes a few steps back. "Cora, watch this." He shakes like a dog, making a funny sputtering noise when he does, dust flicking off.

"You're silly," Cora giggles.

"Better?" he asks me.

"No." I wet a kitchen towel and step outside. Cora is still on the ground with her paintbrush, a wide grin on her cute face. "Here," I say, handing him the towel. As he wipes his face and arms, I brush off his hair and shoulders. A man's hair should not be this soft. "You are so messy!"

159

"It's a gift," he says with a smile.

Our eyes lock as I smile back. He has a wonderful smile. Nice eyes too, a little on the bug-eyed side but so were Daddy's. I feel the first of the butterflies, which is usually followed by blushing, so I look away with a chuckle. "There. Now you're presentable."

"Thank you, ma'am," he says with a tiny nod. "Better get the chicken." With another bright smile my way, he walks inside. Oh hell, there's the blushing.

"Adam's funny," Cora says.

He's something alright. "Come on, you need to wash up too." As Adam carves the chicken on the counter, I shout, "Sophie, dinner!" before washing Cora in the sink.

We sit as Adam dishes out the chicken. "Is Sophie coming down?" he asks, hovering over her plate.

"Don't know," I say with a sigh.

"Let me try." He hands me the platter and walks out. Hope he has better luck.

I finish serving, and Cora and I wait to start eating until everyone is seated. Adam steps in a minute later. "She coming?" I ask.

"Only if you promise not to talk about the you-know-what."

"Fine."

A miserable Sophie steps around Adam, taking her seat, eyes averted. Adam sits next to her, and we exchange a glance that I hope translates into "Thank you." He smiles and nods.

We all eat this indescribably delicious dinner in silence for a few seconds. What a group we are. Across from me is a dusty werewolf, to my right is a paint-covered six-year-old, and to my left is a sullen-beyond-her-years ten-year-old, and I look like Natasha the fat spy.

Adam must have some Southern in him because, like a gentleman, he takes it upon himself to ease the tension. "What do you think? Taste okay?"

"It's wonderful," I say. "What do you call it?"

He glances at Cora. "Beer butt chicken."

Cora giggles. "I knew it."

Adam and I smile at one another before he turns his attention to Miss Misery. "Sophie, do you like my beer butt chicken?" he asks.

"It's okay," she says, still not looking up.

"You know the secret?" He pauses, leaning toward Cora. "The butt."

Her high-pitched laugh brings a huge grin to my face. There is nothing better than a child's laugh. *Nothing.*

"You're gross," Sophie says.

"A lesson on us boys, little one. Telling us we're gross is a compliment. We take great pride in our grossness. I am quite proud of my 'Best Belcher' trophy at home."

"Whatever," she mutters.

I don't know how she does it but that one word drags all the mirth out of the room. Adam shrugs. He tried. I smile sympathetically. Goddess bless this man. My turn. "So how was school? Sophie, did you have play practice?"

"Yeah," she says, taking a bite.

"I can't wait to see it. Everyone's going to be there: Tamara, Clay, Aunt Debbie, Greg."

"Why? I only have two lines."

"Because we're all proud of you."

She doesn't say a word, just picks at her food like an anorexic teenager.

"I watched a video on the planets today," Cora says. "I like Neptune, it's pretty. Adam, what's your favorite?"

"I'm partial to Mars myself. I like Martians."

"There are no such things as Martians," Sophie says.

"Well, people think there are no such things as werewolves and witches, and here we are," I point out. "I have faith in Martians as well."

"Then you're stupid," Sophie says.

My breaking point has officially been reached. I toss down my fork. "Okay, I have had just about enough of your mouth."

"Then send me away like you wanted to," the girl snarls.

"I didn't want to … it seemed like a … I am not sending you away!"

"Only because Adam told you not to! What happens when he leaves?"

"I'm not sending you anywhere!"

She's not listening. She leaps out of her chair and scampers out. Wonderful. I follow behind, reaching her as she's about to leave the living room. I grab her arm to stop her, but she yanks it away. "Go away! I hate you!" I try to pull her into a hug, but she flails around, smacking my face a few times on accident. "You don't love us! You're just like them!"

"I'm not! Just stop. Stop!" I get a good grip this time and get her into my arms. "Calm down, honey. Calm down." I envelop her, stroking her hair and kissing it. Her body relaxes as the seconds pass. "I'm sorry, okay? I'm sorry. I wasn't thinking clearly this morning. Even grown-ups mess up sometimes, okay? You and your sister aren't going anywhere. Ever. This is your home. Always will be. No matter what, okay? I promise. I promise."

"You promise?"

"On my life."

This is what she wanted to hear because those small arms wrap around my waist, hugging me back. "I'm sorry I called you stupid. You're not. You're real smart."

I kiss her again. "Apology accepted, if you accept mine. I'm sorry I scared you."

"I forgive you."

With a smile, I lift up her head and kiss her nose. "I have the best nieces ever, you know that?" I kiss her nose again. Her reluctant smile fades back to apprehension. "You still feel a little bad?"

"A little," she admits.

"Then you know what we must do." I pull her off me and walk to the iPod player.

"No, not that," she whines.

"Oh, stop it. You love it."

Mommy started this tradition with Daddy, who kept it going after she died. Whenever us girls fought or were down in the dumps, she'd turn on the music and make us dance until all our tension or aggravation was gone with the wind. Worked like a charm bag. Some of my best memories are of all four of us cutting loose like we were having seizures. I carried on the silliness with Debbie and now the girls. Family tradition is most important.

I select Kenny Chesney's "Ain't Back Yet." It always makes me want to dance. As the guitar riff begins, I start grooving to the beat, swaying my hips and head, and lip syncing like a *mo-ron*. But it sure is fun. I take Sophie's wrists, lift up her arms, and start moving them around like a puppeteer until she does it on her own. A second later she's mimicking me, giggling at the stupidity. It's catching.

"I want to dance!" Cora says as she sprints in. She leaps onto the couch and starts bouncing while shaking her arms around like a monkey. I think dance camp this summer for her.

We have an audience. Adam leans against the wall, the widest grin on his face as he watches us crazies. I wiggle my finger at him to come to me. He does, his shoulders bouncing to the music as he grooves toward me. After a second our bodies get in sync, pivoting, gyrating, hell even laughing in time to each other at the music. He takes my hands and moves my arms like a bicycle, forcing me to bend back as his body presses toward mine then brings me up again. He breaks away, and I bust a gut as he "raises the roof" while puckering his lips like a fish. Damn is he adorable. Just as the song ends, he takes my hand again, spins me away, then toward him again. At the last beat, he dips me as if we were in an old movie, our grinning mouths an inch from each other while panting as if we've just ... hell's bells.

The song ends, and we just stay like that for a second. I realize his chest is pressed against mine, and the only thing holding me upright is his strong arm around my waist. Our smiles slowly falter as our eyes meet. A large jolt of I-don't-know-what cascades over me, and boy does it feel wonderful like a warm rain. He might feel it too—or it could be that the most romantic song ever, "Somebody" by Reba McEntire starts playing—because I swear there's lust in those baby blues. My breath catches. I think I want to kiss him. Okay, I *definitely* want to kiss him. Among other things. His eyes read mine as I read his, and I suddenly feel naked. Exposed. Crap.

I look away and press myself up before pushing him away. "Can't dance to this song," I chuckle nervously. I leap away to shut off the stereo. I give myself a second to compose myself, and plant a smile on my face before turning to face the girls. "Well, I feel better. How about we finish dinner, huh?" I smooth my hair and walk away.

What the hell was that?

• *Operation: Hoochie House*

Between cleaning up dinner, getting the girls to bed, and preparing for tonight's B&E, there isn't time to obsess over whatever happened in that living room. I all but blink, and it's time for Adam to leave on his date. He pokes his freshly showered head into my office to let me know he's leaving. I don't look up from my scrying but nod. This isn't working. I need something of the demon's in the pendulum to locate it. Stupid idea.

For some reason, when I hear the front door shut downstairs, I relax a little. I avoided eye contact at dinner and made it a point to stay away from him after that. He probably didn't even notice in the living room or at dinner. It was all in my head. Besides, there are more important things to worry about than momentary lust. I have to go commit a felony.

As I'm gathering all my charms for the break-in, I call Auntie Sara. I check on the girls, who are still asleep. They won't even know I left. Auntie Sara stands at the invisible barrier clutching onto her cardigan and nervously scanning the street for baddies. I open the barrier, and she walks over to me. "This is a bad idea."

I extend my hand. "Car keys, please?"

She gives them to me. "A very bad idea."

I kiss her cheek. "I'll be an hour. If they wake up, tell them I'll be back soon."

I close the barrier behind myself and run next door to where her Monte Carlo sits in the driveway. Driving it is like steering an ancient tank that coughs exhaust. Low profile I am not. As I drive closer and closer to the south side of town, the rock in my stomach grows. I miss the butterflies from before. I got caught last time, and I'll probably get caught this time too. I can never get away with anything. The one time I jaywalked I got a ticket. When I'd fake sick to stay home from school, two days later I'd actually get sick. I'm on the universe's watch list. Step out on line even an inch and be fed to the crocodiles. Cheyenne raises a demon to kill me then gets to make out with Adam. How is that fair?

I cruise past Cheyenne's and notice the lights are still on, and my car is in the driveway. Get going guys. I park a block down where the house is still visible and shut off the engine. A minute later, the happy couple saunters out. If that girl's skirt was any shorter I'd be able to see what half the men in town already have. Adam says something and Cheyenne throws back her head with laughter, touching his chest because she can. I scoff. He opens the car door for her, and she kisses his cheek. He just opened a damn door, he didn't rescue your kitten from a tree, you tramp. Keep your paws to yourself. The car starts and pulls out, coming my way. I duck down as it passes. Time to go.

I pull out the power triangle amulet from my purse then take off my Mohammedan circle of protection one. I hold up the new amulet, calling the magic before putting it on. When I open my eyes, I hold out my hand but can see right through it. That's a little freaky. I have a hard time opening the car door as I can't seem to get my hand in the right position. Yeah, expert cat burglar here. Can't even open a door.

When it does open, I jump out and rush my butt down the street. Instead of using the front door, I go around the back to the sliding glass door. Adam was supposed to unlock it, and as always he is a man of his word. Now I'll only be arrested for entering. The house is dark, so I pull out my tiny flashlight from my waistband. Even with the flashlight I hit my leg on the end table, beer cans clattering and falling to the ground. Okay, I really suck at this. I take off the amulet, and my body appears. Should make things easier. Let's get this over with. Bedroom first.

I walk down the hall past pictures on the wall. Cheyenne in a bikini at the beach. The unhappy twins about age ten flanking their equally dour parents. Maxine working in the garden. One I took of the twins and Debbie drawing with chalk. If I remember correctly, that day ended with Cheyenne shoving Debbie for using her Barbie comb. Okay, stay off Memory Lane. It just dead ends with the sheriff arresting me for trespassing.

The bedroom is cleaner than I imagined, with the bed made. Not that I want to touch it, mainly because of the mirror above it. Tacky. I check the dresser first. Nothing but a thousand thongs and enough polyester clothes to outfit the cast of *Saturday Night Fever*. No false bottoms either. Nothing under the bed or mattress. The nightstand gives me pause. Not only do I find pot but also a pink vibrator, furry handcuffs, condoms, and some beads that I assume I don't want to touch. Grimacing, I shut the drawer. The closet holds no surprises, just clothes and shoes. I press on all the walls for a secret space but come up empty. Guess she wants to keep her sex and murdering lives separate.

Across the hall is a bedroom converted into an office of sorts. Really there's just a stereo on the end table and a desk filled with ritual items. Jars of herbs, a small cauldron, an athame, and a tiny bookcase filled with books. A few are on black magic, but I don't find the handwritten notebook Meg and Belle told me about. Everything here is within regulations. Some herbs could be combined for black magic spells, but there's no sulfur. She probably used it all last night. Okay, so I have no idea what I expected to find. A bound copy of "How I Intend to Kill Mona" maybe. Hell, I'd settle for matches from Alejandro's club. Photos—

The sound of the deadbolt unlocking down the hall makes my stomach drop to my toes. Of course. I'm going to jail. I click off the flashlight and stand still, afraid even to blink in case she can hear it.

"...so sorry," Cheyenne says as she steps into the other room.

"Not a problem," Adam says. "I'm just going to use the bathroom before we go again."

I hear his heavy footsteps moving toward me, then the shutting of a door. A second later he appears in the doorway, finding me clutching the flashlight to my chest and tense like a virgin on her wedding night. "What happened?" I mouth.

He steps in and whispers, "She forgot her wallet." On accident, I'm sure. "We're leaving again. Just stay quiet." He rushes out again, and a few seconds later, the toilet flushes. "You find it?" he calls out as he walks down the hall again. "Cheyenne? Where—"

He stops mid-sentence. In my heightened fear state, my hearing is phenomenal. He lets out a surprised moan and then I hear lips smacking against each other in a wet kiss. The bitch pounced. "No, wait, stop," he says a few seconds later. "What about dinner?"

"Fuck dinner. We'll order pizza after," she says huskily. I can hear jingling as she undoes his belt.

"But—"

"Just shut up."

There's another groan, then the sound of bodies falling on the couch. Oh hell's bells. There is no way I am going to stand here and listen to them have sex in the next room. I'd rather get arrested. I stick the flashlight back in my pants and re-energize the amulet before tiptoeing down the hall like a ghost. Of course if I stomped through wearing clogs, they wouldn't notice right now. Cheyenne lays on top of Adam making out with him with abandon, as if they'd just discovered the activity. She's even got her shirt off, revealing a leopard print bra. She rubs against him like a cat in heat, hands under his shirt, raking her nails on his chest. His eyes are open, but his hands are busy caressing her naked back. A rage like nothing I've ever felt pours into me like molten lead.

Oh hell no!

A huge gust of wind outside rattles the windows and knocks the patio table over like a Jersey housewife. Both Adam and Cheyenne jolt with surprise, and the game of tonsil hockey is called. "What was that?" Adam asks.

"The wind I think," Cheyenne says.

Adam peels the whore off him and stands. "I better check it out."

"Why? It was just the wind."

As he passes me, I swear he looks right into my eyes, a little embarrassed. Good. He opens the sliding glass door and steps out. Reading his mind, I know what to do. I quickly tiptoe through the kitchenette and out the open door. The problem is that Cheyenne is a few steps behind me. I barely have time to step aside before she plows past. "Told you it was just the wind."

"These days you can't be too careful," Adam says, picking up the table. "There is a demon running around town."

Cheyenne rolls her eyes. "Oh, spare me from demon talk. I'm so over it."

"You're not afraid? It was here a few hours ago."

She runs her hand down his chest. "It takes a lot to scare me."

"But Mona—"

She pulls her hand away while rolling her eyes again. "Oh, please shut up about her. All day all I've heard is demon, Mona, demon, Mona! I am sick of that fat, sad, know-it-all. She ain't as great or mighty as she pretends to be. She's only Priestess because her grandmother knew she'd have nothing else in her life. She felt sad for her like we all do. Hell, I wouldn't be surprised if she summoned that damn demon herself just to show how powerful she thinks she is when she kills it or whatever, and give her something to do. It's downright pathetic."

It takes every ounce of my willpower not to choke her. Or cry.

"Don't—don't talk about her that way, okay? She's my … cousin," Adam says.

"Mine too, but you don't know her as well as I do. I've been around her all my life. She's always been the same. Arrogant, prissy, thinks her shit don't stink. Hell, I'm pretty sure she's still a virgin. She has no passion. Cold, frigid bitch from birth. Now I, on the other hand," she says, running her tentacle through his hair, "do not have that problem." She kisses him again. "Let's go back inside, and I'll prove it." She takes Adam's hand and leads him inside.

With a shudder, I let out the breath I was holding. I don't care what that bitch thinks about me. *I don't.* So why are the tears coming? No, no way. I'm not giving her that satisfaction.

I make it back to the car with no trouble, since Cheyenne is once again busy sticking her bilious tongue down Adam's throat. Not for long though. I pull out my cell and call his. He picks up on the sixth ring. "Time to come home," I say.

170

"Hey, Mona—" he says, but I hang up, start the car, and get the hell out of Dodge.

The girls are still asleep when I return home, and Auntie Sara is watching *Antiques Roadshow* and knitting. "How'd it go?" she asks, standing up.

"Could have been better. Thanks for watching them."

She takes her car keys from my hand. "Of course, dear. Will you need me tomorrow night too?"

"Tomorrow?"

"The auction. You're still going, right?"

She knows about that? Of course she does, she's a one-woman gossip mill. "I totally forgot about it," I say, shaking my head. "We'll see. Let me walk you home."

She puts on her coat, and we walk out. "Did you find anything?" she asks.

"No. Still at square one after three days. To be honest, I really have no idea what I'm doing. We keep making it up as we go. Miss Marple makes it look so easy. I mean, it might not even be Cheyenne."

"Of course it is," Auntie Sara says as we stroll. "That girl is just like her grandmother: crazy and mean as hell. And Maxine's mama was the same. I don't know what Daddy was thinking when he took up with Jackie. He usually had better taste in mistresses than that. Mind you, they were normally poor trash, but they knew to keep their traps shut and cash the damn checks. Except Jackie. She kept showing up on our porch begging and threatening. I mean he gave her money, what more did they want? Not even Granny Ramona could back them off."

"That must have been horrible for you."

"Well, having to go to school with your half-sisters and pretend you're not related was a strain. I wanted nothing to do with them.

171

Sally, your granny, on the other hand, went out of her way to be friendly, even to Maxine. That one blew up in her face more than once," she says with a scoff. "The worst time was right before her wedding. Sally wanted to invite the whole town, Maxine included. Well, your granny was walking down the street with Albert and me when all of a sudden Maxine comes barreling out the general store screaming like a banshee about Sally rubbing her rich wedding in her face, calling poor Sally a million names." Sara shakes her head. "I'll never forget it. Your grandfather stepped right in front of us, looked Maxine square in the eye, and as cool as a cucumber said, 'If you don't stop talking to her like that, I swear to God above I will strike you down so you never utter another word again. *Leave.*' And damned if she didn't. I knew right then, despite what everyone in town said about Sally marrying a lowly mechanic, that they'd be together forever."

We reach her porch but don't go in. "Papa really loved her, huh?"

"Oh yes. You saw it, I know you did. True love is a beautiful thing. Your mama and daddy had it too. So did Lawrence and I. Goddess, I loved that man. He made my body sing. My greatest regret was not marrying him before he shipped off to Germany." I vaguely remember Granny mentioning Sara's beau, Lawrence, but nothing else. She sighs. "You'll have a great love too. I know you will, Mona Leigh."

She's the only one in town who does, apparently. "Well, whoever he is, he's taking his sweet time getting here, huh?"

My Acura rolling down the street draws our attention. Adam climbs out of the car and nods at us, bed hair wild as he moves. He does a quick walk of shame into the house. My lips purse in disapproval "That boy needs to brush his hair," Auntie Sara says.

I kiss her cheek. "Thanks again. Love you." I hustle back to the house, turning on the barrier before going inside. The faucet's running in the kitchen where I find Adam filling a glass with water. "So what happened?"

He chugs the water then sighs. "She forgot her wallet. I texted you."

"I left my cell in the car." Really have to stop doing that. "Why didn't you offer to pay for dinner?"

"I did! She said she was worried about getting carded. She insisted, what could I do? I'm sorry. Did you have a chance to find anything?"

"In the five whole minutes I had, no. Nothing except a porno set in her bedroom," I say with a shudder. "And I can't believe you fell for that wallet trick. What are you, a fifteen-year-old girl? She just wanted to lure you back to her lair so she could suck your soul out."

"Then I'm glad you were there to rescue me," he says with a grin. "And here I thought you'd be mad."

"Why?"

"Seemed like you were enjoying yourself a little on that couch."

"Hell, no. She tasted like cigarettes and smelled like cheap perfume, and that was before she said that bullshit about you. I couldn't get out of there fast enough." He shakes his head. "Are you okay? I mean, she was pretty fucking evil. If it wouldn't have blown our cover, I would have slapped the words out of her mouth."

I grow a little warm inside and can't stop the smile from crossing my face. "Like I care what that ho thinks about me," I lie, but only a little. I pull out bread, cold cuts, and a knife to make the girls' lunches. "Besides, it's nothing I haven't heard before."

"What? Really?"

I shrug and spread mayo on the bread. "That I have no life, no passion. I'll die alone and childless, blah de dah. Though, just for the record, I am not a virgin. I had a boyfriend, just to be clear. He was a lying, cheating asshole, but still."

"Thank you for letting me know?" Adam says in a confused tone, getting snacks for the lunches.

"I'm just saying I'm not as pathetic as she made me sound. I'm picky, that's all. I sure as hell don't need a man to validate or complete me, unlike some. The man who ends up with me has to be pretty damn special."

He hands me the saran wrap, meeting my eyes. "I don't doubt it for a minute."

Oh hell's bells. Another damn sliver of lust moves through me again. I think I'm starting to like them. I look away and clear my throat. "So what now? Where do we go from here? Because I am fresh out of ideas."

"Then I guess we go to bed."

My gaze whips to him, eyes wide. Thank the goddess his back is to me as he locks the back door because I feel my cheeks flare up again. I look down at the counter, willing them to return to normal. Doesn't work, especially as an image of him shirtless and sweaty on my bed surrounded by rose petals pops into my head. "Good idea. Sleep. Always helps." I gotta get out of here before I pull a Cheyenne and pounce. I quickly wrap the sandwiches, put them in the bags, and stick them in the fridge. "Night."

"Goodnight."

I rush out, all but running up the stairs to my bedroom. Okay, what on Gaia's green earth is the matter with me? A hug, a dance, a little eye contact and I've suddenly lost twenty years of my life and am a teenager again, creating some grand love story out of next to nothing. Sophomore year and Peter Lee all over again. It's the situation, that's all. Men and women thrown together in intense situations always go a little lo—*lust* crazy. I mean, I've always thought he was attractive, I'm not gonna lie. But his rudeness and complete lack of interest in me quashed mine. I try not to fight losing battles. Though now … no. Stop it. Any designs he may or may not have on me are purely sexual due to our close proximity and his role as protector, and I don't do casual sex. He's leaving Saturday. There's no future. Damn it.

Cheyenne's right, I am pathetic. And disloyal. There's Guy to think about now. Tomorrow we start officially dating, and I am no cheater. No, I'm just grateful for Adam's help, but that does not mean I need or want to jump into bed with him. There. That's settled. Good.

I throw on my pajamas, brush my teeth, and hop in bed. Big day tomorrow. I have a date with my future husband. In less than twenty-four hours, we'll be taking the first step into our future. I'll prove them all wrong.

Even the witch ends up with Prince Charming sometimes.

WEDNESDAY TO DO:

- *Continue with investigation*
- *Paint store window*
- *Make sure to check online orders*
- *Buy pantyhose/eyeliner/hairspray/~~condoms?~~*
- *Find something to wear!!!*
- *More demon research*
- *Try breaking into Cheyenne's again*
- *Get ready for auction*
- *Look into getting a prescription for Valium
  so don't have panic attack*

FOR THE FIRST TIME in almost a week, I get a full night's sleep. I wake the next morning with two little girls and a cat nestled in bed with me feeling pretty darn good. My favorite way to start the morning. The mountain of French toast Adam cooks and we scarf down like Hoovers just makes the whole day that much brighter. I can even look at him without blushing. Definite progress. We walk the girls to the bus stop and head to the store to resume the huge task of fixing the shop. I crank up the music and start removing all the statues from the shelves. It's gonna be hard for people to find merchandise, but I don't have a doubt it'll be perfect when it's done.

We're busy after the shipment of herbs arrived, then later when scared witches come in for them. More than one—hell, more than five—hang around pretending to browse while not so covertly checking out the guy stretching and flexing as he drills holes in the wall. It is like a porno for women: tight jeans, sweaty brow, power tools. I should sell tickets.

When things calm down, I check my e-mails. Four potion and five charm orders, one from George, and a couple from other co-op members asking to add items on the agenda. I open the letter from George last. The financial records of my suspects are ready. In the past three months, all but Shirley have used their credit cards in Richmond. Cheyenne and Erica had charges at Alejandro's club, Cheyenne more than once. It is the most popular club in Richmond, so I'm not that surprised. At least Collins is off the hook.

Before I can begin making the orders, the bell rings in the shop, and I get up. Clay maneuvers through the mess and waves at Adam, who nods before returning to his noisy drilling. I'm gonna have a headache by noon. "It's official business," Clay says.

"Come on back." I usher him in and shut the curtain. "What's up?"

"I need a quote from you. We're running a story in tomorrow's paper about why there are dozens of occult carvings and paintings around town. People are a little freaked."

Great, that's all I need. "I don't know what to tell you."

"How about the truth, and then we'll brainstorm on the official story?" So we sit and I tell him. "I ... have no idea how to spin that. A *demon?*"

"Just say they're family crests for the Goode and Knight families. We put them up in honor of Founders' Week. You can quote me as saying anything. I'll back you up."

"Mona, people should know there's a dangerous monster running around."

"It doesn't want them, it wants me. I wouldn't have said a word, except half the damn town felt the thing. Besides, you know you can't print the truth. It'll destroy your credibility."

"What if this thing starts killing?"

"Then other scary monsters with big guns will come, exterminate it, and arrest the person who summoned it. Speaking of, any news on that front?"

"I called a few of the names my friend at the paper gave me of Erica's acquaintances. The general consensus is she poisoned her husband, not that they have proof or seem to care. And they all know that Thomas guy and a few knew Alejandro. She was always flirty with both, but especially Thomas until about a year ago. He started seeing someone and cut the flirting, though she never gave any real indication that she cared."

"A jilted egomaniac is never a good thing. I'll ask her about it tonight."

"You're still going to the auction?" Clay asks, more than a little surprised.

"Of course. I have a date. Are you covering it?"

"I'll be there."

"I hear Bethany Harmon signed up," I say in sing-song. More than once I've caught him glancing at her and turning bright red. Must be genetic. "Bring your checkbook." The bell rings again, and I stand. "Hell, bring it anyway. I may need you to bid on me the way my week is going."

And the hits keep coming. As I walk to the front area, the Whore of Babylon with her low-cut jeans and off-the-shoulder shirt sans bra worms her way through the store toward Adam. "What a mess," she says, nose scrunched.

"And good morning to you too, Cheyenne," I say. "What can I help you with?"

"Nothing." She reaches Adam and smiles. He smiles back. "I was on my way to work and saw you in the window," she says, as if Clay and I aren't even on the planet. "Just … wanted to thank you for last night."

Clay clears his throat. "I better get back to work," he says, kissing my cheek. "I'll see you tonight at the country club. Adam. Cheyenne." He gives me a pitying look before walking out.

Cheyenne sneers at me. "You're going to that thing? Why?" she asks snootily.

"I promised *Doctor* Sutcliffe I would. He was most insistent I attend."

Cue eye roll. "Whatever."

I have no desire to watch the coming farce. "Excuse me. I have work in the back." I step into the back room and shut the curtain, then stand right behind it. I said I didn't want to watch; *hearing* is another story.

"That hot doctor is really into her?" Cheyenne asks.

"So it would appear," Adam says with little enthusiasm.

"Huh, no accounting for taste."

"She can probably hear you, you know," he says in a low tone.

"So?" Bitch. "She ruined our night with her minor drama, and you know she did it on purpose. Probably busted that pipe herself."

"It's an old house," he counters, "pipes burst."

"Whatever. Look, are you busy tonight? We can finish what we started."

"I promised Mona I'd watch the girls. Sorry."

"I can come over and help," she says.

"I don't think Mona would be comfortable with that." Damn straight. "Maybe Thursday, okay?" I can hear the smack of lips on lips and grimace. "I have to get back to work too."

"Fine," she says shortly. Seconds later I hear the bell on the door. The bitch is gone.

I toss the curtain back and step out. "Okay, we *so* need to find a way to nail that c-word."

"I am in total agreement," he says. "We should go finish the search at her house."

"Is that a good idea? We keep almost getting caught."

"Any better ideas?"

I think for a second. "Waterboarding? Worked in Salem." He shakes his head no. "Okay, then the house it is."

They do say the third time's a charm.

• *Continue investigation*

After Alice arrives an hour later, and after walking past the diner to make sure Cheyenne's there, we drive to her house and break in. Again. Adam takes the bedroom and I the office. I re-examine the books on black magic she has, but they are innocuous, with a watered-down version of the demon summoning spell in one. It wouldn't work since it's missing a bloodstone ingredient. I feel along the walls and floor for false panels but find none. Twenty minutes and nothing to show for it. Adam has since finished in the bedroom and has moved onto the living room where I join him. "Any luck?"

He lifts up the couch one handed as if it were made of marshmallow. "Anything under the couch?"

Yeah, I should probably take my eyes off him and check. "Just wrappers and dust."

He lowers the couch. "Bedroom was clear. This one too."

"I'll check the kitchen, you take the bathroom." As he walks to the bookcase, I rifle through her cabinets. Snack foods and empty boxes of snack foods. No goat heads or baby's blood in the fridge either. "Nothing here. This is a bust." There's nothing here I can nail her with. Waterboarding is looking more and more viable by the minute. I flop down on the couch. "Maybe it's time to confront her. Haul her in, be the bad cop to your good."

"We have no proof," Adam calls from the bathroom. He steps out a second later. "And if it isn't her, you might tip off the real person."

I groan. "This is so aggravating! Everywhere we turn, we hit a brick wall."

"Well, we've gone through this place top to bottom. We should get out of here."

"And do what? Go where?"

"We'll figure it out." He stretches out his hand to me and pulls me off the couch with a smile. Goddess do I love that smile. "Come on."

Since we can't see each other with the invisibility amulets, we hold hands all the way back to the car. First time I've strolled down a street holding a man's hand. It's nice. From here on out, I won't roll my eyes when I see couples do this. We make it back to the car and replace the invisibility amulet with the psychic protection one. I already feel naked without it. I start the car but have no destination in mind. Back to the shop I guess; but if I do that, it's kind of like I've failed. Given up. That leaves a bad taste in my mouth.

"Careful. Your face might stick like that," Adam says of my scrunched face.

I force it back to normal. "Hardy har."

"I had a thought. Why don't we go to the barn where the demon was summoned? I might be able to pick up scent or find a clue the police missed. It's been over a day, but it's worth a shot. We probably should have done it yesterday, but I just thought of it now." He shakes his head. "I am not very good at this investigating crap. Jason and Vivian usually handle that part. I just go and do as I'm told."

"Does that bother you? Being bossed around like that?" I ask.

"No," he says. "I'm his Beta, it's my job. It's why he picked me."

"You never wanted to rise up? Usurp the throne?" I ask dramatically.

"No thank you."

"Never even gave it a thought?"

"Not a once. I'm not like you and Jason. I have no desire to be a leader. It's not in my nature. I'm not that ambitious. Too much trouble anyway. I much prefer being in the background, helping when needed. It's just as important."

If not more so. "Well, Jason's lucky to have you." I pause for a second. "Me too for that matter. I … I don't think I've thanked you for everything you've done for me. I doubt I would have made it this far without you."

"You're selling yourself short."

"I don't think so. You've been great, better than great. You're like my hero," I say with a chuckle. "So … thank you. From the bottom of my heart, thank you."

"You're welcome, Mona," he says solemnly. "I'm happy to do it."

Before I can stop myself, I ruin this beautiful moment by blurting out, "Why?"

"Maybe someday I'll tell you," he says with a mischievous grin.

The few minutes to the barn are spent in silence except for a Shania Twain block on the radio. Normally I'd be belting right along with her, but not with a cute boy in the car. He's already seen my horrible dance skills, don't want to scare him with my singing too. There's a car I don't recognize already parked outside the barn when we arrive. Adam and I exchange a look and grab our respective weapons: charms and potion for me, and my .38 from the locked glove box for him. We exit the car, slowly approaching the barn. Though faint, my skin prickles from the demon. Rap music booms inside mingled with a girl's giggles. Adam and I glance at each other again and put away our weapons. Demons do not giggle.

Off in the corner near the back lying on a sleeping bag, Jace Brown has his hand inside Amber Kermer's bra. They're too busy making out to notice us step in. Ah, young love. I loudly clear my throat and they jolt apart. "Sorry to interrupt."

The teens scramble for their clothes. "Oh shit," Jace mutters as he zips up his pants.

"Shouldn't y'all be in school?" I ask.

"Yeah, um," Amber says as she stands, "we were just—"

"Hasn't been *that* long, hon," I say. "But you two know better—this place is dangerous."

"I know. We saw all the Satan stuff on the floor," Jace says, collecting the sleeping bag. "I heard they were sacrificing virgins here or something."

"Don't think you two have to worry then," Adam says.

The mortified couple walk toward us heads hung. "Um, bye," Amber says. They practically run to their car.

Adam and I chuckle. "Youth is wasted on the young," he says.

"I was never *that* young," I say as I walk in.

Adam follows me. "What, you never ditched school to go make out in a barn?"

"No, I was too busy taking care of my hellion sisters and being groomed to be Queen of the Witches." I scoff. "That and my teenage years weren't my best style wise. I hit the trifecta: zits, overweight, and braces all four years. I looked like a troll."

"Trust me, you weren't that bad," Adam says. "I thought you were kind of cute actually."

"Thank you for that wonderful lie," I say as I examine the reverse pentagram, minus a plank of wood in the center, with splotches of blood, yellow powder, and wax around. I step into it and the barbs of pure evil grow worse, like literal pinpricks hard enough to draw blood. I'm standing on a portal to hell. I get a little sick to my stomach and step out.

"It's not a lie," he says as he steps toward me. He grimaces. "God."

"You feel it too?"

"Yeah. And it reeks. Sulfur and blood mostly. Ugh."

"What about tacky perfume and cigarettes?"

He steps away. "This is where teenagers come to party, that's all I'm getting. Nothing specifically Cheyenne, sorry."

"What about the evidence the police collected? Think you'd have more luck there?"

"Probably, but no guarantees."

I check my watch. "I think we have time. Okay, police station it is."

"Great," he says with a sneer.

"Got a better idea?"

He shrugs. "We could stay here, and I could help you make up for lost time."

"What? Oh … " A flash of me throwing myself into his muscled arms and sticking my tongue down his throat fills my vision. I go a little gooey inside for a few seconds. I mean, if I get it out of my system, maybe … I glance up and find the real Adam smiling mischievously. Lust is replaced with embarrassment. He's kidding, of course. Of course. To think I … ugh! To regain some dignity, I straighten my back. "Cute. Let's go," I order, my voice hard as concrete. I spin around.

"Mona, I wasn't—"

A stiff breeze wafts through the barn. I hear the crack above but don't have time to put the source and noise together. I glance up and just watch like an *mo-ron* as a piece of wood falls from the roof toward me. I feel a scream coming, but the force of two hundred pounds of muscle grabbing and spinning me out of the way stifles it. The moment we stop moving, the plank smacks right where I was standing. I gasp and clutch onto Adam's shirt. "Hell's bells," I say.

My rescuer and I both breathe heavily, our chests moving in rhythm. I realize they're pressed together, and we're embracing each other like lovers. The adrenaline sends my senses into overload. His raspy breathing echoes, his hot body mingles with mine, and the scent of soap mixed with stale sweat intoxicates me.

"Are you okay?" he asks. I nod. "Come on." Arm still enveloping me, he leads me out of the barn. When we're safely outside he gazes at me, checking my head and forehead for damage. When he doesn't find any, his body relaxes a little. He doesn't let me go though. "Thank God. Are you sure you're okay?"

As long as we stay exactly like this, all is right in the world. "I—I'm fine."

"I swear, I think you're cursed," he says with a laugh. "A walking damn disaster area."

"Th—that's me," I say with an awkward chuckle.

Still smiling, he smoothes my hair and finally meets my eyes, that beautiful smile slowly wavering to nothing. He searches intently for something in my eyes, but I give nothing but anticipation and lust. There's nothing but *this*. This is it, the right moment. He can throw me down and have his way with me, and I won't resist. Oh *please*... damn it!

All mirth leaves his eyes a second later. If I didn't know better, I'd say he was disappointed. All emotion vanishes, replaced with a blank screen. He pulls away with a smile. "We better get out of here before it starts raining brimstone and frogs. Come on." He starts walking back to the car, leaving me shivering from the adrenaline and frigidity left in his wake. I hug myself to stop it. It doesn't work. Only one thing can fix it and he's walking away. I can't take much more of this, whatever *this* is.

I give myself a second to collect myself, forcing the mortification and deep regret down. Years of practice pay off once again. I square my shoulders then amble back to the car as if nothing happened. Without a word, I get into the car and start the engine, nary even a glance at Adam. I can't wait to get to the police station. Maybe one of the officers will let me borrow their gun so I can shoot myself for being such a mo-ron.

· *Review evidence with Sheriff Andrews*

The Gardenia County Sheriff's station is located one town over in Juniper. They have a satellite office in Goodnight with two part-time officers posted there, but Sheriff Andrews works out of this one-story brick building. I've only been here a few times with Daddy when we had to pick up Ivy after she got caught being scandalous. It hasn't changed a lick since those days, with a drab waiting area and wooden counter for reception. The officer at the front runs back to get the sheriff for us. Andrews appears a second later, all smiles. "Miss McGregor. Nice to see you."

"This is my cousin, A.J.," I say of the silent man behind me. Hasn't uttered a word since the barn, thank the goddess. "We were wondering if you had a minute?"

"Of course," he says, lifting the partition. "Come on back." Andrews leads us into his cluttered office filled with boxes of files. We sit in the chairs across from him. "I've been meaning to call you."

"Same here. We wanted to stop by to maybe get a look at what you collected from the barn."

"There wasn't much there, I'm afraid. Some blood on that pentagram, wax from candles, dust, and salt. We took photos before we collected all the paraphernalia." He takes the top file off and hands it to me. The white paint of the inverted pentagram is stained red with blood with pools of black wax on the sides of it. Circled around that is salt to trap the demon. Near the bottom of the pentagram the salt has been removed to let the demon out after he agreed to do her dirty work. The next few photos are of the same area at different angles.

"There weren't any gemstones or other ritual items?" I ask.

"Nope, that's all we found."

"So there's no chance of fingerprints or DNA?" I ask, dejected.

"Sorry," Andrews says. "I can tell you that the blood came from a dog, but we didn't find the carcass."

"Did anyone report any pets missing?" Adam asks. "She might have stolen one."

"We checked into that. The few that weren't found at the pound, I spoke to their owners. No one saw anyone steal them, and they found their gates open."

Another freaking dead end. "Would it be possible to see what you collected from the barn?" I ask.

"Sure." He moves his chair back, bends down, and pulls out a box, which Adam takes. "Right now all we have is a case of animal cruelty. I can't exactly arrest someone for summoning a demon."

Adam opens the box and pulls out the baggies with the residue of four candles, a small plank of wood, a vial of powder, and another with salt. He opens the evidence bag with a candle.

Andrews balks. "You can't do that."

Adam ignores him, inhaling the scent. "Sulfur mostly," Adam says, "blood, and cigarettes. Faint but there. Also a latex smell."

"Probably wore gloves so she didn't ruin her nails," I offer.

He opens the other bags, with Andrews grimacing each time, and sniffs. "More of the same, though the wood smells of ectoplasm and fire."

"You don't get anything else? No perfume or personal scent?" I ask.

"I can barely pick up the latex and cigarettes, and with those I can't be a hundred percent positive. The sulfur is overpowering."

"Crap." It's official. I am beyond frustrated in every conceivable way. Can just one darn thing go my way? "Thanks for your help, Sheriff." I walk out of his office and the station without looking at another living soul. I'm not feeling very up with people right now. They're either disappointing me, trying to kill me, or sending me mixed signals, all of which are doing my head in. The gray sky isn't helping matters either. Demon, take me now.

Adam catches up to me as I step outside. "We should go back to Cheyenne's house and gather her ritual knives. They might still have dog blood on them."

"I examined them. They were spotless. Plus Andrews would want to know where we got them or he'd drag Cheyenne in, and we'd lose our element of surprise."

He grabs my arm and pulls me to a standstill. "But—"

I jerk my arm away and keep walking. I just want to go back to my shop and hide in the back until it's time to go home, where I fully intend to crawl into bed and pull the covers over my head until this is all over. I get into the car and start it. Adam has three seconds to get in here or he's walking. He just makes it.

If the ride here was uncomfortable, the ride back is downright painful. I keep pushing the radio button but there's nothing on. I shut the damn thing off. But thirty seconds of silence is worse, so I turn it back on and settle on a commercial.

"I know this is a stupid question," Adam says, "but are you okay?"

I scoff. "If you know it's stupid, why ask it?"

"I'll take that as a no." He pauses. "Was it something I did?"

Yeah, you jerk. You let me think for a second I was desirable, *twice,* then all but laughed in my face at my stupidity. Okay, maybe that's a tad harsh, but my Achilles' Heel was exposed and he cut it, intentionally or not. Can't let him know this though. "Of course not. You saved my life today. I'm just…" sad, confused, scared, frustrated, "tired. I just want things to go back to normal." I glance at him. "I'm sure you do too."

"Yeah," he says after a pause. And for the rest of the ride, the only sounds come from Miranda Lambert.

Alice, with her narrowed eyes and folded arms, does not hide her annoyance at my extended lunch break, but I glare as I pass. The perk of being the boss: no castigation from my subordinates. I shut the curtain and plop my head down at my desk with a sigh. A few seconds later the drill starts, doing nothing to improve my mood. Just think a week ahead. A week from now everything will have settled down. No meetings, no festival, no wedding, goddess-willing Cheyenne will be behind bars, and Adam will be back in Maryland howling at the moon. I will be able to repress everything about this week. Maybe I'll even make a forgetting potion. Best damn idea I've had all week.

I sit up and smooth my hair. That's when I notice what's right in front of me, the flowers on my desk. More red roses. The day's events have taken their toll already, because I feel no thrill like before. I pull out the card and put on my reading glasses. "*Mona, Can't wait for tonight. Guy.*"

Ugh, I totally forgot about tonight. Really. How the hell could I have forgotten my first date with the man of my dreams? Maybe I should call and cancel. I have neither the desire nor energy for being funny or flirting. The image of Cheyenne and Adam on that couch last night springs to mind, and I grimace. No, if I cancel I'm letting that ho-bag win. No passion? Not desirable? Hell, I'll show her. If there's even half a chance of it, I'm gonna sleep with him. A lot. That'll show them all.

With my head up and flowers in hand, I stroll into the front. Adam is leveling a shelf and eyes me as I come out. I stick the flowers on the counter. "Alice, I have an errand to run. Do you need anything at the drugstore?"

"I could use some Excedrin if he's going to be keeping that up," Alice says with a sneer.

"You got it. Oh, and if Dr. Sutcliffe calls, thank him for the flowers, and tell him I can't wait either. Be right back."

As I knew he would, Adam trails me out without my say-so. Every time he reaches my side, I pick up the pace so he's a step behind. The drugstore is just around the corner, and Maynard Jefferts holds the door for me as I enter. I pick up a basket and start shopping. Excedrin for Alice. Hair dye a few shades darker than mine to cover the stray gray hairs, red nail polish, mascara, eyeliner, and three new lipsticks to match my new hair all go in the basket. Too bad they don't sell dresses too. I have no clue what I'll wear tonight. I also grab pantyhose, control top if you must know. Have to break out the Spanx too. I'll just change out of it before we do the nasty. Thinking of…

I move down Aisle Four feeling like a self-conscious weirdo, checking over my shoulder to see if people are judging me. They all know why I'm coming down here. There are about a dozen multi-colored boxes of condoms all with different boasts. For his pleasure, for her pleasure, ribbed, lubricated, ultra-smooth. I am way out of my element.

I've only had sex three times in my life. The first hurt like hell, the second wasn't much better, and the third was over in a literal minute. And that was fifteen years ago. My bravado tanks. This is insane. I can't do this. Sex on a first date? Hell, any sex at all with a man who's prettier than me? What if he wants to see me naked? There isn't enough darkness in the world to conceal my cellulite.

Crap. Abort mission! Abort! I'm about to slink away when Adam strides down the aisle with a razor and four packets of beef jerky in his hands. Double crap. My back straightens, and I pick up a lubricated box, examining it. "You're a guy. Which of these is the best?" I ask nonchalantly.

He dumps his items in the basket and walks away without a word. I smirk to myself and grab the ultra-thins and some K-Y just in case. Adam is nowhere to be found, but I check out anyway. I turn beet red when Rosie scans my items, but her face stays neutral. I hustle out of the shop before anyone else can see my shame.

Adam waits outside, phone pressed to his ear. "...don't know how much longer I can keep this up, Viv. I'm going out of my fucking mind. I—" He sees me and balks as if I've caught him hiding a body. "Um, yeah, I have to go. Thanks." He turns off the phone. "That was Vivian." Jason's wife.

"Oh. Next time you talk to her, give her my best." I pull out one of the jerkys and toss it to him. "Jerky's on me."

And I strut away like a supermodel, my smile dropping when he's out of sight.

• *Be subjected to hours of torture in the name of beauty*

The minutes turn to hours far too slowly. Customers filter in, but Alice has them well in hand. I'm feeling creative so I stencil in the rest of the new window and start painting. Adam finishes about two thirds of the shelves before leaving to pick up the girls. We don't utter a word to one another except, "Bye," the whole time. He didn't even offer me any jerky.

At five, just as I'm cleaning up the paint, Hurricane Tamara rolls in. She's out of breath as she steps over to me, eyes bugging out of her head. "You're not ready to go? We only have three hours to get you beautiful."

"It won't take that long," I say.

"Oh lord, sometimes I think you don't have a feminine bone in your body! Get your purse. We have a lot of work to do." She literally pushes me into the back.

"I have to close alone?" Alice asks.

"You can handle it," Tamara says, still pushing.

I put away all the paints, shut off the computer, and grab my purse. Tam examines the flowers, and just as she's about to peek inside the drugstore bag, I snatch it away. "No."

Saying goodnight to the perturbed Alice, I follow the impatient Tamara out of the store. "So are you excited?" she asks when we get to her car.

"It's just a date, Tam."

"With a gorgeous doctor who you fell in crush at first sight with." She pauses. "And who, judging from the contents of your bag, you plan on getting down and dirty with."

"What? I—"

"I saw the condoms. You intend to play nurse with the doctor, you slut you."

"I just—I—in case," I stammer. "You know."

"Hey, no judgments here," she says with a chuckle. "I think it's a damn fine idea."

"It probably won't get that far anyway."

"The man sent you flowers twice this week. You damn well better give him something in return. It is the polite thing to do."

I throw up my hands. "I don't want to talk about this anymore."

"I'll bet all that prudery melts away when you've got your ankles over his shoulders."

I smack her, and she chuckles. "Enough smut talk. Have you found out anything on Cheyenne or Erica?"

"Erica, no. But Cheyenne has been in rare form the past few days. She won't shut up about Adam. Keeps asking all the McGregor's about him."

"Crap. What have they been saying?"

"That they don't know him."

"Think she's suspicious?" I ask.

"I think she wouldn't give a damn if someone told her he was a serial killer."

Nothing clouds judgment quite like lust, as this week has taught me. "What about when people talk about the demon or me?"

"Well, when Meg came in, I did hear Cheyenne say it was probably you who summoned it so you could play demon slayer. Oh, and she gave me a message to give to you. I'm paraphrasing, but the gist is, 'Just because you're not getting any, the people around you shouldn't suffer. Next time call a plumber.' What happened?"

I fill her in on my various crimes, and the rest comes spilling out. What Cheyenne said about me, the barn, police station, the whole shebang. "What the hell is the matter with me?"

"You're horny," she states plainly. "I'm sure the doctor can give you a prescription for it."

I'm surprised to see Debbie's car in the driveway. We walk up to the house and find the girls sitting in front of the TV. I was half expecting the smell of pot roast or something equally delectable, but not tonight. "Hey, girls."

"Aunt Debbie's here," Sophie says. "She's in the attic."

"Where's Adam?" I ask.

"He left when Aunt Debbie came," Cora reports. "He wanted to run away."

My stomach clenches and intense fear grips me. "He's gone?"

"He went for a run," Sophie clarifies. "He said he'd be back soon."

I literally breathe a sigh of relief. "Oh. Okay."

"This is all fascinating, but we need to get cracking," Tamara says. "You girls behave while I doll up your aunt for her big date." She pushes me up the stairs and into my bedroom. There are three dresses on my bed that Debbie must have pulled, all black and at least ten years out of style. I really do have nothing to wear. Tamara grimaces. "Ugh. Oh well, first things first. Let's dye your hair."

I change into my black ratty bra, then Tam gets to work. The goop reeks but such is the price of beauty. Just as she finishes covering my head, Debbie swans in, still dressed in her work suit with a bright smile on her face. "Hey," she says.

"Hey. What are you doing here?" I ask. "I thought you and Collins were checking the wedding flowers tonight."

"I called in reinforcements," Tamara says.

"Good thing she did. Never would have found Granny's dresses otherwise."

"What?"

Debbie dashes back into the bedroom, then returns with two of the most beautiful gowns I've ever seen. They're both from the fifties. Full skirts down to the knee with netting underneath. The one on the right is bright red velvet and sleeveless like a pin-up girl would wear. The other is off the shoulder and made of a light pink metallic material with crystal stars across the neckline. I love them both.

"Those were Granny's?" I ask.

"Yeah. I remember finding them a few months ago when I was looking for Daddy's law books for Greg. These are the only two not needing mending. Now, I think both will fit and look great, but my vote is for the red one. You'll look sexy as hell."

"Especially with your darker hair," Tamara adds.

"I don't know. It's so … red. And my arms aren't made for it."

"That's why you'll have your black shawl and that way you can wear black shoes," Debbie says.

"Two against one," Tamara says. "You're wearing the red one, and that's that."

Oh boy.

Debbie leaves in search of shoes, jewelry, and the shawl while Tam continues on my hair. I feel like I'm on one of those makeover shows. Always turns out well for them. Tam wraps my head in saran wrap to keep it in place, and as I don't look ridiculous enough, smooshes avocado mask all over my face. Debbie returns and chuckles. "You look like dinner."

"Funny," I say as I stand from the toilet. "Speaking of. I should start on—"

"Stop," Debbie says. "I'll take care of it. You aren't allowed to leave this room until the big reveal."

Debbie walks out to feed the little monsters while Tam paints my nails and then toenails bright red. She leaves me to call her kids as I gingerly switch to shorts so I can shave my legs. I read somewhere this is a no-no for a first date because it means you intend to sleep with him. Since I sort of do—fifty-fifty at this point—I go for it. I manage to finish the first leg with only a tiny nick and no ruined nails when the sound of running water from the girls' bathroom next door overshadows Carrie Underwood's singing. "Oh crap."

I grab a towel to cover my bra and rush out of the bedroom. The water continues to run as I step into the hallway and pound on the bathroom door. "Sophie, take a shower later! I—"

The door flies open and the entire English language is zapped from my brain. Instead of a cute ten-year-old, I'm greeted by a sweaty werewolf in nothing but a tiny towel wrapped around his waist. Hell's bells. The animal part of my brain takes the wheel. I drink him in as if I was dehydrated. His legs are as muscular as the rest of him. I can't take my eyes off them. Okay, I can't unglue them from the gap where the slit of the towel reaches his hipbone. If he moves I might be able to … I suppress a whimper. I better sleep with Guy tonight or pretty soon I'll be jumping the mailman. "Yeah?" he asks.

"Um … " Say something! "You're sweaty."

"I went running."

All I can manage is an, "Oh."

"Do you … want something, Mona?"

Hell, yes. I go to play with my hair like I do when I'm nervous but touch plastic. Reality, or really mortification, hits me. I'm in shorts, a ratty bra, my face is green, and I have goo in my hair. I am the bog monster from the planet Ick. "Shower! I'm dyeing my hair, and I need a shower in ten minutes."

"I'll be done by then. I'll just take a quick one."

"Okay, great, bye," I say quickly as I scurry back to my bedroom and shut the door. And I just killed any chance of him ever having romantic feelings for me. Dead. Yeah. Ugh! I groan and shake my head before shuffling to the bathroom to beautify myself for a man I still have a chance with.

I shave, trim, shower, shave some more in a place I never thought to before—per Tamara and *Cosmo*'s advice—moisturize, exfoliate, blow dry, straighten, and keep perfectly still as my sister and best friend apply makeup as if they were painting a Monet. What we women go through while men just shave, brush their hair, and walk out the door. So unfair.

Finally, after over two hours of torture, I pull on my Spanx and dress—which barely zips—and step out in my faux velvet heels. "Tada!" I say with little enthusiasm.

"Oh. My. God," Tamara says, eyes bulging.

"Wow," Debbie adds with a similar expression.

I go to the full length mirror and join the eye-bulging brigade. I look … amazing. The darker hair and red lipstick off-set my skin, making it almost glow. My brown eyes pop with the eyeliner and shadow even brings out the gold flecks. But that's nothing to what this dress does to my figure. It's almost a perfect hourglass with just enough cleavage to be sexy yet not trashy. I should wear heels more often because my hearty calves look muscular. Hell's bells, I'm a babe.

"Sutcliffe won't know what hit him," Tamara says with a proud smile.

Per their instructions, I wait in the hallway as Tam and Debbie gather everyone for the big reveal. "Does she look pretty?" Cora asks downstairs.

"Very," Debbie says. "Got the camera ready?"

"All set," Tamara says. "Presenting the most eligible bachelorette in Gardenia County, though I guarantee not for long after tonight, the spectacular Mona McGregor!"

That's my cue. They all applaud as I step onto the landing. I'm greeted by shock and awe below. Sophie smiles, Cora squeals, and Adam … his hands stop mid-clap and his jaw drops a little. Goodbye bog monster, hello gorgeous. "How do I look?" I ask the audience.

"Awesome," Sophie says.

"You're so pretty!" Cora squeals.

"Thank you," I say to them before turning to the still shocked Adam. "Adam? Male perspective?"

"Um…" He pauses. Seems he's caught speechlessness from me. He looks at me as if there is nothing else in the world. "Beautiful. No other word for it. You're simply beautiful."

His words come close to bringing tears to my eyes. I want to stop in time and live in this moment. "Thank you," I say, voice quaking with emotion.

But it's not to be. "Picture time!" Tamara says, killing the mood.

I pose for about five pictures without my usual protest, as I'm sure I'll never look this good again. When I descend the stairs, the girls insist on hugging me and petting my dress. Adam keeps glancing at my chest when he thinks no one is looking. I do have a great rack. "Guys, I gotta go. I'll be late."

Debbie turns to Adam. "You're not going dressed like that, are you?" she asks the gray shirt and blue jeaned man.

"He's staying here," I say.

"But he's your bodyguard," Debbie says. "What if the demon—"

"He's not going on my date with me," I state. "End of story."

"Yeah, she's going to need privacy," Tamara says with a wink.

"Why?" Cora asks.

"Duh," Sophie says, "she's going to have sex with Dr. Sutcliffe."

"O-kay," I chuckle before she can elaborate further, "it is definitely time for me to leave." I kiss the girls' heads. "Behave." I look at Adam, who wears the remnants of a scowl. "I guess I'll be home… whenever."

"Fine," he says curtly.

I give a quick hug to my fairy godmothers, grab my car keys, and hustle out the door before I lose my nerve.

Here goes everything.

• *Bachelorette auction*

For a non-member of the Gardenia Country Club, I am here quite frequently. Just this year I've graced its halls seven times, mostly with Debbie and Greg to coordinate the wedding with the staff. On any normal year I come here about half a dozen times for various weddings, birthday parties, or when Clay is nice enough to bring me as a guest so he can whip my butt at golf. Tonight it is as elegant as always with the gas lamps flickering up the driveway, white globe string lights hung on the lawn amid the Spanish moss and willow trees, all leading to the entrance over perfect grassy hills. The cherubic fountain alternating colors spews its water in front of the cobblestone building and waiting valets. I drive past and down a hill, over a wooden bridge to the parking lot. It's about half full with BMWs, Lexuses, and the odd Ferrari scattered around. My Acura sticks out like a model's hipbones.

I started getting nervous when I left the town proper, the non-fun butterflies multiplying as the miles passed. Now as I re-apply my lipstick, my hands tremble. My confidence and determination have completely left the building. Or really, I just don't want to do this. It's a bad idea of epic proportions. I am well aware of this fact. Now. On the way over I realized this could all be a set-up to humiliate or kill me. If Erica is the one who wants me dead, she could have recruited Guy to lure me here. They could be lovers in cahoots. I don't have a shred of evidence, but that doesn't mean a damn thing. Oh this is such a bad idea. I wish Adam was here. I was an *idiot* to make him stay behind. He was probably right that day in the store. Why the hell would Guy all of a sudden be interested in *me*?

Okay, stop it. Just stop it. You'll be surrounded by people, you have all your protection charms and amulets, and you made a damn commitment. You gave your word, and that is sacrosanct. *Get out of the frigging car.*

So I do. I walk over the wooden bridge above the creek and up the paved hill, my shawl wrapped around me, clutch bag in hand, and head back. *Fake it till you make it.* The valets nod as I pass and Jimmy, the doorman, smiles as I walk in. The décor is old money with white painted walls and burgundy carpet. Paintings of Confederate soldiers and huntsmen hang on each panel. The hallway opens onto the hexagonal reception area, where three middle-aged men dressed in business suits pace around and shout into their iPhones. I consider myself a feminist but damned if my self-image doesn't sky-rocket as each of the men eyes me up and down like I'm prime rib.

The party is in the Jefferson Hall where Debbie's reception will be, but tonight it's sparsely furnished for the cocktail party before the auction. I give my name at the door so I don't have to pay the hundred-dollar cover charge. Lining the walls are vendors selling their jewelry and other items for the silent auction. More men in suits and women in ornate cocktail dresses chat and swill champagne that waiters cart around on trays. Damn, those lamb chops look good. I scan the crowd for familiar faces, spotting Clay off to the side interviewing homecoming queen Naomi Ferguson. She looks spectacular in a sparkly pink dress a little too high in the skirt for my taste. My self-image gets knocked down a peg or nine.

"…all about charity," Naomi says into Clay's recorder as I join them. "It's so important."

Clay turns off his recorder. "Thank you," he says to Naomi, who smiles and slinks off to mingle. He takes one look at me and his jaw almost drops. "Holy crap. Mona?"

I grab a passing champagne glass. "The one and only."

"You ... you look great!" We kiss cheeks. "I barely recognized you."

My eyes narrow. "Thanks, Clay," I say sarcastically.

"You know what I mean. Did you just get here? Erica was looking for you." But I'm only half paying attention as I check the crowd for my date. Clay notices. "He's here too."

"He is?" Oh thank the universe. "Where?"

Clay points to the other side of the room at one of the silent auction tables near the bachelorette stage. And there he is. He looks damn fine in his dark suit and glasses, but my heart doesn't do the usual pitter-pat. Huh. Must be the nerves. Whatever, let's do this. I smooth my hair, lick any lipstick off my teeth, and force myself across the room. The few people who know me either seem shocked or confused when they see me. My cousin Dickie stops serving crab cakes to get a look. I nod. I definitely need to wear red more often.

Guy is scribbling a bid on a golf lesson with a tournament pro when I reach him. "Hi."

He looks up and, like the rest, cannot believe his eyes. Was I really such a troll before? "Mona? You—you look wonderful."

"Wanted you to get your money's worth," I quip with a chuckle.

"I, um ... wow." He's speechless. I've rendered another man speechless. I rule.

"You're sweet," I say with another chuckle.

"Mona?" Erica asks behind me. I spin around and find my scowling cousin dressed in a low-cut silver and black beaded dress. "There you are. You're late. You missed the orientation." She looks at Guy.

"Please excuse us." He and I share a small smile as Erica ushers me out of the hall. "Did you have to wear all those amulets and charms? Honestly."

We end up in a smaller conference room with papers all over the desk. "There is still a demon on the loose," I say. "You're not wearing your wards?"

"I'm fairly sure a demon has better things to do than bother me," Erica says as she shuffles papers around. She finds the one she wants. "Here. I need you to sign these."

I read them over, just liability wavers and a contract. I know my way around them and see nothing wrong. "Here you go."

She stuffs them in a folder. "Thank you. We're going in alphabetical order, and you're number nine. I suggest you mingle and chat with the gentlemen. Let them get to know you. The auction starts in thirty minutes, then you and your date will be escorted to the patio for dinner. They're serving braised ham, salmon, or filet mignon prepared by celebrity chef Louis Nabrone from New York. Tell the men this, okay?"

"Got it."

She eyes me up and down. "And don't feel bad if you make the least amount. Every little bit helps," she says with a smile.

"I understand." You bitch from hell. "Oh, before I forget, did you ever get around to phoning Lord Thomas or Alejandro? They haven't called me."

"I'm sorry, I totally forgot. I've been swamped."

"That's okay. I shouldn't have asked anyway. I know you and Thomas had a falling out after he started seeing that girl, but I thought since you and Alejandro were closer now you could go through him."

If it wasn't for the Botox, her forehead would crinkle as her eyes narrow. "Excuse me? Who said that?"

"Just something I heard. I wouldn't blame you. Revenge sex is hot, or so I've been told."

"I did not have revenge sex," Erica says. "It wasn't like that."

"What was it like?"

"It—" Her mouth snaps shut. "Why am I discussing this with you? It's none of your business. Get a life, Mona." She sets the folder down and stalks out of the room.

I think I hit a nerve. So she *did* sleep with Alejandro. Oh hell. A horrible realization whammies me. Maybe it isn't Cheyenne. I mean, Erica's always been in the running, but I haven't seriously considered her a threat. She is better skilled to raise a demon, and she has a better motive, at least against Thomas. She could have wanted to control the coven to advance Alejandro's agenda, and now she wants me dead to avenge her lover. Have I let my prejudice against Cheyenne cloud my judgment? Hell's bells.

Clay is nervously interviewing Bethany Harmon, who looks radiant in her knee-length blue and black print dress, her blonde hair loose in curls around her round face. He's had a crush on her for years. I feel kind of guilty interrupting them but do anyway. "Bethany, mind if I borrow my handsome cousin for a minute?"

"What the hell are you—" But I pull him away.

"Life or death, cuz."

I know Erica drives a silver Mercedes but have five to choose from when Clay and I reach the parking lot. I look in the first one but the interior is wrong. "And you need me for what exactly?" Clay asks.

"I need a lookout. I have to break into Erica's car." Not this one either.

"So you dragged me away from Bethany to commit a felony?"

"I think it's only a misdemeanor, if it makes you feel better." Ah. A luck amulet on the dash. Found it. "Plus, now you'll get to save the conversation for when you win her tonight."

"Yeah, forcing her to eat with me. Just how I envisioned our first date."

I close my eyes, call the magic, and the lock pops open. I am good. I slip into the car and start ransacking it. Nothing under the seats or the glove box. I pop the trunk before climbing into the back, but there isn't even a gum wrapper. I lock the doors again before moving to the trunk. Clay, who is about to jump out of his damn skin judging from the jittering, scans the lot. Jackpot. Both her gym bag and purse are in the trunk. The gym bag is a dead end with nothing but clothes and shoes. Her purse proves more interesting. Not just because of the pearl-handled .22, but because of the smell of sulfur wafting from the charm bag at the bottom. Sulfur is used in a number of spells and wards, so it could be a coincidence. The muti bag in a hidden zipper sends my suspicions over the edge. This bag is hoodoo, a distant cousin of witchcraft, and very dangerous. There are human teeth, herbs, and charms in the deerskin pouch. Use of any human body part indicates black magic. Erica just became my prime suspect.

I take out my cell to get pictures of these items for use in her ex-communication and possible arrest. Now I just have to find a link between her and the demon. I suppose tomorrow Adam and I can break into her house. That's always fun. She's gotta have—

"Someone's coming!"

I shut the trunk and rush over to Clay just as Guy strolls over the wooden bridge. "Guy!" I squeak. "What are you doing down here?"

"Looking for you," he says suspiciously. "Someone saw you leave. Am I interrupting?"

"No, I was just … I forgot my cell phone," I say, holding it up. "Clay offered to accompany me."

"Nice to see you again," Clay says with a guilty smile.

"So you're staying for the auction?" Guy asks.

"Of course! Just … cell phone!" I say, holding it up again. "Let's get back in there. Erica will kill me if I don't mingle." Among other reasons. I lock my arm in Guy's and lead him back to the party.

Guy and I find an isolated corner, and he begins talking. Nonstop. The man sure does like to jaw about himself. I think he asks me about two questions about me in half an hour, but I find myself tuning out, so maybe he's just carrying the conversation since I'm not up to the task. How the hell am I supposed to break into Erica's house? It's a huge refurbished antebellum with about a dozen rooms, servants milling around, and it's ensconced in a gated community. Maybe Adam will have some ideas. At least this time I won't have to watch him feel up another woman. At least I hope I not.

"Am I boring you?" Guy asks, bringing me back to the present.

"What? No. You were talking about your residency."

He starts another monologue, and I make the appropriate noises and head nods, occasionally glancing at my cousin. Erica is chatting with a bald man across the room, occasionally touching his arm for effect. She feels me staring and glances my way. She nods and smiles before turning back to baldy. Could she really want me dead? It makes about as much sense as Cheyenne wanting to kill me. Regardless, tonight would be the perfect time to strike. I go to the bathroom alone and she hexes me, or hell, just shoots me. Goddess, I wish Adam was here. I should have brought him. Why the hell didn't I? Guy can't defend me, and for all I know he's in on it. As he chatters on, I study his face. There's no hint of malice, just pride and good cheer. I've misjudged men before. Have I just been a sucker for a handsome face?

"Why did you ask me to do this tonight?" I blurt out.

"What?" he asks, taken aback.

"Why didn't you ask me on a regular date? Why here? Tonight?"

"I—I don't know. I thought it would be romantic, me declaring my intentions in front of everyone. And it's for a good cause. Do you not want to? We can leave ... "

"No, I was just wondering." Plausible enough. "So no one put you up to it?"

"Of course not," he says, a little offended. "Why?"

"It's just that I didn't think I was your type. Then, out of nowhere, I am. I was wondering what changed."

He thinks for a moment. "I—"

"Attention," a man says over a microphone. "The auction will begin in five minutes. Will the ladies please assemble at the appointed location?"

Crap. To be continued. The fifteen of us excuse ourselves and follow Erica into the next room. "God, I hope that sweaty guy doesn't win me," Naomi says to Bethany as we walk. There are chairs set up around a table for us to sit. The majority of us kick off our heels the moment we can.

"Now, Miranda you're up first with Julie-Ann next. Y'all know your order," Erica says as she sits too. "Listen for your cue, and for God's sake, *smile*."

"You look real nice tonight," Bethany says to me. "I like your hair."

"Thanks," I say. Normally I'd take this opportunity to sing Clay's praises to his paramour, but I can't focus on anything but Erica. Enough pussyfooting around. This ends now. I pick up my shoes and stand. "Excuse me, Bethany. My cousin Clay likes you. He's a good man but shy. You should ask him out. You won't regret it." There. If I die tonight at least I helped out a friend. Hope they name their daughter after me. I walk over to her majesty and loom over her. "Erica?"

"Yes?" she asks.

"May I speak to you in private for a minute?"

"Now? I don't—"

"It's important."

"Oh lord," she says as she stands. I lead her out onto the patio, shutting the door behind myself. "If you want to quit, it's too late. I—"

"Why do you have a muti bag with human teeth in your purse?"

Her collagen infused lips open in surprise. "How do you know that?"

"Someone came to me in confidence and told me. What is it for?"

She starts playing with her diamond pendant. "I—none of your business."

"I am your High Priestess, and if you are involved in black magic, it is my business. Especially considering recent demonic events."

"And you think I had something to do with that? Why on earth would I?" Her eyes narrow at me.

"To kill me. That was the plan, right? The one you concocted with Alejandro?"

Her mouth drops open. "Mona McGregor, you have lost your freaking mind. I do not have to listen to this." She takes a step to leave, but I grab her arm. "Don't touch me."

I don't let go. "What was the plan? Enlist your friend Dr. Sutcliffe to lure me here, get me alone, and have your demon murder me on the golf course?"

"I don't even know a Dr. Sutcliffe. And why would I conspire with anyone to kill you? That is beyond ridiculous." She shakes her head. "I really do think you have lost your damn mind. Get help, Mona. Now let me go before I scream," she says calmly.

She's afraid of *me*. That's rich. I do release her. "You do know it's not too late to stop this. No one's been hurt yet. Just send the demon back and forget the whole scheme." I meet her eyes. "But you should know if any harm comes to me or anyone because of you, the F.R.E.A.K.S. will show up on your doorstep and drag you to their secret prison never to be heard from again. Do you hear me, Erica? Nothing is worth that fate."

Erica glares at me, trying to mask her fear with indignity. "For the last time, I have no idea what you're talking about. Now, if you'll excuse me, I have to get back to my party." With a last glare, she strolls back inside as if the entire conversation never happened, smiling at all the women. I think they've been watching us the whole time. I'm sure I came off as the crazy one.

I turn my back to them and take a deep breath. That could have gone better. I think I just made a large tactical error, tipping my hand. What if this pushes her over the edge? What if she has Guy poison my champagne? Goddess, I wish I had a cigarette. I'd leave, but if Guy is somehow involved in all this, I need to pump him for information. What I really need is backup.

I need Adam.

I rush inside and retrieve my purse before returning to the veranda. Tamara prepared my purse so all I have in here is my license, credit card, keys, condoms, spare underwear (why, I do not know), and my cell phone. I very much doubt I'll put any of those to use aside from the cell. I call home, but the machine picks up.

"Adam, it's Mona. Oh I really hope you get this. Um, can you get Auntie Sara to watch the girls and come to the country club? I—I may have been wrong about Cheyenne. I think it's Erica. Call me or just get here. The address is on the fridge. Bye." Maybe he was outside. I try his cell.

This time he picks up. "Hello?"

"Oh thank the goddess. It's Mona."

"Are you okay?" he asks over the voices in the background.

"I guess. Where are you? I hear people, and you didn't answer the house phone."

"I'm … watching TV. I didn't hear the phone, sorry."

"Whatever. Um, can you meet me at the club? I'll fill you in when you get here."

"Are you in danger?"

"Not right now. Just get here."

"I'm—I'm on my way. Stay around people."

The door opens and Bethany pokes her head out. "Hey, two girls have already gone. You better get in here or you'll miss your cue."

I press my hand over the cell. "Be right there." When she's gone I tell Adam, "Hurry," and hang up.

Erica refuses to look at me when I slink back in and sit. Luckily there are only about two minutes we have to be in the same room before it's her turn on the auction block. She doesn't return. Maybe she'll actually listen and this will be the end of the nightmare. She'll send the demon back, suppress her murderous impulses, and we can go back to silently disliking each other. Yeah, while I'm in Fantasyland, maybe I'll win the lotto too.

Sooner than I'd anticipated, Nadine LaPlante leaves for her turn and I'm the next bachelorette to face her fate. My stomach does somersaults as I walk to the door to listen for my name. All thoughts of my death are momentarily overshadowed by the intense fear that I'm about to be laughed at the moment I set foot out there. What if my humiliation is part of the plan? I think I'm about to throw up.

I hear applause, which means Nadine has successfully paired off, and it's my turn. Okay, let's just get this over with. This is the South, some gentleman will take pity on me if nobody makes an offer. I smooth my hair, throw my shoulders back, plaster a smile on, and walk out. Yep, definitely about to throw up.

"And here is our next bachelorette, Miss Mona McGregor," the auctioneer says as I enter. The spotlight follows me through the dark room. People politely applaud as I make my way up to the stage. I can't see the majority of the audience for which I am grateful, though Guy stands right at the front, all smiles and pride. "Miss McGregor hails from Goodnight and is the proprietress of Midnight Magic. She is active in the community there and enjoys going to the movies," the man reads off the card. It's really sad that I had to make up a hobby. "As always, we'll start the bidding at one hundred dollars."

"Three hundred," Guy says with a proud smile.

"Five hundred," I think Clay says, goddess bless him.

"Six," Guy says, beaming up at me.

This is going better than I thought. "Seven," Clay says.

"Eight," from Guy.

There's a moment of silence before the auctioneer says, "Do we have any other—"

"Two thousand dollars," a new man says, though the voice is too faint to place.

The audience gasps along with me. I can't have heard that right. What on earth? Everyone, a shocked Guy too, turns to get a glimpse of the man. Damn these lights! The auctioneer clears his throat. "Um, we have two thousand from the gentleman in the back."

"Twenty-one hundred," Guy says.

"Twenty-five," the man in the back says.

Guy's lips purse in disapproval. "Three thousand," he says with a hard edge.

"Four," the mystery man says without missing a beat.

There is dead silence for a few seconds. This is madness. Wonderful madness, but still. Guy just stands there scowling, indecision visible even from here. It breaks like a fever. "Six thousand dollars. And well worth it."

"We have six thousand for Miss Mona McGregor. Do I hear seven?" There's no answer. "Sir in the back?" I shield my eyes to get a look but to no avail. "No? Then sold to the gentleman in the front for six thousand dollars!"

Hell's bells.

The audience applauds as I step carefully offstage in my heels. That went well. When I take the final step Guy is by my side, wrapping his arm around my waist and waving to the people. "Almost lost you there for a second," he says to me.

As he leads me out of the room, I scan it for the man in back. "Who was the other bidder?"

Guy looks around, then kisses my cheek. "Forget him. You're all mine now."

I sigh. Oh lucky me.

· Go on a date with a possibly evil doctor

At least Guy will get his money's worth with the food even if I'm a mess inside right now. We join the other couples on the candlelit patio. Paper lanterns hang above with magnolias floating in water and candles next to them as centerpieces. A string quartet plays romantic music off to the side. I pass the other women, who are at least pretending to enjoy themselves. Bethany ended up with Royal Lorrel, the owner of Lorrel Dodge, poor thing. She just smiles as his mouth moves as quickly as his cars. Erica glances up at me for a moment, face blank, then back to her date.

Cousin Dickie pulls out my chair for me, and the date officially begins. The quite pleased with himself Guy smiles at me, and I manage one back. Even if I didn't now suspect he had ulterior motives I'd be nervous. The man did shell out six grand for a meal with me. No pressure there. Dickie pours our wine then walks away. Guy holds up his glass and I follow suit. "To our first date. May it be one of many."

We clink glasses. "Let's just hope all aren't as expensive," I say as I sip.

"True. Not that it isn't worth it," he adds. "And it's a tax write-off."

"How did I compare to the others?"

"Before you the highest was fifteen hundred for the homecoming queen."

"Hell's bells," I say.

"I like to win," Guy says. His hand slides across the table and touches mine. "Especially with the important things."

Dickie returns with our salads, and I take the opportunity to pull my hand away. We place our orders, which he brings right away (I'm guessing they were prepared in advance), and Dickie scoots off again. I spy Erica looking at me, but she glances away when I catch her. "This looks good," I say as I pick up my fork.

"So do you," he says. "You look wonderful tonight."

"Yeah, I clean up good," I say, shoving filet into my mouth.

He sits back in his chair, examining me. "It's more than that. I—I look at you and I just … you're so wonderful, how you take care of those kids. How you run your own business. I think you're the most spectacular, beautiful woman I've ever seen in my life."

And with those words, my heart breaks along with any illusions I've harbored. I physically hurt. "Okay, you need to stop talking now."

"Why? I didn't … did I offend you? I've come on too strong, haven't I?"

I press my fingers against my temples to stop the oncoming headache. "Just stop it, okay? I don't believe a word coming out of your mouth."

He's shocked. "What? Why—"

"Listen, I don't know why you're involved in this, why you lured me here tonight. Maybe you and Erica have some sort of relationship, but—"

"Who's Erica?"

"*But* whatever she's convinced you to do, it is a bad idea. I'm onto you both now. And if you tell me everything she's told you, I will make sure that men with guns do not show up on your doorstep, okay?"

He leans forward. "Mona, I have no clue what you are talking about," he states emphatically. "*None.* I don't know an Erica, and I didn't lure you here. I wanted to be romantic and—and show you how much I care about you. I—I like you more than any woman I've ever met, including my ex-wife." He pauses to find the words. "I—I think I'm in love with you, Mona."

"Oh please. We've spent a total of twenty minutes together," I point out.

"I know it's not rational, and it makes no sense to me either because you're not really my type," he says with a chuckle, "but I do. You're all I think about all day. I even dream about you. I've driven by your house, even your shop a dozen times just to get a glimpse of you. I can't concentrate, especially when you're right in front of me. It's taking all my resolve not to jump across this table and... you know. If that's not love, I don't know what it is."

I do. I know what this is. And I am a total idiot for not seeing it right away. Of course. At least he doesn't want to kill me. "Guy, when did you start having these feelings?"

"Um... the moment I saw you in the exam room on Saturday. You took my breath away."

"I'm sure I did," I say with an eye roll. "And nothing prior to then?"

He thinks. "No. It was like I was seeing you for the first time."

"You saw me in the lobby the same day. In-between those two times, did someone give you something to drink or a piece of jewelry or a little bag?"

"You mean the bracelet Sophie gave me?" He pushes up his jacket to the wrist and reveals a blue and pink braided bracelet I now remember her working on. You have got to be kidding me. That girl.

"Yeah," I say with a sigh. I signal Dickie over. "Hey. I need a glass of mineral water, a clean bowl, sea salt, some sage, and if the kitchen has it, cinnamon as well." He nods and walks away, leaving me with the lovelorn doctor. "I need to apologize for my accusations. I see now they're unfounded. I also apologize for my niece. She will be punished for this."

"For what?"

"I'll tell you in a minute. Just know I'm sorry, and I had no idea she did this to you." An agonizing minute later, Dickie returns with all my tools. All the other couples, who have been pretending not to watch since his declaration, glance over again. "Can you take off the bracelet please?" He does. "Do you feel any different?"

"How so?" Take that as a no. I light the sucker on fire with the candle at our romantic table. "What? Why are you—"

"Trust me." I set the burning cloth on the empty bread plate and add the salt, sage, and cinnamon to the mineral water. Mixing with my finger, I close my eyes and call the magic, infusing the water with it. When I open them, all eyes are on me and not bothering to hide it. A confused Guy watches as I dump the ashes into the water and mix again. "Give me your wrist." He reaches across, and I take it. I dab two fingers into the murky water then run them along the area where the bracelet touched. He grimaces but doesn't pull away. I raise my fingers an inch above the area. "Look into my eyes." His eyes meet mine, and I savor this moment. This is the first and probably last time a man will look at me with love, false or not. It was nice while it lasted. I take a deep breath, then say, *"Purgo,"* at the same time I touch his wrist, magic flowing out of my fingertips.

The change is instantaneous. Love morphs into shock, then confusion tinged with anger. I have no idea what to say or do except wait for him to lead the way. He blinks and moves as far from me as possible. With the "love" that was clouding his mind gone, he glances around the room at all the staring people. "What the hell is going on?" he asks.

"It's … hard to explain."

"What did you do to me? I feel … strange."

"I know, and I'm sorry."

"Did you drug me?" he hisses in a whisper.

"Uh, in a way. But you're completely healed now, okay? I'm, uh, going to go now," I say as I move to stand.

Guy reaches across the table and seizes my hand, shocking me. "Sit down."

I obey. "I don't know what else I can tell you."

"Ten seconds ago I wanted to marry you, and then you did that … whatever and now …" He shakes his head. "What the hell is going on?"

I hate having this conversation. I'm only authorized to have it in circumstances such as this, when I have no choice. I'm about to override his entire belief system. It never goes well. "Okay, you're going to find this very hard to believe. Just keep an open mind, okay?"

"Fine," he says gruffly.

I sigh. "You were enchanted. By a love spell. The bracelet sort of brainwashed you into thinking you were in love with me."

"That doesn't make any sense," Guy says.

"It does if you believe in witchcraft. *Real* witchcraft, not just Wicca. I'm a witch."

Guy stares at me for a second, then breaks into laughter. "Yeah, right."

Ugh, I hate resorting to parlor tricks, but I want to leave. Now. I reach over toward one of the candles and call the fire. The flame does as I command. It rises in a spiral as I move my finger the same way. Guy's eyes grow wide as it glides up inches. When I move my hand away, the flame dies. In case he still doesn't believe, I do the same with the water in the centerpiece. The water carries the magnolia up and up in a column. When the water splashes down again, Guy jumps in his chair. He glances from the water, to me, eyes wild with fear.

"Believe me now?"

"Holy shit." The shaking man stands, knocking over his chair. He backs away from me as if I was a rabid dog. "Fu—don't ... oh fuck." He hits the table behind and it rattles, sending wine glasses rolling. The other couples murmur at the spectacle.

I stand and hold up my hands. "Guy, please calm down."

"Stay the hell away from me you ... you ... monster."

"Son, there's no cause to speak to the lady like that," Erica's date says.

"She—she fucking put a spell on me to make me love her! She's a fucking witch!"

"Guy ... " I say as I take a step.

"Don't come near me, you fat bitch!" And he storms off inside as fast as he can.

For a moment, I'm too shocked to move. I know all the people are staring and murmuring, but they're far away from me. I feel nothing. Not the air, not the ground beneath my feet, not even my own body. I want to stay in this void forever. Then someone says my name and touches my arm. My head whips toward the source: a concerned Bethany.

"Are you alright?"

I don't answer her. I can't stand all those pitying eyes on me. They almost burn. I dash toward the door into the hallway, my panting mouth covered by my hand. I will not cry in front of anyone, I *won't*. Bethany follows me out, calling my name, but I keep sprinting past the other partygoers. I can feel their stares as well and pick up the pace. Tears well in my eyes, but I keep them at bay as I hurry down the driveway to the parking lot. I'm an idiot. I am such a freaking idiot. What ...

Oh fuck.

As I walk over the bridge to the lot, the relief I should feel turns into sheer panic. My skin is stabbed with tiny pins, and my stomach lurches. *It's here.* I gasp and shudder as I scan the area, but there's nobody in sight, just trees, cars, and the night. "Oh shit," I whisper. What the hell do I do? Do I run back inside? Can I even make it? The car. Get to the car. I kick off my heels and run off like a flash. My protection amulet burns against my skin. He's trying something psychic. I half expect trees to come alive or fall on me, but I make it to the car intact.

But I'm a moron. I left my keys in my purse, which is on the ground back at the country club. Worse, all four of my tires are flat. "Oh shit, oh shit," I mutter. I can't stay out in the open. I pop the lock with a spell and jump in. If there's a spell to start the car, I don't know it. My whole body is quaking with fear and adrenaline. I can't think. What the hell am I going to do? I'm a sitting duck in here. Just focus. *Focus.*

Wait, I prepared for this. My trembling hands open the glove box and I pull out chalk, a crystal, and athame. There are three small crystals already in place in the car and when I put this one in the corner and energize it, the perimeter goes up. Even my amulet stops burning. Now I just have to wait. Adam's on his way. He'll get here in time. We'll … as I look around the lot, I notice Auntie Sara's Monte Carlo. He's here already. What … I honk the horn in Morse code for S.O.S. Thank the goddess Mommy signed me up for Girl Scouts. With his werewolf hearing, he's bound to hear this. He has to. Oh hell, then what?

There is movement to my left, but I keep honking. The door of a pickup opens and a pretty girl about ten years younger than me climbs out. She's wearing a black sweater and jeans, and she grimaces and covers her ears as she approaches. I've seen her before, but I can't place her. "Are you okay?" she shouts.

I stop honking. "You need to get out of here!" I shout.

"What? Why? Open the window, I can barely hear you," she says.

"I can't! Just go up to the club! It's not safe here!"

She stops right beside the car and reaches for the handle, but the barrier won't allow it. "Shit! Fucking witches!" She hits the barrier with her fist, and the car tilts to the right from the sheer force.

Oh hell's bells.

Clarity comes too late. She was outside Cheyenne's house with Cray Bradshaw. When the demon was there. When *she* was there. No, demons come as men. There's only one female demon we know of that visits this plane.

"Lilith," I say.

She smiles. "Nice to meet you. *Now get out of the fucking car!*" she roars. She pushes against it and the car jerks again. I hate super-strength. I scream as I fall to the side. The chalk in the passenger seat rolls; it'll have to do. I reach for it, and as she pushes the car again, I quickly draw a banishing sigil on the dash. She tries again, this time the car lifts a few inches off the ground. I stab my finger with the knife to draw blood as I bounce back to earth. She lifts again, but when I press my blood onto the sigil and scream, "*Absentis!*" she jolts with a scream and stumbles three feet back. She can't touch the car now, can't even get within a few feet of it. She shakes her head to clear it.

"Shit!"

"Who summoned you?" I scream.

"Get out and I'll tell you," she says with a smile. I definitely see Cheyenne in her. Same cold blue eyes with a mocking grin. "Might as well. I'm getting bored being stuck in this town. I promise if you do,

I'll make it painless. Barely even feel it. It'll be just like going to sleep. But if I have to come after you tomorrow, I *swear* after I'm done with you, I'll go after those two brats of yours. They'll keep me energized for weeks. Children's life forces are so much more delicious."

That's right. The myth is that she's a succubus, draining energy like a psychic vampire. Most do it with sex, but she can probably do it with her mind. If I wasn't wearing the amulet I would have keeled over days ago of an apparent heart attack. No one would even think let alone prove murder.

"You stay the hell away from them!"

She isn't paying attention to me. She stares off behind me and a huge grin forms on her face. "Or I can feed now."

I turn around. Three people, two men and a woman, walk over the bridge. The woman stops before the men do right under the streetlight. It's Bethany with Clay and Adam. The relief I should feel is just bone-deep terror. The smiling demon closes her eyes and in the same instant Clay doubles over. No. No! Bethany grabs him to keep him upright. Oh crap. Oh goddess no. She's killing my best friend! Why the hell didn't I make him a fucking protection amulet too?

Adam is faster on the uptake than I was. He must see the woman by my car and just *know*. He takes off running as Clay falls to the ground with a hysterical Bethany beside him. *No.* I smash the nearest crystal. The barrier lifts. I call to the wind and she listens. Everything from the trees to the cars shake as a monster gale wind rushes through the parking lot aimed right at her. Anything not weighing a literal ton is knocked down then back as if on rollers into the wooded area. The demon smacks against a tree, her head lolling to the side. She's knocked out. She won't stay like that for long.

I leap out of the car, taking off in the opposite direction. A few seconds later I all but throw myself into Adam's arms, hugging onto his gray sweater with all my strength. Why this makes me feel so much better, I don't know. He squeezes back. "Did it hurt you?" he asks, breathless.

"No." I pull away and take his hand. "Come on."

Bethany is helping the still shaky Clay up when we reach them. "Was that the demon?" Bethany asks, voice quaking.

"Yeah. We need to get up to the club," I say. Bethany's breath becomes ragged, and I follow her gaze. Lilith stands and brushes the dirt off her clothes. *"Now."*

"I got her. Go," Adam says.

"What? No! I'm not leaving you!"

He grabs my face, rough palms pressing against my soft cheeks. His hard blue eyes burn into mine. "Mona, help your friends. I'll be fine, I promise. *Go.*"

He's right. I nod and he releases me. "Don't let her touch you." I throw Clay's arm over my shoulder like Bethany has, and we start running as best we can. Clay can barely keep his feet moving. My back, my arms, my legs all cry out in pain as we trudge up the hill.

"What did she do to him?" Bethany asks.

"Sucked out his life force," I pant.

"Will he be okay?"

Tears fall from my eyes. "I—I don't know." He'll be fine. We all will. If that bitch so much as musses Adam's hair ... no. He's strong. He's got an amulet, he can take her. He has to. He promised.

A minute later, far too long, the bored valets spot us, immediately toss down their cigarettes, and run over to us. The boys take Clay. "What happened?" one asks.

"He collapsed," I say, now completely out of breath. "Call an ambulance."

Bethany follows the men into the club, but when she sees me staying put, she stops. "Mona, what—"

"Take care of him. Keep everyone inside. I have to go back."

"No, Mona, no. That's suicide."

"Bethany, keep everyone inside," I say, my voice hard. "That is an order."

I grab a lighter from the valet stand, the closest thing to a weapon available. Maybe I can set her hair on fire. I spin around and sprint down the hill again. Nothing. There are no sounds beyond my footfalls on the pavement. No birds, crickets, not even the wind. This is so stupid. All I have is a lighter and tiny knife. I don't even have my kit. My kit! It's in the trunk. Salt, charms, potions. Good. A plan.

The prickling starts sooner this time, right when the bridge comes into view. Where are they? If that bitch hurt him … I full on run now, scanning the horizon for her. But I don't find her, I find him.

Oh fuck. No.

As I run over the bridge I see a body floating face down in the creek. My pounding heart comes to a standstill. He looks dead. He is dead. Goddess, don't let him be dead.

Without a second thought, I leap off the bridge and wade into the creek. The cold water only reaches my knees but people have drowned in less. I put the lighter into my cleavage, grab his body, and hoist it up onto the creek bed. There's a gash in his head that's still bleeding and the beginnings of a black eye, but his head is otherwise intact. Except he's not breathing, and he doesn't have a heartbeat. He could have been in the water for ten seconds or two minutes. I have to do CPR. I—

A hand touches my bare shoulder, and all the air is sucked out of my lungs. I don't think, I react. The ground violently shakes while the wind gusts. The hand is gone, but I fall flat on my back on the muddy creek bed beside Adam's cool body and my athame. I reach for the athame. Lilith is up before me, slim hand once again reaching for me. One swift upward movement and the blade jams through that hand. Screaming, she stumbles away as I find my feet. She pulls the blade out of her hand, tossing it to the ground. "Bitch."

Crouching, I let loose another gale, knocking her down again, before I spring up and take off running. There is nothing else I can do but pump my legs as fast as they'll go away from her. I used to make fun of people in horror movies who ran into the creepy house or an isolated area, but I never will again. When a psychopath is chasing you, it's very hard to strategize. The only two words that cycle through my head are *run* and *faster*. My feet are taking me up the hill to the club. I have maybe a five-second head start, which from her nearby cussing I quickly lose because she's in better shape than I am. "Stop running, Mona," Lilith calls, "you're just pissing me off!"

I keep going but don't get far. Since my life has become a horror movie, I do what the victim always does. I trip and fall. I'm so shocked I scream until the wind is knocked out of me when my stomach hits the ground. That's it. I'm done. My body won't move. I'm going to die. The girls will be orphans. Cheyenne will take over the coven and ruin it. I'll never get married or have children of my own. No man's ever truly loved me. It's so fucking unfair.

The demon grabs my wrist and flings me onto my back with a triumphant grin on her pretty face. The air is sucked out again like a vacuum. My heart rate increases ten-fold from overwork. I watch as my veins rise to my skin like worms, and my skin turns to ice as she pulls the life out of every one of my cells. She glows like a lantern as my life becomes hers. If I had breath, I'd scream. Did Adam feel like this when she killed him? Oh, Adam, I'm sorry. I'm so sorry.

Within moments the world becomes fuzzy, and I have the strongest urge to fall asleep.

"What the ... " Lilith says, staring behind me. I don't have the energy to look but there's no need to. What looks like a battalion of super-bright fireflies glides over me like a wave toward the demon, swarming her.

"This way!" I hear a woman shout.

Lilith releases me to swat at the horde enveloping her. Sprites. She's being attacked by spirit energy. I gulp the air back into my lungs and cough. "They're here!" Bethany shouts.

Four people—Bethany, Dickie, cousin Julie-Ann, and Erica—all run into the clearing toward me. Bethany rushes over to me, cradling my coughing body, and the other three move toward the overwhelmed demon. There isn't an inch of her that isn't engulfed by light. Erica waves her hand, and the sprites fly off. That's when I notice the Glock in her other hand, which she raises like Dirty Harry. "Ruin *my* party?" Erica fires twice into the demon's head. I almost vomit over Bethany as the back of Lilith's head explodes, tiny particles of blood and skull flying like fairy dust. The body crumples to the grass in a heap beside me. Hell's bells. "We don't have much time before she recovers," Erica says.

"Cut off her head?" Dickie suggests.

"What with?" Erica asks.

"Cleaver from the kitchen?" Dickie asks.

"Look at her! She's already healing! We don't have that kind of time!"

"Does anyone know a ritual to un-summon it?" Julie-Ann asks.

"Dear Lord in heaven," Erica mutters. "Yeah, I carry all the ingredients in my bra!"

The fog has cleared from my head enough to actually form a thought. "I have an idea." Bethany helps me up, and the world spins a little. "Erica, I think I'll need your help. I'm a little weak right now." She hands the gun to Dickie, before I take her hand and fall to my knees on the ground. She does the same, and we place our hands on the grass. "Call deep, *deep* into the soil and ask it to part." She nods. We close our eyes and push our power into the earth. Within seconds, it starts to rumble and fall in on itself. I open my eyes just as a slim crack parts in the grass. It'll do. "Push the bitch in."

Dickie picks up the still unconscious demon and chucks her down into the abyss. Erica and I close the crack. That's the end of that. She's either crushed flat or it will take her a hundred years to claw out of there. It's over. "Thank you," I say to Erica, who nods.

"Is it over?" Julie-Ann asks. "That wasn't so bad."

"Are you okay?" Bethany asks me. "Do you need a doctor?"

"I'm fine. I'll be fine."

"What about Adam?" she asks.

Oh crap. "Adam! He wasn't breathing!" I leap up and start running again even though I'm still dizzy. "Get a doctor!"

What felt like seconds before when I was chased feels like hours as I race back to the creek. No. He hasn't moved an inch or regained consciousness. I fall to the ground beside him, resting my head on his chest. Still no heartbeat or breath. "No, no, no, no, no," I whisper.

Dickie and Bethany stop a few feet away. "Is he dead?" Dickie asks.

That word hits me like a knife to the gut. "No!" I roar. "Help me!"

I start CPR, hesitating only a millisecond about putting my mouth on his. Some of the creek water dribbles out of the side of his mouth. "Come on, Adam, please," I mutter as I pump. I press and press with all my strength. It's enough. It has to be enough. I have to stop the second round of chest compressions for a second to wipe my tears because I can't see. I breathe into him. Once. Twice. Another round, then another. My arms are killing me, but I push the pain away. Fifth round, still nothing. I can do this. I *will* do this.

A minute passes. No reaction. Fuck. This isn't working. Why isn't this working? It has to work. I look down at him and gasp. He's so pale, so peaceful. That beautiful light of his has vanished. Extinguished. He's gone. He's ... left me. I pull my hands away. It's over. He's ...

No, a voice inside my head says. *No!* He wouldn't give up on me. *Never.* Rage fills me like an invading spirit. You can't have him. Not today. He's mine.

With all my strength, I pound over his heart. More water dribbles out. "No!" I shriek with another pound. "No, you will not do this! Not now!" I slap his face more from fear than anger. The tears can't stop now. I start CPR again, breathe into him, and then let a sob escape me. "Don't leave me alone! Fight!"

"Mona ... " Bethany says, touching my shoulder, "he's—"

"No!" I breathe twice into his mouth again and start compressions. "He cannot leave me! He promised!" My arms are close to buckling and there are spots in my vision, but I keep going. I will until the ambulance gets here. "You promised," I whisper. I place my mouth on his, my tears rolling off my cheeks onto his eyes. "Please, don't leave me."

"Wait! His eyes!' Dickie says. My lips touch his again, and his body jerks. Adam sputters water into my mouth with a cough, and I pull away. His body is wracked by coughs as more water spills out.

He's ... he's ... I'm too happy to do anything but sob. Dickie smacks Adam's back to help as Bethany chuckles from joy.

"Oh god," Adam croaks. "Ow." The three of us chuckle at the absurdity of that statement. Adam grabs onto my skirt and pulls his head into my lap. I can't stop chuckling and crying, even as I kiss his wet hair then plant kisses in his cheeks and forehead. "What—what happened?"

"You died," I chuckle/cry. "Don't ever do that to me again, okay?"

"Oh. Okay. I promise."

I don't take my arms off him until the ambulance arrives.

· *Go to the hospital—again*

Medical mysteries become miraculous recoveries. Both Clay and Adam fight going to the medical center, but Bethany, Dr. Sutcliffe, and I all insist. Though he may be a complete asshole, he is a good doctor. Bethany rides with Clay, Sutcliffe with Adam, and I follow behind in Auntie Sara's Monte Carlo. My car will have to be towed, thanks to the four flat tires, and as I drive, I arrange for Clay's and Bethany's to be taken to their homes. Least I can do after almost getting them killed.

I refuse to leave Adam's side even as Dr. Sutcliffe examines him while occasionally shooting daggers at me. Doesn't penetrate my armor a lick. He checks Adam's lungs and heart, both of which are going strong. Less than an hour ago he was dead and now he's sitting up in bed, holding my hand and asking when he can leave. Sutcliffe can't find a single thing wrong with him except the rapidly healing gash and black eye. In light of tonight's revelation and his intense need to stay as far from me as possible, he listens when Adam gruffly tells him where to stick his blood tests and CT scan. I do convince Adam to stay another hour attached to the monitors just to be safe. He passes out the minute the doctor leaves. Dying takes it out of you.

Clay is on the mend too, though I don't know if it's to do with the electrolytes being pumped into him or the fact Bethany is fussing over him. I called Auntie Sara from the car to tell her to bring the girls to her house since I didn't know when I'd be home and the phone's been ringing off the hook. I had her do a little research on Lilith. All Clay needs is twelve hours of sleep and a few good meals. There should be no permanent damage. He and Bethany look so cozy smiling and whispering, so I just slink away. At least some good came out of this mess.

Adam is still asleep when I return. I stand at the door, staring at him. He looks so peaceful lying there, my heart wrenches. *I almost lost him,* a voice whispers inside my head. My stomach lurches at this thought. If he died, I … I feel fresh tears coming and push them away. He needs me strong. I sit next to him, take his hand, and rest my head over his beating heart. I fall asleep to that strong rhythm.

THURSDAY TO DO:

- *Get Adam to bed*
- *Check on Clay*
- *Send Erica a gift basket for saving my life/accusing her of murder*
- *Work*
- *Pick up my car from the garage*
- *Send e-mail about dead demon*
- *E-mail George*
- *Help set up for the festival*
- *Wedding rehearsal*
- *Gas up Sara's car, new tires on mine*
- *Video store*
- *Finish fixing the shop*
- *Clean the litter box*

TWO HOURS LATER, AROUND one in the morning, we're woken by the nurse with Adam's discharge papers. Dr. Sutcliffe's orders. They're keeping Clay overnight for observation. He's asleep, so we drive Bethany home. We're all silent for the few minutes it takes. It's been a night. Bethany thanks me for the ride home, and I wait until she's inside before pulling away. I owe that woman my life.

I thought he'd sleep the second he got in the car, but Adam just stares out the window. His clothes were covered in mud, so they gave him sweatpants from lost and found and a white undershirt. The black eye is already yellowing and I doubt he even needs the bandage over his cut anymore. He died tonight and still looks good, except for the scowl. As the minutes pass, the scowl deepens as he grows angrier and angrier to such an extent I can feel it coming from him.

"Are you okay?" I ask.

"I'm fine," he replies harshly. "Fine. Fine!" he says as he hits the door hard enough to shake it. He growls then runs his hands through his hair, making it stick up.

"What?" I ask.

"I just, I … nothing. Forget it."

"No. Talk to me." I touch his hand. "Please."

Violently, he pulls his hand away and bunches it into a fist. I tense, not because I'm afraid he'll hit me—I know he'd never lay a finger on me—but he would hit himself. As we drive under a streetlamp I see the twinkle of tears in his eyes, which brings fresh ones into mine. I am a damn wreck. He takes a few deep breaths to calm himself. "I failed."

"What?"

He turns to me, eyes wild. "I failed you! I couldn't protect you! You had to save *me*! You would have died if they hadn't shown up. It's my job—*mine*—to keep you safe. And I failed."

"You didn't fail me, Adam," I say, voice cracking. "You—you died trying to protect me. You were *dead,* Adam! You had no breath and no heartbeat for minutes because of me. Don't you fucking dare beat yourself up. Me. Be angry at me for putting you in that position. You died because of me."

"You brought me back," he says.

I roughly wipe the tears off my cheeks and sniffle. "You shouldn't have been there in the first place! My life is not worth yours! I am not worth it!"

He's quiet for a moment, then says, "Yes, you are."

I pull into my driveway and shut off the car. "I'm really not."

I'm about to get out of the car when he grabs my wrist, pulling me back in. His serious eyes bore into mine. My breath catches. "You are to me."

A million emotions run through me as I stare into those eyes. Fear, joy, apprehension, and I can't handle a single one of them right now. "Let go," I whisper. I yank my arm away and leap out of the car. All the lights are turned off in the house, but I don't need them. I run up the stairs into my safe haven, turn on the light, and slam the door shut. The world needs to go away. I can't do this anymore. He—

I gasp when I see myself in the mirror. My once glorious hair is now a frizzy mess with some patches plastered to my head and others sticking up. I have dirt and mud all over my body and black splotches on my cheeks from the mascara. The dress, Granny's beautiful dress, is caked in mud and ripped on the side. *Fat bitch…monster.* I'm an idiot. I am such a fucking idiot. I close my eyes but that offers no relief. The image of Clay lying in that hospital bed morphs into Adam on the ground the moment I actually considered giving up. I almost gave up on him. He almost…

My eyes fly open, and I start to hyperventilate as huge sobs escape that cannot be contained.

"Mona?" Adam asks as he rushes through the door. His warm arms wrap around me, and I practically collapse against him. "It's okay, baby. It's okay," he whispers. "Just breathe. Breathe." I inhale but the sobs don't stop. "Good. There you go, baby." I cling onto him, digging my nails into his back. He hugs me tighter.

"I'm sorry," I sob. "I'm so sorry."

He kisses the top of my head. "There's nothing to be sorry about. *Nothing.*" Another kiss to my forehead follows. "Oh baby," he says after another kiss. "Don't cry." Another kiss. "Don't be sad. Don't cry." And another. "It'll all be okay. I promise."

As he says it, I believe him. With his arms around me, his heart pounding against mine, his warm breath against my exposed skin, I have faith for the first time in a long time. Faith in *him*. The sobs lessen enough for me to lift my head off his shoulder. He gazes down at me, his eyes filled with sadness. Not for long. The moment I meet them lust explodes out of me. If he wasn't holding me, my legs would buckle. He doesn't move. He can't. His breathing stops from shock. "Adam ... " I whisper.

His lips are on mine before I can say another word, soft and tentative then as hard and greedy as mine. I brush my tongue against his pursed lips. He opens his mouth to accept me in. Oh hell's bells, can he kiss. He sucks on my tongue and the taste of him is better than chocolate. This isn't enough. Not nearly enough. The hand running my fingers through his soft hair moves to his hardness. Me. I did that. The moment I touch it, he breaks the kiss and groans, eyes glazing over in ecstasy. My reprieve lasts only a second before those lips find mine again with fierce intensity as his hand tries to breach my top. The fucking dress it too tight. That doesn't stop him. He rips the fabric right off and pushes up my bra, tongue finding my nipple. I almost orgasm right then.

Even this isn't enough for us. Not by a long shot. We fall on the bed, literally tearing each other's clothes off. Before I realize it, we're naked. Oh goddess, he is a sight to see. Hard muscles everywhere, flat stomach, and more than ample manhood. He's gorgeous. Absolutely gorgeous. Then panic grips me. I'm naked and the lights are still on. I do not look good naked. I really don't. Instinctively, I grab the quilt on the bed, but Adam's hand grasps my wrist. He pins mine down and kisses me again, slow and lingering as if savoring the taste of me. I return the favor. His free hand runs a feather light finger from my knee upwards, moving a trail over the sensitive inner slope of my thigh into the core of me. I cry out in shock and pleasure, lost in a dream of amazing sensations, then again as another finger joins in. I'm so slick and ready for him. "You are so beautiful," he whispers. I believe him.

The fingers disappear. It's a surprise, but nothing compares to the shock of his tip replacing them. He thrusts inside me, and I shudder. It's been so damn long I might as well have re-grown my virginity. I'd forgotten what it feels like to be invaded, but it isn't unpleasant. Adam tenses and looks down at me, concerned once again. "Did I hurt you?" he asks. "Do you want me to stop?"

I grip his cheeks with my hands and look him dead in the eye. "Don't you fucking dare." I smile and pull his lips to mine again. He plunges in deeper, and I cry out from pleasure this time loud enough to wake the dead. Glorious.

I get the hang of it very soon, and within seconds we're completely lost in each other. My hips thrust to meet his strokes over and over and over again as I grip onto his luscious butt. The beautiful tension I feel grows and grows with each coupling overtaking my entire body and soul with its brilliance until I scream and shatter into a million pieces underneath him. He groans at the same time, his fingers tangling in my hair, spilling inside me.

Then there's nothing but stillness and silence except for our ragged breathing. I open my eyes and see him staring down at me, content and surprised at the same time. He rolls off me, out of me. I'm shocked by the void left in his wake. It feels unnatural. We lay next to each other, unable to do anything but catch our breaths for a few seconds. "That was ... unexpected," I say through the pants.

"Yeah," he says though his own. I hear him lick his lips and turn his head. I turn mine. Goddess, he's sexy. "Want to do it again?"

I take a few more breaths, then say, "Oh hell, yeah." We both chuckle then do even better things with our mouths.

What a night.

• *Figure out what the hell happened last night*

Meowing wakes me. I blink a few times and see the Captain a foot away on the nightstand. Probably hungry. I'll get up in a minute. Goddess, am I sore. I pull the arm around my naked body in tighter and close my eyes again, only to have them fly open with a gasp. What the ...

I'm naked. There is an aroused man pressed against me and breathing on my neck. The night's events come back to me. The auction. The demon. Hospital. And ... Adam. I had sex with Adam. Two, no wait, three times. I almost forgot that time we were half asleep, and I somehow ended up on top riding him like a bucking bronco before falling back asleep. My sore nethers tingle from the memory. The pleasure doesn't last long. The Captain meows again and leaps off the nightstand, right on top of my pillow. Hell's bells, it's past ten. The girls, the shop. I have to get out of this freaking bed.

Since I don't have time for a long, awkward conversation, I gently lower Adam's arm onto the mattress and slowly crawl out of bed. Even that hurts. I grab some clothes from the open closet and silently retrieve undies from my drawer before tiptoeing to the girls' bathroom. I turn on the shower and wash the night away. The dirt, the mud, the stickiness from between my legs. Oh holy shit, we didn't use protection. I bought the damn things then … ugh! After the trillion safe sex talks I gave to Ivy and Debbie through the years, it'd serve me right to get knocked up. For a second, just a second, I happily contemplate this idea but push the thought away. No. No. A baby is the last thing in this universe I need right now. First on the agenda is to whip up a prevention potion. Never had a dissatisfied customer.

I don't linger in the shower or over hair and makeup. When I creep back in, Adam is still asleep on his side with a tiny smile on his face and torso exposed. This sight stops me dead again. Damn is he sexy. Lust rushes down my spine, though it's just a snowflake compared to the blizzard from last night. I could just slink back into bed and … no. Last night was last night, and today is today. Besides, I have no time. I sneak in and grab my shoes. The Captain, who has taken my spot on the bed, meows again. Wonderful. At least I know the potion to make him tolerate Adam is working.

Adam groans and shifts. I freeze. He feels for me but finds only fur. I don't wait to see how this ends. I scoop up my purse and run as fast as my sore legs will take me.

I check over my shoulder for sexy werewolves as I scurry next door. I keep knocking until Auntie Sara opens the door and don't wait to be invited in. "Hi! Did the girls get to school?"

"Of course."

"Great. Good," I say quickly. "Listen, I need your car for today, but I'll bring it back tonight. Is that okay?"

"It's fine. Are you alright? You seem skittish."

"No. Fine. Just real late. I'll be at the store until noon, and then the park until five. Adam will bring the car back around three. Um, I think that's it."

"Okay." She touches my shoulder right over one of Adam's love bites, and I try not to wince. "Mona, are you sure you're okay? Maybe you should take the day off in light of—"

"I'm fine." I kiss her cheek. "Thank you for everything. Love you. Bye."

I check to see if the coast is clear then make a mad dash to the car and peel out of the driveway. When the house is out of sight, I can breathe again. Damn, I hurt. Gonna need a pain potion too, though some of the pain is rather pleasant. I touch the mark on my shoulder and shudder. I have two others, one on my inner thigh and one on my breast. The second time went much slower, though it was equally mind blowing. There wasn't an inch of me he didn't kiss or touch like a maestro. I almost came with each mark he gave me, and did on the third one. Twice. I finally get what the fuss is all about.

I park in the lot and power-walk to the shop. A few people try and chat about last night's event, but I smile and walk on. I don't feel secure until I'm in the shop. But he's everywhere. The shelves are only half complete, and the store's in disarray. It's like a hurricane blew in and complicated every damn thing. I can't even look at it without seeing him, so I run into the back to safety. I take three Advil and start on the prevention potion. There's no real magic to it, just the right combination of herbs. I've just got them all together when the bell rings. I tense and hold my breath. Please don't be—

"Mona?" Tamara asks. I literally breathe a sigh of relief. I have a feeling I'll be doing this all day. She walks in, still in her apron, and gives me a huge bear hug. "Are you okay?"

I pull away. "I'm fine. Just a little sore."

"What the hell happened last night? The whole town is buzzing."

I keep working on the potion. The sooner I take it, the more effective it is. "What have you heard?"

"Just what was in the paper. That the rat bastard doctor freaked out on you, and when Clay, Bethany, and Adam went to check on you, a bear came out of the woods and attacked y'all. Clay fainted or something, and Adam hit his head and almost drowned. Erica heard you screaming, grabbed a gun from her date, and scared the thing away."

"That's the cover story?" I ask with a raised eyebrow.

"Well, everyone knows it's not true. What really happened?" I tell her, leaving out the last part, and she listens with bated breath. "Is Clay okay? Adam?"

"They're both fine. More than fine, I'll bet. Bethany was fawning over Clay at the hospital."

"Well, he did almost die. He should get something out of it." She pauses. "So that doctor really did go off on you like that? Are you making a hex? No one would blame ya."

"Tam, after all that happened, I barely care."

She looks skeptical. "I know you really liked him and had a lot of hopes pinned on his lapel. No one should talk to another person like that. I vote hex."

"A project for another time," I say with a smile. I mix the last herb in. "So what's the bigger story? Me and the not-so-good doctor, or Erica and Smokey the Bear?"

"About even." She glances at the cauldron. "So is she off your suspect list now she saved your bacon?"

"That and the demon didn't look a thing like her. No, I have no doubt it's Cheyenne. Demon even had her smile. I just have to prove it, and my last lead is buried at the country club. I'm screwed." I drink the nasty brew and shudder. For once I can't wait until my period.

"Speaking of, where's Adam?" she asks.

My stomach clenches. "What? What—what do Adam and screwing, I mean being screwed, have to do with each other?"

Her eyes narrow. "Nothing. I just meant he should be here. Cheyenne's still loose and probably more pissed than ever."

"He died last night. He's worn out. I gave him the day off." I turn my back on her, hoping she gets the fact I have no desire to continue with this conversation. "I have a lot to do today. Can I call you later?"

"Sure," she says after a pause. She hugs me from behind. "Glad you're okay."

When she's gone, I fall into my chair with a sigh. Thank the universe I have a trillion things to do today. First I call Clay, but there's no answer on his cell or at home. I try Collins, who tells me he checked out this morning with a clean bill of health. He must be at home asleep. I'll pop by later.

Next up I send a mass e-mail to the coven to tell them the demon is gone. I don't get into details, since I'm sure they have them already. The e-mail to George Black is longer. Maybe now someone came to physical harm, the preter police force my tax dollars pay for will do their damn job.

The bell rings and once again I about jump out of my damn skin. Damn. I force myself out there. Just customers, though they don't want to shop so much as gossip. My scowl does the talking, so they soon leave. I manage to get a few online orders done before the bell

239

rings again. More cousins looking for the skinny. After five minutes of incessant questions, Billie walks in to rescue me. She's changed her hair to ketchup red since I last saw her and smiles as she walks in. I excuse myself, walking to the back room. The bell rings as the cousins leave.

"This place is a mess," Billie says as she comes in. "Hey, I heard. You okay?"

I am getting sick of that question. "Fine. Listen, Alice will be in around one today. I'll be in and out when I can get away from the festival setup. I'll be counting on you in the next three days."

"And I won't let you down. Are you sure you're okay? You seem scattered."

"I said I'm fine," I snap. The bell rings again, and Billie looks at me. Consider my patience gone. I mutter, "Goddess, just make them go away."

I roll my eyes and walk out. Two minutes of peace. I just want two stupid minutes—

I stop dead, all color draining to my toes. My breath catches as it always seems to do around him. I wasn't ready. I can't handle this right now. Just hours ago those lips now pulled into a bright smile were on my most intimate places. Those eyes were full of awe and lust as they roved my naked body. Now as they gaze into mine, all mirth leaves them. His smile fades too. I can't think of anything to say, I don't know what to do, so I flee into the back room. Something to do, I need something to do. I need to get the hell out of here is what I need to do.

"Mona, what the hell—" Billie starts.

"Bank," I blurt out. "I haven't been to the bank. I have to make a deposit, and we need ones." I rush over to the safe and punch in the code. Just as I stand, Adam steps in. I read his face, but can't tell if

240

he's hurt or is just as embarrassed as I am. I can't look at him, I can't … I have to get out of here. "Hello, Adam," I say as I grab my coat. "You're looking well this morning. Billie, I have another million errands to run today. I don't know when I'll be back. I have my cell if things get crazy."

"O-kay," she says, pierced eyebrow raised.

I rush out of the room and worm my way to the front door. "Mona, stop," Adam says coming behind me and taking my arm. "What is—"

I spin around. "I can't deal with this right now," I hiss in a low voice. "I can't be around you today. You need to stay in the store and fix this mess you made, okay? I will be fine alone. I'll be surrounded by people today. Just … do this, please?" I pull my arm away. "I'm sorry."

He lets me go without protest. Don't know how I feel about that. I don't have a damn clue about anything anymore.

· Bank/Clay/phone calls/festival prep

Bank: check. Gas up Auntie Sara's car: check. Video store: check. Thousand phone calls while at Starbucks: check. Visit my best friend who I almost got killed: check. (He's still really tired, so I make him a sandwich and let him nap.) Minutes spent at the shop: two, and Adam and I can't even look at each other, let alone talk. Good.

I give Billie the car keys to give to him before walking to the park where the vendor trucks are lined up and unloading their goodies for Friday's festival. Mechanics are already building the Ferris wheel and carousel, while builders hammer away on the stage for the pageant. I find Mayor Magda yelling at a man with mutton chops at the concession area. As he leaves, I walk over. "Sorry I'm late."

"Mona! How are you? Are you okay?"

If I had a nickel for every time someone asked me that … "Fine. Ready to work."

"If you're up to it. I need someone supervising the games area."

"I'm on it." Just as I get to my station, a familiar silver Mercedes parks across the street, and Erica climbs out. My savior. She eyes a few of the cuter workmen as she saunters into the park. The tens of thousands of dollars she's spent to turn heads pay off as they return the favor. My fellow committee members Eileen and Yvonne all but run over to her.

As they fire questions, she leads them to me. "Well, of course I was afraid, but I just pushed it aside. I couldn't very well let three innocent people die."

"You are so brave," Eileen says. "An absolute hero."

"Oh, please don't call me that," Erica says with fake humility. "I just did what anyone would." She smiles, and I smile back. "Mona. How are you?"

"Fine. Thanks to you."

"And Clay and your other friend?"

"Both much better now."

"Glad to hear it." Erica turns to the women, all smiles. "I can't stay long. I just came to speak to Mona. Will you please excuse us?" As if she's my best friend, she slides her arm through mine and leads us to a more isolated part of the park. "You owe me six grand."

"What?"

"Your doctor friend put a stop on his check this morning."

"I'm sorry," I say.

"I mean, really Mona, after all the preaching about black and gray magic, you're so desperate for a man you compromise your morals?"

"I didn't. It was my nieces. I had no idea."

She pulls out her buzzing phone and begins texting. "Well, I don't suppose your cousin would agree to honor his bid of four thousand for dinner, would he?"

"What cousin? Clay?"

"No, the cute one. Adam, I think his name is? The one who almost died? He was the other bidder."

Well, knock me over with a feather. "He was?"

She keeps texting. "That's what I heard. So, would he?"

"I—I don't think so. Sorry."

"Damn it. Well, this is why I have a lawyer on retainer. I'll get her to call and scare the money out of that doctor. We broke a record, and I intend to keep it." She puts her cell away. "And I assume you know the cover story? About the bear? It was the best I could come up with on such short notice, though everyone knows the real story. At least people can't say I throw a boring party."

"I'm sorry," I say. "For everything."

"For accusing me of trying to kill you? You need to send flowers for that one, hon."

"I know. I was wrong. It's just, someone *is* trying to kill me, and they would have if it wasn't for you. I don't know why you did it, but thank you."

"Well, I couldn't very well have a demon attacking my guests. It's unseemly."

"Thank you just the same."

She nods. "You're welcome. See you at the coven meeting. And try and stay out of trouble." She nods again and walks away. That went better than I thought it would.

Adam was the mystery bidder? That doesn't make any sense. It takes twenty minutes to get to the country club from the house, and

I had called him less than five minutes before I got on the stage. Which means... he was already there. He ignored my order to stay home. But why? Why would he... he was doing his job, protecting me. That's why he bid too, to keep me away from Guy, since he was suspicious of him. That's gotta be it. Right?

Oh hell. The thoughts I've been attempting to keep at bay can no longer be contained. I had sex with Adam last night. The fact is I've *wanted* to have sex with him. For a few days. I admit that now, but the lust from last night was brought on by sadness and fear, the joy of being alive. Intense situations have that effect. We almost died, and there's nothing more life-affirming than sex. We acted on it, and now it's out of our systems. End of story.

I mean, he's leaving Saturday. He'll be almost six hours away and long-distance relationships never work. He has a life up there, a job, a pack that needs him. Last night was an aberration. I've known him for eighteen years. Eighteen years with about thirty words exchanged, though I tried for more. The man would see me coming and walk away. He's probably as uncomfortable and freaked as I am. No, it was a one-off reaction to a life-and-death situation. I will not read anymore into it. I've learned my lesson from Guy. At least I got some orgasms out of it. Back to real life now.

"Hey, you in the wife beater," I shout. "We aren't paying you to check out my cousin's ass! Get to work!"

Ugh. Men.

• Get ready for rehearsal dinner

"Cheyenne came into the store today," Billie tells me as she drives me to Goodnight Autocare. My car has four new tires, and I am officially broke. Thank you, Lilith. May you rot in hell.

"What did the psychopath want?"

"To fawn over Adam. She seemed worried about him."

"She was technically responsible for his death. If she was capable of it, I'm sure she'd be drowning in guilt." I pause. Not that I care, but I ask, "How did he respond?"

"Well, he was in a pissy mood all day, and it didn't get much better when she came. He shrugged her off, and she left in a huff."

"Oh." Good. We pull into the parking lot, and I get out. "Thanks for the ride."

I am so freaking exhausted that I write a five-hundred-dollar check for tires without even hyperventilating. Usually I'd need a Valium to survive that. It helps that I just spent five hours running around like a crazed harpy yelling at lazy workmen and organizing stuffed animals. Took it out of me. At least I was so preoccupied I couldn't brood. Now I can barely sign my own name. My future in-laws are going to think I'm an idiot if they engage me in conversation tonight. Greg's parents, Conrad and Gretchen, are lovely people. I could kiss them for paying for the whole wedding, but they are a tad snobbish. My drooling and grunting when they ask me questions will not improve their opinion of the McGregor clan.

Luckily driving doesn't require complex thought. The house is quiet when I walk in. The girls laze in front of the TV, but both sit straight up when I walk in. They're scared. They should be. If I could muster it, I'd be furious. I'll fake it as best I can. Their wide eyes follow me as I walk to the TV and smack the off button. "Hope you enjoyed that show because it's the last one you'll be watching for a month."

"Aunt Mona—" Sophie says.

"I don't want to hear it," I snap. "Do you have any idea what you did? Do you have any idea how illegal what you did was, not to mention just plain *wrong*? You took away a man's free will. He could press charges and the F.R.E.A.K.S. could take you away. What the hell were ya'll thinking?"

"We knew you liked him," Sophie says, "and we liked him too. We wanted you to be happy. If he loved you, you'd be happy."

"That isn't love," I say. "It's trickery and manipulation and downright evil toying with a person like that. *Two* people. I just... I am so disappointed in you. Both. I can barely even look at you. Get upstairs. Get ready for the rehearsal. Get out of my sight."

Sophie hangs her head and takes her sister's hand, leading her past me. "Sorry, Aunt Mona," Cora says. A few seconds later a door shuts upstairs.

"Kind of hard on them, weren't you?" Adam asks.

I turn my gaze to the kitchen entrance where he stands. "What they did was illegal and dangerous. I have merely begun."

"Their hearts were in the right place."

"Well, if last night has taught me anything, it's letting your heart override your head only leads to misery. It is not a mistake I will ever make again."

"Then you're in for a very lonely existence."

I scoff. "Yeah, well, I've known *that* since I was twelve. Such is life."

He steps toward me. "Doesn't have to be."

I glance at his impassive face, my damn stomach clenching again. Just stop it. "I have to get ready. Excuse me."

"Mona, we really need to—"

"Not now."

"When?"

"Not. Now."

I half expect him to follow me—and yes a little part of me wants him to—but he doesn't. When I get to my bedroom my stomach seizes again as I stare at the remnants from last night lying on the floor. Granny's old dress is nothing but rags, along with the Spanx and bra. Don't know how my panties survived the onslaught. I just want it all gone. Out of my damn sight.

The Captain meows and jumps off the bed as I rip off the rumpled sheets. No reminders from my bad judgment can remain. I need to add laundry to my To Do list. After I make the bed, I start on myself. Oh joy of joys, I get to return to the country club to go through the ceremony and have dinner with the families. I'm sure the staff from my previous sojourn will be there tonight, and I will get many pitying looks. I settle on a light blue blouse and white skirt with sandals, slap on makeup, and brush my hair before stepping out. If the way I feel is any indication, I still look like hell.

When I walk in the girls' room, they're both lying on Sophie's bed looking at a magazine and wearing their best floral print dresses and white sweaters. Without a word, I remove their TV and PS3, hiding them in my closet. The girls haven't moved when I return. "That is punishment number one. Of twenty. Put your shoes on, we gotta go."

"Do you hate us?" Cora asks pitifully. "Are you going to send us away now?"

She looks so much like Ivy at that age. She used to do this exact thing to Daddy when he punished her. The pout, the "if you loved me, you wouldn't do this" eyes. Manipulation at its finest. Not buying it. "No. Put your shoes on."

They do, and I all but push them down the hall. Adam is coming up the stairs just as we reach them. He smiles at the girls, saying, "You all look very pretty tonight."

"We're rehearsing dinner," Cora says.

"We should be back in about two, three hours," I say.

"You're not coming?" Sophie asks him.

"Girls, go wait by the door," I order. They obey without hesitation. "It's a small party. I wouldn't know how to explain you to Greg's family. The demon's dead, Cheyenne won't be there. I'll be safe."

I expect protests, but instead he says, "Fine. You're the boss. I could use a night off anyway." He walks up the stairs past me. "Being your houseboy takes it out of me."

"Excuse me? My what?"

He spins around, face hard and angry as a rattler. "Houseboy. You know, slave? Unpaid babysitter, cook, manual laborer, hell even sex toy."

"Keep your voice down," I hiss in a low voice as I step toward him. "And you volunteered to be here. I didn't ask you to do *any* of this."

"No, you're right. You didn't," he says with attitude. "Don't know what the hell I was thinking. I forgot, you're the woman who needs nothing and no one. Well, since you don't seem to need a bodyguard or anything else anymore, maybe it's time I left you and your delusions of grandeur alone."

"Well, maybe you should if you think I'm such a selfish, delusional bitch."

"Maybe I will."

"Good! Great!"

"Fine!" He stomps toward his room and slams the door shut.

"Perfect!" I shout before I stamp down the stairs. The girls stand there with the fear of God on their faces. "What? Move your butts! We're late!" I slam the door shut with a sad sigh.

Yeah, we have to go celebrate love. So why do I feel like I just gave its eulogy?

• Rehearsal dinner

I thought I'd have a breakdown or panic attack when I got to the country club, but there are no PTSD flashbacks or even apprehension as I pull up. The girls and I didn't say a word the whole ride, but by the looks on their faces they're about as miserable as I am. Hope we don't infect the rest of the party with our gloom.

They wedding party and families are assembled in the garden by the fountain with the two swans. The wedding planner, Jocasta, talks to the Reverend Potter, going over the details and pointing to the flowers on the hedges. Representing the McGregors are the beaming Debbie, Collins, and bridesmaids Becca, Kaylee, and Chelsea. I recognize Greg's parents, but the groomsmen and ushers, along with a crying three-year-old boy held by a thin woman, are strangers. Not for long, I'd guess. "Sorry we're late," I say as the girls and I walk down the steps. "Insane day."

"We heard," Gretchen, Greg's mother, says. "It must have been so frightening for you."

"What happened?" one of the groomsmen asks.

"There was a bear here last night," Gretchen says. "It attacked Mona here."

"Is it still around?" Becca asks.

"Animal control got it," I lie. "We'll be fine. Just a freak thing."

"Well, we're glad you're safe and sound," Conrad, Greg's father, says. "Reverend?"

The Reverend Potter smiles. "Everyone please follow me."

We meander down the gray pebble path toward the seven-foot-tall arch that will be covered with pink roses and daisies on Sunday. Jocasta takes over, telling us where to go, stand, and what to do. On the day I'll walk Debbie from the clubhouse, past the two hundred plus guests on either side of the path to the arch, where she will pledge her undying love to Greg. The rehearsal goes well with the girls relishing their flower girl duties, tossing imaginary petals with abandon. The ring bearer does begin to cry halfway through, but Debbie's future sister-in-law takes him away. We go through it twice, which takes an hour, then it's dinner time.

Jocasta leads us to the patio, the scene of last night's horror show. Dickie, who adds water to the glasses, is almost grimacing when he sees me. I nod reverently, and he returns the gesture. Debbie leaves her fiancé's side for the first time tonight to come over to me. "Can we talk?"

"Sure. Girls, behave."

"I'll keep an eye on them," Collins says.

Debbie drags me to the side. "Are you okay? I was so worried. I tried calling a million times."

"I was very busy. And I'm fine. A hundred percent fine. Don't worry about me, just worry about buying sunscreen for your honeymoon," I say, rubbing her arm.

"Of course I'm worried. You had your heart broken, and then almost died."

"Really," I chuckle, "I'm fine. It'd take a lot more than a few ugly words and a demon to bring me down. You know that. It's done, it's over, I've moved on."

She looks skeptical but says, "Okay. And how are Clay and … Adam?"

"Fine. We were all very lucky."

"Why isn't he here tonight? Shouldn't he be guarding you?"

"Um, we sort of decided it was time for him to go home." I start playing with my pendant. "You know, the demon's dead, and it's only a matter of time before I can prove Cheyenne's guilt. He has a life in Maryland. It's time."

"You *both* decided this?" she asks.

"Yes. Now stop worrying about me. This is your night. You're getting married!" I hug her. "I'm so proud of you." I release her. "Come on. I'm starving."

I actually get to enjoy my dinner tonight, and the only scenes that are caused are when Collins and Greg toast Debbie. Everyone has a great time. Groomsmen flirt with the bridesmaids, the girls play with the ring bearer, and the happy couple only has eyes for each other. I manage to keep a pleasant smile on my face watching the joy, but inside…

I'm just exhausted. Emotionally, physically, hell even spiritually. I mean…a *houseboy?* Is he kidding? I never, *not once,* took him for granted. I saved his freaking life last night. I didn't give up on him even when they told me to. I was safe, I didn't have to go back for him. And I'm paying him for the work on the store, and he never asked for money for cooking and watching the girls. I give him free room and board. And if memory serves, he used me for sex as much as I did him. Houseboy, indeed.

Maybe it would be best if he left. He could stop resenting me and I can stop…the same. He needs to go back to his pack. He needs to go back to his life; once Cheyenne is neutralized, I can go back to mine. Yippee. I can't wait.

Collins grimaces as a boisterous groomsman talks, and talks, and talks. She needs a rescue, and I need to speak with her. Win win. I grab two salt shakers, putting them in my purse, before going over. "Collins, take a walk with me?"

She glances at the wine-chugging man. "Love to." She follows me down the patio steps to the grassy hills. "Where are we going?"

"To tie up a loose end from last night."

"I heard what happened. What was the demon doing here?"

"It was here to kill me," I say nonchalantly.

"What?" she asks, shocked. "Why?"

I stop walking and turn to her. "Because your sister wants me dead." I start strolling alone as I let those words sink in, but within a few seconds she runs to my side. Before she can bombard me with questions, we reach the grave. It's just a mound of dirt where the earth cracked. More than she deserves. I pull out the two shakers and hand one to Collins. "We need to salt the ground just to be safe." I pour salt into my hand and sprinkle it like seed. She follows my lead. "She teamed up with a vampire in Richmond named Alejandro. Has Cheyenne ever mentioned him?"

"I—I don't know," she says. "I can never keep her boyfriends straight."

"You know it's kind of odd you haven't jumped to her defense yet. If you accused Debbie of the same thing, I'd probably claw your eyes out. Talk to me, Collins."

She pauses, then asks, "Do you have any proof?"

"I know she's been to Alejandro's club. I know she has a black magic grimoire stashed somewhere. I know the demon was around her house. I know I'm not her favorite person. I know there are only four people in line for my job, and she's one of them."

"So am I, but … that's why you asked me if I wanted to be Priestess. You were testing me."

"And you passed. That and you're one of the few without a single tie to Alejandro. I ruled Erica out last night, can't see Shirley doing it, Whitney is fourteen, so Cheyenne it is. The demon even looked like her. I just need proof."

"I—I can't help you. I'm sorry."

252

"A lot of people almost died last night, Collins. She did that. Next time it could be the girls. Or Debbie." I walk over to her. "Listen, I know she's your sister. I know deep down that you love her and want to protect her, but she's dangerous. To us all. I'm asking, no I'm *begging,* not only as your High Priestess but as the woman who helped you get ready for junior prom. Who took you to the doctor to get on the pill. Who baked your birthday cake four years in a row. I need your help. *Please.*"

She opens and closes her mouth a few times, but words don't come out. I know this is tough on her. I hate myself for asking, but I'm out of options. If she doesn't help me, that's it. Finally, she says, "Of course."

I hug the girl. "Thank you. Thank you so much."

She pulls away. "I'm not surprised, you know. She's damn jealous of you and Debbie, has been since we were kids. Meemaw's doing, I guess. She hates your grandmother even now. And there's always been something wrong with Cheyenne, that's not news. When we were kids, she used to catch butterflies then burn them with a magnifying glass and laugh. She tried to starve our pets too. Daddy would smack her, but she kept at it." Collins shakes her head. "What do you need exactly?"

"We searched her house and locker at work but didn't find anything. I just need proof she's linked to Alejandro or the demon. Anything. That grimoire would be useful too."

"I'll see what I can do." She pauses again. "Did you really suspect me? Seriously?"

"For all of three seconds. I mean, you're practically my sister too. You're more a sister to me than Ivy even."

She smiles. "I think the same about you. I kind of always wished it was true."

"Thank you." I take a deep breath and sigh. "Okay, let's finish up here. Even with it dead, I feel the evil." I start throwing salt again.

"Are you sure it can't come back?"

"Nope. But even *I'm* not that unlucky."

"Famous last words."

Goddess, I hope not.

· *Sleep for twenty years*

I make my excuses to the party, going with the always-effective school night defense, and herd the girls to the curb. After last night I decided to splurge and valet the car. Our chariot arrives a minute later, and we're out of there. It's almost their bedtime, so they slump in the back with heavy eyes. I feel the same way. I can't wait to climb under the covers and fade into oblivion.

About halfway home Cora says, "Aunt Mona, why did you yell at Adam?"

"I didn't yell. We had a discussion." Loudly.

"Is he going to his home now?" Cora asks.

"I—I don't know, sweetie. But if he is, we'll be okay. We're tough chicks, we don't need him."

"I don't want him to leave," she whines.

I bite my lower lip. "He has a life, sweetie. He has a job, and friends, and a home he needs to get back to."

"He won't leave," Sophie says with certainty. "He promised he'd film the pageant."

"Honey, I can film it," I say.

"I know, but he promised. He won't leave until then," she says with finality. She pauses, and then asks, "We really can't watch TV for a month?" I shake my head no. "That sucks."

"Language!"

The rest of the ride not a word is uttered. As the miles pass I grow more and more apprehensive, and by the time we pull into the driveway, my whole body might as well be made of stone. All the lights are off. No life inside. He must have called a taxi to the train station. Damn it. I start playing with my hair. I don't want to go into that house. I know I'm not going to like what I find in there. The girls have no such worries. Getting a second wind, they leap out and run to the door like race cars. I pull my wrecked body upright and slowly amble toward the door, unlocking it.

Cora squeezes in before it's all the way open, shouting, "Adam?"

I turn on the foyer light with a sigh. No noise except us. Cora stomps up the stairs shouting his name. I set down my purse as Sophie moves into the dark living room and kitchen. Cora stops shouting. The silence is maddening. That's when it hits me like a two by four. He really left. He's gone. A wave of sadness ripples through me. He wouldn't. No. He promised. He—

"What kind of flowers did you imagine?"

I inhale a ragged breath. I must have stopped breathing. Hell's bells.

Adam and Cora walk onto the landing, both smiling. "Roses and daisies. My dress has daisies on it too."

"I can't wait to see it." He looks down at me. "Hey."

"Hi," I squeak. Oh thank you goddess. Thank you.

Sophie comes into the foyer with a glass of water. "Told you not to worry. I knew he'd be here."

"Yes, you did," I say with a little laugh. "Okay, um, it's bedtime. Showers, pajamas, bed. Big day tomorrow. Go on."

Sophie treads up the stairs, and as she passes Adam, he ruffles her hair before walking down to me. "You were worried?"

"Not really," I say with bravado.

"I'm not going to lie, I almost left," he says. "Vivian talked me down though."

"You called Jason's wife?"

"Yeah. Needed a woman's perspective. She convinced me to stick it out, at least until the Saturday deadline."

Goddess bless that woman. "Well, it's your choice," I say. "We're glad to have you until then. Excuse me." I turn my back on him and start up the steps.

"We need to talk," he says when I'm halfway up. "About us."

And my happiness buzz is swatted away. I stop, groan, and spin around. "Can it please wait until tomorrow? I'm exhausted."

"No, I've put it off long enough."

I sigh. Great. "Okay, fine." I take a step down. "We had sex, big whoop. I take full responsibility for what happened. I didn't really mean to turn you into my sex toy like you said, but I'm not sorry about it either. It was wonderful. You are phenomenal in bed, but I don't expect *anything* from you. I know you're leaving soon, and it was a one-off, and—"

"I'm in love with you," he states as fact.

Did he … *what?*

My mouth snaps shut like a bear trap, and my eyes bug out of my head. He just stands there as if waiting for a damn bus. How the hell can he just act as if those words never happened? A trillion thoughts run through my mind in a flash, and I can't keep them straight.

"What—you—no—what?" I stammer. He's in love. With me. *Me.* No way. No . . .

The shock wears off, and one thought pushes through. My shoulders slump. Of course. "Oh damn. Not again." I take a step down. "Did one of the girls give you a piece of jewelry or something to drink right before you started feeling this way? Because—"

"I've been in love with you for eighteen years. Since the moment I saw you. You're my mate."

I'm his . . . werewolves have an evolutionary advantage when it comes to love. When they meet "the one" they instantly know it. Call it pheromones or magic, but they *just know.* I'm his mate. For some reason this thought makes me dizzy.

"What? No. *No.* You—you hated me. You avoided me like the plague whenever I got near you."

He takes a step toward me. "I avoided you because it was the only way for me to control myself around you." He steps. "I avoided you because the only other alternative was for me to pin you against the wall and screw you senseless."

"But—but I had braces, and pimples, and . . . no. No."

He steps onto the stairs, gazing up at me with fierce determination. "I have loved you since I first saw you, and that love has grown and grown through the years so that . . . I can barely stand it anymore. I love you. It isn't a spell, it isn't a figment of my imagination, it is a stone cold fact. I love you."

I can't move or even blink. I'm paralyzed. I have no idea what to say or do, or, hell, even feel. Because I believe him. "Why—why didn't you say something?" I whisper.

For the first time, he looks away. "Because. Couple reasons, I guess. The first being you barely knew I was alive. I was just one of Jason's werewolves you saw a couple times a year then forgot about."

"If you had talked to me, maybe asked me out, that might have changed," I point out.

"I know that. I thought about it every time I knew I was going to see you. I'd psych myself up saying, 'This time. This is the time I tell her.' Then I'd talk myself out of it."

"Why?" I ask shrilly.

"My second reason." He looks up at me again, face a little angry. "I can't be with you."

These words are like an icicle to my heart. "You—why—why not?"

"You're a witch. A *powerful* witch. If we mated, our children would be considered hybrids by pack law. They're considered a threat to the pack. I'd have to leave it, go rogue, and I wasn't ready to do that. It was too big a gamble."

"'Was?'" I ask, my voice cracking.

He takes a step up, then looks me square in the eyes. "We heard about the threat to you, and I ... lost it. I took off, didn't even wait for my Alpha's approval. You were in danger, and that was all that mattered."

"You could have died. You were tortured!"

"And you patched me up."

"And last night?"

"I don't know what it meant to you, but ... " He shrugs. "It was better than I ever imagined. And I imagined it a lot," he chuckles. The laughs subside a second later. This is no laughing matter, not to me. "Sorry."

"Stop apologizing to me!" I all but shout. Eighteen years of experiences and looks and ... hell's bells. "So it's me or the pack?"

"Yes."

"Wh—what about dating? We can't even date?"

"Mona, you're my mate. Werewolves mate for life. I can't just date you then walk away. I'm not a masochist."

"I can't … this, this is too much to process. I—I don't know what to say or do or … "

"You don't have to say or do anything. I just, I had to tell you. Just … just once. You don't have to say anything back. I just thought … hell, I don't know what I thought. Never mind." Without looking at me, he walks up the stairs and I step to the side to let him pass. His shoulder brushes against mine, and I freeze up. "Excuse me," he says.

I can't let him leave like this. "Adam?" I ask. He turns around, face slack in misery. My heart all but snaps in two for him. "What happens Saturday?"

"That's the day I have to decide. Either I stay here, or I go back and never see you again."

"Oh," I more groan than say. "And will—will you stay until then?"

His eyes burrow into mine, down to my soul. "Do you want me to?"

I hesitate, my heart pounding so fast, then whisper, "Yes. Yes, I do."

The briefest of smiles passes over his face. "Okay, then. I guess I'll see you in the morning. Sweet dreams, Mona." And he turns around and walks to his bedroom without another syllable.

My legs finally give out when I hear his door shut. I slump onto the stairs, just staring into space, my mind reeling. No complex thought is able to form in my brain except those three words: He loves me. He *loves* me. He loves *me*. "Hell's bells," I whisper.

A laugh escapes, then another, then they won't stop. I don't have a clue why I'm cackling like a witch on meth, but I can't stop. I guess the sheer insanity of it all. All of it. The demon, Guy, Cheyenne, eighteen years of unrequited love, hell, throw in five hundred dollars for tires. I mean, five hundred dollars? That's highway robbery! I laugh harder.

I don't know how long I'm on those stairs laughing, but I don't stop until Cora, wrapped in a towel, touches my shoulder. "Aunt Mona, why are you laughing?"

I pull her into a hug, holding her as if she were a life raft. "Oh, sweetie, because life is so freaking ridiculous."

FRIDAY TO DO:

- *Continue working at festival*
- *Work*
- *Attend pageant*
- *Start agendas for co-op meetings tomorrow*
- *Finish store renovation*
- *Keep investigating, if possible*
- *Send reminder e-mail about meetings*

EXHAUSTION SAVED ME AROUND midnight from analyzing eighteen years of memories and inventorying my feelings. I came up with nothing but a headache. The alarm buzzes at seven and my eyes fly open. I pull my body out of bed and into the bathroom. After taking great pains to put on makeup and tame my hair, I guess for *the werewolf who loves me,* I go to wake up the girls but they're not in their room and neither is Adam. His bedroom door is open. There are clothes strewn everywhere, and the covers on the bed are in a tangle. He had a fitful night. The smell of eggs draws me into the kitchen, where the girls sit at the table chewing on toast while Adam stands with his back to me at the stove. *He loves me…*

"Morning," he says, still cooking. "Omelet'll be done in a minute. Can you get the ketchup?"

"Uh, sure," I practically whisper. Not taking my eyes off him, I pour myself coffee and get the ketchup, but he doesn't look back. "You girls, uh, sleep well?" I ask as I sit.

"I guess," Sophie says.

"Eggs!" Adam says as he turns, skillet in hand. "There's cheese and peppers in here. Hope that's okay." He dishes it out, the whole time smiling pleasantly at us. When it's my turn, I feel a blush reddening my cheeks. His smile never wavers even as he sits across from me. I quickly smile and look down at my plate. "What do you think?"

"It's yummy," Cora says.

It is. "Thank you for making breakfast again," I say.

"My pleasure," he says before turning his attention to Sophie. "Are you excited for tonight? The pageant?"

"I guess," she says with her usual enthusiasm.

"I want to ride the Ferris wheel," Cora says to Adam. "Will you take me?"

Adam chuckles. "We'll see. I don't really like heights."

"You don't? I didn't know that," I say.

"Well, there's a lot about me you don't know," he says with a grin.

I gaze down at my plate and clear my throat. "No rides for either of you. Consider it part of your punishment."

"Really?" Cora whines. "Can I at least get cotton candy? Play games?"

I feel someone cross the psychic barrier out front, so I stand. "We'll see. Excuse me." I reach the front door the moment there's a knock. "Who is it?"

"George Black."

Oh. The F.R.E.A.K.S. have arrived. About damn time. I open the door just as Adam and the girls walk in. Dr. George Black, Ph.D., stands on my porch with two serious-looking men in dark suits behind him, one with olive skin and the other with a scar in his eyebrow. I don't know exactly how old George is, but in the twenty odd years I've known him, he's barely changed. He's still painfully thin with gray hair cut like a helmet, tan skin, and an always perfectly pressed suit. He is a sight for sore eyes.

"Uh, hi," I say.

"Aunt Mona?" Sophie asks.

"It's okay. It's, uh, the police. Come in." Better late than never. As they walk in, I notice the girls move behind then press themselves against Adam. "Want some coffee?"

"Yes, please," the agent with the scar says.

"Girls, go get your breakfast and take it upstairs. Get ready for school."

"Go on," Adam whispers to them. Not taking her narrowed eyes off the men, Sophie clasps Cora's hand and leads her to the kitchen. Adam walks toward us. "Well, gentlemen. Took you long enough to get here."

"It turned out there was another wraith," George says. "The team just finished late last night and had to re-supply before we flew here."

I start walking to the kitchen and the men follow. The girls pass us with their heads down and plates out. "And we thank you for coming," I say. "We've hit a wall." As I fill up the coffee cups and dispense them, I update them on the too-few developments since Wednesday night. "So we know it's her, but we can't prove it."

"We'll see what we can dig up," Olive skin says. "We'll need a list of her friends, family, boyfriends, and so on."

"Then she'll know we're after her," Adam points out. "That's exactly what we've been trying to avoid."

"We'll be as discreet as possible, but at this point it's unavoidable," Scar says. "We have been in touch with your local police, and they have her under surveillance as of this morning. If she comes near you we'll know it."

George pats my hand. "Don't you worry. We've done this a thousand times."

Adam gulps the rest of his coffee. "Excuse me. I'm going to check on the girls." He leaves the cup on the counter and walks out.

"We may need you both on the takedown," Olive Skin says. "Think you can handle that?"

"It would be my great pleasure," I say honestly.

"You're sure the demon's dead?" the other agent asks.

"She's gone. Do you guys fight a lot of demons?"

"Not often," George answers. "Last one was nine years ago. If you ever want a job…"

"I have several," I say with a smile before standing. "Alright, let me get the girls to the bus, and then I'll get you that list. Make yourselves at home." I leave the F.R.E.A.K.S. in my kitchen to fend for themselves and run upstairs. I feel a little better knowing they're here. If they can't nail her, nobody can. Adam closes the girls' door as I step into the hall. "They getting ready?"

"Yeah. You should probably talk to them. They're afraid those guys are here to arrest them for the love charm. I told them they weren't, but it'd be better coming from you."

I stop walking as I get a few feet away. That's close enough for now. "Okay. I will. Thanks."

"You're welcome," he says. "What now?"

I shrug. "We let them do their thing. Help when asked, I guess."

He takes a small step toward me. "And ... what about me? What do I do?"

You could kiss me. "What?"

"Well, your backup's here. You have several bodyguards. No need for me to stay."

"I ... " I don't know what to say. The thought of him leaving literally makes me sick to my stomach. "You—you promised you'd stay for the pageant. And my store is still a mess. You can't just leave it like that. You're not going anywhere." I nod and start walking past him. "Excuse me."

"Mona?"

"Yes?"

He grabs my wrist, spins me around, and pulls me toward him. I smash into his body, and before I stop moving, his lips are on mine. I'm surprised at first, but that lasts less than a blink. All of me grows gloriously warm and my knees go wobbly as we kiss. Just as soon as it began, he moves away, leaving a vacuum in his wake. Lips still parted, I look up through my lashes to his smiling face.

"Whatever you say," he says before kissing my nose. "Don't just stand there. We're going to be late." He steps toward his room, shutting the door behind himself.

I don't move for a few seconds, not until the feel of him on my lips vanishes. So much for pretending. I shuffle to my bedroom and quietly shut the door, resting my back against it with a sigh. A demon attack I can apparently handle, but a quick kiss from the man who loves me discombobulates me to the point where I can barely think. Those lips are dangerous. They make a lady forget herself and all logic, something this lady cannot afford to do.

But boy do I want to.

• *Go to work*

The squad is hard at work making a case. As I help customers, at least twice I see one or more men in suits I recognize driving or walking down Courtland Street. I only know this because I can't stop gazing out the window; the alternative view is far more distracting. The shelves are almost up, and I finish painting the window so I can keep my back to Adam as much as possible. The few times I've caught him gazing at me, or vice versa, our eyes lingered. I'm always the first to look away, embarrassed by the thoughts running through my head. We don't say a word, not a syllable since the squad left the house. The ride here was unbearable. I think he's waiting for me to make the next move. When I know what that is, I'll let him know.

Billie is running late, which means I'm running late too. Magda and her committee cronies are going to give me hell. With the window done, I flip through *Cosmo* impatiently as Adam puts up the last shelf. I glance up to see him smiling with self-satisfaction. I don't think I've seen a man who smiles so often, and each one of them is so full of glee and earnestness. A cock-eyed optimist. I guess people are attracted to their opposite. "Good job," I say. "It looks great."

He turns, and the smile grows. "Thank you. Is there anything else that needs fixing? I already took care of the floorboards and sink in the back."

"You've done more than enough," I say with a chuckle. "Thank you. I already feel like I've taken advantage of you."

"I have no problem with you taking advantage of me, Mona," he says as his smile grows mischievous. "As I remember, it was *quite* enjoyable."

I blush from the memories and look back at the magazine. "You know what I mean. I don't want to talk about that."

His smile wavers a little. "Not going to make this easy on me, are you?"

That's the problem. It's all too damn easy. I stand and turn around. "I'm going to check the online orders. Excuse me." I walk into the back and take a deep breath, letting it out slowly before I reach the desk. Damn it, Billie, get here before I lose my damn mind. I don't—

I sense him before I even spin around. By the time I do his arms are already around me, pulling me into him. Those delicious lips find mine, instantly matching his intensity on instinct. Oh … *mama.*

I press my body into his as his tongue parts my lips. He tastes good. Never tasted anything better. I swear he's drugged me. I'm already a damn addict. I clutch onto his back to anchor myself, as he does me. Something real and solid to keep us from being swept away. I barely notice my legs hit the altar as he backs me into it. As he lifts me onto it, his lips move to my ear, whispering, "See how easy this is," before trailing my neck with light kisses down to my collarbone. I go cross-eyed as he gives me a playful nibble. I wrap my legs around his waist, and his bulge bears down on my engorged nethers, sending me into frenzy. I hate clothes. We are never wearing them again. His mouth is on mine, giving me another fix, as his hand sneaks up my shirt to my breast. I groan, scraping my nails down his back. Heaven. We kiss and kiss, and rub and rub, and …

"Oh shit!"

I make the mistake of opening my eyes only to find Billie standing at the door, mouth agape. I didn't hear the bell. He has his hand under my shirt, and I've been writhing like a cat in heat. My legs drop, and I push Adam away, beyond mortified. "Um … " I say.

"Sorry to interrupt," Billie says through her chuckles. "Don't stop on my account."

I straighten my shirt and hop off the altar as Adam smoothes his hair. "We were just—"

"I can figure it out." She puts her purse on the hook. "Carry on," she quips as she leaves.

We're alone again. Not good. "I'm late," I mutter. I step toward the door and so does he. *Don't look at him.* "No. Stay. Just ... stay." I grab my purse and hightail it out of there. "Alice will be here in two hours. Call if you need me," I tell Billie as I rush out.

Air. Now that I'm outside I can breathe again. Through the window I see him step out of the back room, and I sprint down the sidewalk like a coward. At least I make it to the park faster. Things are shaping up here. Rides are being tested, the food is being brought in, and stuffed animals are being hung in the booths. The world carries on.

I find the overwhelmed mayor screeching into her cell phone about missing tables. I simply wave and rush off to find a task. Overseeing the setup of the stage for Sophie's show tonight will do. All thoughts of Adam are pushed aside as I decorate the replica of our town—well, most of the time. Bits of the scene on my altar flash through my mind, sending my body into a frenzy all over again. I just stop, close my eyes, and will the feelings away. I'm a master after so many years. About thirty minutes in, my cell buzzes. "Hello?"

"Where are you?" Tamara asks.

"The park by the stage. Why?"

"Oh, I see you." She hangs up. A second later I spot her coming my way. I walk off the stage as she reaches me. Before I say a word, she grabs my arm and pulls me away from the crowd. "The FBI just interviewed everyone at the diner about Cheyenne, and it's all over town they're here about her. What the hell is going on now?"

"They're the preternatural police. They're here to build a case. What did they ask?"

"Strange behavior, grudge against you, stuff like that. If she hasn't heard, she damn well will pretty soon. What if she tries to shoot you or something?"

"Then the squad will arrest her, and all will return to normal."

She puts her hand on her hip. "You should still have Adam with you just in case."

"That … is not a good idea," I say.

"Why the hell not? Let the man do what he came here for."

"I can't be around him right now, okay?"

"Why? Because you slept with him?" My mouth drops open. "Oh, save the protests. I saw the love bites, and I'd know the stink of your pregnancy protection potion anywhere. I didn't say anything yesterday because I know you're weird about sex stuff." She smiles. "Reprieve over. Was it good?"

I want to lie but can't keep it in anymore. "Fucking fantastic," I laugh. I take her hands and drag her even farther away. "It was incredible. One second I was crying, and the next we were attacking each other. It was like he knew what each inch of my body wanted."

"Oh, hon. I'm so happy for you. You had your first real orgasm."

"I had more than one," I chuckle. My smile fades. "But then I woke up the next morning and panicked. I didn't know what it all meant. Then … Tam, he says he's in love with me. He has been for years."

I expect surprise but no emotion surfaces. "So he finally told you, huh? Damn, I owe Debbie twenty bucks. I bet he'd tell you right before he left."

"*What?*" I ask, eyes bugging out of my head.

269

She laughs. "Come on. I had my suspicions from the start. We all did. I mean, why would a guy risk his life otherwise? And the way he looked at you. *Damn.* I'd give my right arm for a man to look at me like that again. Debbie and I got the truth out of him right after you left for the auction. We even convinced him to go, bid you away from that doctor, and confess his love right there. Did he tell you then, I mean before he died and all?"

"He told me last night."

"A whole day after you slept with him? Well, what'd you say?"

"I … what could I say?"

"Uh, how about, 'I love you too'? It's tried and true for a reason."

"But I don't … know if I do," I say weakly.

"Oh bull-fucking-shit girl. It's written all over your face, has been for days. You light up! It's adorable. Even Clay noticed for God's sake." She pauses. "He's a good man, Mona. He may not be a doctor, and he may turn furry once a month, but he loves you. Hell, I think he even loves those troublemakers of yours. He already proved he'd die for you. What more do you want?"

Oh fuck. No. No. *Yes,* that voice says inside my head. Oh shit. She's right. She is so right. It's been staring me in the damn face for days, but I just wouldn't open my eyes. I love him. I've fallen in love with him. Hell's bells. I should be happy, right? That's the appropriate response. Then why am I petrified?

"I have to get back to work," I say, stepping away.

"Mona, we are not done talking about this," she says, following me.

"Oh yes we are. I'm busy."

She takes my arm and swings me around. "You cannot bury your head in the sand this time. You can't. If you do, I guarantee you will live to regret it. This is a gift you've been given. True love is pretty fucking rare, don't throw it away cause you're scared. Sometimes things do work out the way we want them to. Real stories can have a happy ending. You just gotta have faith."

Faith. The word turns my stomach.

"I have to get back to work," I whisper. I rub her arm. "Thank you." This time she doesn't follow me.

Tamara's right about one thing: real stories can have happy endings. I just have no faith that mine is one of them. Faith. I used to be capable of it. Faith that Daddy would always be there. That Granny would pull through. That the universe would balance good and evil. Something can only let you down so much before you shun it, even hate it a little. Faith broke my heart and now it's knocking on my door, begging to be let in again. I just don't think I can turn that knob. Not for him. Not for anything. I just don't think I have it in me.

So that's that. The end.

· Emergency call

After the stage is dressed, I move onto stocking the game booths with fluffy bunnies and toy guns. Before I know it, it's one thirty and I'm starving. Time for a meal break. I start walking up the street when my cell buzzes. "Hello?"

"Mona, it's Collins. I need to talk to you," she says, sounding scared.

"What is it?"

"Cheyenne. I—I can't believe it."

"What happened?"

"Those agents came and interviewed Meemaw. She called me all upset, so I came over and ... I need to show you something."

"You're at Maxine's?" I ask, speed walking toward the shop.

"Yeah. Get here soon. Meemaw called Cheyenne, and she's on her way too. I have to go." She hangs up.

"Crap." I take off in a run to the shop. Alice is behind the counter helping a customer and Billie is replacing our stock on the new shelves when I rush in. "Adam?" I call.

"He's not here," Billie says. "He took off a few minutes after you."

"Shit. Did he take my car?"

"No. An SUV picked him up."

"Great." I run into the back, getting an athame and protection amulet before sprinting out of the shop toward the parking lot. When I get there, I peel out of the lot and down Courtland as I pull out my cell and call George, rattling out the facts and Maxine's address before hanging up. Adam's next. He deserves to be there for the take down.

"Hello?" he asks, with another man's voice in the background.

"It's Mona. Collins found something. I'm on my way to Maxine's now."

"I'm with the squad," he says through the pants. He's running. "We just heard. Wait for us to get there before you go in, okay?"

"How far are you?"

"Most of us are at the barn. Others might get there sooner. Just wait, okay? Please?"

"I'll try. Just get there."

I'm about to hang up but he says, "I love you."

"I lo—" I stop myself. "Bye." I hang up.

A minute later, I pull into Maxine's driveway, the only free space for blocks, and cut off the engine. There's no sign of Cheyenne. I beat her here. I guess now I wait. They better—

The front door is tossed open, and Maxine barrels out, scowling as usual. "You get the hell off my property, Mona McGregor!"

So much for waiting. I climb out of the car, all smiles. "Hello, Maxine."

The scowl grows. "Troublemaker! Liar! Get out of here!"

Collins steps out. "I called her, Meemaw."

"Collie, how dare you invite this viper here! You know what she's been saying!"

"With reason," Collins says. "Come in." I don't think I have a choice now. I walk up the driveway, past Maxine's death stare, into the house. It reeks of cigarette smoke and cat pee with shabby furniture scattered around. This must be where Cheyenne learned to decorate.

"Collins, what is going on?" Maxine asks.

Collins leads me into a small bedroom with only bunk beds and a small TV on a rickety stand. She immediately moves to the closet, bending down inside. "Cheyenne used to keep stuff Meemaw wouldn't like in here. Drugs, booze, you know." She pulls up a floorboard and extracts an athame, books, charm bags, potions, and a small notebook with red splotches on it. Blood. "I found this."

The books are worn, one on black magic, another on necromancy, and the last about demons with a page marked. Lilith's page. It gives her biography, powers, and there's even a picture of her in her true form with six breasts, fangs, and twisted body. Dang. The notebook is what really draws my attention. There are some pretty serious spells in here. Love potions, memory erase charms, hexes, spells to paralyze, raise the dead, kill, and raise a demon. "I leafed through it," Collins says. "I can't believe she would do this."

"Meemaw?" the wicked witch of Goodnight says in the front room before the door shuts. "Are you okay?" Crap. Adam, get your ass here *now*. I follow Maxine into the living room where Cheyenne stands. I take one step out of the door and our eyes lock, stopping me dead. "You bitch. Get out of here!"

I'm the bitch? My blood boils, and I have to fight the urge to leap across the room and slug her. "We found your secret stash."

"What the fuck are you talking about?" she asks.

"The notebook. The demonology book. I know you summoned Lilith."

"*What?*" she shrieks. "Notebook? What ... ? Meemaw?"

"My granddaughter would not do that," Maxine shouts. "You get out of my house!"

"Stop covering for her, Meemaw," Collins says behind me. I turn. She's almost next to me, leaning in the doorway. "You know she's a bad seed. Always was."

"Fuck you, Collins," Cheyenne spits. "You're just a jealous bitch." She glares at me. "Both of you. What, because your cousin would rather screw me than put his dick in your cobwebbed vag, you're framing me? Why the fuck would I summon a demon?"

"Because you want me dead, and you're too much of a coward to do it face to face. First you got Alejandro to do your dirty work, and when that failed, you brought in a demon!"

"My Cheyenne didn't do any of that," Maxine shouts. "You're crazy. Why would she?"

"Because she's tired of being the town whore," Collins says. "High Priestess has a better sound to it."

Cheyenne's eyes narrow. "What?" Her eyes dart behind me. "I don't—"

"Stop lying," Collins cuts in. "No one's buying your bullshit anymore. Goddess, are you so fucking dumb you don't get that?"

"Will you shut the fuck up!"

"It's over," Collins shouts. "Like everything else in your life, you've failed!"

"Shut up."

"Collins," I warn.

There's no stopping her. "You're not going to lie or fuck your way out of this one! You're going to prison for the rest of your miserable life!"

"What? No!" Cheyenne shrieks.

"They're gonna come here with guns ... "

"No," Cheyenne whimpers.

"Slap those cuffs on you ... "

"No ... "

"That's if they don't shoot your dumb ass on sight!"

"No!"

It's so tense in here the thump on the front door makes all four of us jolt and scream. Collins leaps behind me, pressing against my back and clutching onto my shirt for protection. I momentarily close my eyes, and when I open them across the room I see Cheyenne's hand raising out of her purse with something shiny. My instincts know what it is before my brain catches on because all my muscles clench. Oh hell. The small revolver points at me first, then Collins, then back to me as its owner breathes heavily, eyes bugging out of her head. "Nobody fucking move!"

"Cheyenne!" Maxine shouts.

"Don't move, Meemaw. I'm sorry," she says through the pants.

"Cheyenne, put the gun down," I say calmly. Collins clutches even harder.

"Shut up!"

"Cheyenne, the police were following you and agents are on their way. If they see you pointing that gun at us, they will shoot you on sight! Do you hear me?"

Her hands shake violently. "No, no," she whimpers.

"Right now all you are guilty of is attempted murder. If you kill one of us, that's murder. You will never get out. Is that what you want? Put the gun down."

"Put it down, doll," Maxine says. "She's right. Put it down."

With a whimper, Cheyenne's tear-filled eyes move to her grandmother's. She's still that scared, angry little girl I used to try to play dolls with twenty years ago. I think she might listen. She lowers the gun halfway, but then that pitiful gaze moves back to me and the fear morphs into anger as if a switch was flicked. "Stop looking at me like that."

I avert my eyes. "Sorry."

She's quiet for a second. "You ... " she whispers, *"you* did this!" she shouts. "You bitch! I fucking hate you!"

"Cheyenne ... " Collins says behind me.

"Fuck you!"

It's true: the world slows to a crawl when you're about to die. My cousin raises the gun again, and I can see the dust particles in the air shift in her wake like flakes of silver in the light. My brain works in overdrive trying to figure out a solution in the second before death. Rushing her, trying to grab the gun, just running are all discounted because of the distance. She's too close. I'm done. That's it. I'm going to die.

My eyes close, and my life flashes by like I was flipping through a picture book. Mommy pushing me and Ivy on swings. Us all dancing in our old living room, with Daddy dipping Mommy and kissing her nose. Mommy's coffin lowering into the ground as I held baby Debbie. The last time I saw Daddy as he waved goodbye from the driveway. The first time I saw Adam as he was walking inside a party with Jason, that bright smile turning to shock when he laid eyes on me. Granny and Papa doing dishes together side-by-side.

Cuddling with Debbie after Papa's funeral. Opening the front door and finding Ivy and the girls on my porch, all haunted by whatever they had just escaped. The first time Sophie hugged me after months of shrinking away from my touch. Adam gazing up at me the night of the auction as if I was the only woman in the universe. I stop there. That's the moment. That's the moment I fell in love with him. When he made me believe I was beautiful. It's the image I want to take with me. One brimming with love.

Okay. I'm ready.

"Excessum!"

My eyes fly open just in time to see Cheyenne's eyes roll back into their sockets and her body crumple to the carpet, the gun dropping beside her. What the … ? My head whips to my left where Collins's arm is still outstretched over my shoulder with her finger pointed right where her sister was. A curse. She cursed her. She's dead.

A bloodcurdling scream fills the room as Maxine falls to her knees beside her granddaughter, touching her dead skin. I spin around. A trembling Collins is staring at her sister in disbelief. "I had to," she whispers. "I had to. It was the only one I remembered from the notebook."

I take her in my arms, hugging her tight. She doesn't respond. "It's okay. It'll all be okay." I lead Collins past the sobbing Maxine and out the front door. Away from the crime scene. We make it all the way to the sidewalk when the police car down the street starts its engine and guns toward us. The Gardenia Sheriff's Department will not be getting a donation from me this year, that is for damn sure. Two dark SUVs also round the corner, reaching us a few seconds after the police get out of their cruiser. "She's in shock," I tell the police as I help Collins sit on the curb.

"Mona?" Adam shouts. He bounds out of the barely stopped SUV and starts running toward me. I leap up and do the same, all but crashing into his open arms. I close my eyes and savor this. His wonderful smell, his beating heart, those arms that hold me tight enough to believe as long as they're around me nothing bad can touch me. That I am loved. "Baby, are you okay? What happened?" he asks desperately.

"Cheyenne's dead. She was going to shoot me, but Collins stopped her."

"What?"

"Just hold me, okay? Don't let me go."

He showers kisses all over my face. "Never. *Never.*"

I believe him.

· Go home

He's as good as his word. Adam doesn't leave my side as the circus unfolds around us. Maxine has to be sedated and taken to the hospital. After giving her statement, Collins goes with her grandmother. I don't think I'll be welcome there, so I call Debbie to meet Collins. She'll need someone by her side now. The four F.R.E.A.K.S. agents collect all the evidence, snap a few pictures, load up Cheyenne's body, and drive off to sort out this mess. I give my statement to a short man wearing gloves, and they allow Adam to drive me home. The end of the nightmare. He's been glancing at me with worried eyes the whole time, but it gets worse in the car. Maybe I'll break down later, but right now I'm just tired. So tired. I could sleep for a week.

When he pulls into my driveway, Auntie Sara rushes out of her house. The news has spread like a virus. "Are you okay?" she asks as I get out of the car.

"I wasn't hurt. I'm fine."

"Is she really dead? Did Collins really kill her? What—"

"Sara," Adam snaps, "leave her alone. Now."

Her mouth shuts. "Well, then. Sorry."

I muster a smile and round the car over to them. "It's okay."

"I'm going to take Mona inside to lay down," Adam says. "The bus will be here soon. Can you get the girls from the bus stop for us?"

"Of course."

Adam nods, slips his arm around my waist, and we start walking toward the house. It's quiet inside. I used to love the quiet, now it just feels aberrant. Life should not be quiet. It should be filled with laughter and music and conversation. I'll never take those for granted again. Our footsteps on the steps and then the hallway fill the void, as does the Captain's meow when we trudge into the bedroom. I crawl in beside him on the bed and run my fingers through his fur. "Good boy."

Adam lingers by the door, fidgeting and glancing around the room. "Do you need anything? Water, or—"

"Can you just hold me a little longer?"

"I … of course." He kicks off his shoes and climbs into bed, spooning me, while one arm rests on my waist and the other under my head. I wrap my fingers in his, bringing his arm up to nuzzle against. We just lay like this for a minute, his breath tickling the back of my neck. "Are you okay?"

I snuggle closer. "Am now."

He's quiet again, and then says, "I'm so sorry."

"About what?"

"I should have been there. I failed. Again."

"You're here now. I need you more right now than I did then. I don't need grand gestures, and I don't need rescuing. I need this. *This.* No one can do it but you."

"I—"

"Don't talk anymore, please. Just … let's have this moment, okay? Where there's nothing but you and me. No past, no future, no coven, no pack. No murderer, nothing in this universe but us and how this feels." I think I can feel him smile.

He holds me, occasionally kissing the back of my neck for I don't know how long. Time has no place here. I savor each second, banking them away like precious jewels so I'll always remember the first time in my life where I was well and truly happy. Where faith won.

• *Go to the pageant*

I fight sleep as long as possible, wanting this to never end, but it sweeps over me far too soon. I wake with a start alone in my bed. The house is still, and it's dark outside. The clock reads 6:30 p.m. Crap, the pageant. Double crap. My car is gone. I have to walk. I quickly change into a burgundy sweater and sneakers before running out. It's a beautiful night in the low sixties without clouds to hide the few stars already out. It feels good to walk. I should do it more often, maybe get Auntie Sara to come with me. The pounds would melt off. Have a reason to care now.

It takes me twenty minutes to get to the park. I'm always amazed how well things come together. Happy families walk around stuffing their faces with sweets while others chat with their neighbors. Oldies play over the loudspeaker as the rides twirl. I don't even care that people keep giving me sideways glances as I pass. I even see a few members of the F.R.E.A.K.S. walking around. The teenager with bangs walks arm in arm with a blind man while the man with gloves trails behind eating cotton candy. They've earned some fun. I don't stop to say hello as I spot a grinning Clay and Bethany at the ring toss. He misses. "Shoot."

"It's okay," Bethany says, touching his arm. Even from several feet away I can see him blush.

"Hey, guys," I say.

The moment I stop moving, Clay pulls me into a tight hug. "Oh my God. Are you okay?"

"I'm fine. Not even a bruise." He releases me. "It's over."

"I can't believe it was Cheyenne," Bethany says. "How's Collins?"

"I called Debbie on the walk over. She's with her. She's holding up pretty well. Collins is a strong girl; she'll be fine with time."

"Poor thing," Bethany says. "I can't even imagine it."

"Oh my God!" I hear Tamara shout. She all but body blocks people out of her way to get to me. I get another bear hug. "I heard! Are you okay?"

I pull away to breathe. "I'm fine. Little shaken. I really don't want to talk about it yet. I'm still … processing."

"Of course," Clay says, "but if you need us, we're here."

Tamara hugs me again. "I'm just so glad you're okay."

"Thanks." I pull away. "Have you guys seen the girls or Adam?"

"Yeah, they're over by the stage," Clay says.

"Thanks. Have fun, okay?"

A few people stop me and try to get the gory details while feigning concern, but I quickly excuse myself. I want Sophie to know I'm here cheering her on before she goes up there.

Inside the tent there are about thirty kids all dressed in costumes ranging from pilgrims to dance leotards. Pilgrim Sophie is off to the side with tutued Melody Yates playing cat's cradle. She glances up, shocked to see me. "Aunt Mona! You came!"

I scoop her up, giving her a huge hug. "Of course I came. I wouldn't miss this for anything." I release her. "You look so authentic! Are you nervous?"

"Not really," she lies. "Are you okay? Adam told us what happened."

"I'm okay. Really, I'm okay. It's all over, honey. No one's gonna hurt us again."

She nods. "Good."

"No parents backstage!" one of the teachers shouts.

Ugh. "I better go find a place to watch. You're gonna be great." I kiss her. "Break a leg."

Parents are beginning to assemble near the stage as Magda and the A/V tech check the microphones. Adam isn't among them. They're not at games or rides, so I stroll over to the concession area, and there they are. My family. Adam hands Auntie Sara and Cora corndogs with a smile. I really do love that smile of his. It brings one to my face and makes me tingly at the same time. He says something to Cora, who giggles, then he looks up and spots me. Our smiles grow in time to each other. But his falls a second later.

"Mona?" a man asks behind me.

I turn around and, to my surprise, find Guy standing there. Strange, but I feel nothing. Not lust, not anger, nothing. "Hello, Dr. Sutcliffe."

"I, uh, heard what happened today. I was at the hospital when Collins arrived. I'm glad to see you're alright."

"Thank you. It's been quite a week."

"Yes," he says, looking over my shoulder toward Adam. "I'm happy to see your cousin is doing well too. It was a miraculous recovery."

"He's not really my cousin."

"Oh." We're quiet for a few seconds as he gathers strength. "Well, I just wanted to … I've had time to get over my understandable shock and reflect on my behavior that night."

"Good for you."

"Yeah, I just wanted to apologize. I was … unnecessarily cruel, and you didn't deserve that. I'm sorry."

"I accept. I hope there weren't any after effects, dreams and whatnot. If there are, they should fade in a week or two. The girls have been punished."

"Good." He pauses. "I am sorry. You *are* a wonderful woman."

"I know. See you around!" With a hop in my step, I turn around and walk over to my inquisitive family. Cora barrels through the crowd as a glaring Adam follows behind her. "Hi!" Cora runs into my arms, and I sweep her up. "Oh, I love you sweetie pie!"

"I love you too, Aunt Mona. Adam bought me a corndog, but I'm not allowed cotton candy. I can have some if you say I can. He did win me a goldfish! Can I keep him? His name is Nemo, like the movie. Auntie Sara has him in her purse. I love him."

"Of course you can keep him. Just don't let the Captain get jealous."

"I won't." She pauses for a breath. "Are you mad we didn't wake you up? Adam said not to."

I glance at Adam, who shrugs. "No, it was the exact right thing to do."

"Attention, please," Magda says over the loudspeaker. "We are about to begin the festival pageant. Please join us by the stage on the south side of the park. Thank you."

"Guess we better get over there," I say as I put Cora down. She runs a little ahead with us adults following behind. I smile at Adam. "Thank you for bringing them."

"You're welcome," he says. "What did the doctor want?"

"To apologize."

"Oh. Good." He pauses. "I still think I should kick his ass."

"He's not worth it. Never was."

We join the crowd beside Tamara's family, Clay, and Bethany. Tamara eyes Adam and me with a sly smile. I pretend not to notice. Magda walks onstage a minute later and after a speech about what a success the week has been, she thanks the committee and we all applaud. "I can't see," Cora says.

"We'll fix that," Adam says. He picks her up, placing her on his shoulders like a few of the other fathers before taking the video camera from Auntie Sara and starting to film. Anyone looking at us right now would think we were just like everyone else. A family. A week ago he wasn't here. He was on the fringes of my life, seen but unseen. Now…

As the opening act, Miss Blanchard's dance class, taps across stage, I keep stealing glances at the smiling werewolf who is too busy channeling Spielberg to notice. When the dance is over, the parents applaud as the pilgrims filter onstage. Sophie stands in the back clutching onto her skirt for dear life. Adam's smile grows when he sets eyes on her. The time comes for Sophie's first line, and she delivers it like a pro. Adam's smile matches my own. It's so full of pride it all but explodes out of him. If I didn't know he wasn't her real father the thought would never cross my mind. It moves me to no end. He must feel me staring because he looks at me, still beaming. His smile wavers from confusion as he studies my awed face. He's about to ask me what's wrong, but I smile and slip my hand into his. His brow furrows as he looks down at our hands, then back up at me for verification that this is real. My tear-filled eyes express the words I haven't managed to get out yet. His say the same thing. We hear Sophie's next cue and both turn back to the performance to support the family. Our family.

Hand in hand.

· *Get everyone to bed*

Adam carries the sleeping Cora through the front door with Sophie and I behind. Silently he passes her off to me, and I give him Nemo's bag before starting up the stairs. We're all pooped. As I put her sister to bed, Sophie changes into her pajamas and crawls into bed too. Showers can wait until morning. I tuck our star in, giving her a quick kiss. "I am so proud of you," I whisper.

"Was I good? Really?" Sophie whispers back.

"The best up there. No question," I say with a grin.

She smiles back then looks away. "I was really scared. I almost didn't go on."

"But you did. You didn't let fear stop you. You're a brave girl. Never had any doubt." She still won't look at me. "What is it?"

"Were you scared? Today?"

I sit on her bed. "Yeah. A lot. But it's all over now."

She nods, pausing for a few seconds, then says, "Does that mean Adam's leaving?"

"Why? I thought you hated him."

She shrugs. "He's okay."

"Would you like him to stay?"

"I don't know. I guess. You smile a lot around him."

"Do I?"

His ears must be burning as the man himself walks into the room, carrying a vase with our newest member Nemo floating in it. She's right: one look and I'm beaming. "This is all I could find," he whispers. He sets the vase on Cora's nightstand. "Welcome home, Nemo." He looks at us. "I'll leave you ladies alone."

He's about to leave when Sophie whispers, "Adam?"

"Yeah?"

"Thank you."

He winks. "Anything for one of my favorite people, doll face. You were great tonight. Sleep tight." He walks out.

I turn back to my smiling niece and kiss her forehead. "I love you." I kiss her again. "Dream only good dreams." I stand up and walk out. Adam's leaning against the wall in the hallway smirking when I step out. I walk over to him, take his hand, and lead him down the stairs. "Come on. We can still watch the fireworks from the porch."

The street is bustling with families walking or driving home from the park. They smile and nod, and we reciprocate as we lower ourselves onto the porch swing. As if he's been doing it for years, he drapes his arm around me, pulling me toward him. I cuddle close and rest my head on his shoulder. The Jordans next door eye us as they pass. "I think I'm ruining your reputation," Adam says with a grin.

"Thank the goddess for that," I say as I snuggle closer. We sit like this for a minute, just rocking. "Sophie wants you to stay."

We rock for a few seconds before he says, "What do you want?"

"I want ... to not need you."

"What?"

I sigh. "This is so easy. You and me. You fit so seamlessly into my life, like a peg in a hole I never knew existed. Now it's filled ... you have the potential to break my heart so thoroughly nothing could repair it. The thought of you leaving ... never coming back ... " I shake my head. "A big part of me can't believe this is happening. I'm not sure I can trust it."

"I know," he whispers. "I'm sitting here with you in my arms, like I've imagined a million times, and it still doesn't feel real." He pauses. "It is, isn't it? You haven't said."

I sit up and look at him square in the eye. "Before we do this, and there's no going back, I need to set a few things straight. I'm not a teenager. I have massive baggage. I have a house and a shop that is always a hair's breadth from going into the red."

"Then I guess I'll have to pass the state licensing board and be a contractor here. Shouldn't be too hard. Two incomes are better than one."

"I only have a few years before middle age hits. I'm just gonna get fatter and grayer. My granny had facial hair too."

"Baby, I almost threw you to the floor when you had green gunk and hair dye on. I don't think me wanting you is ever going to be a problem."

My scowl deepens. "Okay, how about this? My sister is bound to crawl out from under her rock and try to get those girls back, and there is no way in hell I am giving them to her. It will get ugly."

His smile drops like a ton of bricks. "I will fight to my dying breath for them. Anyone who wants them is going to have to get through me. I promise you that."

"Well, what about—"

He takes my hands in his. "Listen, just stop, okay? I know all of this. I know you're scared. I'm scared too. I know what loving you will cost me. It's been drilled in my head for eighteen years, and I have fought against this very situation every one of those days. But after one week with you, with those girls, seeing how strong and smart and caring you are with everyone, I just know ... no matter what life tosses at us, I want you by my side. And I can't promise it's all going to be easy for either of us. I can be damn stubborn, and territorial, not to mention the whole werewolf factor, which is going to be a bigger problem than you realize. I just … I can't not wake up next to you, and dance with you, and … and … you make me smile just by being in the same room. You make me *happy*. Happier than I ever thought I could be. And I can't promise we won't fight, and we won't drive each other crazy, but I can promise I will always be there when you need me. Through thick, through thin, through sickness and health, through crazy relatives, and burst pipes, and whatever else life throws at us. Because I love you. Always have. Always will."

I'm speechless as tears stream down my face. I close my eyes and shake my head. This is it. He's it. I take a deep breath, open them again, and grin. Here we go. "In that case, Adam Blue, I would like to extend you membership into the McGregor pack of Goodnight, Virginia. We can offer you residence in a creaky old house, nosy and sometimes homicidal neighbors, and the deep, unwavering love of the town spinster until your dying day. What do you say?" I extend my hand. "You in?"

He glances at my hand, then slyly smiles. He shakes my hand with a nod. "All the way, baby." He draws me into him, kissing me with all his considerable worth before I lead him inside and up to our bedroom to seal the deal all night.

The fireworks outside ain't got nothing on the ones we have in here.

SATURDAY TO DO:

- *Wake up in Adam's arms*
- *Try not to think about Jason coming*
- *Agendas for meetings (type/print)*
- *Put together packet for coven meeting*
- *Send Auntie Sara to printers with documents*
- *Coven meeting*
- *Co-op meeting*
- *Decide on outfit for wedding tomorrow*
- *Check on Collins*

GODDESS IS HE SEXY. I don't think there's a thing about him that doesn't do something for me. I love his lips, how the lower one is plumper than the top, his curling eyelashes, even his ears. I've never seen such perfect ears before. I kind of wish Cheyenne was still alive so I could thank her for trying to kill me. If she hadn't I would have just let him pass me by, a need that never got filled because I didn't even know I needed it so bad.

We lay in bed, naked limbs entangled. I could definitely get used to this, waking up with the man I love. Though I have to pee. Real bad. I know, I'll get up and make him breakfast in bed. I quietly toss the covers to the side when his hand clamps on my wrist and he yanks me back on top of him. "Can't get away from me that easily," he says before planting a kiss on my lips.

We flip over so he's pinning me. "I was going to make you breakfast."

He kisses down my neck, sending pleasant shivers all over. "There's only one thing I feel like eating right now," he whispers as the kisses go lower.

I giggle as his lips move south of the equator. I can *definitely* get used to this.

Just as he's reached his destination, there's a knock on the door. "Aunt Mona? It's past ten," Cora says on the other side. She tries to open the door, but it's locked.

"Crap," I mutter. "Be out in a minute." I gaze down at Adam and pout. "Welcome to your new life."

He smiles that smile of his and moves up to kiss me. "Rain check."

The girls are in the kitchen with bowls of cereal watching TV when I come in. I glare and shut it off. "Care to make it *two* months?"

Adam follows a second later with a spring in his step. He kisses my neck as I pour coffee. "And how are we all this gorgeous Saturday morning?"

"You just kissed her!" a wide-eyed Cora says.

"That I did," Adam says. "You want one too?" She grins and nods. He walks over and smooches the top of her head as she giggles. He moves over to Sophie with a quick peck to her head too. "Figured I'd complete the whole set."

"Cereal okay?" I get two bowls and Raisin Bran before sitting. "You girls sleep well?"

"Your music woke me up, but I fell back asleep," Cora says.

I turned on a CD to mask our adult noises. Adam and I exchange a guilty glance. "Sorry, sweetie."

"Why were you listening to music so late? Could you not sleep?" Cora asks.

"They were having sex and didn't want us to hear," Sophie informs her.

"Sophie!" I say in shock.

"What? You were."

"We—I—you—" I stammer.

"It's not polite to talk about things like that," Adam instructs her. She shrugs. "Oh sorry."

"Are you going to be our new Daddy? Are you two getting married? Can I be your flower girl too? Am I getting a baby cousin? Do we have to move?" Cora rapidly fires.

"Hold your horses," I say. "No one is getting married or pregnant. Yet."

"But eventually yes," Adam says to me.

"Let's be a couple for more than twenty-four hours before we have this conversation, okay?" I ask with a chuckle. "But the answer to your last question is no. We're not moving."

"You're living with us?" Sophie asks.

His smile wavers at this thought for a second, but then he says, "Looks that way. That is, if it's okay with you two. We want your blessing. Think you can stand to have me around?"

Cora leaps out of her seat and runs to Adam, throwing her arms around him. "I love you."

He hugs and kisses her, closing his eyes for a second to relish this. "Love you too, kiddo." He looks at Sophie. "Sophie?"

She studies his face, looking for subterfuge, but when she doesn't find it, she shrugs. "I don't care."

Knowing that's the equivalent of Cora's reaction, he smiles. "Thank you."

"Okay, then. That's settled," I say, though I feel like breaking into song. I take a bite of cereal. "So I don't have to do anything until two. What should we do until then?"

We all glance at each other. "I have an idea," Adam finally says. "You gals ever go fishing?"

· *Teach the girls to fish*

I know the perfect spot, the same place Mommy and Daddy took us when Ivy and I learned to fish. Being girls never stopped Daddy from teaching us guy things like how to throw a punch or play baseball, or, heck, even shoot. Fishing was my least favorite of these pastimes because I never caught a thing. Ivy did every time. She so cheated.

The girls officially inherit our old poles that have been stashed in the attic for years. As Adam shows them the proper way to cast off on the riverbank, I clean up our lunch under the same tree from my childhood and field my seventh phone call in the last hour. "Didn't anyone get the damn e-mail? It's at the playhouse like always. Just bring questions, okay? I gotta go." I hang up on Julie-Ann and lay on the blanket with a sigh. So much for relaxing. I barely have time to sigh before it rings again. "Mona here."

"Mona, it's Debbie," she says, voice panicky.

"What is it? Is Collins okay?"

"She's fine. She still wants to be in the wedding, can you believe it? No, it's everything else! I know all you've been through, but I am freaking out! The bow ties for the groomsmen are white, not ivory, so they clash with the boutonnieres. Seven of Greg's relatives just today RSVP'd so I have to re-do the seating charts. Both Becca and Kaylee hooked up with the best man and now they won't be in the same room! The DJ just cancelled because his father had a heart attack, and I just realized I don't have anything blue! What am I going to do? I'm hyperventilating."

"Calm down for one," I say with an eye roll. I have been dealing with wedding crap for six months. Everything is a crisis. "It'll work itself out. Jocasta can handle it." Adam strolls up, face scrunched in confusion. I roll my eyes again. "You just—"

Adam swipes the phone from me. "Debbie? It's Adam. How are you? Look, I am holding your sister hostage right now. You will get her back at two o'clock. Do not call unless someone is bleeding, okay? Bye." He hangs up. "I'm turning this thing off. The world will not end if you fall off the grid for a few hours." He tosses the phone on the grass and lowers that gorgeous bod beside mine. "Come here." We lie down, and I rest my head on his chest. We just remain like this amid the swaying grass, watching Sophie and Cora casting off for a few minutes. My tension dissipates with each beat of his heart, and soon I have never felt so serene in my life. My eyes start leaking. "Baby, why are you crying?"

"Because this is really happening," I say with a chuckle. "I'm happy. Really happy."

"Well, get used to it."

I smile and wipe my tears before gazing up at him. "I love you."

"God, I love you too," he says intensely. His lips press against mine in a hungry kiss.

We make out with abandon for a few seconds until I hear, "Eww, they're kissing," from the riverbank. "Impressionable children here!"

"So don't look!" Adam shouts back. "Keep fishing!" He kisses me again.

"Gross," Sophie says. "I think that's against the law."

Adam and I chuckle and shake our heads. "Sure we can't give them away?" he asks.

"This is boring, Adam! Do we have to do this?" Cora shouts.

"I could be convinced," I chuckle. He rolls off me, still smiling. I sit up. "Consider this part of your punishment!" I call over.

"You are *evil*," Adam says.

I kiss him. "Diabolical." And we're off again, traumatizing the youth of Virginia with our PDA.

The buzzing on *his* belt breaks the lust spell. Shit. He pulls the phone off and looks at the display. Double shit. I thought we had a few more hours. His face falls. "It's Jason."

My heart seizes. "Are you going to answer it?" His brow furrows, and I read the indecision in his eyes. No. *No.* Not now. I can't face this now. "Don't."

Years of obedience overshadow my protest. He accepts the call. "Jason, hey. What's up?" He listens. "Have a good drive down? Who's with you?" He laughs. "Really? That's great!"

I remove myself from our oasis. I really don't want to hear this. I look to the girls and start walking as he continues talking. For some reason my hands are trembling. I ball them into fists, though I smile at the girls. "Catch anything yet?"

"Do we have to do this? It's so boring!" Cora whines.

"Who's Adam talking to?" Sophie asks.

"His pack leader."

"He looks happy," she says.

I turn around. Adam is pacing and nodding as he laughs. My stomach clenches again, but I keep my smile. "Yes, he does."

He hangs up a few seconds later. The smile he has wavers a little when he notices us staring. That waver scares me more than being held at gunpoint. "Sorry about that," he says as he saunters toward us. "Catch anything yet?"

"No," Cora says. "This is stupid."

Yes, our fairy tale lunch is more than over. "I'm ready to go too."

"Yeah," Adam says. "Okay, fishing lesson over. Let's head back." The girls hand him the poles and race to the car, leaving us to pick up after them. As I'm folding the blanket he says, "Aren't you going to ask?"

"Okay. What did Jason want?"

"He's swinging by the house at one."

"Oh. That should be interesting." I pause. "You've missed them, haven't you?"

He studies my poker face. "Hey." He wraps his arm around me and brings me in close before giving me one of those soulful kisses I'm now addicted to. "I love you."

"I know. I love you too," I say with a half smile before walking away.

That bitch faith better not let me down this time.

· *Coven and co-op meetings*

I have a trillion things to do with the coven and co-op meetings tonight, but I can't get in the right mindset. I try to type the agendas at the dining room table as the girls staple packets together, but can't stop looking at the clock. It's five past one, and he still hasn't arrived. Auntie Sara glances at me. I've bitten my lip for so long it's raw. "Mona Leigh, are you okay? Are you having the PTSD?"

"The what? No, I'm fine." The knock on the door proves otherwise. I jerk and leap up. Oh hell. "Excuse me."

Get a hold of yourself. Show no fear because you should have none. He loves me. He wants to be here with me. He's not going anywhere. I have … faith. I square my shoulders before opening the door. Jason and the same two wolves that showed up Sunday to cart Adam away stand there with the same scowls. "Mona," Jason says.

"Nice to see you," I say icily.

"You as well," he says, voice like stone. "I'm glad your troubles have ended. You must be relieved."

"I am, thank you." We stand in silence, more or less glaring at each other. I know this is a challenge and his wolf wants to go for my jugular, but I don't look away.

We both turn when Adam walks down the steps. "Hey, guys!" I step aside to let the men in. The underlings, one in his mid-twenties with thick brown hair and the other thin as a rail and pale, do that whole bro-hug thing as the girls watch.

"You ready to go?" Jason asks gruffly.

"Where's he going?" Cora asks.

"I'm just going to visit with my friends," Adam says. "I'll be back." Jason scowls at this response but when Adam gives me a peck it deepens. "See you tonight."

He steps toward the men again but I grab him by the collar, kissing him with my all. He returns my passion with abandon. Neither of us can breathe when we break apart. "See you tonight."

Now all the men are scowling. Adam walks out with them, but Jason turns around and says, "See you at the meeting."

"Can't wait," I say with a smirk. I shut the door in his face. "Jerk."

"He's coming back, right?" Sophie asks.

"He said he was," I say. I compose myself and turn around. "Come on. Lots to do."

I field more phone calls from witches and people in the co-op, but my mind isn't on the task. Every five seconds I think, "What are they doing?" or "What if he decides to leave?" This is one of the reasons I hate relationships, they make me nuts and an ineffective leader. At least I get through to Debbie, who has since calmed down. I'm being a crappy mother of the bride. I should be by her side putting out fires. I'm useless today.

Keeping busy is key, and in that regard I'm lucky. Pressing supernatural matters abound. I have to appear strong, capable, focused or I'll lose all their respect. If they knew my hands were trembling as I fold Adam's clothes before putting them in my bedroom, they'd never take me seriously again. Faith, Mona. Faith. When we finally arrive at the playhouse with *The Crucible* set still up, it's as if a switch is flicked, and I'm all business. This is my domain. They need me, and I will not let them down.

At four thirty, my witches start arriving. Auntie Sara and Billie hand out the agenda and packets as they walk in. I wait backstage with the girls as the cacophony of voices grows louder by the minute. I'm a tad nervous but when five rolls around faster than I wish it to, I push the nerves down and walk onto that stage with my head up. I scan the audience. Erica is in the third row, typing on her iPhone. Bethany talks with Dickie a few rows back. No Collins or Debbie.

"Good evening and thank you all for coming," I begin. "Before I start, I feel I must address yesterday's events. Since it is still an open case, I cannot say much except it appears that Cheyenne Bell was the one who summoned the demon. When confronted, she grew violent and ... died. I also understand there is a rumor going around that she summoned it to cause me harm. To save her family further grief, I will not comment on this. I will simply say…we all have our demons, pun intended. Some are simply stronger than others. What happened was a tragedy, and I can only pray we learn from it and grow stronger as a community. As a family. Because that is what we are."

I sigh. "This week has been trying. We've faced elements few have, and we made it through by sticking together, looking after one another. I just want to thank each and every one of you for that. This is what makes us great. This is what makes us a force to be reckoned with. This is what makes me so proud to be your leader. *Thank you.*"

The audience burst into applause. Even Erica seems impressed.

"Now, if you please, turn to the first page of your packets. I have received many requests for additional protection charms and spells. Let's go over some."

I spend half an hour going over spells, then forty minutes answering questions or concerns about demons and black magic. A few attempt to get details about Cheyenne, but I evade. All in all it's a good meeting, though I'm glad I won't have to have another for a few weeks until we celebrate the Sabbat Beltane. I have to spend another ten minutes being fawned over and asked a dozen times if I'm alright before I have no choice but to excuse myself. One down. Now I have all of ten minutes to eat and change for the co-op summit at City Hall.

When we walk in the door at home, I half expect to find Adam in the kitchen, but the house is empty. Not even a message. Okay, now I'm just kind of pissed. He has to know I'm worried. Whatever. I rush around the house eating my tuna fish sandwich, collecting my papers for the meeting. Since I'm about to walk into a room with the scariest creatures on the planet, and these summits usually end with screaming or the occasional fist fight, I need to look serious. I change into my only black suit and put my hair in a French twist. Time to play with the big boys.

Auntie Sara watches the girls, and I drive to City Hall. There are a few cars and even limos in the parking lot. I roll my eyes: vampires. No sign of Jason's SUV. I hurry to find two thirds of the co-op members have arrived. It's mostly vampires who like to use this summit to suck up to the F.R.E.A.K.S. and witches from their areas. Per usual there is a bloodsucking crowd around George. All look like they belong in magazines with perfect figures and glossy hair. Lord Thomas, dressed in a white Armani suit that elongates his short frame, isn't playing. He sits at the table looking bored. The vampire gives me a long, respectful nod that I suppose concludes our involvement, then returns to his cuticles. Jerk. I work the room, speaking mostly to the other High Priestesses who are not being flirted with by vampires. I barely pay attention, nodding and smiling seems to placate them, keeping my eyes on the door. A few lone psychics and vampires come in, but no werewolves.

As I'm listening to the Priestess of Chicago complain about the weather, I glance back for the millionth time just as the werewolf contingent walks in. Jason scowls but Adam grins at me. I want to run over and leap into his arms, but that would be unprofessional. Instead I excuse myself, yank down my suit jacket, and stroll over to the men. "Thought you weren't going to make it."

"We lost track of time," Adam says with a half smile. He wraps his arm around my waist and kisses my cheek. "Hey."

The other three men's eyes narrow. "We better get our seats," Jason says.

As they move to the table, I back Adam through the door, pull him to the side in the hallway, and kiss him as if we've been separated for a decade. Chuckling from the door makes me pull away. We just smile as the Lord of D.C. walks into the conference. "There goes my rep."

"I missed you too," he says.

"Did you ... enjoy yourself?"

"Yeah. We went and got lunch at this barbeque place and ate the place out. Then we went for a run," he chuckles, "and I ended up getting into a wrestling match with Rory. Then we went for drinks, which is why we're late."

Here I thought Jason was all brawn and no brains. He played this beautifully, giving Adam all that I can't. Familiarity, male bonding, kinship. The light in Adam's eyes stings my heart. "I'm glad you had fun," I say with a fake smile.

"It was a great sendoff," he says, kissing my forehead.

One of the F.R.E.A.K.S. agents, I think his name's Chandler, steps into the hallway. "George wants to begin."

"Thanks," I say. The man nods his head and walks in. "Time to be diplomatic."

George, Lord Peter of D.C., Jason, and I, as the founding members or their successors, sit at the head of the table while the others sit along the columns with their attendants sitting in chairs behind them. George begins by giving crime statistics, talking a little about the cases the squad handled this year. Zombies, vampires, trolls, wraiths, and even a rogue pack of werewolves. I helped with that last one. A few vampires raise their hands to ask questions about the law, covering their own butts, but I'm too busy taking notes and trying to ignore the glares coming from the werewolf on my right. George finishes with his report, and it's my turn. I address the questions and comments sent in, and the applicable person answers. Finally, Jason takes a break from glaring at me to glare at everyone else as he spends two minutes filling us in on werewolf news. Short and sweet.

We break after that for a few minutes, per usual. Next the peanut gallery gets to speak. As I'm standing, a tight vise grips my elbow. "I need to speak with you in private," Jason growls.

Crap. This should be fun. "Of course."

We take a few steps before Adam approaches. "What's going on?"

"It's fine," I say.

Adam looks at Jason. "What are you doing?"

"Do not question me, Beta," Jason snaps. "You haven't left yet."

I can see the struggle in his eyes. He wants to obey his Alpha as he always has, but he wants to protect me too. It's killing him he can't do both. Oh hell. "Adam, really it's okay," I say, saving him. "I can take him." I look up at the seething werewolf. "Outside."

Adam doesn't move as I yank my arm from the Alpha's grip and walk out with Jason behind me. The moment the front door shuts, Jason asks, "You saw it too, didn't you?"

I spin around. "You're an asshole, you know that? *You're* the one doing this to him, and you have for eighteen fucking years! A good friend, a *true* friend, would be happy, not threatening to kick him out of the family."

"In this case I cannot be his friend, I must be his Alpha. I have an entire pack to consider. There are rules and safeguards for a reason. I cannot break them. Not for him, not for anyone."

"I'm your ally! I helped you and the pack many times without question. Did it ever cross your mind that these hypothetical children we may or may not have might be good for the pack?"

The hard exterior cracks just a smidge. "As a matter of fact, it did. I have broached the subject to the other two Alphas on more than one occasion, and I have been shot down every time. It would set precedence, and it would only take one to topple us all. If I could make an exception, I would."

I hug myself. I'm losing. "This is wrong, Jason. It's unfair."

He nods. "I know that. If there was anything I could have done, I would have by now. Despite appearances, I do like you. More, I respect you and under other circumstances I'd be honored to have you in my pack. It cut me deep every time I saw him looking at you all these years, knowing what it was costing him. I can sympathize in ways you can't fathom. That's why I gave him the week."

"That was nice of you."

"It was fair of me. I didn't think it would work. You're a hard woman, Mona. A lot like me in most respects. All business, pragmatic, keeping emotion out of the equation. I should have known better. Love ... there is nothing more powerful in this universe."

"Yeah." I sigh. "Where is this going, Jason? What do you want from me?"

"I want you to give *me* a week. If half of what he's told me about the past week is true, then you've been through hell together. It's been constant intensity and danger. I know from experience how those two elements can draw people together. How they can make you do something you swore you'd never do. But you're still in that bubble. You both need time to think and reflect because if you're wrong about this, about how you feel, you've ruined his life. Once he leaves the pack, I can't take him back." He steps toward me. "I'm asking you to be smart. Be sure. If it's meant to be, it will be."

I stand as still as a corpse as those words sink in. There isn't time. Chandler steps out, telling us we're back in session. Like a zombie I follow Jason back in. The other two wolves are making Adam smile with conversation when we enter. Adam puts one, I think Rory, into a headlock and gives him a noogie. When he sees us, he releases his friend, and the smile drops. I half smile to reassure him but hold up my hand to stop him from coming over. He gets too close to me and all logic fades.

Needless to say I barely pay attention for the rest of the summit. I could give a damn about territory borders or a local newspaper outing a psychic because I know Jason's right, and I'm failing at convincing myself otherwise. I love Adam, and he loves me. I know it, just as I know I didn't fall in love with him when he was chasing the demon or breaking into houses with me. It was when he made us dinner, danced with me, walked the girls to the bus, smiled with his whole heart. But love isn't enough. What if he's just so happy to have caught me after all these years he's not thinking clearly? What if in a month, a year, a day, whenever, the doubts start to creep in and he begins to resent me for making him choose? This is forever we're talking about. No going back. I think I have to let him go. I have to trust.

The Thirty-First Annual Preternatural Co-Op Summit ends forty minutes later. What we accomplished or decided, I couldn't tell you. As we get up, Jason glances at me, but I look away. "Are you alright?" George asks.

"Fine."

"When everyone leaves, I need to speak to you about yesterday," George says. "We—"

"Fine. Whatever. Excuse me." I walk over to the wolves. "Let me walk you to the car."

Even though his arm wraps around my waist and he smiles, I can read Adam's face like a book. The sadness and apprehension is etched in every muscle. The others seem just about as happy, and Rory is downright hostile. For a moment I close my eyes, recording the feel of him against me, his smell, that arm circling my waist. I can do this. I can do this for him.

When we reach their SUV the tension is palpable. "So," Jason says.

"So," Adam says, voice cracking a little. "I, uh, guess this is it."

"I guess so," Jason says.

His arm drops from my waist. "I, um—"

"You need to go with them," I blurt out.

Adam's eyes narrow. "What?"

"You need to go back with them," I whisper.

His eyes grow triple their size in disbelief, then grow enraged as he turns to Jason. "What the hell did you say to her?" he roars.

"Nothing she didn't already know."

Adam cocks his fist back and is about to lunge, but I grab his arm. "No!" I pull him away from the group, who takes their cue to climb into the car.

"Did he threaten you?" Adam asks. "What—"

"I love you."

He does a double take. "I don't understand this. You love me, but you want me to leave?"

I chuckle as I wipe the falling tears from my eyes. "I don't want you to leave. But you need to. So you can come back."

"Baby, I have no idea what you're talking about."

"I love you, and you love me. I don't doubt it for a second ... but I think there's a tiny part of you that still does. And it should. We— we've been in this bubble, on this rollercoaster, and it's been exhilarating and scary and romantic and a whirlwind, and on it I found exactly what I needed." I cup his cheeks in my hands. "*You.* Now it's time for me to give you what you need, and you need this. There is a reason you didn't tell me for eighteen years. This is your life, your *whole* life you are giving up. If there is a doubt, even an inkling, you need to get in that car. You need to get off this rollercoaster and think, really think about what you are giving up. You love those men in that car too. I see it all over your face. And they love you too, probably a little less than I do," I chuckle, "but they do. They deserve a fair fight." I sniffle. "You know I'm right. I want you here, no I *need* you here, but all of you. I'm giving it all to you, all my love, all my faith, hell, my soul is yours. No one else's. I just ask the same in return."

He blinks his own tears away. "This is so unfair."

I smile. "I know," I say, wiping his cheeks, "but I have faith. In you, in *us*. I know you'll come back to me. I've waited thirty-five years for you, I can wait a little longer. You're worth it."

He pulls me into a hug, and we cling to each other. "I love you so much," he whispers.

"I love you too."

"You really trust I'll come back?"

"More than anything."

We kiss as if the world is ending. He's the one who pulls away, as I knew he would be. "I'm coming back."

"I know."

"I love you."

"I know that too." I pause. "I'll be here waiting for you, Adam Blue." I kiss him again. "See you soon." I run away before I lose all my resolve, without a glance back. No need. I'll see him soon enough.

There isn't a doubt in my mind.

• *Comfort the bride-to-be*

I drive around for a while, trying to calm down before going home. I just want to get into bed with some ice cream and watch *Persuasion* with my own Captain Wentworth purring beside me. I'm not that lucky. Collins's Ford Focus is parked on the street. My work is never done.

With a sigh, I walk into chaos. My baby sister is sobbing on the couch while her best friend smoothes her hair. Sophie and Cora sit on the stairs, and with one glare from me, scurry upstairs. "What on earth is going on?"

Debbie sits up and breaks into more sobs. "Oh, Mona." She leaps up and squeezes me tight. I can smell the whiskey on her breath. "I'm—I'm a horrible person!"

I glance at Collins, who rolls her eyes. "Why sweetie?"

"It's not going to work. It's not. He's too good for me!"

"Where did this come from?" I chuckle.

"He—he was flirting with Becca tonight, so—so I kissed this guy," she sobs.

I look at Collins for confirmation. "We all went out for drinks, and she obviously got plastered. She barely touched his lips, then busted into tears and insisted I bring her here."

I mouth, "I'm sorry," and Collins shrugs. I rub my sister's back and shush her. "Calm down, sweetie, calm down. It's okay."

"I'm a horrible person," she sobs. "How could I do this to him? I don't love him. I mean, I mustn't to have done this! I have to cancel the wedding. I have to!"

Ugh. I pull away, and hold her by the shoulders. "Deborah Jean McGregor, you stop all this right now! You are not a horrible person, you are not canceling your wedding, and that is final. You are scared, you are drunk, you are being inconsiderate, and I will not stand for it. You know you love Greg, and he loves you. Your feet are just a little chilly right now. It's normal. You are going to have a wonderful life together, and that life begins tomorrow. If you sober up and still don't want to go through with the wedding, then so be it. But you better be a hundred thousand percent sure, otherwise you will have wrecked the best thing that ever happened to you. Got me?" She nods. "Good. Now, march your drunk butt upstairs to my bedroom and get into bed. You're bunking with me tonight. Go! March!" Sniffling and with her head hung, my baby sister obeys. When I hear the door shut I flop down on the couch next to Collins. "Oh goddess, give me strength."

"Kaylee brought a bottle of rum, and they started drinking it around three," Collins says.

"She'll be fine. Tamara acted the same way. All three times." We both laugh and shake our heads. "And how are you doing?"

"Alright... and I feel bad about it. Right now I'm just focused on the wedding. I figure I'll have a breakdown right after."

"You and me both, hon." I shake my head. "You're a strong girl. You will be amazed what you can survive."

She's quiet for a few seconds. "She was my sister," she whispers sadly. "She wasn't all bad. She was just lost. She had no purpose in life. That's not a way to live."

"How's Maxine?"

"She won't talk to me," she says, voice cracking.

"Oh, honey," I say, hugging her. "She just needs time."

"Meemaw and Debbie are all I have," she cries as she clings to me. "Now Debbie's getting married, and Meemaw hates me. All I ever wanted was for her to be proud of me. I've done everything I could, and now it's all ruined."

"No, it's not. I'm sure she's real proud of you. How could she not be? You're beautiful, smart, a hard worker. Hell, you spend your days saving people."

"I hate that job so much," she cries. "I only became a nurse because Meemaw said I should. I hate my life! Nothing ever works out."

I rub her back. "I know it feels that way sometimes, honey, but take it from me, life can turn on a dime. You just need to have faith."

She sniffles and pulls away. "Oh hell," she says, wiping her face, "I hate crying in front of people. I'm sorry."

"Nothing to apologize for. We're family." I smile. "You want to stay here tonight?"

"That'd be great, thank you. I don't want to be alone."

I squeeze her hand. "You're not alone." With a smile, I stand. "Okay, I'm gonna check on everyone. Why don't you find some sappy movie we can watch and bawl our eyes out to?"

"Sounds great."

"Be right back." I walk upstairs and check on the girls first. They're pretending to sleep. "Goodnight. I love you." Inside my bedroom, Debbie lies on her side sniffling. "Hey," I say, shutting the door. I walk to the bathroom to get her aspirin and water. "Sit up and take these."

She does. "I'm being a brat, aren't I?"

"Yes, but you're my brat, and I love you nonetheless."

"I don't know what's the matter with me. You and Collins are going through all this crap, and you're both taking care of me. I am a horrible person."

"You'll make it up to us," I say with a smile.

"I really don't know what's the matter with me. I love Greg, I do. It's just … this is forever. How do I know he's, you know, the one and only?"

"Is he your best friend?"

She thinks. "Don't tell Collins, but yes. He is."

"Has he been a good partner to you? Being there when you need him to be?"

"He's been great."

"I know you want babies. Will he be a good father?"

"Oh yeah. No question."

"This is the biggie. Can you honestly picture sitting across the breakfast table every day from him for the rest of your lives?"

She considers it. "Yeah."

"Then you got nothing to worry about, I guarantee it."

"Thank you," she whispers. "I love you."

"Love you too." The telephone rings. Now what? "I gotta get this. You try to sleep. Big day tomorrow." I pick up the portable and walk into the hallway. "Hello?"

"Mona?" George asks.

"Hi, George," I say as I walk to the attic for privacy. "What can I do for you?"

"You disappeared after the summit. Is everything okay?"

"Personal stuff. It'll work itself out. What'd you want to talk to me about?" The attic is stuffy and cluttered with boxes on top of boxes, so I sit at the top of the attic stairs.

"I was hoping you could clear up some inconsistencies so we can close the case."

"Try my best."

I hear the rustling of papers on the other end. "You said the demon was summoned early Tuesday morning, correct? Well, we spoke to a Bruce Nettles, and he said Cheyenne arrived at his apartment around one, and Adam Blue alibied her prior to that."

"Couldn't she have slipped out after Bruce was asleep?"

"That is possible, yes. There is something else though. There were three sets of prints on the notebook: yours, Cheyenne's, and her sister Collins's."

"So? We looked through the book."

"One of the fingerprints was in blood. Animal blood. It wasn't Cheyenne's, it was Collins's. We thought maybe she cut herself, but tests just confirmed the blood was from a dog. Also, though the handwriting is very similar, we compared samples from Cheyenne's to the notebook. It wasn't a match."

If I wasn't sitting, I'd fall down. No. *No way.* Not her. That doesn't, it doesn't make sense. She loves me. She saved my life. Cheyenne was going to shoot me. If Collins wanted me dead, she would have let her. *"You… you did this!"* Cheyenne sounded so surprised. Collins was standing right behind me. What if Cheyenne wasn't aiming for me? What if…

I stand up and walk farther into the attic. All that she has in the world is her grandmother and Debbie. She wants respect. Me dead accomplishes that. She's the obvious choice for Priestess since Erica would never take the job. And the wedding. That's why it had to be this week. There's no way they'd go through with it so soon after my death, and who would be there to comfort Debbie? Her best friend. I'm a fucking idiot. "George, get over here. She's—"

"Hang up the phone, Mona." I spin around with a gasp. Collins stands at the door with her finger outstretched, all business. It's the finger that killed her sister yesterday. My heart rate doubles. *"Now."*

My shaking finger presses the button. "Oh, Collins."

"You know, I knew the second I heard you say his name in the hall I was screwed. Just knew it." She clucks her tongue. "I all but gift-wrapped Cheyenne for them. I thought they had the notebooks, they had her trying to kill you, that'd be it. You always made the

F.R.E.A.K.S. seem like all they did was containment. Killing preters. She's dead, end of case. They'd go, I'd kill you a month from now some other way. Car accident, maybe. Best laid plans, huh? I swear, I have the worst fucking luck on the planet. Just *once*, why can't something go my way?"

"You framed Cheyenne."

"Well duh! I had to do something. You weren't supposed to know you were in danger, but that fucking werewolf ruined everything. Then Ale got caught, and I had to move to Plan B."

"How long have you been planning this?"

"Around two months, I guess. Knew I needed help though. I wanted no ties to me, but I don't know many killers. I was at Croatoan and 'accidently' ran into Ale. Introduced myself. You mentioned him a few times. We found out we had a lot in common."

"There were no records of you being at the club," I say.

"I insisted on secrecy for obvious reasons. After that first night, I knew he could help me get rid of you, and I could help him too. That's what the co-op's for, right?" she asks with a smile. "Cooperation?"

"Not exactly. So he died, and you moved to Plan B. The demon."

She takes a step toward me. "I knew you'd found out when you offered to make me your heir and were asking about Richmond. It was kind of obvious, you know. Even Cheyenne would have seen through it," she says with a scoff. "I played it well, don't you think? Telling you Cheyenne wanted the position was really inspired."

"Convinced me."

"I know." She shakes her head and clicks her tongue. "Then my luck turned again. Lilith was just supposed to drive over and suck the life out of you from a safe distance without anyone ever knowing she was here. Let me tell you, there wasn't any indication in a single damn book I read that her presence would wake up the whole damn town. I knew we could feel her evil up close, but not a trillion feet away. So there you were, ahead of me again. At least my plan to frame my bitch sister went better. You bought everything—the demon at her house, my performance at the country club, my frantic phone call—hook, line, and sinker."

"Cheyenne believe you too?"

"I told her you were threatening Meemaw and acting crazy when I called. I even sounded scared. Then things went sideways again," she says, shaking her head. "It was my fault. I had to gloat, and for the first time in her life, she got a clue. She was supposed to shoot you, then me being the brave hero, I'd kill her. Then she aimed the gun at me, and I had no choice."

"But I don't understand. *Why?* Why would you do this to me? You're like my sister. I love you!"

She scoffs. "I was never your sister. If I was, you'd have let me stay here like you'd promised. You had the room."

I think for a second, then remember ten years ago when she had to go back to her parents again. "I was twenty-five, Collins. My grandmother had just died, my grandfather was a walking ghost, I was head of the coven and guardian to a teenager. I'm sorry, okay?"

"No," she says, shaking her head. "You *promised.* After the last time my daddy got arrested, you sat me on that porch and promised I would always have a safe haven here. You lied to me, you bitch. You know what happened the night you sent me home? He raped me. If it wasn't for Meemaw taking us in again, he would have kept at it until one of us was dead."

I shake my head. "I'm sorry. I am so sorry. I had no idea he was—"

"*You're* supposed to take care of us," she says, snarling at me. "That is your job, and you failed. *I* could do a better job. I couldn't stand it another day. You acting all mighty and people bowing to you. I knew it should have been me. The shop, the house, the *respect*. It isn't fair they look up to you and down on me just because Meemaw wasn't the favored daughter. She was going to get her rightful respect, her birthright, and to see me become the most powerful witch in the country. But now … it's all ruined," she says with a sad chuckle. "My life is over."

"It doesn't have to be. I—I can talk to the squad."

"Oh shut up Mona. Don't insult me. I see right through you." She squares her shoulders. "At least I can accomplish what I set out to do. *Ex—*"

I toss the phone at her head, smashing it right into her temple, while at the same time saying, *"Calx!"* She stands petrified like stone. Not bad for my first time using it. I run through the mess to the door. The spell only lasts five seconds. Just as I take the last stair down, she points that finger. I barely have time to step into the hall before she shouts the death curse. Its evil stains the hallway a scorched black.

Debbie pokes her head out. "What—"

"Lock the door!"

I lose precious seconds making sure she does. Collins moves into the hall, fury practically making her skin glow. A gust of wind barrels down the hall like a bullet, knocking me back onto the stairs. I grab the banister in time and only fall two steps onto my butt but smack my head too. The world becomes a little fuzzy. Collins runs toward me, finger out again, but I'm still recovering. Part of me knows I need to do something, but I can't get my body to listen. She's gonna kill me, and the almost feral smile on her face is the last thing I'm going to see.

"Bitch," she says.

"*Lapsus!*" a voice yells.

Triumph becomes shock as something invisible grips Collins and tosses her thin body over the banister. She falls the story, screaming all the way until her body hits the hardwood below with a thump. Hell's bells.

"Aunt Mona!" Sophie says as she runs toward me. "Are you okay?"

I mange to sit up just as Cora and Debbie step into the hallway, both terrified. We all gaze down at Collins's lifeless form when they join us. She lies on her stomach with her left leg at an odd angle. "Oh goddess! Collins!" Debbie shouts. "What—"

"It was her. She framed Cheyenne. She wanted to kill me." I look at Sophie. "Where did you learn that spell?"

"Mommy. She used it on the demon Papa summoned."

I pet her hair. "You'll have to teach it to me sometime." I kiss her cheek. "But if you ever do anything that stupid again, I will tan your hide." She nods. "Good. Come here." I groan and pull both girls into a hug, holding tight for a few seconds. "Debbie, help me up." I release the girls, and the crying Debbie gets me off the floor. The world tilts a little but rights itself a second later. I take one step at a time, my eyes never leaving Collins.

"Is she dead?" Sophie asks, voice quaking.

"No, she's still breathing," Debbie says, sounding relieved. "She couldn't have—"

"She did," I say. "She murdered Cheyenne in cold blood too."

"Why?" Debbie asks.

"Because she thought I was lucky. Because I failed her." I stifle the tears that want to come. That poor girl. We make it down the stairs, then stop and all gaze down at our cousin. She hasn't moved an inch. "Debbie, take the girls over to Sara's and stay there. The squad is on its way."

"What about—"

"Debbie, *go!*" I don't take my eyes off Collins with my finger pointed out as Debbie grabs the girls and runs out. They don't even close the front door. Her breathing is shallow. The wind from outside blows in, and I get a chill. A big part of me is happy she's still alive. Murderer or not, she's still the girl whose knees I put bandages on. "Oh, Collins."

"Adam!" Cora shouts outside.

I spin around to see Adam standing next to an SUV on the street. I almost faint from relief. He looks confused and concerned as Cora sprints over to him. The other wolves get out too, but the movement out of the corner of my eye makes my head whip around. Collins's finger is pointed right at me, as deadly as a gun. Her bloody grin chills me to the bone.

"Mona!" Adam shouts, panicked.

"My fucking luck," she mutters as she flips over. "Guess I need a hostage. Hands up."

Adam is through the door as she sits up. "What—"

"With one word, I kill her, loverboy. You know I can do it. Move and I will." Her hate-filled gaze whips toward me. "Hands fucking up, Mona! You're not as skilled in black magic as I am. Your finger is just a finger right now." I raise my hands and she smiles, a tooth falling to the floor while blood and saliva dribbles down her chin. I may throw up. "Shit." It takes effort but she gets to her feet. "Fuck, I think I broke my leg."

"You hurt her, and I will rip you apart limb by limb," Adam growls.

"Blah, blah, blah. By the way, if you're supposed to be her bodyguard, you really suck at it. Get on the lawn, loverboy. Go!"

He listens. With her free hand, she grabs and spins me around, using me for support and holding her finger to my temple. "Walk, oh mighty Priestess." Slowly, we shuffle to the door as she groans in pain with each step. My eyes never leave Adam, who waits outside tight as a spring. His eyes keep shifting to my right to signal me. Okay.

I take the first step onto the porch and see Jason to my right waiting to pounce. The moment she sets her good foot outside, I elbow my cousin in the stomach just as Jason grabs for her arm. She's so shocked she releases me. Jason grips her arm as she struggles, wiggling like a worm on a hook. Her mouth opens to say something, but I cock my fist, spin around, and slug her in the face with all my might, just like Daddy taught me to.

She slumps against Jason, down for the count. Her luck has run out. "You are so excommunicated." I sigh and look at Jason. "Now *that's* what I call cooperation."

· *Enjoy being alive*

The F.R.E.A.K.S. arrive five minutes later to find Auntie Sara serving the werewolves coffee, Adam icing my tender hand, and Collins tied up and gagged on the couch, still unconscious. Sadly, I'll bet this isn't the strangest crime scene they've pulled up to.

They take Collins to their mobile command center to be treated and shipped off to a secret prison never to be heard from again. In spite of everything, my heart breaks for her as they wheel her out on a gurney, hands cuffed. I let her down. I did. I'll never forgive myself for that. As I'm beating myself up, my hand is checked by the F.R.E.A.K.S. doctor and deemed fine. Bruised and battered, but I'll keep going. Always do.

About an hour later, after they separated us to get our statements, I'm allowed to bring the girls back from Auntie Sara's and put them to bed. To my amazement they fall asleep almost immediately. They've been through worse, I guess. Never again. Debbie called Greg, who rushed right over. Pretty sure he kissed away her cold feet before taking her home. Guess the wedding's back on.

The wolves are willing to take over helping the squad, so I can have a few minutes of peace out on the porch. What a week. This is how Adam finds me, curled up on the swing staring into space. I move to make room for him and rest my head on his chest as he puts his arm around me. We just rock for a few minutes. Heaven.

"So," I finally say, "how long did it take you to realize you couldn't live without me?"

He looks down at me with a sly smile. "About five minutes. Took me longer to convince them to turn the car around though."

I raise an eyebrow. "Five whole minutes, huh?"

"Shut up. It took you eighteen years."

"True. You definitely have the smarts in this family."

"Then let's hope our kids get my brains and your beauty. And your right hook." I grin and he returns the favor. "She was right though. I do make a lousy bodyguard."

"My love, for the nine hundredth time, I do not need you to save me."

"Then what do you need from me?"

I gaze up into his bright blue eyes. "Just for you to be yourself. And love me."

"Think I can handle that," he says after a kiss.

I pause and move my head to its spot right over his heart. "And sex. Lots and lots and lots of sex. I have a whole slew of years to make up for."

"More than happy to oblige, ma'am."

George and two of the squad walk out of the front door. "We're finished in here," George says. "If we have follow-up questions, we'll call."

"We'll be here," Adam says.

George smiles and follows his men to the car. "See you next year, George!" I shout.

A few seconds after the SUVs pull away, Jason and his wolves come onto the porch. Adam doesn't move, he just smiles at them as I do. "Y'all leaving too?" I ask.

"Yeah," Jason says.

"Thank you for all your help tonight," I say.

"I'll think of a way for you to repay me," he says, voice icy as always. Can't wait. He looks at Adam. "Are you absolutely sure about this?"

"Never been more sure of anything in my life." He pauses. "Better make it official. I, Adam Paul Blue, do hereby renounce any and all allegiance to the Eastern Pack of America, and in doing so am declaring myself a Rogue with all that entails."

Jason bows. "Very well, then. Goodbye, brother. You will be missed." He steps off the porch with his men, then turns around. "Oh, Mona. Vivian wanted me to invite you to our Frankie's birthday party next month. All the pack will be there. You can bring a guest if you like."

Both Adam and I smirk. "We will definitely be there," I say.

"Good," he says with a nod. With that, he leaves. I am actually beginning to like that guy.

I sit up and stretch. "Well then," I say with a sigh. I stand and look down at Adam. "All our guests are gone, the girls are tucked into bed, and we have nothing on the agenda for almost twelve hours. Whatever shall we do?"

He raises an eyebrow, smiles mischievously, and grabs for my leg, but I leap away, giggling. Can't make it too easy for him. I take off inside running with him hot on my heels. He catches me halfway up the stairs, tosses me over his shoulder, and carries me to our bedroom.

Goddess, I do love this man.

SUNDAY TO DO:

- ~~Iron mine and the girls dresses~~
- ~~Find a suit for Adam~~
- ~~Answer the million phone calls about last night~~
- ~~Try to get a few online orders done~~
- ~~Shower and makeup~~
- ~~Go over to Debbie's and help out~~
- ~~Run errands for Jocasta~~
- ~~Sit patiently while get hair done~~
- ~~Help Debbie on with her dress~~
- ~~Wedding~~
- ~~Reception~~
- Get the girls home

As QUIETLY AS WE can, Adam and I creep into the house carrying our slumbering girls. The wedding really took it out of them. Debbie decided to go through with it—no surprise there—and Kaylee became maid of honor. It's such a shame Collins skipped town without a word to anyone but me. Everyone, save Maxine, understood. Still, a lot of tongues were wagging. I didn't care. Debbie looked glorious and Greg got teary when he saw her. I raised her right. They'll make it.

As for me, I had a blast. I did the "Electric Slide" with Tamara, got to see Clay and Bethany making out under the gazebo, heard Auntie Sara gossip with everyone, watched as Adam taught the girls "Y.M.C.A.," and felt pretty darn good as all those people who usually come up to me and say, "Don't worry, you'll be next," held their tongues as Adam spun me around on the dance floor in-between kisses. Yep, best wedding ever. At least until mine.

We put the girls in their beds, tuck them in, and both stand by the door for a few seconds watching them sleep in their flower girl dresses, dreaming only good dreams. He kisses my head, takes my hand, and leads me into our bedroom. "You know, nine people tonight asked me when I was making an honest woman out of you," he says, taking off my daddy's old tie. "*Nine.* I kept count."

"Welcome to Goodnight," I say, falling face first into bed.

A few seconds later he climbs in too, spooning me. "So. The shop's fixed, the demon slayed, the coven meeting and co-op over with, the evil witch is in jail, your sister is married and on her honeymoon, and even the litter box is clean. What's on the agenda for this week?"

"Shut up," I mutter.

"Because, you see, the full moon is Thursday, my birthday is Friday and you have to find a schoolgirl uniform and a can of whipped cream to celebrate. Not to mention all of my stuff is still at my house in Maryland and needs to be moved, the house itself has to be put on the market, those showers of yours are in dire need of grouting, and—"

I flip over and press my hand over his smirking mouth. "Baby," I say, "I love you to death, but shut the hell up and kiss—" He brushes my hand away, and raises his lips to mine. The whole world stops as it always does. He rolls me onto my back and pulls away, gazing down at me with such love I feel like I'm made of stardust. "Hell's bells, I love you."

The biggest smile I've ever had is only for him. Hell's bells are ringing indeed.

MONDAY TO DO:

- *Lie in bed all day with the man I love*

ACKNOWLEDGEMENTS

First, I just want to acknowledge all of you who sent me letters and e-mails telling me how awesome I am and how much you enjoy my books. They mean more to me than words can express. Keep them coming.

Thanks as always to my agent, Sandy Lu, for all her hard work and determination. She keeps going even when I fumble.

Thanks to Terri Bischoff for loving this book so much she championed me to another three-book deal. You have changed my life. I owe you a million thanks.

Thanks to everyone else at Midnight Ink, especially Nicole Nugent for her edits and Courtney Colton for being a wonderful publicist.

Thanks to my Beta Bunch: Susan Dowis, Jill Kardell, Ginny Dowis, and Theresa Fredrich for their honest criticisms and for helping me make this book better.

A special thanks to my good friend Lydia Vigna for including me in her wedding so I knew a little about what they entail. It was beautiful.

Also to the Prince William and Fairfax Library systems, for giving me a place to go and work—I would definitely be considered a shut-in otherwise.

As always, thanks to my family for all their support both mentally and monetarily. I love y'all.

Finally, to all the Wiccans out there, including my aunt and late great-grandmother: blessed be.

© Bill Fitz-Patrick

ABOUT THE AUTHOR

Jennifer Harlow (Manassas, VA) earned a BA from the University of Virginia in Psychology. Her eclectic work experience ranges from government investigator to radio DJ to lab assistant. Visit her website www.jenniferharlowbooks.com to read her blog, *Tales From the Darkside*; listen to the soundtrack to this book; and more.